CW01066476

The author is a former ꜰᴀʀᴍᴇʀ ᴡʜᴏ ʜᴀꜱ ʙᴇᴇɴ ᴀ reader of mainly historical and biographical books all his life. His other interests are in boating, fishing, sailing, scuba diving, golf and guns. He lives in Australia with his wife; his married daughter, her husband and children live close by.

To my darling wife

C. M. Davis

THE LAGOON

AUSTIN MACAULEY
PUBLISHERS LTD.

A CIP catalogue record for this title is available from the British Library.

This story and the characters in it in no way refer to events or people, either living or dead.

ISBN 9781786123725 (Paperback)
ISBN 9781786123732 (Hardback)
ISBN 9781786123749 (E-Book)
www.austinmacauley.com

First Published (2016)
Austin Macauley Publishers Ltd.
25 Canada Square
Canary Wharf
London
E14 5LQ

Acknowledgements

I wish to thank the team at Austin Macauley for undertaking to publish my work, as a first time author. It is very much appreciated.

Thanks also to "Diver Steve."

Chapter 1

Perfume really filled the air, both physically and metaphorically, thought Freddie as he withdrew from the small group he was with and eased back up the few steps to the elevated lawn. He paused and looked around at the colorful, animated gathering of graduates, parents and friends and hugged his gown around himself in spite of the increasingly hot day. The whole occasion was mildly intoxicating.

An incredibly clear blue sky rested above this perfect setting, the magnificently proportioned buildings forming the Quadrangle: some were covered with ivy, some with cloisters, all with beautifully arched windows, and all constructed from the warm reddish brown stone that he had become so attached to.

The green of the ivy, some in shadow, some in the direct sunlight, stood in a harmonized contrast to the stone; and the green of the elevated lawn, a completely different shade of green, together with its superb array of his favorite flowers, roses, set the whole spectacle off in a way Freddie thought could not be adequately described.

He couldn't stop thinking about Lettice, and wondered if the feelings he had for her would ever wane. To think that someone who he had known all his life could suddenly after so many years become such a preoccupation with him, to be in his thoughts constantly, almost to the extent that it hurt, and almost put him off studying. In fact, if she had in any way been playing games with him, which she had not, he may have lost his way completely. The reality was just the opposite.

He came out of his reverie and gazed around and found himself, looking squarely at eye level at a most magnificent rose on a bush that was planted at the corner of the lawn. Taking a pace along the step and leaning forward to smell it, he realized that he would have to tilt his mortarboard back a little. In doing so out of the corner of his eye he could see two girls, fellow graduates, looking up at him.

Without giving any indication that he knew he was being watched, he drew his gown a little closer and, cupping his right hand behind the rose and with his nose held high—reminiscent, he hoped, of a jack rabbit sniffing the morning air—waved the aroma of the rose towards him as one would when taking the bouquet of a vintage wine. Executing a delicate swoon and a slight recovering of balance, he turned to eyeball the girls with a look of mock incredulity.

The girls were hanging onto each other absolutely in hysterics as they then turned away. As he backed up the last two steps in order to command a better view, he looked down momentarily at Lettice and Alice, his mother; it suddenly struck him that whilst they looked sensational apart, together they looked something else again. Unlike most at the gathering they looked as fresh as could be, despite the heat.

Whilst he had always thought that Lettice looked beautiful, he hadn't actually ascribed that to his mother. She was his mother, after all. Today, however, the day of his graduation as an Engineer with several distinctions, it suddenly hit him.

An incredible feeling of warmth for her overcame him as if for the first time he fully understood and appreciated what she meant to him. He had realized for years, on reflection, how people, both men and women, responded to her. She was approachable and always well dressed and beautifully groomed, all without too much fuss, and it didn't appear to matter what she was wearing.

She had style. The easy confidence born of the Tobacco Aristocracy, not to mention cattle, cotton and fishing, enabled her to mix with anyone who crossed her path. Freddie thought that the two of them standing chatting with the Dean looked fabulous together. Lettice with her strawberry blonde hair and fair complexion, and his mother with her black hair and olive complexion, looked more like friends rather than prospective daughter- and mother-in-law. In fact, it was really only the height of the two different hemlines, and perhaps the different shades of their hose, that from a distance indicated the difference in age between the two of them.

For his part the Dean seemed to be enjoying himself immensely. He almost seemed to be in a barely suppressed state of excitement. He was positively gushing, and was dominating the conversation. Freddie felt another surge of warmth and pride mixed with a fleeting sadness at the memory of the other two people who should have been there.

A movement in the happy crowd caught his eye, and there she was, the Prairie Oyster: well, she couldn't touch any of them now. He chuckled to himself. Whoever dubbed her the Prairie Oyster must have been a real wag; it was spot on. The Dean's wife required nothing more in a nickname than something that was funny, frivolous and apt. It suited her down to the ground. Whilst she played no part in the academic life of the University, she certainly dominated the social, to say nothing of the moral, side of it, which was quite ironic, given that she was a tippler.

If she were a battleship you would say that she had a full head of steam. She was enormous and cut a lumbering swathe through the crowd that brooked no interruption. She was looking for the poor old Dean.

Freddie watched in great anticipation, thinking that if he could capture the next few moments on a movie camera, he could make a fortune. All of a sudden she straightened momentarily: the Dean was spotted and the Prairie Oyster set off, and as she did so, put the Dean's companions into perspective, two trim well-dressed women, and she started to move real fine.

The Dean was so rapt in conversation that he didn't see her until she drew abreast of them, placing herself squarely between him and the two women. Drawing herself up and clutching her handbag in front of her, she towered over the Dean like a positive thunderclap. The Dean, needless to say a little put off by this sudden intrusion, blurted out an introduction and Freddie, for the first time in all his years at the University, saw the Prairie Oyster outdone. She became almost coy.

He thought that it was time to go to the rescue; he moved down the steps and across to them and eased his tall athletic frame in between Lettice and his mother.

They chatted for a while and then excused themselves as soon as they felt they politely could, and set about gathering up the rest of their group: Billy, Chuck and their families. This took the best part of an hour, and it took another half hour or so before they were all back at the hotel where they had spent the previous night.

They decided to have a rest up in their rooms prior to meeting back downstairs for a drink before dinner. Freddie's mother and Lettice had a suite and Freddie had a room just across the passage from them. As they arrived at the suite, Freddie announced that he was going to put his feet up for a while; it had been quite a day and it wasn't over yet. "Just you wait, Letty, your day will come." Lettice was two years behind Freddie at university, studying Pharmacy.

Alice agreed; she was certainly going to have a rest. "What about me?" cried Lettice in a tremulous voice, feigning mock horror at the prospect of being left to her own. Alice wiggled over to her, putting her arms around her.

"You can have a kip on the couch if you like, darling, or have a lie down on your own bed, as long as you don't make a noise," she added as she disentangled herself and slipped away.

They really are incredible, thought Freddie as he wandered off to his room, having given Lettice a wink and a slight inclination of his head towards the door, which was unobtrusively acknowledged.

"Oh, Mom, what did you say to the Prairie Oyster?"

"I'll tell you later, darling," she called out.

"How do you do, Mrs. Marsh, I have been so looking forward to meeting you!" he mimicked.

He entered his room, took off his jacket and after throwing it onto a chair went to the john, washed his hands and threw a little water over his face. It was swelteringly hot. He then stripped off to his shorts, and after pulling down the bedclothes but leaving the sheets he flopped down onto the bed, putting his arms behind his head.

Lying there he mulled over the day past, the evening ahead and the events that led up to the day, waiting for Lettice. She appeared a few minutes later, wearing a dressing gown. Having locked the door, she crept over to the bed and slipped out of the gown. He took a silent gasp at the sight of her: no wonder she had been crowned "Miss Heavenly" in an inaugural beauty competition a few months ago. One the judges

5

commented to the amusement of those within hearing, "She has a most arresting countenance." She had protested vehemently against entering the competition but was prevailed upon by all and sundry. She vowed never again to enter such a competition, even though it was one in swimsuits.

With his heart nearly beating out of his chest he rose to meet her; cupping her face in his hands, he leant forward and gently kissed her. He then put his arms around her and, stepping back slightly, they fell onto the bed in a serpentine embrace.

His whole body began to tingle as he held her and buried his head in her neck, running his tongue ever so lightly over it, and down to her shoulder, bringing his hands down to clasp her soft but firm buttocks. The rare smell of her, and her "special" perfume, made him feel slightly woozy. It had been given to her by her grandmother, who had told her that it was extremely expensive. She had bought it in a souk in Cairo, Egypt, from what she imagined to be one of the leading perfumeries in the souk. It smelt absolutely divine, the whole family agreed, and her grandmother had given all the women in the family a small bottle of it. They each had "to treasure it and not use it for everyday use," and when they did, "to use it sparingly." Enough to give the merest of lingering wafts, as she used to say.

They kissed. He moved slightly and again cupped her face in his hands. He traced his fingers across her lips and ever so tentatively moved one of them between her teeth, to be met by her tongue. This imparted an almost electric shock to him, and repositioning himself slightly he removed his finger and suckled her breast, which was covered in a bath of perspiration.

Still suckling her he moved to a kneeling position over her and gently moved himself until he was running his tongue over the barely visible film of perspiration on

6

her stomach. Abruptly, slowly he eased back down beside her.

"What's wrong?" she murmured dreamily.

He sighed. "I'm sorry, I was all fired up and then I thought of Dad and Edie!"

After a long silence, she turned towards him. "Do you know what?"

He shook his head.

"That's one of the reasons I'm so very much in love with you!" she whispered.

He sighed. "Oh, you know."

"You have never actually said that to me in so many words; and I actually feel the same way about you too. Aren't we lucky?"

"Do you know what?" he enquired, his heart still beating madly.

"What? No!" she managed to utter.

"I'm going to wax philosophical!"

"Oh my God!"

"No, seriously. I'm lying here thinking that on the one hand I'm in another world with you, and at the same time we are doing something that is very special."

"Continue!"

"Well what do you in this immediate context think we are?"

"Oooh; rabbits, stoats perhaps; or trying to be!" She gave him a slight dig in the ribs, immediately falling into his reverie. He shook his head.

"Oh no, no, I think we are becoming a couple of eels!"

"What do you mean?"

"Well. We're lying here bathed in perspiration, it's stinking hot, and you feel so slippery and absolutely wonderful."

"Like an eel I suppose!"

"No no, I didn't mean it like that. I don't go for eels much. But nevertheless..." He trailed off as she put a finger over his lips. He went on. "I know one thing for sure!"

"What is that?"

"When we all arrive back for your graduation we're not staying here again!"

"Oh?"

"It may be the nicest hotel in town, but not at this time of year. Old world charm can only be carried too far. They need to put in air conditioning. Every other hotel seems to be gradually putting it in."

"So you don't like lying with me and playing eels?"

"I'll tell you what; wherever we are, I'll be like a bag of them." He snuggled her closer still.

She continued, "I'd be happy to come back here. Having thought about it, I don't mind this eel business. It's also a bit like being in a pool of maple syrup with you!" She straddled him. Sometime later she gave him a kiss and rose up, and after putting the gown back on, quietly tiptoed out of the room, and across the passageway back to the suite, to find the door into Alice's room still closed, and made for the bathroom.

Chapter 2

Freddie lay back in a dozy state, absolutely exhausted. His mind wandered back years, as it did whenever he became reflective, back to that memorable weekend when his whole life changed forever. He had grown up in the state of Marilina, in a town at the junction of the Lagoon Creek and the Chicamanoke River which led into Chesapeake Bay. His idyllic childhood up until he was twelve years of age had been spent with his parents and sister in the small town of "White Oak." In those days in the 'forties and early 'fifties, it was a town of around two thousand people, and everybody knew just about everybody else. It was also a town that, through some quirk, had never known segregation.

Freddie's mother, Alice, was a local girl coming from an old family which owned the biggest spread in the County, if not the state. The property was known as "The Lagoon" after the lagoon, which it encompassed, and to all intents and purposes it sat on top of the town, both geographically and economically.

Freddie's father had a similar background, but was from out of state. He and Freddie's mother had met as children and were childhood sweethearts. Whilst his father also had a cotton and tobacco background, he had gone off to university, had studied law and before the War had become a partner in a leading city law firm. The

Lagoon was run by Alice's Uncle Edward, a widower who had lost two young children and who adored Alice and everything about her. He was a leader in the community and county and, whilst he had the air of a patrician, he was quite approachable.

The five thousand acres of lagoon was pristine. It was filled from a vast up-country catchment and fed from the north by this and small streams, forming the headwaters of the tidal "Lagoon Creek." The creek itself began its meandering after leaving the lagoon, and wandered through vast, untouched expanses of marsh and timbered country which itself was home to countless birds of every description, various animals and of course fish.

The marsh water came and went with each modest tide and the drainage was hastened by a series of gutters or "guts." These guts in some instances allowed for more ready access to the otherwise inaccessible reaches of the marsh and were used on a regular basis by all sorts of folk for fishing and shooting. Between the wars there had been some recreational activity such as camping and picnicking. Most who went in were hunting for the "pot" as they used to say.

A lot of people had boats that were tied up along the creek, small jetties and the odd dock that festooned the banks by the town. It was also reassuring to know that all adults when down by the water were continually on the lookout whenever they saw small children by the water, in case they happened to fall in.

Nevertheless, something else was needed to discourage children from wandering off. This was most important when discouraging them from going near the gut. In Freddie's parents' day, it was: "If you go near the gut, Ginny Greenteeth will get you!"

In Freddie's day it was: "Ole Snakesbreath will get you." Whatever horrific images were conjured up by children at the thought of Ginny Greenteeth getting them, by the time they were old enough to swim, they had realized that she was mythical, but she certainly served her purpose. Snakesbreath on the other hand was real. Most children had seen him and were terrified.

Leading up to the day in question, Freddie and his two friends, Chuck and Billy, had eventually convinced their parents that they were old enough to go camping in the stretch of woods between the town and the gut. They were twelve years of age.

They had an old handcart and a two-man tent, quite adequate to sleep three twelve-year-olds, sleeping bags, a ground sheet, a flashlight, a length of rope, a lantern, a skillet, a couple of Billy cans, a tomahawk and a large water container; in addition, Freddie and Chuck had their father's military water bottles. Each of them had a slingshot which they carried everywhere when they were not at school. They had provisions for three meals. They were to set off from Freddie's place, which was on the edge of town near the road leading to the woods. Their parents and siblings, including Freddie's sister Edith, known as "Sunny," saw them off.

Sunny was six and was beautiful. She had a captivating slight lisp. She was a constant source of delight to all those around her, although no one was quite sure what she was going to come out with next. She was great fun, loved her parents and simply idolized Freddie who adored her.

Sunny of course wanted to go with the boys, and (almost) a battle royal had been waged for days to this end. All to no avail, although she eventually settled down the night before when her father took her on his knee and explained to her that it was only after great deliberation and agreement with the other boy's parents that they had been allowed to go.

One of the concerns, in fact the main concern that all the parents had, was the possibility that there may be "bars" in the marsh. "Barth?" asked Sunny, eyes wide with wonder.

"Bears," said her father, and added that if there had been the most remote possibility, of them being about, the boys would not have been allowed to go. "Mom and I and Billy and Chuck's parents checked the whole bear situation out independently of each other and no bears had been seen for sixty years or so."

The boys had been wishing to go for years, were older than her, and there were three of them. In time, certainly Sunny could go, but not this time. Even when she would be allowed to go she would require at least one other girl with her. She would just have to wait.

They were going to review the situation anyway, upon the boys' return. It was no light matter. The logic in all this was accepted by her and she was in great spirits.

It was a Saturday morning and Chuck's and Billy's parents arrived with them, also bringing their respective younger siblings. There was a real party atmosphere as the cart was inspected, packed and then re-packed and the stores made secure. You would have thought that they were heading off for the Yukon.

Lettice, Billy's sister, stood back a little apart from the other children with a smile playing upon her face which lit up momentarily whenever Freddie looked in her direction. This went completely unnoticed by Freddie himself, however not by their respective parents who had been aware of her attraction to him for some time. Whilst they were all comfortable with the obvious infatuation, they weren't at all concerned as they were only ten and twelve respectfully. Alice thought that it was quite sweet actually as Freddie was completely oblivious to the fact that he was the object of someone's affection.

Whilst Sunny played with the other younger ones she appeared to be taking more and more interest in the impending departure of the three campers than the other younger children as the time of departure came closer although Lettice watched the preparations from the sidelines. All the while Sunny had been clutching a small package, and kept looking at her mother for a sign.

The great moment eventually arrived and by this time she was standing beside her mother jumping up and down with excitement. Her mother looked down and nodded in agreement and Sunny went up to Freddie and announced to him that she thought he and the other boys should have a little extra something for the cart. She handed him the packet with a hug and then bounced back to between her parents. "What is this, Sunny?" asked Freddie. "I thought we had everything that we are likely to need."

"Have a look, Freddie," muttered Sunny.

"Yes, come on," said Chuck, "let's have a look, Sunny wouldn't give us something we didn't need."

Freddie opened the package and found to his amazement that it was a small first aid kit with a triangular bandage, a gauze bandage, and some sticking plaster, and amongst other things, some small scissors. "Why thank you Sunny," chorused the boys, and almost in unison, "but we really won't need any of it!" Sunny's face was a study through all this and she looked up at her father for encouragement

All of the parents were rolling their eyes at each other slightly at this exchange and then Billy's father hosed it down by saying that "We all hope so, but you never know when you go camping, and a good camper is a prepared one." All of the parents chimed in on cue, and the boys hastily lost their reticence and thanked Sunny a little more enthusiastically.

"Mom altho told me to tell you to take it with you even if you leave the camp!" cried Sunny, quickly regaining her confidence. The boys without any encouragement, indeed without even looking at each other, said that yes they would.

"Well, guys," said Alice, "off you go and have a terrific time and remember, make sure that you are back mid-afternoon tomorrow. Don't forget to eat the sandwiches we have cut for you either, and just remember, if you go near the gut, Ol' Snakesbreath will get you."

The boys drew back in mock indignation and, without a word, set off with the parents barely containing their mirth. "Billy, darling," his mother called out, "aren't you going to give your old mom a kiss?"

"Aw, Mom," Billy threw over his shoulder and away they went.

At the mention of Ol' Snakesbreath, Sunny really pricked up her ears, something that did not go unnoticed by her parents. When the boys had gone a short distance and disappeared around the corner of the street, the parents were starting to chat amongst themselves.

"Thnakethbreath, Ol' Thnakethbreath, who ith he? What ith he?" she enquired of her father, jumping up beside him and tugging his arm.

"The sun is nearly over the yardarm, folks!" said her father. "Why don't we have a drink before we have a shuffle?" He picked Sunny up, leading them into the house.

"He gobbles up little girls who go near the gut," he said to the wriggling Sunny, who by this time he had cradled in his arms, and was now beginning to be put over his shoulder.

"Oh he doethn't, he doethn't."

"No of course he doesn't. He cooks them up in a big pot first."

"Oh, Father, don't be thilly. Well, Daddy who ith he?" she said, falling back to a less demanding stance. Alice and all the other parents were looking at George

14

enquiringly, some with their heads slightly inclined, as if to say—Come on George, let us see you get out of this one.

This, needless to say, put George on his mettle so once they were inside he sat Sunny on his knee and said to her. "Darling I'm surprised you haven't heard of him. We have obviously missed something in your education. Now I'll do a deal with…"

"Daddy, Daddy."

"No, Sunny darling, I'll do a deal with you. OK?"

"Yeth, Daddy."

"Well the boys have gone off on a—we hope—a wonderful adventure. Now if they come back and don't have something to say about Snakesbreath, I will be surprised, however it is a long story and we have guests. I promise you that I will tell you all about him later this afternoon. Now is that a fair thing? It really isn't the time now, and with all our friends here it would just take too long." And he whispered in her ear, "I have to get the drinks," as he gave her a quick tickle. "Is that a deal?"

"Yeth, OK a deal."

Everyone rolled their eyes again as George stood up and, bowing slightly to them all, swept out to get the drinks. "Oh and Sunny, are you going to stand quietly beside me and take in the finer points of bridge?"

"No, Father, thank you, no." And she ran off to play with the other children, calling over her shoulder, "Dadda, can I let Chippie off his chain now pleath?"

"Not yet darlin'. He may run after the boys. Wait a little longer!"

Chip was Freddie's Collie dog and constant companion, although on this occasion he was not allowed to go with the boys.

"Darling," Alice said to Lettice. "I see you have a book. Would you like to sit in a chair over by the window?" She looked fondly at her.

"Thank you, Mrs. Gardiner, I will. Can I help you with anything first?"

"No thank you dear, we can manage."

The boys meanwhile had trudged to the end of the town and had taken one of the roads that as yet were unmade, that led to the woods. They hadn't gone far when Billy exclaimed, "I wonder if there are many stones in the woods."

"Why?" the other two rejoined.

"For the slingshots, and look what is up ahead."

They looked and really couldn't see anything except road, grass, trees, woods, and sky; and said so.

"No look, that pile of beautiful stones."

There off to the side of the road was a heap of stones just the right size for slingshots. "Great, we'll fill our pockets." They were stones that the County had put there for some of their roadwork.

They continued on until they were in the woods proper, and could not see any sign of the town, and it seemed a lot quieter. "Why don't we stop and have a bite," said Freddie, "I've just about had it."

So they stopped pushing and looking around saw a log, and taking the sandwiches from the cart, walked over, and sat down on it.

As they ate and took swigs of water from the water bottles, they fired their slingshots at birds that were nearby, and just about anything else that took their fancy. They were, they agreed, pretty good shots. Eventually they stood up and got going once more, pushing further and further in until the road petered out into a track. They pushed for perhaps another half an hour or so and then the trees began to thin out a little, and they realized that they must be close to the "gut"

16

country. They had agreed that when they reached this stage it would be time to look around for a campsite.

It didn't take them at all long to find a spot to set up the tent. There seemed to be plenty of firewood about, and whilst the country was generally flat, the place that they chose was on the edge of where it began to shelve away to marshy-type country, where they supposed the gut was.

They spread the tent out on the ground and began to trace out the lines for a small trench that they had been told to dig around the perimeter so that the ground inside the tent would not be damp.

Whilst they took this advice, they didn't accept the recommendation that they also dig hip holes so that they would get a good night's sleep. This seemed a bit too far-fetched for them; they had felt that their fathers were pulling their legs. Just as they disregarded the evasion tactics to put into place when being attacked by a hoop snake. It was at this stage that they found that they had come away without the two tent poles. "Well, this is great," said Billy. "What do we do now?"

"Well we can't go back and get them, that's for sure," said Freddie. "We'll just have to put our thinking caps on. How about we run the rope through the eyelets each end of the tent and tie it off on a tree each end?"

"You know, Freddie," said Chuck, "you are just so clever."

"I was just about to say the same thing myself."

So they hunted around in the cart for the rope, then looked for two trees that were close enough to tie off each end. It didn't take them long to find the two trees, but they then found that the rope was a little too thick to pass through the eyelets.

Chuck pondered. "The guys are lighter than the rope. We can tie off the rope, run the guy ropes through, and tie it off each end to the main rope. How is that?"

"We just won't get into any serious trouble at all with you two crack woodsmen," said Billy. "All I have to do is keep you happy with my cooking."

They tied off the heavy rope, then they threaded the lighter guy ropes through the eyelets, forming a knot inside each eyelet to enable them to tension the tent ridge; and tied off each end. Then they pulled out each corner of the tent, and hammered in the corner tent pegs with the back of the tomahawk. They managed to get the height of the main rope correct first up, and needed to make only a slight adjustment so that the ridge could be tensioned. Freddie and Chuck then continued with the tent while Billy set off around the campsite collecting firewood. There was plenty of it and it was not long before he had the fire going.

There were no stones of any size at all in the vicinity, so he pulled a couple of greenish heavy fallen branches and set them up each side of the fire so that he could rest the skillet over it. He also cleared the leaves and sticks from around it so that the fire didn't creep.

Freddie and Chuck chopped out the trench with the tomahawk, and scooped the soil out with their hands, and pretty soon the whole camp looked as though the marines had set it up, they opined amongst themselves.

"What have you got for us to eat, Billy?" said Chuck.

"Chuckie, I've got a beautiful steak each, a great big potato that I will do in the coals, and a tomato that will be done in the skillet."

"It sounds fantastic," both Chuck and Freddie agreed.

"I've even got ketchup and salt and pepper, butter for the spuds. We'll have to wait until the fire has gone down a lot before we put them in, according to Mom," Billy continued. "They have to be done in coals and not in flames."

"Why don't we walk down to the gut and see what it looks like?" said Freddie, so off they set, having put some more wood on the fire.

The gut wasn't quite what they had expected. They could see where they thought it was but there were too many reeds and tall grassy sort of stuff in the way, and the ground had become soggier the further down the slope they went.

It was quite dank. They decided to take a better look in the morning as they were getting quite hungry and it was beginning to get late in the day to do too much exploring. They trudged off back up the slope and back to the campsite. They found that the fire had gone down and that there was a very good bed of coals. Billy put the three potatoes, the boys' favorite vegetable, well down into them.

"As Mom said that they could take an hour why don't we get the rest of our gear out of the cart and put it in the tent?" said Billy.

The others thought this was a good idea, and began to go through the cart. The ground sheet was already in the tent so it was really just a matter of putting the sleeping bags, the flashlight and pillows inside. It was then that they realized that they did not have pillows. "We'll just have to roll up our dungarees and use them as pillows," said Freddie.

"These bugs are starting to get me, too," the exchange went on.

"I suppose we'll be eaten alive without anything to keep them off us. You'd think with all these frogs croaking and crickets chirping it would be enough to keep them away," said Freddie, "but I suppose that when it gets dark and we light the lantern they will all flock to it and keep off us."

"You're amazing," said Chuck, "what made you think of that?"

Freddie looked at him and shook his head.

"I can't work this out. First the poles and now the pillows; I wonder what else we have forgotten," murmured Chuck.

"Chuckie, I seem to remember a couple of weeks ago when we were all talking about the camp with our parents, you said that we wanted to do the whole thing ourselves, that we had discussed it amongst ourselves and knew exactly what was needed. They have probably all been having a great laugh at our expense."

"I know, I know," he responded. "Your mother even suggested a check list and we laughed, and said that between the three of us we couldn't forget a thing."

"Well," said Freddie, "we'll get over it."

Freddie, who was becoming very hungry by this time, went over to the fire and poked around at the potatoes and opined that they were well enough along the way to now put the skillet on and cook the steaks.

It wasn't long before the smell of them cooking took over and they could hardly wait, they looked so good. The tomatoes were put on and the plates made ready. They had tipped the cart over on its front and it made a pretty good table apart from where the wheels were, but they did not worry too much about that. They also had bread and butter to go with the steak, and when it was cooked, hunkered down with their plates by the fire, which they had built up again.

They had about the most wonderful meal that any of them could remember. They made a great fuss over Billy's cooking, and told him that he could be cook forever. He was not sure whether to be pleased or not. They had hardly finished the meal when they decided that it was too dark to try and clean up the dishes, and that they should light the lanterns and build the fire up again. The fire was no sooner burning away brightly than they all mutually agreed that it was time to turn in.

Freddie took a look around the camp. The cart was still on its front, the dishes, which were tin plates, were on the cart, and the skillet was down at the corner of the fire. The rest of the food was in a large wooden box which was beside the cart. It had a pad bolt on it, and for some reason Freddie shot it home. He felt that everything looked pretty good, and walked over to the tent and, getting down on his hands and knees, crawled inside. The other two by this time were down to their shorts, and were struggling into their sleeping bags, by the meager glow of the flashlight.

It was not long before they were all lying side by side like three peas in a pod, simply bursting with excitement—although, whilst they would not admit it, they could hardly contain it. They chatted about what they would do on the 'morrow, and seemed to be nearly settled when Chuck announced that he had to go to the john. Of course they all struggled out and, barefoot, crept out across to the camp's edge.

Back inside the tent the talk turned once more to tomorrow's activities, and then gradually tapered off as one by one they drifted off to sleep. In the years to come they often had a great laugh at what happened that night.

They were not quite sure what time it was but they were awakened by the sound of running or scampering, and the odd muffled squeak. At first they just lay there almost frozen with fear until they were well and truly awake, and the noises began to take on a sort of rhythm.

"They are dogs," said Freddie, in a very low voice. "They must be dogs from the town." He had no sooner said this than there was a crash or clatter as some of the plates fell off the cart.

"They are wrecking the camp," said Chuck, "we'll have to stop them."

"Where is the flashlight? I'll fix them," said Billy.

Freddie found the flashlight and passed it to Billy who by this time was by the flap of the tent. He slowly undid the tapes and, whispering to the others to hang on, slowly eased himself out a little and taking a deep breath suddenly let out a blood-curdling shriek that frightened the daylights out of the other boys, let alone the dogs. As he yelled he turned the flashlight on. There was almost pandemonium outside.

Billy said later that there were at least four dogs, and there could have been more, and one was on top of the cart. When he yelled it flung itself off the cart, and got caught up in the wheel and fell onto another dog, and the whole lot of them took off, with some of them giving frightened yaps.

The boys all clambered out of the tent and by flashlight hunted around for the lantern which they found on its side by the cart. After lighting it they surveyed the scene of devastation. It appeared that the dogs had licked all the plates and the skillet, which did not really impress them, but fortunately the food box was intact although it was on its side. They stood it up. It was decided they couldn't do anything in the dark as far as cleaning up was concerned, and that they would have to wait until the morning, so returned to the tent. After about another half hour of discussion, they gradually drifted off to sleep again.

In no time at all or so they thought, there was something trying to get into the tent. This was quite different from the dog encounter: there was no noise, and it took some time for them to realize, in their sleepy state, that it was not actually one of themselves wanting more room.

"The flashlight, the flashlight," whispered Freddie.

The flashlight was duly produced and shone at the inside of the tent wall where the "object" was.

"What can it be?" two of them said.

"Heavens knows," said Freddie, "but we are in trouble if it comes in. It looks pretty big. Hey can anyone smell anything? It seems to have a smell." They looked at each other in the flow of the flashlight

"Say," said Billy, "it couldn't be a skunk could it?"

None of the boys had smelt a skunk, but they all agreed that is what it could be.

"If it gets in we have had it," said Freddie, "we'll be the laughing stock of our families and the school. We'll have to get rid of it."

"How?" said Chuck and Billy in unison.

"We'll have to whack it with something hard from inside the tent and hope that it does not make a smell when it gets a fright," Freddie replied.

"Well that's just when they do make a smell," said Chuck.

"I know, Chuckie, but have you any other suggestions?"

"Of course I don't," said Chuck. "If we go outside it may really take fright and let one go, and we can't take the risk of just letting it carry on the way it is. What do you think, Billy?"

"I agree, we'll have to whack it."

Freddie picked around until he had one of their Keds. "We don't have the tomahawk, do we?" he asked.

"It's outside by the fire," said Chuck

"Well," said Freddie, "we have to get it in one, and I'll need as much room as possible. Why don't one of you shine the flashlight on it while you both lie flat so that I can get a good swing at it," he said hefting the ked.

The "skunk" seemed to be most intent on getting in at one place up near the end of one of the sides, and it was relatively stable as Freddie hauled off and, after steadying himself, brought the ked down hard. Whatever it was took off and they lay there panting waiting for the dreaded pungent odor. After what seemed like an eternity, they decided that they were in the clear and eventually managed to get back to sleep for the third time.

Freddie awoke just before dawn and after lying there listening to the rhythmic breathing of the other two, realized that he needed to go to the john. Trying not to disturb them, he slowly moved his sleeping bag down past his knees, and then eased the rest of it away with his feet. He then had to get out. He was in the middle, not where he started off last night.

Propping himself up on one elbow, he had trouble remembering when he had felt as stiff. He had a terrible crick in his neck and his back felt like an old man's. He thought that he could only improve, but was worried that he may fall on one of the others. However, he managed to extricate himself and get out of the tent without disturbing them.

There was just a slight chill in the air, but not too much to worry about. He crept across the clearing in bare feet, through the gloom, hobbling along as though he was walking on eggshells although the ground was not at all hard. In fact, there was a very good bed of slightly damp decaying leaves that he was walking on. He was aching in every joint and felt even stiffer.

He could hear the soft drumming on the earth as he relieved himself, and as he did was conscious for the very first time of the pungent ammonia smell. There was something else.

At first he couldn't quite work out what it was, and as he did for another very first time, became aware of the stillness of the dawn. He stood there as though transfixed, which in a way, he was. It was as though he was enveloped in a cocoon.

There was something else he was conscious of. He usually tried to see how far he could piss. For some reason that he could not understand, he had not even

24

thought of it. Again something else intruded. There was only a waft and it was then he recognized the barely detectable smell of the camp fire, that to all appearances had looked dead.

He kept standing still. There was the merest pinprick of sound. He realized it was an ember popping and just the slightest hint of a chill in the air. Those who have watched the dawn come up will have experienced the moment. The night has run its course, the land has cooled, and now the coming of the new day. He was not at all cold.

Looking out towards the east, through the depression of the course that the gut had provided, even in its meanderings, he was unconsciously aware of the distinction between the land in the distance, an inky black, and the black of the sky, where the horizon was just about to be proclaimed more definitively.

He watched almost mesmerized at the beauty or anticipation just about to unfold, something that he had never seen before, but something that he instinctively knew was without doubt going to be beautiful. More beautiful because he was sharing it with no one.

It would be a private experience. Not that he wouldn't have shared it. It was only the circumstances that dictated it.

As these thoughts tumbled out, the spectacular unfolded before him. The first spiking rays that ever so softly grew in its intensity. A further dimension was added when there was a movement of air, warmer air, that only for a moment seemed to move around him so gently that if he had not been completely focused on what was unfolding around him, it would have passed unnoticed.

Then a sound that made him tingle: a cock crowed. It was just the faintest sound. It would have come from one of the outlying houses between the town proper and the woods. Again, further off he heard a response. He felt his heart begin to beat a little faster. The sun by this time was just beginning to visibly intrude itself into his vision, and he began to take in the unfolding miracle of the "stillness of the dawn." He stood until the black gave way to a yellowish, whitish blue, then blue; and was transfixed as the sun broke free.

Out of the corner of his eye, on a bush some six feet from him, a little to his left he saw a spider suspended in its web. The web had just the hint of dew on it, and Freddie, who had never liked spiders, thought that it was one of the most beautiful things he had ever beheld. As he watched, the droplets of dew began to take on the semblance of diamonds.

He was almost too afraid to move. It was almost magical. He let his eyes do the wandering. A movement further off to his left and a little behind him caught his attention: there was a jack rabbit that had come from behind a clump of tussock. It slowly rose up on its haunches and began sniffing the morning air, its nose twitching, front feet still, then executed a paddling action, before, reassured that all was well, it resumed its nibbling course, oblivious to the fact that it had been observed.

Freddie then returned his gaze to the east and there, from his slightly elevated position above the gut country, was the wavy, ghost-like, white mist sitting above the marsh with, as though punctuating it every so often, an enormous tree, some of it with foliage, some dead. Behind and beyond there was the slowly climbing sun gradually asserting itself over the whole vista. He shivered a little. Not with the cold, but with the awe-inspiring majesty of it. In fact, he felt quite goosey.

There he was; the blackness of the sky had completely vanished. The day had dawned. Slowly he turned towards the tent giving his head a little shake, as if to clear it, and there it was with its two occupants still in the land of slumber. He thought that he should get the fire going without disturbing them and set off towards some sticks that he could see beyond the camp, still in a kind of reverie.

He moved around the camp area with as little noise as possible and got the fire started. He had no sooner got a good blaze going than there was a muffled cough, then voices. The spell was broken. Picking up more sticks he walked towards the fire and suddenly realized that he was no longer stiff. "It will be interesting to see how the others feel when they come out of the tent," he mused.

He walked over to it and bending down poked his head through the flap and enquired as to how they had slept. This was met by a badly aimed ked which hit the flap at about knee level.

"Oh you had a good one, Chuckie, did you?" Chuck and then Billy began moaning as to show how stiff they both were and Freddie told them that it would be worse when they got up, so they had better stay there.

"Can't," they chorused. "Gotta go to the john."

"Come on," said Freddie. "The day is nearly over."

"What time is it?"

"No idea Chuckie, my watch is still in my pocket, but it is mighty early, the sun has just come up."

"Haven't you got any clothes on Freddie?"

"Only my shorts, Billy. I had to go to the john too, and I was just starting to gather some firewood for you so that you can cook us a magnificent breakfast when you both woke up. Would you mind throwing me a sweat shirt?"

He watched as they both, lying on their backs, began to move their bags down towards their feet, and then withdrew to begin collecting more firewood.

Struggling into their sweatshirts, they came out of the tent and didn't disappoint him. They both were as stiff as boards, or so they said. He decided that he would not tell them about his experience with the dawn. The time was not right and he secretly wondered if they would appreciate, or even understand, what he would be trying to describe to them.

Thinking about it he concluded that you really couldn't put it into words. There was something mystical about it, and at the same time, he thought that if they ever went camping again, they surely would eventually have the same experience. Whether or not it would affect them the way it had him, only time would tell.

Whatever their mixed thoughts were that morning they were really brought back to reality when the realized the full extent of what the dogs' foray had done. To begin with the milk, whilst they had not lost all of it, had ruined most of the bread. It had slopped everywhere inside the wooden box. It had even got into the greaseproof paper that the bacon was wrapped in and the bacon had become all the more greasy. Freddie was quietly pleased that he had shot the pad bolt home the night before.

They had started off with six eggs and now had five, with one of them slightly cracked. They thought that they may be able to salvage it, but someone was going to only have one. "Don't worry," said Billy, "I'll do a deal, more bacon for me, but you will have to clean up the things."

"I remember reading somewhere," said Freddie, "that sand and plenty of it with water will clean up cooking pots and pans."

"Come on then, Freddie," Chuck said cheerfully, "we'll get them so clean that Billy will miss out on his own bacon completely, and Freddie, just think, after we have cooked the bacon, we could fry the milky bread with some egg and butter—and have fried bread. What do you reckon?" Freddie and Billy looked at him in mock amazement.

When they had gathered up all the plates, knives and forks, mugs and the skillet, they found that it was quite cumbersome for them to carry conveniently. So they decided that they would have to carry it all in some sort of container, but of course they didn't have one. They eventually settled on the ground sheet so with one at each end holding two corners, they set off for the "gut."

They wrestled the ground sheet down the slope and then out through the reeds towards a low marshy-looking patch of relatively open ground. The going became quite squelchy a lot sooner than it had the evening before, and Freddie said that the tide must be higher.

When they were at the spot they knelt down. They were still in their shorts and dug down to see if they could bring up any mud. They found some without too much trouble and began scouring all the utensils. They put a lot of time into making sure that everything was as clean as could be, as they didn't want to catch anything from the dogs. They could see some water further over and decided to investigate after breakfast. By the time they had scoured everything out to their satisfaction and dragged it back to the camp, Billy had a good fire settled down and had cleaned up the mess that the dogs had made.

"The camp looks quite orderly, Billy," said Chuck, "I'm most impressed."

"Well, Chuckie, I knew you would be on my back if I had lit the fire and gone back to bed. Don't you think, Freddie?"

"I sure do," he responded.

They managed to have a good solid breakfast under the circumstances and pondered about what to do next. Chuck suggested that they clean everything up and pack it up and then do a bit of exploring before lunch. The cart was too heavy to pull in the terrain so they could return to it after they had explored. "Good idea," said the others.

Understandably they were all exhausted, but it would never do to arrive home to their parents around mid-morning admitting defeat, so they decided to stick it out; however, the best laid plans…!

Chapter 3

They slowly packed up the camp and walked down to the gut and surveyed it. They had all, without too much discussion, unanimously agreed that today they would cross the gut, Snakesbreath or no Snakesbreath. Today was the day. Moving off in a northerly direction, they worked their way along the edge of the gut. They had to push their way through some quite long grass and rushes at times and pick their way through clumps of trees.

In some places the gut meandered and it seemed as though they were not making much headway. The fact that they were intermittently shooting stones with the slingshots at birds, trees and anything else that took their fancy, slowed the progress on one hand, and made the time pass quite quickly on the other.

They walked on for an hour or so and then suddenly the trees around them and at the edge of the gut thinned out and they could see further than they had before. To their amazement they could plainly see, not too far away, a gigantic dead white oak with an enormous eagle's nest perched on top of it. They stood transfixed. The tree rose majestically above all the others and quite mesmerized them. They looked at each other and without a word set off in that direction. They left the gut and then came to the gut again and realized that they must be quite a way into the swamp as the gut really didn't present a formidable obstacle to them.

It was certainly more squelchy underfoot and deeper over their ankles, but did not give them any trouble at all. On the other side they actually found firmer ground and had no trouble making better time although they suddenly realized that they had lost sight of the eagle's nest. They decided to continue to the next bend of the gut and hopefully they would pick it up again but they were side-tracked.

A little way up ahead they came to a muskrat pool. Whilst they had never seen one before they knew what it was and they began to speak in whispers. Hopefully they might see one. Suddenly, slowly and furtively one came into view. It was a little over two feet long and in deep shade. Chuck, who happened to be in the lead at the time, signaled the others to stop.

The rat was about thirty feet away and had not seen them. Chuck took a stone from his pocket and placing it in the slingshot slowly and carefully bought it up and took aim. Billy and Freddie's hearts were nearly in their mouths as they held their breaths.

Thirty feet was nothing at all in weakening the muzzle velocity from a slingshot; however, he did have to hit it and they all knew if one of the three had any hope at all it was Chuck. It seemed an eternity as they watched. He appeared to be taking his time but of course wasn't. Suddenly the stone was gone and the muskrat was hit right on the head. They couldn't believe it. Chuck looked around at them with a look on his face that almost begged for confirmation.

The look on the faces of his friends told it all. They rushed past him sweeping him up as they descended on the rat and the three of them did a war dance around it. They whooped and hollered like a band of Indians as they executed the dance around it.

Suddenly Freddie said, "Look!"

They stopped and looked down and it had gone. "Here," said Billy, and turning around they first caught a glimpse of the rat rustling into the reeds about forty feet away.

They looked at each other breathlessly and in amazement in their excitement they hadn't seen the rat stir, shake its head and then set off. The whole thing broke them up. They laughed and laughed until the tears rolled down their cheeks.

"Well, killer," said Freddie, looking at Chuck, "what are we going to eat now?" And they all burst out laughing again.

"Now you come to mention it," said Billy, "I am getting peckish." Without them realizing it these things had happened in relatively quick succession. They had only about five stones left between them for the slingshots. This upset them as they took great delight in letting fly at anything that moved and a lot that didn't.

They were suddenly very hungry. They had been wandering along for around four hours and although they had taken a snack with them, they had eaten it and had also been swigging away on the water bottles and didn't have too much of it left either. "We can't eat or drink Sunny's first aid kit, can we?" said Chuck.

The other thing they dreaded had actually come to pass. They were lost. They hadn't seen the eagle tree for some time which could have been a point of reference although they agreed they didn't know where north, south, east or west was.

"Well, what are we going to do?" said Billy.

"Well, we're not going to panic," said Freddie.

"Why not, Freddie?" said Chuck.

"Why not? Because only common people panic."

"Who said that?" he responded.

"My Great Uncle, if you want to know!"

"Well," said Billy, "he is about the only person I know who could come out with something like that."

"I agree," said Chuck, "but what do we do?"

They had a "council of war" and decided that all they could do was keep walking on the higher ground and hopefully keep on course and hopefully come to a track which must lead to somewhere. As they walked they discussed the muskrat.

"He was quite big, didn't you think?" said Billy.

"He was," the other two agreed.

"I thought they only came out at night," said Freddie.

"Yes," said Billy, "but they obviously don't always."

Chuck said, "Well it was pretty shady where he was. I had great trouble even seeing him," he added with a grin.

It was about half an hour after they had set off again that they came to a well-used track and went down it in the direction they thought would take them back to town.

This wasn't to be. They hadn't gone far before they came to a clearing with buildings on the other side. It could only be Ol' Snakesbreath's lair. The fear was almost palpable. Their hearts were almost coming out of their mouths and without a word they turned around without a second look and headed off in the other direction.

They walked for about an hour and then rounding a bend in the track they came upon two little black boys of their own age who they instantly recognized from school. One was very short, almost tiny. The other was of normal height.

It should be pointed out now that whilst much has been written, observed and filmed of racial segregation in the American school system, it never was an issue in their relatively small community. Whilst segregation formally ended in the U.S. in 1954 it had never been practiced in White Oak, certainly since the end of the war and historically perhaps long before that. The historical events of the past fifteen years or so had put paid to any current issues.

They went from the Great Depression into a catastrophic (for some people anyway) World War and most folks in the community honestly believed that there was much more to life than maintaining old prejudices, as they were just too sickened at what had happened on the other side of the world, which many had seen first-hand of course; most of the men in the town had served in the armed forces, both black and white, in the Pacific, Europe, the occupation of both Germany and Japan, or Korea If they had not, they were either too old or had some kind of sickness or physical impediment. They were a very small community, proud to be American and all that that meant.

So here they were, lost in the woods having come across two other little boys who were obviously lost too, and whilst they all instantly recognized each other, up until then they really hadn't had anything to do with each other at all. One of the black boys, the smallest boy in the school, was obviously hurt. His shoulder had dropped and he was in great pain, but he bore up very well.

They walked past each other in silence, and then the three heroes stopped and turned around. "Are you guys lost?" Chuck called.

They chorused, "Yes." They were laughing at their mutual predicament. "But Lofty is hurt," the taller of the two said. The other was called "Lofty" for obvious reasons.

"Is it bad, Lofty?" they asked.

"It sure is." He looked back as he replied.

"Well there is only one thing for it," Freddie said. "We will have to go back to Snakesbreath's place and see if he can help."

Lofty and Ben looked at them in horror. "Snakesbreath, you know where he is?"

"Yes we do and you are too hurt to argue," said Freddie.

"I suppose I am, he can only kill us, in fact most of you will be able to get away while he is killing me."

So off they set. It was mid-afternoon by the time they arrived back at Snakesbreath's cabin. They were exhausted and they didn't know how old Lofty kept up, but he certainly did with no signs of a complaint. It had never occurred to them to put his arm in a sling.

Whilst they had never had a conversation with the black boys at school, there was certainly no animosity; if anything there was or appeared to exist a latent desire for some catalyst to manifest itself to throw them together in order to understand the others' point of view, outlook, call it what you may. This may probably sound too far-fetched coming from a twelve-year-old, but there you are; it existed in some shape or form even though they never fully understood it.

The fact of the matter, looking back, is that the community as a whole was not at all bigoted. They just wanted to live and let live and get on with their lives. They took people at face value, black, white or brindle. If you shaped up, fine that was what was expected of you; if you didn't, well, no one was going to deride you.

In retrospect, it could be said that it was "progressive" albeit a backwater. It may seem utopian but it existed.

To say they just "breezed" into the clearing and over to the cabin was far from the truth: getting there was one thing, actually plucking up their collective courage to venture right up to the cabin and knock on the door was no mean feat.

All this was under the watchful eye of Snakesbreath who had spotted them when they first approached the clearing earlier on, but being who he was, decided to remain out of sight and let things develop—if that was what was going to happen, as he correctly opined that they were lost. He also noticed that Lofty was hurt.

They positively crept across the open ground and finally knocked on the door. There was no response from within, not a sound. They knocked harder and the door slowly, soundlessly opened wide but with no response. Peering in with their hearts nearly coming out of their mouths with fear, they beheld what to twelve-year-old boys was a veritable Aladdin's cave.

The cabin was just one great big room with a bench running almost the full length of the wall opposite the door. They didn't notice it but there was only one doorway and they were in it. Above the bench was a long window which let in a lot of light and in the unlined roof there were several of those skylights made of frosted glass with wire mesh, so the room was quite bright. There was nothing dark and forbidding about it. One wall to their right was taken up with an open fireplace with shelves around from floor to ceiling with books on either side. It was a long wall, and they had never seen so many books. There appeared to be all sorts in all shapes, sizes and colors.

The place smelt of paraffin and leather and oil and books. There were several of those paraffin gas mantle lanterns hanging from the rafters. There was a neatly made bed in one corner, a pot-bellied stove, a table, chairs and a big armchair with a slightly smaller one, each on either side of the stove. There were fishing rods, model boats; there was an enormous tanned cowhide. There was a gun rack with several rifles in it. There were saddles, bridles. There was a saddle being made on a bench. There was a work bench with a vice, there were saws, there were hammers, nails, screws, ropes, paint and all sorts of wonderful things.

They had not realized, but the room had drawn them in like a magnet and was the most wonderful room any of them had ever seen. They just stood there slowly drinking it in, when this sound that they would never forget seemed to gradually fill the room. Freddie felt his whole body constrict and he thought that he was going to if not faint, fall over. His heart almost stopped and the hair on his head rose up as though he had been given an electric shock. His head swam.

The sound was like nothing he had ever heard before, wasn't loud but it seemed to fill the room. It seemed to come from somewhere deep down in the throat of an enormous animal. It only lasted a few seconds but it was enough to make them huddle together even as they turned around to face it; in fact two of them collided and almost fell over. What they beheld very nearly made them burst into tears, throw up or fling themselves to the floor.

There in the doorway was Snakesbreath with about the biggest dog they had ever seen before or since. To say it looked mean would not do it justice. Snakesbreath himself was enormous. You couldn't say that he looked mean but in the context of the whole thing he looked positively terrifying. He was about six foot six, wore old clothes, had the most enormous hands they had ever seen, wore a peculiar looking hat that was made out of snakeskin, had stubble but not a beard and nonchalantly carried a shotgun. They were also to find that he spoke with the most superb economy of words.

"Well, have I got me a mess of varmints!" The dog, which was right behind him, uttered another of those throaty sounds and they unconsciously moved closer together again. "Savage," Snakesbreath said, and Savage cut off the sound in mid-breath.

Taking a quick look at Lofty who appeared just about to swoon, Freddie was hoping that he would have the courage to speak; his heart was pounding, his throat seemed dry, and then he suddenly became aware of his own voice actually speaking before he knew it. When it dawned on him, he hoped that it was not quaking.

"We are not varmints, sir, we are respectable folk and we are lost, and one of us is hurt and we have come to you for help." He felt as though his heart was going to leap out of his throat.

"I see, is that so?" said Snakesbreath, looking at them with a new kind of respect. "I see, now which one of you is hurt?"

"This one, sir," said Freddie, standing aside and gently pushing Lofty to the front. Poor old Lofty, however, looked as though he was going to die, but manfully stood and looked up at Snakesbreath. He was in fact trembling like a leaf, and looked as though he could faint.

"Well little fella, you sure are hurt, come let me see." Snakesbreath put the gun down beside the door and moved over to a chair by the table. Savage, they noticed, stayed by the door. So there was no escape at all. Lofty stood there, still quaking with fear.

"Come, little fella, I am not going to hurt you or any of your friends." He gave a big reassuring smile. "I suspect you have dislocated your shoulder. How did you do it?"

"We were playing on a big fallen log, sir, and I slipped off and fell on it and it hurts a lot," murmured Lofty.

"We had better have a look at it. Now don't go woozy," he said, producing an enormous knife from his belt. "We will have to cut your shirt off as we don't want to hurt that old shoulder any more than it is already." With that he gently turned Lofty around to face the others and deftly cut the shirt from the neck down to the waistline with the knife. He then quickly removed the

39

shirt. There was poor little Lofty looking like a perfectly formed piece of ebony apart from the drooping shoulder.

Snakesbreath placed his enormous hands either side of him which made Lofty look even smaller. He turned him around to face himself, "My, my, you sure have a dislocation, and you sure are one tough fella. Now you respectable folks here, you are under my roof, in trouble and have obviously been on the track for quite a few hours, without water or food."

"Yes, sir," they chorused.

"Well there's a jug of water over on the bench and some mugs in that cupboard if you would like to help yourselves. Now what do they call you?"

"Lofty, sir."

"Lofty, well." Snakesbreath nearly chuckled, but restrained himself. "That's a mighty fine nickname. Lofty, I think we should sweeten things up before we fix your arm."

"You can fix it, Snakesbreath?" Lofty said. It was out before Lofty knew it. The others all froze. They all looked at Snakesbreath. The fear returning. Snakesbreath stood up and moved away to the bench, his shoulders shaking as he leant over, placing his hands on it.

Savage began uttering that frightful growl again. "Savage," Snakesbreath managed to get out. Savage stopped. They were all terrified. Ben and Freddie moved over towards Lofty who was just about keeling over. Snakesbreath composed himself and returned to the chair, his face wreathed in smiles and tears streaming down his face.

"Yes, Lofty, I can fix it." Lofty fell against Ben, on his good side fortunately.

"Please, sir, what are we to call you?" Freddie managed to blurt out.

"Why Snakesbreath of course. Lofty knows who I am. I am Snakesbreath! Now you fellas better tell me what your names are."

They all visibly relaxed and Snakesbreath said, "Over in that cupboard is a blueberry pie, a great big one. Why don't one of you get it and we'll all have some?"

The pie was duly put on the table and Snakesbreath cut it into seven generous slices with his enormous knife and offered them all a piece. It was delicious, needless to say. By now they were quite relaxed. Savage had left the doorway and had even smooched up to Ben, Lofty's friend.

"Now, Lofty, let's have a look at this old arm." He took Lofty and his enormous hands enveloped the small black body. "Now let's lift up your good arm. Let's have it right out to the side." Lofty lifted the good arm as far as he could but the higher he went with it, the more it appeared to hurt the other one. "That's good Lofty, keep it there."

To this day they don't quite know what he did. He gently took Lofty's shoulder between thumb and fingers of his enormous right hand as he quietly told Lofty that he was going to do something which would hurt a little and then there would only be a sort of numbness. He had no sooner said it than he had done it. Lofty gave a soft sort of a grunt, staggered a little but Snakesbreath steadied him. He also momentarily turned a light shade of grey, but his color gradually returned and Snakesbreath slowly let him go.

Lofty stood there and felt his shoulder with his good hand. "Oh, Snakesbreath," he muttered looking up at Snakesbreath for approval. Snakesbreath nodded, and Lofty went on, "You have fixed it, thank you, thank you." Snakesbreath just smiled and nodded.

"Now we have a problem," Snakesbreath said, and looking at Lofty he drew Lofty's gaze down to the seventh and last piece of pie. "That's yours, Lofty, all yours. Now when you have finished the pie, Lofty, move your arm a little and gradually swing it from side to side and bring it up over your head and do that for a while to gradually get it going again, and before long you won't even remember which one was hurt."

"Snakesbreath," said Ben tremulously.

"Yes, Ben?"

"You have an awful lot of books! We only have one at home."

"I see Ben, and I betya I know which one it is. It's the Bible, am I right?"

"Yes you are, but why do you have so many?" They all seemed to be hanging on every word.

"Ben, fellas, books are the windows to the world!"

After Lofty had finished the pie, Snakesbreath said, "Well I suppose we had better get you guys home otherwise your parents will get worried."

"Yessir Snakesbreath," they all said, "but how?"

"Follow me," he said and they all trooped outside after him, over to a small shed. "We'll go in the Duck," Snakesbreath said.

"The Duck, what is the Duck?" Chuck asked. The Duck turned out to be a DUKW or small amphibious jeep. Thousands of them had been made during the war and Snakesbreath had one which he had cut down. They were like a seagoing jeep in part, and Snakesbreath had cut the nose or flotation tank off the front and it looked quite ungainly and blunt.

He told them all about it, saying he really only needed it as a jeep, and they asked if they could have a look at the propeller. He told them that he had removed it and he showed them where it had been. He said that Savage had nearly scalped himself on it a few years ago. Well, they all piled in with Lofty having pride of place up front with the other four on the back seat. They had about five

42

miles to go back to the town and on the way Snakesbreath asked them what they had been doing.

They told him about the campsite and the dogs, the skunk and the rat. He had a great laugh about it and suggested that as the camp was all packed up they could probably leave it until the next day.

"Now where can I take you all to?"

It was agreed that it would be Freddie's place and Snakesbreath said that Lofty should be taken to the doctor just in case, though he felt sure he would be all right.

"When will we see you again, Snakesbreath?" they said.

"Whenever you like. Why don't you have someone drive you out tomorrow at about the same time? I'll pick up the camping gear if you tell me where it is."

They were all dropped off at Freddie's place and when his mother heard the Duck pull up and then drive off she came out and you can imagine was quite surprised to see the five of them all standing there looking back at the fast disappearing Duck. "What have you boys been up to?" she enquired.

"Well, Mom, it's a long story. We have been with Ol' Snakesbreath," ventured Freddie.

"Snakesbreath?" she said. "Come along inside—you too, boys," she said to Lofty and Ben. "What are your names?" Lofty and Ben responded. "Well come along inside and tell me all about it."

When she heard that Lofty had been hurt and that Snakesbreath had fixed him up, Alice became quite concerned and said that she would take him straight to the doctor via Lofty's house. They all piled into the Chevy and Lofty directed them to his house on the other side of town. Sunny for once in her life was as quiet as a mouse.

Lofty's parents didn't have a phone. They got quite a surprise when the Chevy pulled up. Alice suggested that Lofty's Mom, Molly, should go with them around to the doctors so that he could do a thorough inspection of the arm and she could get the word straight from the horse's mouth, so to speak.

They arrived at the doctor Eric Holmes' house and in they all went. The doctor was quite happy to see Lofty when Alice told him what had happened. To their amazement the doctor only gave Lofty a perfunctory kind of a check up, and when Alice queried this he sat back, pulled out his pipe and filled it as he said, "Let me tell you a story. Snakesbreath, or Alex Arbuthnot, I suspect, would be a much better doctor than most, if he had continued to practice."

"What," Alice said, "he's a doctor?"

"Well, yes and no. He was a doctor in the first war and had a very tough time of it in France patching up the most horrific wounds. After the war he was still quite young of course and he had had an absolute gut-full of medicine. He went back to University on one of those rehabilitation courses that they have for veterans and did engineering—civil and mechanical engineering. He can do just about anything!

"Now, if he fixed up the little fellow's arm, I can assure you that no one could have done a better job, so you can all rest easy. When the bruising comes out in a few days he won't even be able to tell which arm it was. I bet ya! Now what else did Alex say?"

"Well, doctor, he suggested that tomorrow our parents take us back to see him so that he can see for himself how Lofty is and our parents can meet him themselves," said Freddie.

The doctor smiled and looking at Freddie's mother said, "Ali, why don't you pick me up at about four tomorrow, with the boys, and we'll all go and see him?

Actually he is a good friend of mine, we play bridge together once a week!"

As they prepared to leave, Freddie commented on the fact that whilst bridge had never interested him in the past, it could bear further looking into. The other boys agreed. His mother and the doctor rolled their eyes.

Chapter 4

Just prior to this, the recently-appointed school headmaster, having convinced a very progressive PTA that it was his intention to put together the very best teachers on offer for their school, struck gold. He had advertised for a Math and an English teacher and got them in one: a married couple in their early thirties with no children. He could not believe his luck. Neither could the PTA. They were well balanced, had excellent references to their most impressive qualifications and they both wanted to teach and not administrate.

They were from Canada, although the husband was an American, and when courting they were on her father's ranch and had both contracted the C.A.B. Brucellosis germ from an infected cow that had aborted. Whilst they had been devastated that they could never have children either together or independently, they both loved children.

They were teachers after all and had decided that they would seek out a school and make it their life's work. They preferred a semi-rural community and had no qualms about being associated with a school that happened to have a few black children under its roof, although these children were taught separately.

It was this as much as anything that impressed the headmaster. Whilst there were quite a lot of applicants for the positions, it came down to the final winners who were very nearly pipped at the post by another couple where the husband was also a math teacher and had a most presentable wife who could have taken the English class if the position depended on it, but would rather wait for a year or so as she had two small children.

If anything they were better on paper than the two who eventually took the positions, but the husband failed what was to become known as the "Gate Test," which went like this.

After the interviews had narrowed the field to the two last applicant couples, the School President, Uncle Ted, together with the headmaster, invited them separately out to The Lagoon to have lunch and a look around in a more relaxed atmosphere. This enabled the headmaster and President to see if they knew how to hold a knife and fork amongst other things, and conduct themselves in an informal social atmosphere.

Part of the afternoon involved taking the men with their wives around the spread to enable the two interviewers to see whether or not the applicants were practical. It bemused both of them to find that the most qualified one could hold forth on virtually any subject, was knowledgeable on a host of things, was amiable and didn't ram things down their throats, but literally did not know how to open a gate.

As anyone who has had any experience on a ranch will know, there are a wide variety of gate catches; gates are swung from the left or right as you approach them and some open towards you and some away, and of course some either way. Some with sag have to be carried, and if some have too much strain on them you may have to stand on them to release the chain. Whilst The Lagoon was a beautifully maintained spread it was enormous, so there were plenty of gates to cater for just about any type of problem you wished to subject anyone to.

The first fellow could not take a trick, he would walk to up the hinged end—he had been sat in the front of the station brake so that he had to open the gates, and look for a chain. He would pull when he should push and with some catches he had to ponder over how they worked. The other thing that amazed his two hosts was that he gave no indication that he was having trouble or that this was all new to him.

The one, who was slightly less qualified, got the job. He had no trouble with any of them. In fact, even told old Unc as he was getting out of the vehicle for one gate that he would have to back off a little as he was too close to the gate which had to be opened back towards them.

After they had dealt with the first fellow Unc opined that he could only get the job if the second applicant was worse, which he frankly thought was quite impossible. The successful pair was a perfectly rounded couple for their age and they appeared to greatly impress everyone concerned with their application for the positions and also got along with them all. So much so that Unc made a decision that he and quite a few others came to regret. He offered them a house to live in. He had several houses in the town that he rented out and this one had recently become vacant. It was not nearly as good as the headmaster's house but was much nicer than the one the school owned, which they would normally have had to live in. It had lawns, a garden, shrubs and all in all a lot of charm. Unc told them that they could have it for what they would have had to pay in rent for the schoolhouse.

They were overwhelmed. They let it come out over a period of time that whilst the schoolhouse would have suited them admirably it was too close to the school itself and they preferred, if at all possible, not to live on the job, no matter how dedicated they were.

In the usual course of events the couple would have blended into the community at whatever level their station was and that would have been that. But no. That was not what fate had in mind for them. They were involved quite early in their tenure in one of the most contentious events that ever shook the town. An event that would rock it to its very foundations.

All the locals, both those who knew Freddie's family and those who didn't, whilst they had a great respect for them, also had a soft spot for Alice after all that had happened to her. The immediate family had within a generation on the male side, been whittled away to two people: Freddie's Great Uncle and his brother, who was Freddie's Grandfather, although they had a host of distant relatives living elsewhere in the States and overseas.

Freddie's Great Uncle had four brothers and two sisters and whilst the brothers all went off to France in the First World War only two came home. Freddie's Grandfather and Grandmother, Alice's parents, were killed on a European tour when his mother, the only child, was thirteen years of age.

His Great Uncle who was at home on The Lagoon lost his wife and two children when the horse that was pulling their buckboard around The Lagoon on an inspection, bolted when it came upon a snake and crashed the buckboard into a tree.

"Unc" was thrown clear but the other three were killed instantly, as was the horse. This was some years prior to the death of Freddie's grandparents. The two old aunts had each married and lived overseas. All this over the course of twenty years, with the once extensive vibrant family, a great contributor to the County and the state, reduced to a thirty-something-year-old man and his thirteen-year-old niece, Alice, Freddie's mom.

She would always remember their first meeting after her parents and brother were killed. She was in Switzerland at a hotel in Geneva, where one of Unc's business associates and his wife had taken her after the accident. The couple could not have been more sympathetic or efficient. He took care of all the formalities with the bodies and arranged for them to be shipped home. She, the older woman, could not have been more attuned to Alice's traumatic experience—devastating for anyone, let alone a young girl of thirteen on the other side of the world on her own, and coming into a very difficult age, if she wasn't already there.

Her uncle was with her inside of a week which wasn't too bad under the circumstances. He was shown up to the suite that they were staying in and after the initial welcome the other couple excused themselves and said that they would be back in an hour or so.

Unc showed them out and returned to Alice who was standing over by the windows. She turned as he approached, and looked up at him. He looked down at her beautiful little face, a face that he had never known to show anything other than vitality and enthusiasm with a little bit of impishness thrown in. He tenderly took her face in both hands and gently wiped away the tears that were silently streaming down her cheeks with his thumbs.

Whilst she had her face turned up towards him she lowered her eyes and spoke ever so softly but clearly, "Now I am all alone."

He tilted her head up just a little and said, "Oh, Chickie, oh, Chickie, my darling." He paused. "You will never be alone as long as I have a breath in my body!"

He slowly bought her forward and tilted her head a little more and gently kissed her on the forehead and lowering his arms drew her to him. "You know, Chickie, life deals up some darned awful hard times and our family has had its share over the years, and all the money in the world can't stave it off. But never you mind, whilst things could not be worse at the present time, we will come through it together." He drew back and, taking each of her hands in his, peered at her closely. "Now you look at me, Chickie, I am not yet forty and you may think that is old, but I can tell you, I will be around for a long time yet, and you can take it from me that I will never let you down, ever. You are the most precious thing to me and I will be your rock. Now come over here and we'll sit by the window."

He led her over to the couch by the window with the magnificent view over the lake and sat her down. "Now hang on a tick and I'll order some coffee and something light to eat." He rang room service and ordered something to be sent up and then returned to the window and sat down. He patted her on the knee and said, "Now this is what I propose we do. I've had a lot of time to think over the past week."

What he proposed was relatively straightforward but when he discussed it with their extended family, whilst they agreed, they felt that he was oversimplifying the proposal. As much as his two sisters wanted to help they had their own young families and lived too far away from The Lagoon.

They all agreed that Alice should grow up at The Lagoon if at all possible. The step entailed Unc becoming her legal guardian. This was a procedural matter as no one objected and of course they were a family of substance in the state. They then had to look at the position with The Lagoon itself. When Unc's wife and children were killed, Unc and Alice's father completely reorganized their affairs, leaving Alice's side of the family with what they termed the more rural pursuits and Unc with the industrial pursuits.

The Lagoon was put into a trust for her family and subsequent children. It was an enormous operation with cotton, tobacco, corn, cattle and hogs, orchards; it even had a fishing fleet. There were around two hundred black workers employed on The Lagoon with white managers and overseers. There was also an excellent General Manager under Alice's father. For all this, Alice's father had taken a keen day-to-day involvement in the enterprise and everything ran like a top.

Whilst Unc wasn't at all concerned about the business side of The Lagoon, it was really the domestic side that he had to get right. Having taken care of the guardianship aspect, he now addressed the other issue that had been concerning him. He was a stickler for having everything in little boxes. Things didn't have to fit perfectly, he was too practical for that. But there was a scheme of things and that was that. Nothing was to stray too far.

Needless to say they had always had black house servants and a black cook and butler. Unc felt that they needed a more appropriate arrangement under the circumstances and came up with an excellent well-presented woman in her fifties who was a widow with grown up children who had left home. She had a Southern background and an easygoing nature which immediately defused any likelihood of friction between their old loved black retainers. Alice took to her immediately.

He then, wonder of wonders, and to the amazement of everyone, announced that Alice couldn't grow up in a house full of old people and he had a solution. If it didn't work out after two months they wouldn't continue with it, however they had nothing to lose.

"What do you propose?" asked Alice, when the idea was first mooted.

"Well it only struck me recently when I learnt about the mess that the son of an old friend of mine had got into. They are from Missoura and the nineteen-year-old son has unfortunately got a bit too close to the eighteen-year-old daughter of a neighbor, and what with one thing and another, the girl has had a baby just prior to the wedding, which had to be called off as the boy died. He was bucked off a horse into some rails, and died of the injuries.

"Now whilst the girl's family are respectable, they are battlers and my old friend's wife really can't abide the girl's mother and both families are at a loss as what to do. This leaves the girl and the baby—a girl also— between the devil and the deep blue sea. It occurred to me that if the girl and baby were to come down here we might be able to give her a nice family atmosphere for some years or so and, who knows, we may all benefit by it."

Well of course everyone thought that the whole thing coming together like that was a pipe dream, indeed far-fetched in the extreme, but Unc cajoled all his extended family and the Missourians as well, and they duly arrived. The baby girl soon had everyone including Unc wrapped around her little finger. The whole group, after an initial settling in, fell into the ways of a normal family with the woman, Eloise, presiding over most matters pertaining to the house and girls, with help from Unc when it was needed.

Thinking back over it all some years on, Alice marveled at how well it did work out. Eventually she married her childhood sweetheart and whilst they lived in New York and had Freddie before the war, they moved back into White Oak after it, but not to The Lagoon. Alice wanted Freddie and Sunny, who was born after the war, to have closer companionship with other children, unlike her own experience at the same age; and they would only get that in town.

The girl and the baby, who had of course grown and developed into a lovely young woman herself, had moved back to Missouri, taken up their lives again, and prospered.

Eloise had gone her separate way eventually, and the whole business, they all agreed, had lent another dimension to their lives which they would all cherish. This of course gave Unc no end of satisfaction.

Freddie's father George had been severely wounded in the head during the war and been invalided out. Whilst the wound had not affected his faculties at all he just didn't want to return to the day-to-day pressure of a high-powered law firm in New York. He did a refresher degree, and gradually involved himself in the myriad affairs of The Lagoon with Unc's encouragement. He had a rather full plate as he came from a similar background himself and had a substantial involvement in his own family's affairs as well. Alice called him "Gordos." He had graduated Phi Beta Kappa, and she, being the trick that she was, wanted to maintain the Greek connotation.

Chapter 5

Alice said to the doctor—"You actually play Bridge once a week with him."

"Why yes, we do," said the doctor. "Once a week. He comes in each Thursday evening and he has a bath, and collects his laundry."

"A bath?" said Alice curiously.

"Yes, as you can imagine the place out beyond the gut is fairly primitive although comfortable and whilst he had rigged up a kind of a shower which he has each day, there is nothing like a good old soak."

"No there is not, but how did you come to be in this situation?"

"Aha," said the doctor, who knew her very well. "What say I tell you on the way out there tomorrow evening?"

Alice felt that she could not press him any further on the matter and agreed. "We have to go out to fetch the handcart anyway, so I'll pick you up at four o'clock. Will you have finished with your patients by then?"

"I hope so, I'll see you then."

Alice couldn't wait for three-thirty to come around. Sunny was also in quite a high state of excitement and Alice drove around the town picking up all the other children in the Chevy. The handcart would easily fit into the back of it, with the wheels off. Lofty's mother stayed behind—she felt she was getting a little too out of her depth—and so Alice arrived at the doctors with five boys in the back and Sunny on the seat behind her.

She collected the doctor and set off. He could sense that Alice was nearly beside herself with anticipation so more or less immediately began his amazing story.

He had first met Alex on one of the Pacific Islands during the war. They were island-hopping and Alex was the Captain of an engineering company responsible for building airstrips. The island was also a staging post for medical evacuees. They were stabilized there before they were flown or shipped back to the States or Australia. Their wounds were assessed and they either flew or went by sea, depending on their condition.

"Well, to cut a long story short the Japs staged one of their very few attacks—they were in retreat at this stage as you may remember, and they bombed the airstrip, the officer's quarters beside the hospital, and killed all the doctors except three, out of twenty. They also killed a lot of the orderlies.

"Well to the amazement of everyone when they met to organize themselves after the raid, in a formal sense, Alex, who had been helping out with all the other able-bodied men, announced that he would be happy to take over the hospital.

"The ranking officer—a one-star General—asked a Colonel who he was. Alex said, 'Give me five minutes, General,' and disappeared.

"Now everyone stood around waiting, almost but not quite shaking their heads. Alex had a quiet presence about him and from the Colonel down, as much to his demeanor as his older years, they all liked and respected him. Whilst they couldn't understand where he might be coming from they had to give him the benefit of the doubt. I should point out at this stage I was one of the three remaining doctors, and a young Captain. Alex at the time would have been in his late forties, almost too old to even be enlisted, but we needed engineers. Little did we know.

"A few minutes later Alex came around the corner of the tent wearing the tunic of a First War Major with the most amazing array of decorations including British and French, the Distinguished Service Cross, the Military Cross and the Croix de Guerre. With a sheepish look on his face he announced that he was in fact a doctor and a surgeon and had much experience in these situations in France.

"Well you can imagine we all nearly wept. The General even saluted him and immediately promoted him to full Colonel. Alex took it all in his stride and said quietly, 'Well, shall we do our rounds of the wards?'

"It goes without saying of course that Alex made sure that the engineers were well organized."

"Phew," said Alice, "There are actually people like that alive and well. I never ever expected to meet someone like this. The Distinguished Service Cross, the Military Cross, the Croix de Guerre! There aren't many decorations higher than that, are there?"

"No, and when you have the Congressional Medal of Honor and a host of other American decorations it is most impressive. He was the most highly decorated soldier in his division in the first war and for the two wars, I believe he was in the top ten; not a bad effort.

"The only other thing I would say is that he is a very retiring private person, so just exercise discretion with what I have just told you!"

"Of course," said Alice. "Now boys, Sunny, did you hear what doctor said?" They all murmured assent. Whilst the doctor was relating all this they were very quiet and hanging on every word, and looking at each other with their eyes wide, and looks of amazement on their faces.

"So when he comes in for a bath, you play bridge do you?"

"We do, we play three-handed contract. He's an excellent player and we began, of course, during our island-hopping."

"Did you know he actually came from White Oak?"

"No, I knew he came from the country. It was only in '46 when Annette and I moved to White Oak into the new practice that I found out. I ran into him at the garage and livery."

"You astound me," said Alice. "Are we still on the right track, boys?"

"Yes, Mom."

"He isn't seen around the town very often, is he?" said Alice.

"No he isn't, but that is the way he likes it I suppose. He's certainly involved with the veterans, though."

The boys in the back seat were goggle-eyed at all this talk coming over from the front seat and Sunny who generally didn't stop talking had hardly said a word. "We haven't got far to go now, Ali," said the doctor.

The track widened out slightly as it converged with two other tracks coming in from either side and it then opened out into the open space that the boys had arrived at what to them seemed a lifetime ago. So much had happened.

Snakesbreath appeared with Savage almost immediately and after shaking hands with the doctor introduced himself to Alice and greeted the boys with a twinkle and a broad wink. Savage slowly meandered over to Ben and quietly stood beside him; looking up at him he slowly wagged his tail and leant against him. This didn't go unnoticed by the others, and even Snakesbreath rolled his eyes and smiled.

Alice, who was normally the most composed person, had to confess to herself that she was a little in awe of him. She responded and was in the process of introducing Sunny when he hunkered down in front of her and with a lovely smile and asked, "What is your name, little Missy?" Sunny, who was staying very close to her mother, moved even closer to Alice who put an arm around her and gave her arm a slight squeeze of encouragement.

"Edith, Edith, Elithabeth but they…" quaked Sunny who had almost grown out of her lisp.

To everyone's consternation Snakesbreath went as white as a sheet and rocked backwards and although he recovered quickly his reaction was such that Alice and the doctor looked awkward and the boys threw quick looks at each other.

Mercifully, Alice thought in retrospect, although not at the time, Sunny saved the situation.

Like the others she had been concerned at Snakesbreath's reaction and her normal caring nature more or less instinctively overcame her natural reticence.

"Oh I'm thorry, did I upthet you thomehow? They call me Thunny!"

"Sunny," said her mother.

"No it's OK," said Snakesbreath.

"No no you don't have to explain really," said Alice.

"I know," said Snakesbreath, "I don't, but perhaps it is time I should; come inside." Snakesbreath offered the chairs to Alice and the doctor and invited the children to perch on the table. He looked at Sunny and said "May I?" And lifted her up onto the bench not far from the stool. Which he then sat on.

"You see," he said, "I used to have a little girl named Edie. Before the first war I was married with a wife and two children, a boy and a girl. They were ten and eight and my daughter's name was Edie. Now you can't be expected to know this but I am part Chickamokee and my people lived in this region of the country up until the mid-1800's. They then resettled in what we know as Florida."

The children had amazed expressions on their faces at all this and Snakesbreath smiled, acknowledging this, and continued: "However, they always regarded this as their spiritual ancestral home. Now as I said I am only part Indian and whilst I knew about this area I didn't place too much belief into the story that we would always be drawn back to our ancestral home, until after I had married and the children had reached the age of four and six, we came down here one time and camped.

"We had brought a canoe on the roof of the old car and we stayed in town for a few days and went exploring in the canoe. We had the most wonderful time. But do you know that when we set off on our most extensive days outing, we came to a place where, when we went ashore, I felt as though I had been drawn there by a magnet, and it was this spot that we are on now."

The boys looked at each other, Alice looked at Edie and she seemed mesmerized. The doctor lit his pipe.

"Now the interesting thing was, my two children experienced a similar sensation but my wife didn't and—she had no Indian blood in her at all. She did however appreciate it and told me that when we were here we, the other three, became almost different people.

"She said that it was so intangible that the normal observer would be oblivious to it, but she wasn't. She said that the best way she could describe it was that we quietly began to exude a kind of inner grace. It was quite odd but she was correct. I had never been more at peace with myself, with the world. I had in fact come home, with my children. It was more than that; it wasn't so much the coming home, it was the fact that I knew where it was, I had experienced it, no one could take it away from me. The fact that I had exposed my children to it at such a tender age lent another dimension to it."

He looked at Alice and the doctor—"Do you want me to continue? I'm not boring you am I?"

"No, no," they said as one.

"But really," Alice looked at him, "We don't wish to impose at all."

"I'll put the jug on, would anyone like a cup of tea?" he asked, putting the jug on his pressure burner. "I'm sorry I don't have any coffee." They all accepted apart from the doctor who said that he only drank coffee or whiskey, and that he would survive, with a grin. Snakesbreath pulled out a whiskey bottle and two glasses, saying laughingly that as he only had a few cups for the tea he would have a whiskey although he didn't know about Eric the doctor, it would normally be too early in the day for him. Ha Ha.

He continued to talk as he made the tea and had Sunny help him pass it around. Of course none of the children had drunk tea before so he didn't make it too strong. Alice said that whilst she had always liked tea she never drank it as everyone else drank coffee. "Well," said Snakesbreath, "It's a good habit to get into."

He continued with his story. "We all agreed that this was the place where we would like to holiday or come to, if we had any spare time. I had my business to attend to and was doing a course at University and had free time every so often and we only lived a hundred miles or so away over in Maryland.

"I went to the local Realty and asked them if there was any land for sale in the gut country south of the bottom end of The Lagoon and incredibly there was 50 acres available. This 50 acres. It was one of the small parcels that had been overlooked for years. The owners were long gone and the rates hadn't been paid so the County had resumed it, it really was just a piece of rising ground, well drained and a well wooded area in the whole extensive southern lagoon area. And like a fairy story it was our very own spot. The County was going through a tough patch at the time and informed me that if I was to pay the outstanding rates they would give me clear and free title to it, so that is what we did and this is where we used to come wherever we could.

"How is everyone's tea? I'll just pour a couple of whiskeys. Now, it is well over say thirty years ago but it only seems like yesterday. The four of us were out on the lagoon in the canoe and a terrific storm blew up, it was in 1923."

"I was three years old," said Alice.

"Were you?" said Snakesbreath. "At that time I had not got to know your family. Anyway, the canoe was suddenly swamped and Edie, who was eight at the time, was drowned, as were my wife and son. Whilst we found my wife's and son's bodies, we didn't ever find Edie."

"Oh," said Sunny. She was sitting quite close to him and moved over to put her hands on his forearm and inclined her head.

Everyone looked everywhere except at each other and then Snakesbreath broke the spell. "Now it is a very long time ago and I have got over it, but it did give me a jolt when you, Missy, told me your name. I must admit it is odd that I had not heard that Alice had a little girl by that name, but there you are. I suppose really, as everyone calls you Sunny, I couldn't expect to know."

He stood up took a deep breath exhaled and looked at his friend—"Another one Eric?"

"No thank you, I think we should be off." The doctor stood up and gave Snakesbreath's arm a squeeze and said, "All we need to do is take the wheels off the cart."

"Yeah, well that won't be too difficult," said Snakesbreath. "Come on you guys!"

He smiled as Alice and Sunny walked past and ahead of him. Sunny looked up at him as did her mother who looked a little as though her head was spinning. Alice quite honestly felt that she was too exhausted by the whole visit.

They slowly drove back to town and after driving in complete silence for some five minutes Alice said to no one in particular, "That was one of the most incredible stories I have ever heard."

The doctor said, "Well, I told you he was an interesting fellow—there is a lot more to him than you would imagine."

The children, who had been quiet up until then, seemed to snap out of their reverie when Sunny asked when they could see him again.

"Well," said Alice, "I don't know."

"Aw come on, Mom," said Freddie and all the others muttered something along the lines that "it would be great Mrs. Gardiner." Alice said that she would discuss it with the doctor and all the parents.

The upshot of the whole visit was that they all agreed that if Snakesbreath was happy to see the children the parents would facilitate it one way or another. Of course it wasn't possible for Sunny to go out into the swamp with the boys but a happy compromise presented itself. Sunny was invited to stay over one night with the doctor and his wife and it just happened to coincide with Snakesbreath's weekly bath night.

So around a week later Sunny was at the Doctors house having dinner with Snakesbreath and the doctor and his wife Annette. After dinner the three adults settled down for their usual game of bridge and Sunny asked if she could sit up for a while and watch. The doctor's wife told her that she could stay for the first rubber and then she would have to go to bed as little girls had to get their sleep.

They explained how the game was structured at her request but not without a certain amount of eye rolling at each other. However, it was not long before they realized that some if not all the questions she was asking them were extremely intelligent coming from someone who had never seen the game before, let alone one so young.

The rubber was over too soon and then she was told that she had to go off to bed. She had been standing more beside Snakesbreath than the others and she leant upwards and gave him a kiss on his cheek and thanked him very much. She then went around the table as Annette was getting out of her chair and kissed the doctor goodnight and thanked him. Annette then took her by the hand and led her off in the direction of the bedrooms saying that she would be back in a moment after she had put her to bed.

The two men sat back not saying a word with old men's smiles on their faces. Annette came back into the room a few minutes later.

"Well, what do you think of our Sunny?" she said, looking at Alex,

"She is an absolute sweetie," he responded. "She sure cottoned on to the bridge, don't you think? Has she ever been exposed to it before?"

"She stays with us perhaps once a month, every six weeks or so, and she has been exposed to it before but has flatly refused to learn. Her parents play and Alice used to play with her uncle when she was younger before she was married when they had Eloise Conroy and Ella Collishaw, the young unmarried mother staying out at The Lagoon. Now I have to tell you something!"

Eric said, "Just a moment, Apple"—his pet name for her—"we have around two more rubbers to play tonight."

"Don't worry, relax, you won't believe what Alice said to me when she dropped Sunny off."

"Well don't keep us in suspense, tell us," said the doctor.

"Give me strength," said Annette, patting him on the shoulder, as she sat down again. "Alice said that Freddie had asked her if he and the boys could learn to play bridge."

"Good heavens," said the doctor.

"Yes," Annette went on, "but the interesting aspect to the whole thing is that the new school teacher and his wife play bridge and they have been trying for the last few weeks to interest the school children, with no success at all with the boys. They have half a dozen girls but the boys won't have a bar of it. Apparently they all believe it is for sissies. No inducement could get one boy.

"Now out of a clear blue sky they have three boys wanting to learn.—Now I wonder what could have changed their minds." She looked knowingly from one to the other.

"I wonder?" said the doctor looking at Snakesbreath and smiling.

"Good heavens," said Snakesbreath.

"Yes," they both said.

"Now Alice said when she dropped Sunny off, that she would like to speak to me at a more opportune time; however, that is the state of play at the moment."

Looking back, it emerged that Alice felt that it took no time at all for the whole bridge debacle to develop.

Chapter 6

However, few things develop in isolation.

Bridge apart, the five boys were allowed to settle into what became an established but casual routine with Snakesbreath.

Once a fortnight one of the parents took the five out to the "land beyond the gut" where they spent the most wonderful hours with him. Sometimes they slept overnight in a large tent that he bought for the purpose.

They had been making these visits for around the sixth time when they arrived to find him with five long packages on the bench. There was a name on each one and they were invited to open theirs.

To their utter joy in each one was a single shot pea rifle. Needless to say they ooed and aahed and thanked him profusely, which he acknowledged but brushed off nonchalantly. He then went on to say that only one of them had handled the gun correctly.

"What do you mean?" they chorused.

He also told them that he had spoken to all the parents and asked them if they would be happy to give them each a rifle and teach them gun lore. "Now we'll put them back again."

He went on. "Well, whenever you pick up a gun for the first time or one that has been out of your sight for a while, you always check to see if it is loaded. Always: it

66

doesn't matter if it's yours or someone else's. You always check it. There are an awful lot of people killed each year by not following this simple rule. You always check them and you never point a gun at anyone.

"Now Ben was the only one who checked to see if his was loaded." Ben looked most embarrassed. "No Ben, you were the only one. Now guys, pick 'em up again and check them."

"I don't know how," said Lofty.

"OK, OK. We'll start at the beginning," said Snakesbreath. "Now, we'll put 'em on the table again, and I'll take you through it."

Picking up one of the rifles he said, "Now, this is what is called the bolt. It is what actually fires the bullet, as it is activated by the trigger. When you pick a rifle up you take the ball of the bolt, lift it up and slide it back. This exposes the breech, which in this case is empty. As it should be." Now, he put his hand in his pocket and pulled out two bullets and placed them on the table.

"If you look closely at them you will see that one is slightly longer than the other. If you look closer you will also see that one has three 'rings' around the actual lead, and the other has two.

"These are known as long and short rifle. The short rifle can be used for target practice, or critters at close range, and the long rifle, which has about 25 percent greater charge, for anything that is a distance away. We then have the foresight and the back sight.

"To aim you close your left eye, squint along the barrel and place the bead of the foresight with the top of the bead, square in the middle of an imaginary line across the top of the 'V' of the back sight. Like this." He held it in the aiming position.

"So here we have a rifle made up of a stock, the wooden part, a barrel, and a breech above the trigger which is attached to the barrel. Here, I'll show you." He undid the knurled screw just forward of the trigger guard and removed the barrel from the stock.

He then reassembled it and further explained the workings of the bolt. "To remove it completely you just pull the trigger and pull the end of the bolt or the ball of the bolt up and back and it will come out. See, now we can take it apart even further, but you will probably never need to do that. But if you hold it you can pull this knob back and then softly let it go: this cocks the rifle. When you don't wish to cock it you pull and hold the knob back and pull the trigger and ease the knob forward.

"The firing pin or mechanism is on the other end of it, and it is this that actually fires the bullet. These small bullets are what are known as rim fire whereas larger caliber bullets are known as center fire. But we'll deal with these at a later time.

"Now we'll do it again: we'll put the bolt back by reversing the process." They were all hanging on every word, he was pleased to see. "To close the breech off we pull on the trigger when the bolt is partially back in and then slide it forward keeping the trigger pulled. Slide it completely home and down and then release the trigger. It is now safe. Now you fellas try that a few times and then we'll go outside and fire a few shots. I can see you're itching to."

He led them outside and down towards the lake. "Now there is another thing about not pointing a gun at anyone, and that is, you always shoot for the pot. Why, you may ask. Well, what are you shooting for? Target practice. Fine. Fire away as much as you like. However, if you want to become a good shot, as most people do, fire single shots. If every shot has to count you will become much better than if you have a full magazine to play with.

68

"It's a bit different if you have a horde of nips coming at you, of course, but that isn't likely."

"What would you need for that Snakesbreath?" asked Ben.

"Well, in the Islands and in Europe we had M1 Carbines. And BARs, and sub machine guns, as well as medium and heavy machine guns. The officers also carried pistols, automatics. As engineers we had M1 Carbines which are much handier than a rifle as they have short barrels. As Medics we were not armed."

"What's a BAR?" asked Chuck.

"A Browning Automatic Rifle. They were quite popular for a range of work," Snakesbreath responded.

The target practice progressed for some weeks until one day Snakesbreath said to them that from today he would like to have them call him Alex. He would feel more comfortable and he suspected that they would also. He then said that next weekend he was going to take them on their first shoot.

"What are we going to shoot, Snakesbreath?" said Chuck, much to his embarrassment. Alex wiggled his finger at him and they all laughed.

"We're going to shoot an elk!"

"What is an elk?" asked Ben.

"A kind of deer," said Billy.

"That's right," said Alex.

"Are these bullets big enough for an elk?" asked Freddie.

"No, they are not, we are going to use a heavier charge, with a scoped rifle: that is a .22 Hornet. It is also a center fire. I've got one on the bench."

They had all been looking at it but hadn't said anything. He passed it to Chuck who was standing closest to him. Mercifully, they all thought, Chuck opened the breech when he took it. He closed it again and asked if they could go outside and look through the scope. Alex nodded and out they trooped.

"The scope is zeroed in at 200 yards," said Alex. "All you do is become comfortable with how far you place your eye behind the telescope. It takes a bit of getting used to, but the trick is to have a clear lens with no dark shadow around what you are aiming at. You place the target in the middle of the cross hairs and there you are.

"With the elk, you must have a head shot. The bullet won't stop it if you hit it anywhere else. So what we need to do now is have some practice with the Hornet."

"What are we going to do with the elk once we have shot it Alex?" Lofty asked.

"A good question, Lofty. We are going to dress it, or skin it. Hang it for three to five days depending on the weather and then cut it up and you can each have some. Actually, I take one into town to the Holmeses every now and again."

"How big are they? What do they taste like?" The questions flooded in.

"They are not much bigger than a big sheep really, but with longer legs and they taste pretty good, but they are almost too gamey or strong-flavored to eat all the time. Say once or twice a year. Of course you then have the hide, which we can peg out and even make moccasins out of if you like."

The target practice began, and the following Friday afternoon when they arrived Alex said, "Well, tonight is the night. We shoot an elk."

"What if we can't find any?"

"We will, we will, I know where to find them."

"In the dark?" asked Chuck.

"We have a spotlight," said Alex. "Look." He led the way into the shack, and there on the bench was a hand-held spotlight and a battery.

"We'll have a bite to eat now and then head off, fellas, on foot. We'll leave Savage here and only take the Hornet, a long pole and a shovel."

Chapter 7

Old Unc was quite tickled when he learnt that the teachers wanted to conduct bridge classes at home. He just shook his head when he was told that none of the boys were interested and impishly commented that the parents obviously had no influence over their children. When told that the boys now wanted to learn, he was delighted and asked what this sudden change of heart could be put down to.

Alice then told him, or enlarged on the meeting that she had with Snakesbreath and the fact that the doctor had told her that Snakesbreath played bridge once a week with them.

"A bit of hero worship don't you think, Unc?"

"Seems like it," said Unc. "He is an incredible fellow all right, he has the most unbelievable war record and more decorations than anyone I am likely to know—did Eric fill you in on that?"

"Yes he did—you know I had always thought that he was an old hermit."

"No, no nothing like it," said Unc. "He is retiring and a little reclusive, but that is his business. He is well liked by the local members of the Legion, however is not quite as involved as he used to be. But I suppose a lot of people are like that, and few, if any, would have his record, but as you can see it is a two-way thing."

"He seems quite taken with Sunny, too," said Alice.

"Well there would be something wrong with him if that little sweetie didn't strike a chord," mused Unc.

"It seems to be a mutual thing."

So it was arranged that the three boys would take bridge lessons and Sunny was invited to play bridge with the doctor once a fortnight.

The peace in the small community was shattered about a month later when Freddie told his mother one afternoon that Lofty and Ben would also like to play bridge. Unbeknownst to their parents the five boys had been seeing a lot of each other at every opportunity at school.

"It is OK, Mom, I have asked the teacher and he said that he would be only too happy to teach them."

"Freddie, you should have discussed it with Dad and me first," she responded in quite an agitated way.

"Why, Mom, don't you like Lofty and Ben?"

"Darling, that is not the point!"

"Well do you, Mom, do you like them or not?"

"Freddie come and sit down. Now look there are some things that in the fullness of time you will learn about, but all I will say now is that the boys—Lofty and Ben— are very nice and I do like them. They are lovely boys, but, and it is an enormous *but*, the fact that the teachers are prepared to take little niggers—and that is what they are, how a lot of people regard them—little niggers into their house and teach them bridge will be taken as an affront to a lot of people. They will be most upset. I can tell you."

"Mom, I…" said Freddie. Alice cut him off.

"Now don't worry, my darling, your dad and I will handle the issue and it will be, or will develop into what I can only predict will be, an unholy brawl. But don't you worry, if this is what you want to do, we will stand behind you—now off you go and don't worry."

That evening after the children had gone to bed, Alice and Gordos discussed the matter and how it would affect them and their relationship with Unc.

Alice said, "Do you know Gordos, darling, I have never had a cross word with Unc, there has never been one iota of friction, he has been the most perfect Uncle Guardian anyone could have ever wished for, but I think this is going to shatter all that."

"Well, Ali, the fat is in the fire alright, when do you think we should tell him?"

"What say we tell him next weekend. The boys are going to play with old Alex and we will leave Sunny with the Holmeses."

The following Saturday they went out to The Lagoon for lunch. Unc had had Mary the cook set up a table on the patio not far from the kitchen, at the front of the mansion, which had an expanse of lawn running away in the direction of the lagoon itself: actually one of the most beautiful outlooks imaginable. There were just the three of them. The day was perfect. They had a most pleasant couple of hours discussing the coming duck season opening which Unc had hosted for as long as anyone could remember.

Since the war it had fallen into an informal routine which involved most of the workload being taken over from Unc by George. All Unc did was formally invite the different hunters to come. He sent out the invitations by post some weeks ahead. It was a most select group and the highly prized invitations endowed the recipient with more than a degree of self-esteem in the County.

If you were on The Lagoon Canard list you were in. They were something that you could only aspire to—you couldn't ask to be included. George in his turn would organize all the boats, the food and the whereabouts. This was dependent on the reed growth around the lagoon and creek, and where the duck appeared to be congregating.

They also told Unc that George would be taking the Swan over to the Mourmill Boatyard at Hampton Roads, to have a new diesel engine put into it. The Swan was a beautiful old wooden boat. It was 45 feet in length and was well fitted out and beautifully maintained. It was a motorboat and had a gasoline engine in it that had seen better days.

George and old Luke, at the head fisherman's suggestion, had decided to fit it out with a diesel engine. This would be much more reliable, had a lot more power but didn't use a lot of fuel at the speed they ran it at. He was also going to have two new 75-gallon copper fuel tanks installed which would give it an excellent range, and they would then probably use it a lot more. The boat had been in the family for years and everyone loved it.

"What make o' diesel are you fitting?" Unc asked.

"A Gardner."

Unc laughed. "A Gardiner with a Gardner."

"Of course." George and Alice grinned. "What else? A 5LW, 75 horse."

"Seventy-five horse," mused Unc. "That'll push her along."

"Yep," said George. "About seven knots we estimate."

"How do they think the propeller will match up with it?"

"Well, they certainly have taken that into their calculations, and interestingly, it was my concern too. Actually they found that when she was running at optimum revs with the old engine, the prop. was slightly cavitating, something that you and I had always suspected as you know. It has never run as well as it should. There has been a mismatch right from the start. Hull, engine, propeller. You remember we always had the feeling we were pushing too much water around about then anyway, and they feel that with the new engine all that may be taken care of. With it being slower revving, and all."

"Yeah," Unc opined. "They just didn't seem to match the original prop.—British, aren't they?" said Unc.

"Yep, they are. They have been about for quite a while, but not long in the States, and a diesel is the only way to go, and at this stage there's not much local to choose from."

"That's right," Unc said. "Gasoline, boats and water can be a volatile mix. Particularly if yo' got a couple o' pipe smokers on board. So old Luke was the moving force for a diesel was he?" Unc went on.

"Yep!" said George. "Not only the diesel but the actual make, and he recommended the Gardner. Actually I'm going to take him with me. It's the off season and he can probably make a contribution to the exercise."

"Good idea," said Unc. "It's a funny old world," he continued. "His father had the best figures of any of our skippers before or since, or should I say just prior to the war. We carried out conversions from sail to gas progressively through the 'thirties, and Luke's father was the most resistant to change. Of all the 'Swashbucklers' his boat was the last to be converted. He was a man of sail first, and then a fisherman, but no one was a better fisherman than he was; anywhere on the bay."

The Lagoon had a small fleet of six fishing boats. They had been part of the operation for several generations, as had the actual crews of them.

Years ago, someone had referred to them as the "Swashbucklers" and it had stuck. Of course there was a very good reason for this, and it was quite a story in itself. There was nothing covertly pejorative about it, and it had an air of cheerful but nautical "Devil may care" about it. All in all, they were about as good a bunch of employees that Unc, George, and their predecessors could have wished for.

Still, employer-employee relationships were a two-way thing. The Lagoon family, so to speak, never took anything for granted; they all worked at giving their very best in their respective areas of responsibility, in the overall scheme of things. Consequently, the whole enterprise was a "very happy ship."

"Now, what do we have, some twenty years on, his son having taken over the reins, or the tiller, from his father, is the one at the forefront of the new engine conversions. Ah've never mentioned this to you," Unc went on. "Old Joe involved himself in all of the original conversions, albeit from a distance. He was the 'Commodore' of course, and he took an intense interest in the whole business. His quizzing of the other skippers nearly drove them around the bend—in a good-natured way, of course.

"Ah've always thought that we should have sought his opinion on the original setting up of the Swan, the problem was, Ah suppose, we didn't really go off cruising in it enough. We just puttered around, real slow, never going fast. His interest and appetite for the knowledge on them, was insatiable.

"Consequently even before his own boat was converted, he was an authority on the whole thing. An' you know what, his figures didn't fall away at all once he was converted. They just gradually began to inch up. He took the whole business in his stride, and only ever lamented to me once. 'Yo' know Mr. Ted,' he said, 'Ah really don't think yo' can get as close to the fish, with these dirty smelly things, as yo' can with sail.'

"Well, no one ever came back with as many fish as he did, including hisself, once he had converted hisself. Dirty smelly, noisy things. Well they may be smelly but

77

yo' could eat off his. Best maintained boat in the whole fleet."

Up until then everything had been absolutely blissful until Alice mentioned rather cautiously that Freddie and the boys had asked the teacher Mr. Grieves if he would also teach the two black boys, Lofty and Ben, to play bridge.

Unc hadn't been at all happy when he was told how they had met up with them in the first place. "I knew it, I knew it," he almost hissed at them. They were quite taken aback.

"Give them an inch and they will take a mile." He jumped up from his chair and began stomping around. "Over my dead body they will. George, Alice, I am telling you it is not going to happen."

He then went off in a mild coughing fit, and pulling his handkerchief out walked to near the edge of the patio and spit on the lawn. He turned and walked back towards them, wiping his mouth, and then stuffed the handkerchief back in his pocket.

Alice tried to soothe him. "Unc, darling, please. Surely it can't hurt. They are only little boys and good heavens it will probably wear off after the first lesson or so, please, please." He seemed to cool down and she thought that he would come to see reason, but no, he was only more controlled.

"That is not the issue—the issue is that it has gone beyond contemplation. The Grieves, apparently at the request of the niggers, albeit through Freddie, have agreed to give them bridge lessons. It is absolutely preposterous and I will not have it."

"They happen to live in my house—for which they pay rent," interjected Alice.

"Don't come that at me, technically it is my house." He continued, "Do you think for one moment I am going

78

to have that sort of thing going on in property in my backyard?—No!

"I would have thought that they would have been more attuned to other people's sensibilities—they have obviously spent too much time in Canada—or at least he has. I simply can't believe it. Anyway, I'll see them at church tomorrow and give them notice."

"Oh Unc please and where do you expect that they will live? You can't possibly throw them out like that."

"Yes I can."

"Well, listen to me for a moment."

"No I won't!"

"You have to! You more than anybody else are responsible for this school being one of best of its kind in the County, if not the state. You have worked for years to make it and keep it so. Now if you go in there and lay about you with a big stick, you are going to, apart from anything else, make an awful fool of yourself. Anyway, they won't be at church tomorrow. They have gone away for the weekend."

"Well, I'll tell them on Monday night. Alice, I have told you, I will not have it!"

"Come on Gordos," said Alice. "We'll be off, darling." She went over to him and gave him a kiss. "Thank you for the lunch, we will see you at church tomorrow." George gave Unc's arm a squeeze.

"Why does life have to be so difficult at times?" Alice said after they had driven in silence for some minutes.

"Well you know why, don't you?" said George.

"Of course I do," she responded, "but you would think in this day and age he would have grown out of it by now."

"You can't be too sure when anything as deep-seated as this comes up; you can never be too sure," said George. "It is odd, though: he has brought you up to be one of the most tolerant people I know, perhaps the most tolerant. Whilst he himself is the perfect gentleman in every respect, and would go out of his way to help just about anybody, he has this blind spot.

"The mere mention of it was like a red rag to a bull— you know, Ali, he couldn't help himself. I think it is going to be extremely difficult to work through this, and the pity of it is that it is going to be so public. So public on one hand, and the two protagonists are to all intents and purposes father and daughter."

"I know, my darling, but unfortunately it can't be helped; it will have to run its course and I haven't the faintest idea as to what the outcome is going to be, if you really want to know. It doesn't bear thinking about. My problem is, I'm not going to back down: I feel very strongly about it, and if this is going to be my Armageddon, so be it."

"Hoo Hoo that's a big word, Ali, darling, do you really think he will go toe to toe with you?"

"Of course he'll have to," she responded. "He is in a corner, the poor old darling; and do you know, for the good of the family as far as the world at large is concerned, it would be more acceptable if I was the one who lost out. You can understand that the social order must be preserved. He will lose such a lot of face over this if I prevail and the bigger the blue the more it will drag us down, and it will be a hollow victory anyway."
As if we don't have enough on our plates at the present time, without all this, Alice thought to herself.

The only way this matter could be resolved before it came to a head of course would have been if the Grieves agreed not to teach Lofty and Ben how to play bridge. Unc, give him his due, and much to everyone's amazement, retreated to a position whereby he informed the Grieves if they lived in his house they could teach the children elsewhere, the black children that is, or they would have to vacate his house.

Their response was that they would endeavor to get some other black children to learn bridge, and if he could give them a month to put a class together elsewhere, it would possibly be feasible. However, it would be extremely difficult, as none of the girls would be interested, and out of all the boys only Lofty and Ben, in their opinion, would really be interested. Unc's response to this was that they could have until the end of the school holidays to resolve it. If they couldn't put a group together by then, they would have to move out and into the house the school secured, ready for the next term. However, under the circumstances, and as the whole matter had originated through his kin, they could include the two boys in their group of white children. As soon as any others came forward they had to go elsewhere and that was that if they wished to keep teaching, however many black children they finished up with.

The Grieves and everyone else, needless to say, were pleased with this. They fully expected to be out of the house within a week or so, once they had realized the significance of their actions and the effect it had on the man who was perhaps the most powerful in the County. Everyone in the town, whether they had children at the school, black or white, had an opinion as to how it would pan out.

Old Unc was untouchable: the whole family had impeccable credentials down through the years, and whilst nothing like this had ever occurred before no one was quite sure who would prevail. The community at large, both black and white, had a certain amount of sympathy for the two protagonists.

Things were a little strained in the family, which was understandable, but they went about their respective business with their heads held high and if you didn't know about all the fuss you would never have known. Some, however, thought Unc was walking a very fine line, as did he. George took the Swan down around the bay to the boat works and Alice left the children to stay over with friends for a few days, as she was going down to pick George up in the car and they would take a few days off for the drive home.

Chapter 8

They arrived back to find that everything was in order, and that their darling Sunny had taken up what she referred to as her "pink look." She announced that everything would be pink from now on. She had a lot of pink in her wardrobe already and the curtains and counterpane were pink, but of course she wanted pink sheets and pillowcases, just about anything that came to mind. She hounded her mother to dye the bedding pink and when told that it would fade in the wash, she said she just didn't care. "It would still be a little bit pink," she maintained.

Like a lot of little girls, she developed the occasional fad and to the delight of the family in particular and the amusement of friends, these fads, whilst they didn't last very long, were fervent in their pursuit. The pink fad was no different. Whilst every item of clothing from socks, shoes and hair ribbons and everything in between had to be catered for and wasn't altogether too difficult for her mother to provide, it did set off in another direction one day.

Her parents had the painters in to paint the exterior woodwork on their house, which was two-storied, quite large and had extensive windows. The painter had an assistant who would fetch and carry, mix paints, sand back and do any other jobs that needed doing whilst the painter got on and did the actual painting. Sunny became great friends with the assistant who arrived a few days ahead of the painter to begin preparing the woodwork. Part of this preparation involved scraping off the old coats of paint by use of a scraper and blowtorch.

Sunny had never seen this in operation before and became fascinated by it. The assistant, Samuel, who was black, was a very cheerful type of person and was only too happy to show her how to light the blow torch. He explained how and why it built up pressure, how to light the flame, make adjustments and prick the injector. She in turn became his little helper and would run out and say, "Good morning, Sam," before she went to school each day, and as soon as she arrived home again after school would find him and continue helping him and offer advice when she thought it was required, and constantly keep up a chatter and a stream of questions.

She arrived home from school one day to find Sam mixing pink primer. The painter had arrived that day and had begun priming the prepared woodwork. She couldn't believe her luck. Pink paint. There appeared to be tins of it offering up endless possibilities to her. She went fossicking in the room behind the car garage—the box room. She knew what she was looking for and found it without too much trouble. It was a two-wheeled hobbyhorse that had belonged to Freddie. He had grown out of it. She had played on it and after she realized that it was really of no interest to anyone, it was consigned to the box room. She pulled it out and gave it a cursory dusting off and dragged it around to Sam and asked him if "we" could paint it pink. Sam rolled his eyes and his face broke into a grin and said, "Why Miss Edie"—he always called her "Miss Edie"—"mercy be, this ole hoss has seen better days. Of course we can paint him pink but wouldn't he be better off, say, white? White hosses are lovely, but pink, never, never heard of a pink one afore!"

"I know, Tham, but I would really like him to be pink."

"Well sure, Miss Edie, we'll fix him up to be the best pink hoss that ever was, but first we got to prepare him, now here's what we'll do."

So Sam got some tools and removed the two screws that held the wheels on, explaining to her that the screws were loose and he would bring some slightly heavier gauge or thicker screws tomorrow, and the bridle was broken because the leather had dried out, so it needed to come off and he would also bring a new strip of leather to replace it. He also suggested to her that he should paint the horse's nostrils, eyes and mane a different color to give them a contrast with the overall pink and that possibly a very light brown would be the best color. He then made up a small sanding block for her and showed her how to sandpaper away all of the old paint on the horse.

"Me?" said Sunny.

"Why sure, Miss Edie, everyone who owns a hoss has to maintain, look after him," rejoined Sam, having great difficulty keeping a straight face.

"Well, OK," and she began to sand it in a clearly not very enthusiastic manner.

Sam was working away a few minutes later around the corner of the house picking up all the paint residue that had been taken off with the blow torch. Most of it had fallen onto the strip of light tarpaulin that he had laid out on the lawn and garden bed below where he was "torchin'," but of course not all of it. He was down on hands and knees when Sunny bounced up to him a few minutes later and announced that she had forgotten to do something for her mother.

"That's fine, Missy," he called after her as she skipped away. "We'll finish it off after school tomorrow." He was nearly killing himself laughing.

Needless to say when Sam eventually arrived back to where the "hoss" and paint and things were kept, he found the "hoss" with barely any paint removed but the sandpaper torn, lying beside the small matchbox-sized block of wood that he had wrapped the paper around. It was no more that you could expect of a small child, he thought as he chuckled to himself. He decanted around half a pint of pink primer into a small can which had a lid, wrapped the component parts of the "hoss" in an old sheet and took it out to the Boss' vehicle. He would take it home and work on it himself tonight.

There would be enough light left in the day for him to work, sanding it, and putting a fresh coat of primer on it. He opined that it would be easy enough in the morning to put another coat on it if need be; he would put plenty of turpentine in the first mix and they could paint the face and mane on when Sunny turned up after school. He would tidy up the two wheels and put them back on and they could put the leather rein on together. He had a couple of nice studded heavy upholstery tacks that would be ideal to tap into the head where the reins led from.

So on the morrow when Sunny was due home after school the "hoss" was there in the garage beside where all the paint was, looking mighty fine, he thought. It looked as though it was brand new, straight off the work bench, just waiting for a new face and the bridle to be put on. He had to admit he was looking forward to her impending arrival with great anticipation. It had been a long time since he had had anything to do with a child so young. All of his were grown and gone, and they had broken the plates, as they say. On top of that he had never come into contact with a little white blonde girl ever. She was such a little sweetie. He wondered if this would last and what fate had in store for her.

Her daddy was rich, he mused, so she was off to a good start, she wouldn't have to worry about too much. Only how to make some lucky cracker happy. She'd break a few hearts before that, of course. Most of these pretty girls did. Still, her Mommy was a sensible type of woman—"Always speaks to me, gives us a cup of coffee and cake or summat to eat three times a day if she is around.

"A real lady, not like a lot of these other Southern Belles. She could probably buy and sell any half dozen or so of 'em anyway. She is seriously rich. Takes after her uncle who brought her up, in a way, although you have to keep your place with him. You never take liberties with him, but that's also the case with the crackers, let alone some of the uppity niggers. She has had a sad life a long time ago, seems to be over it now, and mighty happy too. Not like Ol' Neville, picks me up each morning with a grunt, shows me what to do if need be with a series of more grunts and then drops me home each night with no grunt at all. Still the pay's good, the pays regular and I've been at it for how many years now?—Fifteen or so. Can't complain I suppose... Look out, here she is."

Sunny came bouncing into the garage and was brought up short when she saw the "hoss." She was speechless. She clapped her hands and looked at him in apparent bewilderment.

"Tham, oh thank you. Thank you—I really didn't recognithe him." She bounded over to Sam who was hunkered down decanting more paint and gave him one of the kisses, those kisses completely spontaneous and uninhibited, that little girls give, and all too soon grow out of the spontaneous affection that comes so readily to the young. He couldn't have been more touched by her

87

reaction and suggested to her that they could perhaps paint the face and mane onto the horse and showed her the rein that he had made from an old leather bag and the two upholstery studs that he felt would make excellent bits for the bridle.

She thought all this would be a terrific idea and asked him who he thought should paint the face on. He suggested that he do one side and she do the other and that as he had done quite a few before, he should go first and she could see how it was done, and she could repeat it on the other side. So that was what they did. He had already mixed up a small batch of brown paint at the right shade and he began with the eyes. He painted the eyebrows first and then with a very fine brush he painted the top and bottom eyelids and then the actual eye itself. He then did, much to Sunny's delight, some delicate eyelashes that turned up at the end. He then moved over to the nostrils and painted them in a little more boldly than the eyes and then he painted in the lips, which also had a slight curl to indicate a smile.

Sunny had been standing stock still in rapt attention. Following his every move with little eyes like saucers looking from him and down to the "hoss" which was beginning to take on a personality all of its own.

"There we are Missy, what does he need now do you think before we turn him and you have a go?" Sam turned to her and looked directly into the beautiful wide-eyed little face which seemed to be only inches from his. He hunkered back a little. "What do you think he needs now, Miss Edie?"

"The reinth?" she quavered, looking at him with those questioning eyes.

"No Missy," he said, "I think he needs a topknot and then his mane."

"What ith a top knot?" she asked.

"Here, Ah'll show you." The head of course had been cut out on a band saw and the topknot mane had been outlined, as had the nostrils. They first needed emphasizing.

So Sam dipped the brush into the brown paint again and deftly wiped the bristles on the top of the can after he had withdrawn it and he then began to boldly paint in the slightly curling top knot and then the mane. This of course immediately transformed the head from something bland into something that was quite pretty, he thought—and so did she, as he looked at the little face light up again and as she clapped her hands

"Now," said Sam, "we'll turn old 'Hoss' over and you can have a go, Miss Edie." He dipped the brush into the paint again and then offered it to her. She had been animated until he did this and then she crossed one leg over the other and nearly bent double and looked at him in one of the little girl beseechingly ways. "Oooo, Tham, I don't think I can."

"Look Missy, I'll help you."

"Tham will you do him, you're tho much better than I could be, pleathe?" What could he do? He rested the horse's body over a couple of large paint tins that were on the floor in such a way that the head of the horse was resting on one of them down where the neck was screwed to the body.

He turned to look at her. The little wide-eyed face was looking at him with so much appeal that he found he could not force the issue with her.

"Orright Missy, Ah'll paint him fo' yo'. Yo' jes' watch." She nodded expectantly, and sat down on the ground, with her arms wrapped around her knees, almost on top of him. He had great trouble containing his mirth as he deftly painted in the features of the horse's head. Every once in a while he caught her little face looking up at him, and each time he gave her a wink and a smile.

She responded by hugging her knees a little closer, and with her tiny face lit up once more, returning her gaze back to the horse. All in all, the two of them were having a great time.

He had nearly finished the job when a shadow fell across them, and looking up he found Ol' Neville standing beside him. His heart gave an extra beat; he wasn't at all sure how Neville would accept the fact that he wasn't actually doing something associated with the job, in fact he wasn't at all sure as to whether Neville regarded him as an "Uncle Tom," not that it worried him too much. He wasn't at all, he just liked children, in fact he liked most folks, and there wasn't nothing wrong wid that! Neville was very dour, and although he was married, and quite happily Sam gathered, he had never shown any animation towards children, although he had some that were grown up. Sunny looked up at him quite unperturbed, and said. "Look what we are doing Mr. Waths, ithn't he beautiful!"

"He sure is!" Old Neville responded.

Sam took another couple of brush strokes, and then turned to look directly up at him, and was relieved to see Neville smiling, something he rarely did. Wonder of wonders, he then patted him on the shoulder, something he had never done before, and murmured that they would be packing up for the day shortly. He then quite clearly said "Miss Sunny," as he walked off.

Sam sat back and said to Sunny, "There yo' are Missy, jes' a touch on de nostril, de nose, and de ol' hoss is finished wi' de paintin'. Tomorrow when he's dry we'll put de wheels, and de reins on him, an yo' all be able to take him for a ride."

"Oooh thank you Tham, thank you." She jumped up and gave him a kiss and stepped back. "Tham!"

"Yea Missy."

"I've got thomething elthe to do, could you leave me thome pink paint pleathe, and a bruth?"

"Why yes Missy, an Ah'll leave yo' some turps to put the brush in when yo've finished, how's that?"

"Thank you Tham!"

Sam had no sooner packed everything up for the day, leaving the paint out for her and departed, than she ran around to the box room and pulled out a pair of rubber Billy Boots that Freddie had grown out of. She had tried them on the day before and they came up just above her knees. She could however walk quite comfortably in them, although her parents would have said that she was clomping around in them.

She dragged them around to where the paint was, and gave them a good dusting down. At least one of Sam's lessons had struck home. He had instilled it into her that a good paint job was as much preparation as anything else.

She then set to work applying the pink paint to them. Apart from the fact that she could be said to have as much paint on herself as on the boots, they came up quite well, she thought to herself. She then put the lid on the paint tin and the brush in the can of turps and promptly knocked the can over. She hurriedly stood it up and skipped out of the garage.

She thought that she should tell her parents and rushing into the house found them deep in conversation in the kitchen holding hands over the table, having a cup of coffee. Sunny immediately noticed this and cheerfully asked. "Why are you two holding hanths?" They looked at her with smiles on their faces which then turned to mock concern when they saw that she was liberally covered in paint. Her father hunkered down and holding her out at arm's length said, "Oh, Sunny, baby, what have you been up to?" in a slightly despairing voice.

"Painting, pink painting," said her mother. "I'll get something to take it off."

"Mommy, Daddy."

"Now darlin', let Mom get something to take it off," said her father. She pulled away from her father and ran over to the ice box, and nearly tearing the door of its hinges, took out the milk.

"Easy baby easy," said her father shaking his head and standing up. "Slow down, slow down."

She pulled a glass off the bench and filled it nearly to overflowing and began gulping it down. She put the glass down taking in great gulps of air and her mother mildly admonished her.

"Sunny darling, slow down, you'll be sick, now come on."

"Can we all go and look at what I have been painting first pleathe?" she uttered as she jumped up and down in front of her father.

"Alright, come on Harly." Harlequin was her cat, a big black one and whenever he drank milk he had a big ring of milk like a moustache over his top lip. Whenever one of the family had milk or food around their lips someone invariably called them Harly. It had become a family joke.

"OK, OK," said her mother. "We won't all get covered in it, will we darling?" Sunny quickly nuzzled her face on her father's cuff, wiping the milk away and began pulling him out of the kitchen.

Almost out of control, she led them back to the garage and proudly pointed out the pink boots. Her father seemed more interested in the horse.

"Did you do the horse as well, darlin'?" he asked, winking at Alice.

"Tham did him for me Daddy, ithn't he beautiful, but look at the booth!"

"They look like Freddie's old Bogs!" said George. "My my, did Sam do them too?"

"No Daddy, I did them all by mythelf and Tham doethn't even know, don't you think they are beautiful?"

"Yes they are." Alice laughed and asked Sunny where she intended wearing them.

"Everywhere, Mommy, but firtht I am going to put flowerth on them."

"You're what?" said George. "You're going to put flowers on them, how are you going to do that?"

"We will get thome glue, and I will cut the flowerth out of thome of Mom'th magazinth and we will glue them on."

"We?" said her father quizzically.

"Mom and me."

"Mom and I," he corrected.

"Would you like to help too Daddy?" she said. The little, appealing face looking up at him.

George looked across at Alice and, squatting down beside Sunny, took her hands in his and looking intently at her said, "I couldn't think of anything that I would like to do more, my little darlin'." Alice looked at the two of them, with a flood of emotion. She walked off, saying that she would rustle up some magazines, and get the scissors.

Sunny led her father back into the house, holding him by the hand and jumping all over the place nearly tripping him up once or twice. "Steady, steady," he kept saying. They went straight into the kitchen where Alice had already put a few magazines on the table, and walking on into the house, said that she would scrounge up some others. George pulled Sunny's "grown up" high chair to the table, and told her to start looking for some nice flowers, and that he would fetch three pairs of scissors.

"First my girl we are going to clean up all the pink paint you have all over yourself," said her mother. This took another good ten minutes.

Eventually the three of them were sitting up at the table cutting away at the flowers that Sunny was tearing out page by page.

"How many do you think we will need, darlin'?" asked George. "Do you want to cover all that lovely pink paint? Or do you want each one to be sitting up there on its own? What do you think, Mom?" he asked.

"Darling, why don't we do one boot at a time, and stick a few on; see how they look, and we just keep putting them on until we are happy with them?" Alice said, tweaking Sunny's nose. "Gordos, what say you keep cutting the flowers out, and I'll show Baby Doll how to make some glue?"

"We have to make it Mamma?"

"Well we don't, we could buy it, but it will be a good lesson for you, in that you will learn to make glue from flour and water."

"From flour and water?" Edie asked in an amazed voice.

"Yup," said her father. In the old days they just couldn't go down to the shop. "We have to improvise."

"What's implovithe?" said the tiny voice.

"I m p r o vise," said Alice. "It means if you can't make something or do something the way you usually would, or would like to, you do it another way. That is, of course, if you know how to. Now come and watch."

By this time Alice had taken a small jar out of the cupboard, together with a medium-size mixing bowl, a wooden spoon, some plain flour, and had run some hot water. She put some flour into the bowl, and added some water, and began whipping it into a paste. When she had the right consistency, she spooned it out into the small jar. Sunny took the whole thing in, and asked her mother what was going to happen to what was left in the bowl.

"We just wash it down the drain," responded Alice.

"Won't it glue up the drain, Mommy?" Sunny asked.

"No, darlin', we flush it down with such a lot of water it dilutes it."

"What ith diluths, Mom?" Sunny asked with her elbows on the table and her chin cupped in her hands. Alice looked across at George who was having a great time listening to this exchange between the two of them. She gave him a helpless look, inviting intervention. George just looked at her with a smile on his face, and his head inclined, as much as to say, Come on Ali, you're doing well.

"Well, darling, it means that you weaken it. You see the way it is now, you have about three times as much flour as water, and you have a lovely thick gluey, gooey sort of stuff. If you keep adding water, the glue becomes very runny, and all of a sudden it becomes water with a bit of flour in it. Come on, I'll show you."

"Can I put my hand in it, Mom?"

"You can put your finger in it," responded Alice, "before we water it down, and again just before we start tipping it down the drain."

Sunny had just withdrawn her hand which of course had glue all over it, when Freddie walked in.

"Hi, Mom, Hi, Dad," he called as he bent slightly to meet the rush of the quickly advancing Edie, who literally flung herself at him, wrapping her small arms around his neck and crying.

"Look, look, Fredlieth," her pet name for him. "Look what we are doing." He looked at his parents questioningly and putting his hand around the back of his neck, withdrew it, looking at it and then down at Edie.

"What is this Sunny, what have you got all over your 'fingees?'"

"Ith glue!"

"It's what?" he said with alarm, looking at his mother.

Alice by this time was walking towards him with a damp cloth, shaking her head, saying, "Don't worry, darling, it'll come off without any trouble."

"What are you three doing?" asked Freddie, as Sunny let her mother wipe the glue off her hand, who then turned her attention to the back of her son's neck.

"Yo''ll survive," said Alice. "There's more on yo' collar than yo' neck. There—it's off already." She gave him a playful slap on the butt.

"Come and thee what I've been doing, Fredlieth!" Sunny grabbed him by the arm, and began tugging at him. Freddie let himself be unceremoniously dragged out of the kitchen and around to the garage where the horse and the boots were in all their pink glory. One of the reasons they got along so well was that Freddie always, particularly when they were alone, took more than a passing interest in whatever Edie showed him, or whatever she was doing. At the same time, having a big brother who adored her was just about as good as it gets, for a six-year-old girl.

"Don't they look fantastic," he said.

"You really think tho?" said Sunny.

"I sure do," he responded. "Hasn't the old horse come up well? I remember when I used to ride everywhere on him. He's very good because he never bucks anyone off."

"Oh, thilly!" she replied. "What do you think of your old booth?"

"Well, I have never seen them looking so good. You've done a terrific job on them too. I didn't know that you could paint boots and horses like this."

She stopped, brought up short. "I have to tell you thomething." She looked up at him. "Tham painted the horth!" She looked quite seriously at him. He put his arm around her.

"Well," he said. "Sam has probably painted a paddock full of horses in his day, and I bet you if he hadn't been here, you could have done exactly the same job. There's no doubt about it. Look at the boots." Her little face brightened up immediately.

"Now come back inthide and I'll thow you what we're going to do with the booth." She began pulling him inside again.

"You're going to do something else to the boots?" He asked.

"Yes, come and thee."

They walked back into the kitchen, and there were both parents sitting at the table again, snipping away with the growing pile of flowers of all sorts on the table in front of them.

"Mom, Dad, what are you all doing?" Freddie asked, grinning from ear to ear.

"We are what is known as rejuvenating your old boots."

"What's rejunate, Dad?" said Sunny.

"R e juv en ate," said George. "It means we are fixing them up, making them nearly as good as new. When we stick the flowers on them, they will, in fact, be better than new. They will certainly look better, that's for sure. Come on, sit down Freddie, there is a spare pair of scissors here and we can get them finished a lot quicker. We've only got another thirty or forty magazines to go through."

"Gordos!" said Alice. "Freddie, we only need a dozen or so more flowers. When you have done a few, the whole thing will have been a complete family effort. We can all take some credit for helping Edie's new boots look beautiful."

"Look here little darlin'."

"Whath that dad?"

"A beautiful butterfly, won't he look good on one of the boots?"

"OOOh Dadda, he thertainly will."

Sunny was so excited at all this that she was completely unaware of the rolling of eyes and good-natured exchanges that passed over her between her parents and elder sibling. It didn't take long for them to cut out the few additional flowers and when they had finished them, Alice asked Sunny if she would help her Dad and Freddie clean up all the paper. And put the scissors away, and put the lid on the small jar of glue, and put it in the refrigerator whilst she prepared the evening meal. George said that he had a little bit of office work to do, and would mix Alice and himself a drink, and then disappear upstairs until the meal was ready.

"Just think, baby, this time tomorrow night the boots will have been finished—that is, of course, unless you want to do them as soon as you come home from school."

"No, no, Dadda, I'll wait," she said, as her father tweaked her under the chin.

It was some two weeks later the four of them were having their dinner one evening when George told Freddie and Sunny that he was going down to Hampton Roads in the next few days to collect the Swan. Whilst normally they would all go together, he had some business to do in New York on the way, and that Mom and he couldn't organize the time for all of them to be away, so Mom was going to follow him in a few days. If they were happy with the Swan conversion, they would come back by water. If not or there were some hitches,

98

they would return home via New York, again, and probably stay overnight there.

What they had arranged was that Freddie could stay with Chuck, and Sunny could stay with the Holmeses, or if she liked with one of her little friends. It would however coincide with Snakesbreath's "bath" night, and actually Mrs. Holmes had invited her even before she knew that he and Mom would be away for a few days. Of course if they wanted to stay out at The Lagoon, they knew Unc would love to have them, but Mom thought that they may be just as happy to stay in town. "Hooray," said Sunny. The other three just grinned. As she called out she bought her arms up, completely overlooking the fact that she had food on her spoon, and consequently dropped some onto the floor. Her mother shook her head, and got up from the table and fetched a cloth to wipe it up.

"Ah hope you don't behave like that, waving your arms about, flinging food all over the place when you're at the Holmeses," she admonished with a smile. "Do you, baby?" She nuzzled her as she sat down again.

"No, Mamma, no. I'll be able to play with Thnakethbreath again, ith great fun playing bridge with him. Hooray," she cried again, this time without the spoon.

"Do you actually play a hand, Sunny?" asked Freddie.

"She doesn't," said Alice. "She stands beside him and watches, and he explains to her what he is doing, and why he is doing it."

"How are the other bridge lessons coming along, Freddie?" his father asked.

"They are terrific, Dad. There are only five boys. Just Chuck, Lofty, Billy, Ben and I, and there are eight girls. The girls have had a few more lessons than we have, and we have had a few more than Lofty and Ben."

"How do the Grieveses cope with at least three streams of competency?" asked George. Alice began gathering up the plates.

"What'th competanty Dad?" The inevitable question from Sunny.

"Com pet ency," corrected her father. "It means ability or experience. You know, take the horse: when you have done as much painting as Sam, you will be as good as him, and Sam who hasn't done as much as old Neville isn't as good as him. All the girls started well before the boys, so we would expect them to be playing to a better standard than the boys. How Ben and Lofty are going is anybody's guess. They may not have the aptitude for it anyway."

Again: "What's Ap...?" Her father held his hand up.

"Wait, darling, let Freddie answer my question."

"Dad, Chuck, Billy and I have just about caught up to the girls. Ben and Lofty, who have now had four lessons, will catch us all up, so Mr. Grieves said, at the rate they are going, in another two. Mrs. Grieves taught them how to play two-handed bridge and they play it whenever they can."

"Well, I'll be doggoned," said George. "Who is the best girl, do you think?"

"Oh Lettice, without a doubt," said Freddie, just a little too quickly.

"Oooh, it's a little like that, is it?" his father chided him good-naturedly.

"Aw Dad." Freddie went absolutely crimson.

Alice gave George's arm a playful slap, and said, "Leave the poor boy alone Gordos. Don't you worry, Freddie," she added, "she's a beautiful girl." This only made it worse for Freddie.

"Mom!" he exclaimed, overcome with embarrassment again.

Alice smiled and patted him on the arm as she sat down again. "Why don't you two run along now and Dad and I will do the dishes tonight? We'll let you both off any clearing away or drying up, for a change."

Freddie bolted.

"Why did Freddie run away, Dadda?" Sunny looked enquiringly from her father to her mother.

"Because he's a little boy," said Alice.

"He'th not, he'th a big boy," was the quick response.

"Mommy really meant that he is a young boy, and young boys don't like talking about girls."

"Don't they Mom! But Freddie liketh Lettithe, Dadda!"

"Of course he does darlin', we all do, now off with you, and Dad and I will do the clearing up. Unless you would like to." Alice got up again, giving one of those "happy" looks to George.

After the children had departed, they just looked at each other. They held each other. Alice looked up at him, her eyes growing misty.

"Now look, don't worry," he said. "Everything will be alright. We are in the best of hands."

"I know, I know, but somehow I can't help worrying."

"Well, come on, we'll get through this together. Aren't those two terrific?" he added, giving her a squeeze as he let go of her and picked up a tea towel.

"They really are," she responded "Ah don't know where they get it from." She smiled at him.

"When we get back, the Canard season will be upon us, and I'll have to get the boats ready."

"Yes I know, have you received Unc's invitation yet?"

"No I haven't. I suppose he's left me until the last batch."

"I don't think so," said Alice. "Gardiner would be fairly well up on the list alphabetically from what I can remember. I hope he hasn't gone all precious over the 'bridge' business."

"No, he wouldn't. I actually run the thing for him, at his invitation certainly, but I've been at it for what, twelve or fourteen years. No, it's not like him He may have got a bit cranky, but he's never been petty. Hon', you should know that better than anyone!"

"I suppose so. How is your headache?"

"Well it never lets up, but to be quite honest, I'll cope." He reached out and put his arms around her, "With a little bit of help from a friend!" She buried her head into his shoulder and kissed his neck. *Well that's one thing for certain*, she thought to herself, her eyes misting up again.

Chapter 9

George had been gone a day or so on the Swan, and Alice was walking down the main street in town after school with Sunny, when she ran into one of the regulars of the "Canard season." He doffed his hat to her and patted Sunny on the head, and after making the usual, almost obligatory small talk about the weather, commented on the upcoming shoot, and how excited he was. He had received his invitation a fortnight ago, as had all the other regulars. It was a highlight of his year, and he was really looking forward to it. Old Ted and George always put on a wonderful day, to say nothing of the dinner.

Alice responded, making all the right noises, but was feeling sick. Gordos had not received his invitation. Years before, when Unc had handed the organization of the day over to George, he had made the statement that he felt he should, while he still had his faculties, actually write and send off the invitations himself. Once he felt that it was getting beyond him, he would hand the whole thing over to George.

The system had worked well. It enabled Unc, on one hand, to keep in touch with his old friends, "The Old Guard"—and a lot of them over the years had gone off to "The Big Shoot In The Sky"—and on the other, to develop a relationship with all of the younger ones of

George's generation that were gradually being invited. Each year the age balance shifted imperceptibly, due to people dying off and of course some years there were always folks who just couldn't make it for some reason or other. These of course were few, as for some it was the highlight of their whole year, and they had to be very sure of themselves in the overall social scheme of things to miss one.

It had evolved into a three-day event. Back in the 'thirties when George had been invited to take it over, there were around twenty men who shot. They had arrived in the early dawn of the day of the shoot, and departed, back to their homes, later that day. They were all local plantation owners. Whilst it had gone into recess during the hostilities, it then changed in the mid-'forties, after a hitch when several of them failed to arrive until it was over, due to a bridge being out. This was coupled with the fact that three of the older ones had died, and the vacancies hadn't been filled.

George had resumed control upon his return from the war, but he and Unc hadn't devoted too much time over the numbers and the structure of the shoot, until one day, about a month before the shoot, they decided that they would restructure it.

When, after the shoot, they were all having the usual get-together, Unc and George, who had settled the "problem", put the suggestion to the others that it may be a good idea to have everyone arrive the day before, and stay at The Lagoon. There was plenty of room for more than twenty of them; they could all have one of Mary's slap-up dinners that evening, and be up bright and chirpy the next morning. Bright and chirpy would be the order of the day, Unc added. They all had a good laugh at that, as he was noted for his "table", to say nothing of his wines.

It was left that Unc and George would decide between themselves as to just how the shoot would be revamped. It was their shoot, after all. The two of them decided that a one-nighter involved perhaps nearly as much preparation as a two-nighter. By the time all the beds and rooms were prepared and all the food organized, they concluded that it would be a lot less rushed, and more leisurely, if they were all to stay over for another night, after the shoot. They could then all drift off the following day after a late breakfast. They also decided that they would keep it restricted to thirty people. That was all that they could comfortably accommodate at The Lagoon.

They didn't open up the numbers immediately; they paced themselves into it over many years. So all in all it was a few days eagerly anticipated and looked forward to by those concerned.

Alice had gradually become involved as Unc seemed to depend on her a little more as the years went by. She, with Sunny's help, organized the entire menu, right down to the "survival rations," as she called them, which she gave to each man to take into the swamp. She, together with Sunny, were a great hit.

For all that, the two of them kept well out of the way when the hunters were there. She felt that as it was Unc's "event", she should not in any way intrude. Alice knew that if she made her presence too obvious she could quite easily steal Unc's thunder, and that was the last thing she wanted to do. It was his event, and to a lesser degree Gordos's, and that was the way it would stay.

As they were walking back to the car, Alice asked Sunny who she would like to spend the night with, as she had to go out to The Lagoon early in the morning. She knew Sunny simply wouldn't like to go anywhere early in the morning, so there was no issue there. Sunny nominated the Holmeses, and Alice said that she would ring Mrs. Holmes when they arrived home.

The Holmeses of course were delighted to have her to stay, and said it would be quite alright if Sunny was to arrive any time, as Annette said that she was just about to start baking, and Sunny may like to help her. At this stage all the Holmes children were married, but as yet there were no grandchildren, and Annette loved having small children to help her bake. She liked the mess they made.

Freddie had arrived home when Alice was just about to leave with Sunny, and she asked him if he would like to go with them, and then help her with some shopping. The three of them set off and after Sunny had been dropped off at the Holmeses, Alice told Freddie that she needed to buy some Keds, and she would like his advice. Freddie was intrigued, and looking at his mother, exclaimed, "Why, Mom, I have a good pair and a knock-about pair or two. Why do you want to buy some more? You and Dad don't wear them very often, and you have them already."

"I want them for Lofty and Ben."

"You what?" he said. "Lofty and Ben? Why Mom, they would be the only two black children in the school with shoes, if you were to do that."

"That's right," said Alice, "and it would only be a start."

"Oh Mom," said Freddie, "I hope you know what you're doing. There are about seventy to eighty!"

"Ah know, darlin'," she drawled. "Ah know. After we buy them we are going around to Lofty's house, and we are going to tell him that we are going out to The Lagoon, in the morning, and ask him if he would like to go with us. I'm sure he will want to go."

"What time, Mom?" Freddie asked.

"We will have to pick him up at four-thirty in the morning, darling."

"Four-thirty!" said Freddie in horror. "Four-thirty, why so early? That means we'll have to be up even earlier. Ooh, Mom!"

"I want to show something special to you. Something—now don't look at me like that, you silly—something that very few people have the opportunity to see. Now don't worry."

Freddie looked at his mother out of the corner of his eye, she just looked down at him and smiled.

A few minutes later, they arrived at the store and went in. They asked to see some Keds; Alice told the attendant that she wanted to look at sizes four and six. These were bought out and Alice inspected them, asking Freddie if he thought the small ones would fit Lofty and the larger ones fit Ben. Freddie said that he thought the larger ones would certainly fit Ben, but that the smaller ones would need to be a size up for Lofty. After they had made the purchases they set off for Lofty's place. Making their way across town, they eventually came to the street or dirt road, track, where he lived.

The house was set back a little on the block, and was pretty basic, needless to say. It was the original clapboard shack, although it was a little bigger than most, Alice thought to herself. The other thing that struck her was that it looked neat and well-tended. Amazingly, although it was quite some time ago, she felt that it looked better kept than it had when she first called there the evening that Lofty had had his arm fixed. There wasn't a stick out of place, and the grass—you couldn't call it a lawn—was also well tended. There was no rubbish or old rusty car bodies lying around. Not like some of them that they had driven past. There were also no utilities. There was no running water, although all the houses had rainwater tanks; there was no electricity and

107

there was no sewage system, although there was a weekly collection.

For all that, Alice thought that Lofty and Ben, too, were well brought up, polite and always clean and well-presented, even if their clothing had reached the stage where she herself would have regarded them as rags.

Alice's big Chevy slowly came to a halt in front of the house. She was aware, as they had picked their way through to it, that all the children that were outside playing had got right out of the way of the car. They had stood silently, almost in awe, as it inched on its way. Even the dogs gave it a wide berth, and didn't chase it. It wasn't every day that someone from the other side of town passed through here, let alone called on someone that they knew.

"Just leave the Keds in the trunk, darlin'," Alice told Freddie as they were getting out of the Chevy. "We'll deal with them in the morning." Lofty and his brothers and sisters came tumbling out of the shack, and Alice found herself giving an involuntary but imperceptible shudder. How they can all exist in such a place is a wonder, she mused to herself. They all ran to the Chevy with Lofty's Mom bringing up the rear.

Alice stepped forward and smilingly greeted Lofty's mother, and the whole bunch of them.

"Molly, I was wondering if Lofty would like to go out to The Lagoon with Freddie and me tomorrow morning?" she asked the nervous-looking Molly.

"Why sure, Miss Alice, yo'd like that Lofty son, wouldn't yo'? Stand straight an' look at Miss Alice," she remonstrated.

"Ah sure would," said poor old Lofty, grinning at Freddie for encouragement.

"Well that's fine," said Alice. "We'll collect him at around half past four. I won't sound the horn, as I'd wake everyone up, so you be ready out in front, Lofty son, and we'll see you then." Alice had a great chuckle to herself as she watched the delight go to apprehension, on Lofty's and his mother's face at the mention of the hour. "You know, Lofty, you'll have to be up long before the roosters," she added. She also mentioned the fact that she had wanted Ben to go too but that Freddie had told her that he would be unable to as he was out fishing on one of the big boats with his father. They appeared to know about that.

The following morning Alice and Freddie were walking out of the house to the car, when Alice asked him if he needed to go to the john.

"No Mom, I'm fine," he replied. They set off and were a few minutes from Lofty's place when he announced that he now, did need to go, but would do so at Lofty's.

"No honey, you'll go right here." She pulled up in the middle of the track.

"Here?" he said.

"Yes honey, right here now, out you hop."

He shrugged and opened the door and got out of the car. "Mom," he looked at her. "Will you turn off the gas please?"

"Turn it off, why?" she said in amazement.

"I'd like to listen to the silence!" he replied as he disappeared.

"Why darling!" she said as she reached for the key, and cut the gas.

Freddie walked to the rear of the Chevy, and gradually took in the atmosphere around him. It wasn't cold at all, but it had that pre-dawn feel about it, with a few other things added. He knew that the sunrise was at least an hour and a half away, so it was still very dark, a darkness that he had never experienced before. There were smells, or a smell that he hadn't been aware of in this part of town up until this moment. The most obvious one was

109

that of kerosene fumes, and there was something else. He had no sooner distinguished it from the kerosene, than he realized what it was. Ugh. He finished just as Alice leant out and whispered rather loudly, "Freddie!"

They continued on in silence, for which he was grateful. He sat back thinking that whilst it was certainly quiet, there was another sensation that he couldn't quite put his finger on. Then, just as they were pulling up in front of Lofty's house, it came to him. He felt that he, or they, were being watched by eyes, lots of eyes, and that there were no dogs barking, which was odd. So they must have been friendly eyes. Lofty came out of the loom of the light into the full glare before they stopped, as Alice told Freddie that the new Keds were on the back seat, and he could go over into the back with Lofty if he liked, and she would tell him what was in the box once they had got moving again.

It was quite an emotional Lofty who opened the box with the Keds inside.

"Ohhh, Miss Alice," he murmured. "Ah've never had Keds before. Ohhh," and he burst into tears. "Thank yo', thank yo', Miss Alice. Ohh, can Ah put them on now?"

"Of course yo' can Lofty honey, and just think, if these are the first ones they will be the first of many. Of that I'm sure. Ah just hope they fit. Now put them on. Freddie darling, help him do up the laces. Ah threaded them last night." She quietly thought to herself with a giggle that he would be the closest thing to "Puss in Boots" that she would ever be likely to see, but that she couldn't say that to him.

"Mom!"

'Yes, darlin'?"

"What are we doing going to The Lagoon so early for?" Freddie asked.

"We're going way out to the North Gate and we're going to drive down to the North Reach Bluff."

"Why, Mom?"

The "Bluff" was not really a bluff. It was a promontory of forest that came down right beside the water and there was only the main meandering road that ran right down and through the spread, north to south, between the water and the trees. The North Gate was about forty miles around the main sealed road. From there they had to make their way back down through the vast reaches of the spread. Fortunately, there were only five gates to open in the fifteen miles or thereabouts that they had to go once they were inside the road gate. The water in the main was fenced off from the grazing and other arable land, near the lagoon, which kept it in a pristine state.

They arrived at the gate and Alice jumped out, telling the boys to stay put. She undid the padlock on the chain with a key which she had on her key ring and pushed one of the two gates across, jumped back into the car, drove it through, got out again and closed the gate, making sure the padlock was in place. She then got back in and gunned the engine; the big Chevy leapt forward into the darkness, only lit by the powerful headlights which penetrated the ever-present gloom.

She knew the road like the back of her hand. It was well formed for a private road, and well maintained, as Unc was a stickler for having everything up to scratch. He was in the process of having the whole spread set up with laneways which would allow the easy movement of stock and vehicles from A to B with the minimum of effort.

At the top end, where they were now, the lane system was yet to extend, so Alice had to be careful of cattle on the road, consequently she couldn't travel as fast as she would have liked to. Every now and again she had to almost stop to allow cattle that were camped on the road to move. In the fresh early morning air they would slowly get to their feet and look into the bright headlights of the Chevy with their heads lowered. Each animal appeared to be beset by a swarm of tiny insects which were so obvious in the headlights. She would never blow the horn, but she certainly revved the engine, to hurry them out of the way. The misty steam rising off their bodies, mingled with the breath coming from their nostrils, coupled with the steam rising from the occasional freshly dropped dung, wafted its way into the coolish morning air.

Alice could not really see what time it was on her watch, as she didn't want to slow down to hold it under the light. She felt that they were in good time to be at the Bluff just as the sun was coming up, but she had to keep moving. Every now and again the road went across a stretch of low-lying country, and she had to be extra careful as it became quite greasy in places. It was in one of these that she momentarily lost control, and the Chevy ran along for a few yards with two wheels in the drain at the edge. Mud spewed up all over the hood and windshield, so much so that the wipers couldn't cope.

There was nothing for it but for Alice to stop and clean it off. Fortunately, she always carried a chamois in the glove compartment, and leaning over she pulled it out, and telling the boys to stay there again, jumped out and began wiping the screen. Looking down she could see in the glow of the lights that the water in the drain beside them looked quite clean, so she gently soaked the chamois, cleaning it up, and then soaked it again. She called out to Freddie to turn the wipers on, and as they began to move, she held the chamois over the windshield, and gradually wrung it out, allowing the wipers to do the work.

"That's great, Mom!" Freddie called out. "Do the other side!" Alice did the other side, and taking a quick look at her watch, gave each of the headlights a quick wipe, saying to herself—Less haste, more speed!—as she climbed back into the car.

They continued on at a more leisurely pace and soon they were through the last gateway before the Bluff. As they continued down the last mile or so Alice began to relax. Anywhere along here would be an excellent viewing area, if they had been behind schedule; however, they weren't, so all was well.

The thing the Bluff had going for it, was that as the sun actually came up, you could look back to either side, and behind you, and see it gradually encroach on the reaches of water and the shoreline stretching away into the distance. Unc had taken her out here years ago to observe it, and she never ceased to marvel at it.

She had once taken Gordos very early on in their relationship, and he, too, thought that it was one of the most spectacular sights he had ever seen. In fact, when he came back from the Pacific, her told her once that a lot of the men he served with used to marvel at the dawn coming up on some of the islands they were on. Most of the men he was with were city folk, and had probably never seen the sun come up over anything but a building.

He didn't disagree with them at all, but used to think to himself that he would like to give them the opportunity to see the dawn at The Lagoon. The other thing he mentioned in that context, was that some even wondered if the Japs, wherever they were on the island, also felt the same way. One wag, to everyone's delight, drawled that if they did, he hoped that they were looking at their last one.

She felt that Sunny was a little too young to fully appreciate it, at this stage. However, it was certainly a treat that she was going to let her experience in a year or two. If she was feeling anything else at all that morning, it was guilt that she had not given more thought to taking Chuck, Billy and Ben along with them. The thing was she had decided too late to come out here at all. The feeling of unease that had been developing over the Canard invitations, together with Gordos, was coloring everything at the moment, and was triggered yesterday afternoon. Well, she would have it out with her uncle when they arrived at The Lagoon.

"Lofty honey, how do the Keds feel?" She shook herself out of her reverie.

"Oh Miss Alice they're wonderful!" came the prompt reply.

"Don't you get them dirty when we pull over along here, will you? You mind you don't get mud on them now!"

"No no, Miss Alice. Ah'll be careful."

A few minutes later they came to the slight bend in the road that would lead them out to the Bluff. The road actually cut through a hundred yards short of it, but there was a vehicle track that was virtually "all weather" which took you right to the point. They came to the next bend and she told the boys to hang on as she took the big car gently down off the edge and onto the two-wheeled track that led on out to the point. They drove on another one hundred yards or so, and she cut the engine as they slowly came to a halt.

"What happens now, Mom?" was the inevitable question from Freddie. "What are we going to do now?"

"We are going to get out and walk over to a great big log and sit on it, now out we get, come on boys. It won't be long before something happens." The two boys silently got out and set off behind her, although she was nearly out of sight. Freddie stumbled. "Now come on, old bumble foot," said Alice, "come on, give me your hands, one on either side. Come on." She took them by the hands and led them over to the log, which she could barely see herself. "How are those old Keds, Lofty?"

"They're great, Miss Alice, they're great, they're very comfortable."

"That's wonderful. I hope Ben's fit as well."

"You're giving some to Ben as well, Miss Alice?"

"Ohhh! Of course, you sausage, of course. We can't have him running slower than you, can we?"

Lofty giggled.

Alice sat with a child on either side of her, and gazed out over the not yet visible stretch of water.

"How long, Mom?" whispered Freddie.

"Now we have to be quiet, about five to ten minutes, I think," said Alice in a hushed voice.

Lofty sat there without saying a thing, but thinking, that whatever it was, it must be special. He only hoped he could understand what all the flap was about, and could appreciate it.

Freddie sat there, and it suddenly dawned on him that they were going to see the sun coming up. Mom must have the same sort of feelings that I do. Alice shifted a little. The old tree wasn't at all comfortable, and she had been sitting on some sort of protrusion, probably where a branch had been, a knot. She patted Lofty's hand, and leant over and began whispering something to Freddie, when to her amazement he patted her hand and said, "Hush!"

Somewhat brought up short, she straightened up, thinking to herself that, after all, it was her party, it was her idea. Oh well, he certainly seems to be getting into the mood of it all. She looked intently out into the darkness and a moment or so later, almost imperceptibly, she sensed, rather than saw, the first sign that the "spectacular" was just about to unfold.

There was the ever so faint paling of the sky, and then the first almost hesitant needle-like points of sunlight thrusting out just as they merged into a larger, more all-enveloping glow. The heavens had the merest hint of red, which almost before you were aware of it disappeared, giving way to shades of yellowy white, along the horizon. The loom of light became gradually larger.

Alice took each boy by the hand and she gave them a gentle squeeze, patted them and then withdrew her hands as it began to unfold before them. They were all mute and sitting stock-still. Alice could feel the old familiar beat of her heart as her whole being seemed to apply itself to what was taking place before them. A barely discernible movement of air ghosted over them, and was gone in a moment as the body of the sun protruded into what a second before had been only the loom of its light.

Way out beyond them was a low range of hills in the far distance, and the sun gradually began to detach itself from the hills, from the landmass. Freddie began to wonder if he would hear another cock-crow, but suspected that he wouldn't as they were too far away from any houses. The sun gradually rose higher, and as it did the light began to envelope all in its panoramic diversity. It gradually came out across the water, and past them. Of course they could only look obliquely, as the rays were becoming ever stronger. They suddenly heard the sound of perhaps a hundred or so water birds, taking off from the surface well out from them. They couldn't see them but heard the unmistakable sound and the muted "honk" of one or two of them.

Alice swiveled her head slowly around to her right and watched the light settle on the vast expanse of the lagoon proper. The boys followed her lead. As she was turning back to the left, they all heard the bellowing of one of the cattle way off over the water. As the bellow dissipated, they saw a flock of water fowl, take flight and then immediately settle on the water again. She stole a surreptitious glance at each of the boys, and could easily take in that they had been enveloped by the same

116

"sense of occasion," as she was. It made her feel a little goosey.

She had seen sunrises without number over the years; however, ninety-nine percent of them occurred when they were secondary to whatever she was doing, or involved in. This particular one, she hoped, whilst it was special to her, would be special to the two boys as well. She looked down at Lofty again. He was such a delightful little fellow. He certainly was little, and he had a most engaging personality. It came as no surprise to her when she had found that she was taking up his cause as far as "the bridge" was concerned. This sunrise excursion was just a natural progression from that.

They continued to sit, each wrapped in their own little world, drinking in each exquisite moment. As the minutes ticked by Alice felt a satisfying glow settle over her. Everything the boys did—no movement on their part; each completely, independently of the other— conveyed to her their complete and utter absorption in the wonder transpiring before them. Out of the corner of her eye she saw a jack rabbit emerge just within her peripheral vision. She also sensed that the boys also saw it as well. It hopped, sat right up, hopped again, and repeated this several times before it eventually was lost to their view. The light became brighter and brighter; way off in the distance, down towards where the mansion was, they saw another flock of birds, quite a big one flying low on the horizon.

None of them had said a word, and Alice was beginning to think that it was time to get going again, when she spotted to her great delight a red fox come tentatively trotting, in short bursts, around the water's edge. It was looking for frogs, she supposed. It hadn't seen them, but they, as one, had seen it. Alice was wondering if the boys had had a tingle go up their spine, the way she had. It came closer. None of them moved a

117

muscle; all wondering what the reaction would be when it eventually spotted them.

It kept coming, and Alice realized that it was going to cross the path that the jack rabbit had taken, which was actually quite close to where they sat. Whilst the rabbit hadn't seen them in its deliberations, she felt the fox would. They weren't called foxes for nothing, after all, her impish sense of humor told her. The fox came on, and didn't disappoint them. It got the scent, and homing in on it, it brought it around to about twenty feet in front of them. Oddly, it veered off away from them, just as Alice remembered the rabbit had; however just as it was turning away, that first slight movement of air that so often attends the still of a new day dawning, moved across them, and, taking their scent, moved over and across the fox.

The fox really broke up the party. It seemed, so they discussed later on, to have actually known what it was going to see when it turned around. It had its head down sniffing the rabbit spoor as it was turning away, as the waft of air carrying their scent enveloped it. It nearly rolled over as it reacted like lightning, it looked hilarious; taking everything in, in a split-second, as it was recovering from the initial shock, it turned to face them. Then it was off and away.

The spell was broken. Alice and the boys stood and Alice stretched, raised her arms above her head, and giving a little yawn, dropped her arms and enquired of the boys who were still chuckling, "Well, what did yo' think of that? What did you think Lofty?" she said, tussling his hair, as he grinned and looked up at her.

"Miss Alice, Ah enjoyed it. I've never thought of it that way before, an' Ah've never seen many, thank yo', Miss Alice."

"Well that's right nice of yo' to say so Lofty, thank you! Freddie honey, what'd you think of it?"

"Mom it was better than the first one I saw, but the first one was really special."

"Why Freddie, what was so special, and you have actually seen one before?"

"Yes Mom, when I went camping with Chuck, and Billy. The same day we met Lofty and Ben. The day we all met Snakesbreath."

"You actually saw the sun come up that day, Freddie?" asked Alice.

"Yes Ma'm, I got out of the tent early to go to the john, and saw it then. I saw a spider in its web, and a jack rabbit. I didn't see a fox though, but it was very special, because it was my first, and I was alone. The others were still asleep; but Mom, this place is a place that you can really bring people to. I was just lucky the first time. Can we bring Sunny and the other boys out here sometime?"

"We sure can, honey, we sure can. We'll do it before long."

They had begun making their way back to the car, picking their way slowly over the grass between the water's edge, and the tree line, and over the odd fallen limb.

"My, my, look at where we walked through the dark, without tripping over anything," said Alice, not really soliciting a response. "Oh my, just look at the poor old Chevy," she exclaimed a moment later.

They could see the car a little way ahead, and didn't it look a sight. It was all covered in mud, from top to bottom. It always looked immaculate. It was shiny black with white walled tires, normally, and right now it looked as though it had had someone deliberately thrown buckets of mud all over it. "Oh well," said Alice, "we'll just have to clean it up later."

"We'll wash it, Miss Alice," said Lofty. "Won't we Freddie?"

"I, well, I suppose so," muttered Freddie, with no enthusiasm whatsoever.

"In we hop," said Alice, her thoughts moving on. "It will take another thirty minutes from here to The Lagoon and one of Mary's breakfasts!"

Lofty had no idea just what one of Mary's breakfasts entailed, but thought that he would wait and see. He was still coming to grips at having been taken in, as it were, by this incredible family or woman, and didn't want to appear to be too pushy. His Momma had told him to really only speak to the adults when spoken to and otherwise just act normally, and be his usual cheerful self. It appeared to be working, as Alice couldn't have been more kindly disposed towards him.

Alice slowly inched the Chevy back up onto the road again, and set off for the mansion. Fortunately, the boys were very quiet in the back seat, no doubt reflecting on the events of the past hour or so. She pondered over how she would broach the subject. She had turned the whole thing over in her mind a thousand times, and had come to the same conclusion every time. Gordos—Oh I wish he was here, and we didn't have this nightmare hanging over us—Gordos would know how to handle it. He must have a bee under his bonnet due to the bridge business, and she knew what the actual "bee" was all about. Well, she would just have to have it out with him, it had going on too long. She wasn't going to become hysterical, it just wasn't her, but by gosh she was going to put it fairly and squarely to him. She was going to brook no argument. She felt the only way was to bring the whole matter out into the open.

Chapter 10

It took them another half hour of driving down through this enormous spread before they came to the first sign of yards and outbuildings, as they loomed out of the ever so slight morning mist. She wanted to time their arrival right on seven o'clock, as she knew Unc would be in the kitchen, having had breakfast, and would be having his first cup of coffee at seven, on the knocker. They had passed a few of the workers as they came within a half-mile of the first buildings. The men were either riding out on horseback, or the odd one was on a tractor. They all saluted or waved to the Chevy as it slowly drove by.

They rounded the last bend and there they were, only a few more yards to go. They crept into the main garden and crunched their way across the beautifully raked gravel, right up to the front of the mansion. This house she loved, it all looked so familiar; the gravel, the lawns all neatly cut; the familiar faces of the three gardeners, who all just happened to be in the main garden just as they pulled in; the ready smiles but bemused looks on their faces, as they took in the appearance of the car, and then the incongruous passenger, peering out of one of the rear windows.

Old Norman, the butler, had been sweeping the front steps as they came in. He turned and came bustling down towards them, delight lighting up his face. Alice noted that his eyes didn't flicker as he took in Freddie's companion. He opened both driver and passenger doors, and stepped back.

"Mornin', Miss Alice, morning, Mast'r Freddie." Nothing any of them could say or do, from Unc down, could induce him to address Freddie in any other way, so they had all come to live with it.

"Good morning, Norman," they both chorused.

"Norman, this is Lofty Arkwright. Lofty, say hello to Norman," Alice said as Norman held the front door open for them. "Come along boys," she said as she swept in. "Thank you, Norman."

Norman nodded, and took a few steps out and back down under the portico and catching the eye of one of the gardeners pointed quickly to the mud-splashed Chevy and made a rubbing motion with his right arm. The gardener waved in acknowledgement, indicating that they were going to anyway.

Alice walked down the large entrance hall: looking through the familiar rooms ahead of her, she could see the lawn sweeping away in the distance towards the lagoon. It looked absolutely beautiful at this time of day, she thought, in fact there weren't many days or times of day when it didn't look quite breathtaking. She turned to her right and with the boys still following walked on down to the kitchen, where she knew she would find Unc, in his customary place at the small table by the windows which also overlooked the lagoon, and the long expanse of patio.

Mary, Unc's old cook, looked up, with surprise turning to pleasure, as Alice entered the kitchen. Unc rose out of his chair, smiling, albeit with a look of surprise at seeing her unannounced, and so early in the morning.

"Why Ali," he started to say, "Freddie mah boy," and then he spotted Lofty. Give him his due, Alice thought,

122

he certainly registered surprise, but didn't let himself down.

"Mornin' Unc, morning Mary," she said. Mary looked at her. "One of your breakfasts for two hungry boys, please. They've been up since four o'clock."

"Why yes, Miss Ali, yes, yes. Comin' right up."

"Unc," Alice looked at him rather imperiously, as she indicated with a toss of her head that they would move to the next room. They were no sooner out of the kitchen than she thought to herself that she would have to slow up. She had made the fundamental mistake of not introducing Lofty. Oh well, it may have passed unnoticed.

For his part Unc had made a partial recovery at his surprise at the events confronting him. Never before had Alice arrived completely out of the blue like this, let alone with Freddie in tow, and this little nigger who was obviously the one at the bottom of all this bother, and all tricked up in a new pair of Keds that Alice had no doubt given him. What on earth had come over the girl? Well, they would have it out now alright. He had a bemused smile on his face nevertheless.

She led the way back down the hall and came to his study and, stepping into the doorway, obviously remembered herself, and stepped to the side, awaiting him to enter first. He was almost tempted to continue on and go into the next room, but checked himself. That would make too much of an issue of it. He stopped, and indicating with his hand, graciously allowed her to enter ahead of him. He could sense that she was barely containing herself. He decided to take the bull by the horns.

He walked to the center of the room over by the fireplace, and turning said, "Righto Ali, what in the devil is going on?"

123

She walked half way across to him, and looking straight at him said, "I simply can't believe that you have let this 'bridge' business get at you so much that you haven't sent Gordos an invitation!" Her voice was restrained, but shaking.

"What, what on earth are you talking about? Invitation to what?" He looked quite astounded, she had to admit to herself. She suddenly felt that she was on unsure ground. "Come on, what are you talking about?" She could sense his anger rising.

"His invitation to the Canard!"

"What on earth are you talking about? His Canard invitation! Of course he has been sent an invitation! Women, Ah don't know. Look at this!" He had gone across to the top of the bookcase shelf, and taken the heavy old Canard book in which he kept everything pertaining to the Canard since day one, and plonked it down on the table near where she was standing. "Look, there it is. Everything, every invitation, every damn thing to do with it, all in the book. Only mah rough sheets that Ah doodle on whilst Ah'm bringing the whole thing together, are still in the book as I had forgotten to throw them out. There you are, take a good look."

"No, no, if you say so," she began saying.

He interrupted. "Ah do say so, now you take a good look Missy."

He only ever called her Missy when he was being deadly serious with her. She knew that, and she could see that he was certainly cross now. He had only been cross with her on about three occasions ever, and she could remember every one. He flipped the book open to where the sheets of paper were, and there to her relief was the invitation to Gordos poking out between the sheets, it even had the stamp on it.

124

"Oh mah God," he muttered. "It has obviously been caught between the loose sheets, Ah had them all over the place at one stage before Ah posted them before after I had put the stamps on them, they were all in the book. Ah'm sorry."

"No, no, I'm sorry." She shook her head, turning away, her eyes brimming with tears.

He caught sight of her eyes, and the anguished look on her face before she turned away, and stepping around her, took her by the shoulders, and said, "Oh dear, Oh dear. There's more to it than this, isn't there? Now come on, out with it, Chickie." His tone softening to the old familiar voice that she knew so well. He gave her a gentle squeeze.

She looked up at him, directly into his face, and nodded. He felt a chill run through him. Her very look was a presage of something seriously wrong.

"Gordos is dying!"

"He's what?!" he found himself saying in an unnatural voice. "Oh, oh." He stepped away from her and sat down. "Oh mah God!" He looked up at her with an anguished expression on his face. "Oh mah God!"

She moved towards him, and he put up his hand to stop her as he rose out of the chair. He pulled a handkerchief out of his pocket, he seemed to collect himself, and wiping his eyes said. "Just a moment, Ah won't be long."

He walked to the door, and pulling it open, turned and smiled at her before he left the room quietly closing it behind him. He walked down to the kitchen, composing himself where he found the two boys each tucking in to a big plate of ham, corn grits, eggs and tomato. Mary was over at the stove, making some flapjacks by the look of things. Old Norman was at a cupboard putting the polishing things away. Unc smiled at the boys, as he walked across to Lofty and, putting out his great hand, leant down and proffered it to the somewhat startled child.

"Ah'm Freddie's uncle, son: Mr. Kershaw!"

Lofty put out his tiny hand and said. "Mr. Kershaw sir!"

Well, he's well brought up, Unc thought to himself. "Norman!"

"Yessir, Mr. Ted?"

Unc smiled and, nodding to Norman, looked at Lofty. "Son, yo' all better call me Mr. Ted, everyone else does, OK."

"Yessir Mr. Kershaw!" poor old Lofty blurted out.

Unc smiled and wiggled a finger good-naturedly at him, and smiled. "Norman, will you go across to the office and tell Alan, he should be there by now, that Ah said to drop everything he is doing in a quarter of an hour, and come and fetch the boys and take them with him to see the new quarry being opened up. He's going down there later this morning anyway, and to have the boys away no longer than two hours from when he leaves with them. That is important. Got to be away only two hours. OK."

"Yes sir!" Old Norman scuttled off.

"Mary, will yo' please bring a coffee tray for Miss Alice and Ah to mah study door, and put it on the table outside, and knock on the door when you do. Ah'd appreciate it if you would do that right now. You better put some drop scones on it as well, with some trimmings."

"Yes, Mr. Ted."

"Now yo' fellas have fun with Alan, and don't get in the way of the bulldozer! Mary, we're not to be disturbed." He disappeared.

Alice had watched him go out of the room feeling almost as low as she had in the past few months. They had resisted telling Unc about Gordos, as they were

126

hoping against hope that it may all work out well. However, this was not to be the case. The prognosis could not be worse, although she as yet had not sat across the desk from the doctor, with Gordos, and had the whole thing spelt out, chapter and verse. That would come soon enough.

She turned a few pages of the Canard book in a desultory fashion, as she waited for him to return, and looked around the room. The beautiful room that she had spent so many hours in, with her old wonderful uncle. She knew when he returned, after she had given him the full story on Gordos, he not unreasonably would want to know what her mention of "the bridge" was in reference to. Well, she would deal with that at the time.

The familiar smell of the polished furniture, mingled with the aroma of the enormous vase of assorted roses that he always had on the table when they were in season, leant the room an aura of permanence and stability. She picked up three petals that had fallen from the arrangement and walking over to the windows absently dropped them into the basket by the desk. She peered out over the great sweep of immaculate lawn that ran down to the lagoon and turned and looked over the room again.

The whole house, she knew, was in fact cleaned and polished on an almost daily basis, which contributed to the overall feeling that it was occupied by a large family, instead of one old man. It certainly required upkeep, but the cost of it all was never an issue. It just didn't enter the equation, and for some indefinable reason everything seemed to emanate from his study, from this beautiful, all-too-familiar room, which, she also contemplated with a slight shiver, would become hers one day.

The door opened again quietly and he was back. He went over to the long built-in bookcase, which was set above an equally long series of built-in cupboards beneath a bench top that had sundry books, ornaments, and other knickknacks, including a whole range of family photographs in both silver and wooden frames. To her continual bemusement it also had his Colt revolver on it for as long as she could remember. For the odd varmint, he used to say.

Only one of these cupboard doors had a lock, and taking a key from his pocket, he said, "Now, Chickie; Mary will be here shortly with a tray." He bent down and unlocked the door, and as he was removing a large book—she thought it looked like an album—he went on.

"Ah've been thinking about your reference to the bridge business, and Ah've come to the conclusion that it can only mean one thing." He walked back towards the table, and put the album on it. "Before we continue down that trail can you fill me in as to where we are with George, from the start to where we are at this moment?"

"Ah don't think at all that you would be over-reacting, but Ah really don't know."

"Now come on." He took her hands, gave them a gentle squeeze, and kissed her on the top of the head.

There was a quiet knock on the door. He turned and walked over to it, and opening it called out, "Thank yo' Mary." He went out, picked the tray up and coming back into the room, leant on the door to close it.

"Right," he said. "We won't be interrupted for two hours. Ah've instructed Alan to take the boys down to see the quarry being opened up and oh, Ah introduced myself to Lofty, and Ah even told him to call me Mr. Ted. How's that?" he went on with a smile.

He sat down in front of her and peering closely into her face, and taking her hands in his, said, "Ah'm sorry, Chickie. If Ah hadn't organized all that just now, Ah don't think Ah would have been able to leave the room, after what you had told me." He gave her hands an extra squeeze, and she could see that his eyes were beginning to fill with tears. He wiped his eyes with the handkerchief again.

She returned his gaze, and the two of them looked into the depths. They, it was acknowledged without so much as a word, had together passed this way before. They sat thus, for a few minutes. Alice brought her hands together, still clasped by his, and entwining her fingers in his, gave his hands a comforting squeeze, slowly got to her feet, and bending over kissed him.

She reached for the coffee jug, and stopped to take a handkerchief from her pocket, but fumbled and couldn't find it. He was still clutching his and passed it to her. She wiped her eyes, and put it down on the table between them, and began telling him as she poured the coffee.

"Ever since Gordos has been discharged, with that terrible head wound, I have had this underlying dread, that at some time in the future it may come back to haunt us. My worst fears have come to pass. Two to three months ago, he appeared to be preoccupied with something and I asked him if he was feeling out of sorts. His response was rather offhand, but this preoccupation continued, and shortly before the boys went off on the camping trip into the swamp, you may remember he went off to New York on one of his periodical family board meetings." Unc nodded.

"Now, he was away a day or so longer than was usual, but he explained that away over the 'phone and I thought nothing of it until he arrived back." Alice pointed to the drop scones with the spoon, and Unc nodded his head. "He told me that he had in fact been feeling, not out of sorts, but that he had developed these nagging headaches." She took two scones and put them on a small plate and put some butter on them, and indicating with the spoon the two kinds of jam that Mary had put in small bowls, she put some apricot on the side of the plate and passed it to him. She went on. "Initially they came and went, and he didn't place too much significance on them, but as time went on the frequency and duration increased. Without wanting to alarm me, he thought that he would have them checked out on the quiet, so to speak."

She continued, "We didn't tell you because we wanted to be sure. You never know with this sort of thing. The implications are too great to be going off half-cocked. I'm sorry. I think it is the first thing I've ever kept from you, and now my unseemly performance over the invitation." He reached out a hand, and she put hers in it.

"Don't you worry, Chickie, you were doing it for the right reasons. Now, when did you learn that it was serious?"

"Well after that initial check-up, we were given a referral to a clinic that handles this sort of thing for veterans, as the doctor who saw Gordos felt that the problem related to, or stemmed from, the head wound. This unfortunately seems to be the case. You will remember I went off with Gordos when he went to Mourmills to discuss the new engine for the Swan. We then went on to New York and they took X-rays and did more tests. The results were given to us by Eric Holmes, a few days before Gordos set off in the Swan.

"They could not be worse. They did coincide however with one of Gordos' comfortable periods, as we now refer to them. They usually last for two to three weeks, where he has no pain at all and he can carry on as usual. They then return for a week or two with greater intensity, and so it goes on. We—or Gordos insisted that we—wouldn't mention it to you or anyone until after the Canard. You know what he is like, he doesn't like theatrics. So here we are, going on, just business as usual, and I'm going to meet him in a day or so and we are going to sit down with the doctors and be put completely in the picture, but whatever the order of march is, it won't have a happy ending." She uttered a stifled sob, and stood there with tears streaming down her cheeks.

Unc hunched forward, his chin in his hands. "What has Eric had to say? As Ah understand he would have to coordinate any referrals wouldn't he?"

"Yes, yes, he did, and he has been absolutely marvelous. He has over-extended himself, speaking to everyone in the field, and he has assured us that we are getting the very best attention there is. There are no better people anywhere either here, or in England, France, Canada, you name it. Germany even. We are in the very best hands."

"Well it seems at this stage, there is nothing we can do except pray for a miracle, and keep our hopes up," said Unc softly, reaching out and taking Alice's hand, and giving it a gently squeeze. She just looked down at him, and gave a sniffling nod.

They both continued with their coffee, with Alice resuming her chair. They sat lost in their own thoughts for several minutes, and eventually Alice found her gaze resting on the old album. She looked across at Unc, and clearing her throat a little, got his attention. She looked at the album.

"Oh the album," he said, with a resigned grimace. The album, the bridge, the niggers, the invitation, the silly old fool! He had the grace to look across at her, indicating that he really didn't mean the last reference in the way it could be taken. He put the cup down, and spooned a little apricot jam onto a scone, which he rather unceremoniously stuffed into his mouth, as he reached across for the album.

Opening it, he thumbed through, until he was about a third of the way through it, announcing that it was a

131

family album, and Alice interrupted: "I have never seen it before, have I?"

"No, my dear, you have not, and in bringing about this exposure of it, Ah can only say that you have now met, even exceeded, all mah expectations of you. Ah have hoped on and off over the years that this conversation with regard to it, would come to pass, one day, and now it has. The fact that mah heart could not be heavier, as to how it came about, Ah mean the circumstances, unfortunately hangs heavily upon it."

She could see that where he opened it, it appeared to only have one or two pages of photographs left before it came to pages that were, or looked clear.

"Ah should say at this point that we have never been a family for taking a lot of photographs. So what Ah am going to tell you has been reasonably easy to conceal. Of course it wasn't so long ago that to take even one photograph involved quite a lot of trouble."

He pointed to a photograph of six people. There was one very old man, a big man, but for all that, he was looking very much in control, virile even. Then there was a much younger man who looked slightly browbeaten, but at the same time putting on a brave face. The other four in the picture were boys: two of about fifteen or sixteen, the others around ten to twelve years of age. They all looked quite happy, and there was something vaguely familiar about them. About all of them, in fact, although she had never seen the older one before. It suddenly struck her that the two younger ones were her father and Unc, and their two siblings who had died in the war. The older one was her grandfather. She pointed to her grandfather, and looked at Unc.

"Gramps, Dad and you, and your two brothers who were lost in the War."

"Yes," he said, "and look at Gramps. He doesn't look at all happy or comfortable, does he?"

"I remember him as always very cheerful." She went on, "Why am I being shown these photos for the first time, Unc?" She felt that she had to get to the bottom of it, and that there may be more in the opening of the album than at first met the eye. "And?"

She pointed to the old man, and looked enquiringly at Unc. She already knew of course, and fleetingly suspected with a slight thrill, that there must be a family skeleton in the closet.

She continued to look at her uncle, and could see that a mask had momentarily descended over his countenance, and just as suddenly it began to contort in what she could only describe as pain.

"Unc, what is it?" He held up a hand and cut her off. They sat for a few more moments, and then he suddenly took in a long, deep breath, and let it out as a sigh.

"He is yo' great-grandfather, or Paw." She began to nod, and his hand came up again. "And Ah killed him!" he said softly, but with defiance. Alice felt a thud in the pit of her stomach.

"You what?" she exclaimed. "You…"

He broke in. "Ah don't mean to say," holding his hand up again, "Ah shot him or hit him over the head, Ah did something else." He held up two hands this time, and lowered his head, indicating he wanted time to structure what he was about to say.

"You see, although Ah didn't know at the time, and then Ah suppose Ah wouldn't have even understood, he had the most frightful inferiority complex, why Ah don't know. He had been in England and Europe during the Civil War, as a procurer, buyer, shipper of badly needed materiel for the Southern war effort.

"He had been travelling in both England and France when the war broke out. He was fluent in French and in fact was both a Francophile and an Anglophile. Whilst Ah can't expect you to know, Jefferson Davis had appointed two Southerners to represent us in England and France. They were arrested by a Yankee ship before they got there and Davis cast around and discovered that our Grand Pappy was already over there moving freely between both countries, in fact in very high circles. He was duly contacted and appointed to represent the South. He eventually received a Presidential Citation from Davis. Ah can even show it to yo'.

"All this, and he could never live up to his father's expectations. And having only sisters, when his father died he was going to take over The Lagoon. Well, he came back and when 'Grand Paw,' as they used to call him, died, Paw set himself up as the Great Plantation Owner."

"When your father and the other three of us came along, we were oblivious to all this of course, and to be honest with you, Ah adored him, and Ah suspect, Ah was the 'Apple of his Eye.' All that finished, shortly after this picture was taken.

"His big problem was that he was never wrong, he always had to be in control, he had to dominate every aspect of everything that was his or what he was involved in, particularly the blacks. His whole existence depended on them of course, but he had this blind spot. He had no sense of perspective where they were concerned; everything had an ulterior motive."

Alice was listening to all this as if in a dream. Her mind was going like a threshing machine. All sorts of thoughts were tumbling through her mind. She managed to bring them into focus around the one thing, the underlying fundamental to everything that he had instilled into her since she had been a child—and that was the essence of family, and one's place in it. The family underpinned one's existence according to him, and this she had had no trouble accepting. Whereas now…

He broke in. "You would have heard of lynching."

"Why of course," she responded.

"Well, from time to time they were advertised, and it was from one of these that this whole terrible 'family' business started."

"What on earth can you mean?"

"This, this, relative of ours organized one."

"He what?"

"Yes, he organized one, and Ah knew the man he had lynched, and Ah pleaded with him to let him go to put him back in the jail, and he almost laughed at me."

"Oh Unc, I don't know what to say. What are you leading up to?" She looked at him with a blank but slightly agonized look on her face. "Why are you telling me this now? As if we don't have enough on our plates!" He reached forward, taking her hands.

"Chickie, there is never the right time for coming out with anything like this, Ah know, but if you are ever going to fully know me; this is the time to bring it up! Believe me! It won't take me long, Ah can assure yo'!"

She just looked at him and nodded, a helpless, distressed look on her face. He went on.

"You see he was the local leader of the 'Klan.' As a man of substance in the County, let alone the state, he really couldn't be anything else. He was unassailable, in all things pertaining to the Klan, and most other matters, as yo' can imagine. In fact, he had even been the 'Grand Wizard.'

"Now, Ah know you suspect me of being the Arch Klansman. Well Ah am, but that is only the half of it. Yo' know, Chickie, being the custodian of an enterprise like this has never been easy. We have owned and built up The Lagoon for how long, do you think? It is well over two hundred years and Ah would like to think that we will be here for another two hundred, but we can't

135

always be all things to all people all the time, no matter how much we may like to.

"In any family there is going to be going to be some bad apples. In my opinion he was one of them, but at the same time he was a very good businessman, even though a very bad family man. My parents had a frightful time with him. He was the epitome of everything known as 'Jim Crow.' Whereas Ah became the exact opposite: a 'John Brown,' although a closet one."

"Unc please just tell me how did you kill your grandfather? What did you do? You are beginning to talk in riddles, please get to the point!"

"Well, yes now, how did Ah kill him, well Ah didn't speak to him again after that night, yo' know!"

"You what?" said Alice.

"That's right," he went on. "For some reason or other he took me and my father to the lynching. He didn't take my other brothers, only me. He may have wanted to impress me, Ah don't know. My problem was Ah knew the man they lynched."

"You have already told me that!" said Alice, "But how on earth would you know him?"

"It is quite simple really," Unc went on. "Today most of the vehicles on The Lagoon are motorized. Back then they were horse-drawn, and while we shod the horses and did all the work on the carts and wagons, we didn't have a wheelwright. Whenever something was needed to be done to the wheels, they were taken into White Oak, and attended to there at the farrier's. Where they were also wheelwrights.

"Ah was always interested in things mechanical, and would help out in my own small way whenever anything got broke, and on the odd occasion would go in on the wagon with any of the wheels that needed fixin', and watch. There was this nigger there who was a dab hand at makin' spokes, and I got to know him, as only small boys can. He taught me a few things about wooden wheels and spokes and the like, and Ah don't think anyone really noticed. If Ah had been older perhaps they would have steered me away from being too close to a nigger, but it never happened. At the same time, it wasn't as though Ah was in there every day of the week, although we always seemed to have a wheel or two that needed fixin'. It was a specialist job, yo' know. The other thing was that Ah always went in with one of the men, and of course they weren't in a position to tell me who Ah should or should not talk to."

"Unc, Unc," Alice said despairingly.

"Yes Ah know, Ah know. Ah became friendly with him, and then there was a white girl in the town who was raped by, they said, a black man, and he was accused. Even the girl couldn't really identify him, but he was in the vicinity at the time, and tempers were really runnin' hot. Anyways, they had a trial, and the evidence, as most reasonable folk would accept was inconclusive, and they had a hung jury.

"The upshot of that was that they decided on a retrial upstate, and whilst all this was being gone through the judicial process, with mind yo' being slowed down by vested interests, our ole' Grand Pappy decided to have himself a 'lynchin'!'"

"He what?" exclaimed Alice.

"Oh yes, don't you worry, and the whole thing, as it could be in those days, which Ah might add seems like only yesterday, was advertised in the County press, and, come one come all, along they came on the great day. Or should Ah say, night."

Unc stopped and looked at Alice, as though to collect his thoughts. She didn't interrupt. "Well, Ah was only about twelve years of age, and to be quite honest had no idea what was afoot the evening the three of us, mah Daddy and Paw and me, went off to town into White

137

Oak. Ah do recollect in retrospect that mah Gran and Mommy were having a mild altercation with him but off we went nevertheless!

"We arrived in town and pulled up in the surrey in front of the Court House, which had the lockup beside it, and we held court, if you will, for around an hour or so as the crowd gathered. All sorts of folks came up to mah Grand Pappy as we sat there. He had a word fo' each and every one of them, and really seemed to be enjoying himself. There was even the Sheriff and the head of the local Militia amongst them. They all spoke to mah Daddy as well, of course, although he didn't seem to be as at ease as mah Grand Pappy.

"Ah must confess Ah thought the whole atmosphere had a kind of subdued festiveness, almost expectation about it. There were all sorts of people, both men and women, there were the usual redneck crowd, and there were well-dressed folks; in fact, now Ah think about it, they were the kind of crowd you would get at a race meetin'.

"Then the whole thing just degenerated into what was, for me, a nightmare. Ah had been just going along with the flow, being a minor part of the center of attraction, in that Ah was mah Grand Pappy's grandson, and Ah can tell you, Chickie, it was a mighty hot night, and then Ah became aware of a roar, and then a hush, and then suddenly there Ah was beneath this great tree over the street from the Court House. There was a rope over a limb of the tree, and this black man was led over towards us.

"The light was really bad but there was a procession of men with fiery torches which gave off quite a glow. The procession came right up to us, and there in front of me was the nigger from the farrier's. Ah couldn't quite take it in at first just what was happening, but we were standing perhaps two feet apart, looking at each other,

138

and suddenly a chill came over me, as he saw me, an anguished look on his face. Ah began to feel terribly uneasy.

"He looked me in the eye and said in a low voice, 'Ah didn't do it, Mas' Kershaw.'

"'Do what, Jed?' Ah cried.

"'Rape de girl, Mas' Kershaw! Ah don' know who dunnit!'

"Ah looked at mah Daddy: 'What is going on, sir?' Ah cried!

"'They are going to string this nigger up,' he replied, looking away.

"Ah shook mah Grand Pappy's arm. 'Paw, what are they doing?'

"'Don't you worry, mah boy, we're going to teach these niggers a lesson. They go messing around with white women, and this is what will happen to them!'

"'But Ah know him!' Ah cried, 'and he didn't do it.'

"'Now now, don't you worry boy, he did it all right, and he's going to get what's coming to him, and any others who do the same thing.'

"Ah should say, as a twelve-year-old Ah really didn't know what rape meant, however if he said he didn't do it, that was good enough for me.

"By this time they had brought up a horse and having put the noose around his neck, were lifting him astride it. Ah shook Paw's arm again and pulled him around. 'Stop it!' Ah said. 'Stop! Ah know him and he didn't do it!' Ah flung mahself at Jed's, the nigger's, leg. Paw pulled me off, and said, 'Righto boys,' and the horse was led off from under the nigger.

"Ah heard a kind of grunting sound and there he was hanging with his feet about three feet from the ground, his hands tied behind his back with his legs beginning to flail, and suddenly two niggers broke free through the crush of the crowd, flinging themselves at him and grabbing his legs bore down, to put more weight on him to quicken it and ease his suffering.

"My last recollection was of the sobbin' of the two niggers holding his legs, and he then voided hisself."

"He what? Ugrh, oh," said Alice.

"He voided hisself, and the stench just spilled out almost on top of me; and the terrible heat of the night rose up and hit me, Ah had trouble breathing, and then Ah must confess, Ah passed out, and didn't come around until sometime later when the three of us were jogging back out to The Lagoon in the surrey."

Alice looked at him. He had watery eyes even then, and was almost choking on the emotion. Momentarily she completely forgot the preoccupation that nagged her over Gordos. She leant forward and clasped Unc's hands in hers. She gave them a gentle reassuring squeeze. He recovered, and continued.

"We arrived back at The Lagoon, and Ah feigned sleep and they carried me up to mah room, and mah Mammy tucked me up and gave me a kiss and Ah heard them softly close the door and go off down the stairs. Yo' know it wasn't really late at all, it was around ten o'clock at night, although still very hot.

"Ah lay there for what seemed like an age, runnin' with sweat. With the events of the evening searing into mah brain. It seemed to me that mah Daddy really didn't want any part of what happened, whereas it was all mah Grand Pappy's doing. Ah was proved to be right on that score, Ah can tell you, Missy.

"Ah could not have been more traumatized if they had strung up one of the family. Ah had grown up overnight, and do you know what, Chickie? Ah gradually became aware that something inside o' me had shut down, it dawned on me that it was as though he had been placed to one side, mah Paw that is. It was nothing to do with me, it was all his doing, and do yo' know what? Ah didn't care one iota.

"All feeling for him just kind of dissipated. Not only had that feeling of emptiness towards him crept into me, but Ah decided then and there to do something about it. Never again would such a thing ever take place due to mah kin, if Ah had anything to do with it. All this being decided by a twelve-year-old, Ah might add. As he, Ah, softly cried mahself to sleep!"

He went on. "The next morning, as usual, Ah went down for breakfast, and as everyone drifted in Ah gave them the usual greeting and a kiss for the women, and completely ignored mah Grand Pappy. Well of course this didn't exactly go unnoticed by him or some of the others, and he invited me to 'Give yo' ole Paw a kiss.' Ah looked at him, solemnly for few moments, and turned away, and went on to have mah breakfast, without looking at him again.

"Well, Chickie, to cut a long story short that fairly put the cat amongst the pigeons, as they say. Ah didn't ever speak to him at all, ever again. It took quite a while for this to play itself out, and rent the family of course, but within six months he was dead. He died of shame, perhaps really of loss, if Ah can put it like that. He went off his food, drank more, went off it completely, waxed and waned between anger and remorse, and Ah suppose the amazing thing about it was that no one including mah beautiful Grand Mah really went out of their way to give him solace. There was not one ounce of compassion for him from anyone.

"Whilst he eventually took to his bed, and had all the attention in the world, he died alone, all alone, even though with the exception of me, all the family was there for his last hours. He just withered on the vine, and became a shell of the man that he had been; and Ah had no pity on him. When he finally went it was quite

141

amazing. It was as though a cloud had lifted, and we all emerged from beneath it, quite a different family. There was laughter through this old house for the first time, in a very long time.

"It's a funny thing, Chickie, about three months into this dreadful business, he finally understood or recognized just how mah attitude was affecting him, in that there was no way out for him. Ah would not bend to him; he was doomed.

"The other thing was that Ah did not hate him at all, Ah think he could have dealt with that. Ah just became quite indifferent to him and this is something that is very hard to come to grips with. It can really cut yo' to the core, if yo' think about it. Love and hate are two similar emotions in that they can hurt yo', almost consume yo' with a passion. Indifference is quite another thing. It is devoid of any pain. Yo' just switch off. Yo' don't care about them anymore, in any respect, and yo' have no control over it! From me he had complete and utter rejection, although passively! It's most odd, Ah've never had the experience since, Ah must say, and Ah'm thankful for that.

"Ah must say, though, to the outside world it was business as usual, no one knew about me rejecting him, and his funeral was one of the biggest the State has seen. His reputation was intact. So, Chickie." He looked up at her. "Things aren't always the way they seem—certainly not in our family anyways."

"Oh Unc." She stood up, went to him taking his head, and giving the top of it a kiss, held him to her.

He moved his head up to look at her, and said, "To cut to the chase: what Ah have done, all through mah life since then, has to make things a little better for the nigger, without ever letting on to a soul. Yo' can't imagine today how things were back then. It is an emotive enough subject now. At times even now we still have a lot of unrest, the odd riot, and the Guard are called out, but do you know in the first decade of this century over 750 blacks were lynched, 90 percent in Dixie?

"This County has been the Kershaw Family bailiwick almost since the first settlement. Ah was twelve when Ah attended that lynchin'. Mah Grand Paw was against Reconstruction, whereas mah Pappy was all for it. We were a mixed bunch, this family of ours. Mah Pappy lost two uncles in the war when the Southern States seceded. One joined the Union, and fought against the South, and the other joined the Confederates, and fought against the Union. We were a house divided. Oddly, neither of them apparently was hell bent on the slavery issue. It was the fragmentation of the country that motivated them to take the positions that they took. They both became Captains, and they were both killed within a month of the end of the war. It was terrible; such a waste.

"The whole business is not without its different levels of complexity, no matter what side yo' were on. Historically Ah think it is fair to say, that once folks realized a long time ago that the slaves were an asset to be looked after and fed and housed properly, it, at the risk of oversimplifying it, came down to whether you as an owner were going to be paternalistic, or tyrannical. Ah also think it is fair to say that Grand Pappy fell into more the tyrannical type rather than the paternalistic, and as such, Ah have to admit was as much a product of the times as the next man who was paternalistic. Of course, both attitudes carried on down the years well after the slaves were freed.

"To put things into some sort of context, without excusing what went on, it is all too often forgotten that in the early days there were nearly as many blacks in some Southern States as whites, and there was a fear that if they ever took it upon themselves to revolt, blood would flow. The whites had to keep on top of this possibility, and the way to do this was to keep them constantly in awe of the whites. This extended long after the Civil War, and some believe in it wholeheartedly today. In fact, Ah don't know if we will ever be free of this fear.

"Looking back on it, he was in some ways progressive, and in others feudal. Apparently when it was mooted that each freed slave would be given forty acres and a mule, it was he that had the foresight, with the agreement of the rest of the family, to call a meeting of the responsible freed slaves who remained on the plantation, and eighty percent at least had stayed. This was as much, Ah suspect, because they had nowhere else to go, together with the fact that whilst he was tyrannical, they had been well cared for, and now of course they would be working for a wage. He put it to them that there really was no free land in the State. If there was, it would probably be reclaimed by the previous plantation owners, and he felt that whilst it would be nice for them to at least have a mule, it would be much better for them, in the long run, if he was to arrange for them to be given a cow and a heifer. They could be run as a separate herd on the plantation, and could be joined free of charge to plantation bulls. In the fullness of time they would return them a healthy profit, and the scheme could go on indefinitely. Today ten percent of The Lagoon herd, numbers wise, is owned by the niggers, as yo' well know, with a further five percent owned by the white overseeing staff.

"All this from the only one of them who was really against Reconstruction. He would have kept the slaves in bondage forever given half the chance, but of course he was a pragmatist. Ironically, mah Great Grand Pappy saw fit to send him off to Europe and, give him his due, he certainly kept the goods coming. Of course he was saved from the carnage and his two other brothers weren't. Anyway, Ah'm beginning to ramble. Truth is, Ah've never really told another soul about this.

"What Ah'm coming to is that mah Daddy and Ah became much closer after the lynchin'. He, as was his due, became the leader of most of the organizations dealing with security, like the Militia on one hand, and the Klan on the other, and his policy was to temper everything, to settle everything down, and rely on reason, and the law as he interpreted it. We have never had a lynchin' in the County, since that one of old Jed. All due to the two of us. Only of course because we didn't nail our colors to the mast.

"With the best connections in the State, this, if yo' play yo' cards right, isn't that hard to achieve, and Ah took over where he left off, but it isn't always easy. Some folks have told me to mah face that Ah'm too soft on the niggers, but Ah just face them down, and make some comment like, 'This really ain't an issue we need bother about too much. Ah'd prefer we allow the Law and due process to take care of it!' That's usually enough. If it isn't I jes' ask them would they prefer to go back to the days of lynching, and that generally fixes them.

"Now Ah do have to say to yo', Chickie, Ah suspected that something like the bridge lessons with the niggers would come up, and Ah thought that it was a good excuse for me to show some of our redneck friends that Ah really am on their side, and come out dead against it. If at the end of the day Ah had to eat humble pie over it, well so be it. Ah'm big enough and secure enough to live quite happily with whatever the outcome may be.

"The pity was that Ah really couldn't let you two in on mah little secret, 'cos Ah knew Ah'd be pitted against you, Chickie, and Ah even rehearsed to mahself just how

Ah would react, although Ah have been so proud of you. Yo' know, Chickie, in this respect Ah seem to have been living a lie fo' most of my life in a sense, and Ah've become cynical, in a way with regard to the black issue, and in another sense Ah can turn it on and off like a tap. Ah'm the one who looks at myself in the mirror and Ah've come to terms with it.

"Now of course all that has changed with the news about George. The bridge and the niggers really are no longer an issue. All Ah can suggest in respect of them, is that yo' leave it to me. Ah'll see to it that they can continue to learn without anyone losing too much face."

She looked at him silently with tears streaming down her face, wondering to herself just where he managed to pull these inner reserves of strength from, over all these years.

She pondered. "Did you forgive him? Paw?"

"Yes!" He exhaled a long sigh. "Oh, Chickie, why did you ask? Ah did eventually. In a word, yes, Ah did."

"When?"

He gave another sigh. "Perhaps if Ah say firstly, that the capacity to be able to forgive is possibly one of the most noble attributes one can have! Ah should also say that Ah came to that conclusion some considerable time after Ah actually forgave him.

"After Paw died Ah just didn't go on mah own sweet way. Ah had been traumatized; remember, Ah was only twelve years old."

She started to interrupt. He put up a hand. "Now, Ah quite honestly was unaware that what he did warranted such a thing as forgiveness. Ah don't think Ah had ever heard of such a thing.

"As Ah told yo', I was in a state of complete indifference with regard to him; however, Ah found that as time went on Ah became aware almost subconsciously that there was a sense of underlying, for

146

want of a better word, unease, that was beginning to niggle.

"Ah suppose this was some five or so years on. Ah was quite relaxed in every way except when mah mind wandered to Paw. All of this Ah kept to mahself.

"This went on for a year or so, and one day Ah found mahself with old Harry Wilson who was our parson. We were sitting under a tree at a local something or other and we got to talkin'. Actually when Ah said Ah hadn't spoken to another soul about this there is one exception, and he is it.

"One thing led to another and he got it out of me that Ah was slightly troubled about something. Then Ah told him about Paw, and how Ah had shunned him. It's a funny thing. Looking back on it the parson appeared to regard me in a different light, from then on. But, and it's a big but, he asked me if Ah had forgiven him. Paw, that is. Ah said, what for? What he did was frightful, and whilst Ah hadn't thought about forgiving him, he didn't deserve it anyway.

"Well, off the parson went, in a nice way Ah should add. He said that forgiving was not so much for him, as he was dead and gone, however it would help mah peace of mind no end if Ah could at least consider forgiving him. He was not suggesting that Ah forget it, that would be impossible, but forgiveness is another thing entirely.

"He explained that for mah Paw to go off and meet his Maker with his mind in torment, was one thing, and there is no doubt he brought it upon himself. However, for me to tell him the parson that Ah was troubled was a tellin' sign of mah concern. Now if Ah was to forgive him, there was a very good chance that Ah would feel more at peace over the whole business.

"Beyond that he didn't press the point, and it took me another twelve months or so to finally reach the conclusion that Ah would forgive him. Nevertheless, it was a challenge. You know what, Chickie, when Ah did Ah felt a whole lot better: a weight had been lifted, and from then on Ah have taken the view that forgiveness is the most beautiful gift one can have. Yo' think about it, Chickie, just think about it…

"Now, enough of this talk. What say we leave it at that? Ah find the whole business exhausting."

They sat silently for several minutes, quietly weeping and holding hands. Eventually they composed themselves, and walked out onto the patio waiting for the boys. Their walk drifted them eventually to the front of the mansion, and there to her surprise was the Chevy looking as though it was brand new and straight off the showroom floor, with not a gardener in sight.

"My, my," she exclaimed, "look what they have done!"

"Look what who have done?" said Unc.

"The garden boys!" said Alice. "They have given the Chevy a thorough going-over. It was covered in mud when we arrived. I didn't tell you, but I took them to the Bluff on the way in to see the sunrise, and at one stage nearly left the road, and covered the car in mud. I even had to get out and wipe the windshield, it was so bad. Look, here come the boys now!"

Chapter 11

The next weeks literally flew for all of them. The shoot at one level preoccupied all—*thankfully,* thought Alice, as they had one more appointment with the doctors just after it, and it was giving Gordos a lot to do. All the family moved out to The Lagoon for the ten days or so either side of the Canard, and it was a time that they all looked forward to. No one more than Unc, who loved having the mansion ringing with laughter and young children's voices.

The children were very contented, with Freddie and the other boys spending as much time as they could with Snakesbreath, and Sunny being a little angel, and like the boys having taken to bridge; and according to Annette, it would not be long before they were playing in pairs instead of three-handed.

Alice on top of everything else had been praying that Gordos would have one of his "good" spells in the lead up to the Canard, as there was so much to do. Fortunately, this looked as though it was going to be the case as he had had a really bad week just prior, only coming good six days or so before the big day. So it looked as though he would have a clear run before the headaches set in again a few days after the shoot.

Over breakfast, the morning before the shoot, he announced that he had all the punts ready, and was going to take them around on the truck to the Mosquito Bend. The "Bend" was the spot where the waterborne hunters started from. There were six flat-bottomed punts which each carried two hunters with their guns and hampers. These hunters collected any birds that were too far out for the shore-based shooters to retrieve, and one way or another they collected quite a few. These were apart from any they shot themselves.

Whilst all the hunters were crack shots the bags varied from each one, due of course to how good a shot they were, but also to where they were shooting from. All the positions were balloted the night before over the dinner, and this had in itself developed into an hilarious sideshow to the main event, the total bag being divided so that everyone took a reasonable number home with them.

On hearing that her father was going, Sunny asked if she could go along too. George looked at Alice, and said, "Well I don't see why not, what do you think, Mom?"

"I think it will be fine darlin', but I think you had better go and put some old clothes on, as you don't want to get all your nice pink ones dirty now, do you?"

"No, no Momma, I'll thtay very clean, I won't get a thpeck on me. I won't go anywhere near the mud, and anyway it ith very grathy out at Mothquito Bend."

"Well I suppose so," rejoined Alice, "but do everything Daddy tells you to."

"Of courthe Momma, I alwayth do." She ran around the table to give her mother a kiss, gave Unc, who had been sitting there saying nothing, but grinning from ear to ear, a big hug and a kiss, then she gave Freddie a kiss and, running towards the door, asked her father when he would be leaving.

"In five minutes!" he called after her.

Sunny was in the brake a few minutes later when George arrived, and getting into it he exclaimed, "My, my, don't you look the pretty girl, all in pink." She was wearing Freddie's rubber boots all pink, and with the cut out flowers all over them.

"Haven't the boots come up well? I think they look wonderful, baby. It was a terrific idea of yours, they would probably be still just sitting in the box room if you hadn't cleaned them up. Now off we go to the barn to get the truck. Old Banjo and I loaded the punts on last night and he was going to have the truck all fueled up this morning. Here he is now."

They pulled up beside the barn and walked over to Banjo.

"Morning Banjo," said George and Sunny almost in unison.

"Morning Mist' George, Miss Sunny," he said with a big smile. "My, my don't you look jest the about the prettiest li'l gal Ah've seen?"

"Oh thank you, Banjo! Do you like my booths too?"

"Miss Sunny they'se about the best boots in the County, Ah reckon!" Sunny's day was made.

"Now up we get Missy, you can drive if you like, Banjo!" George said, lifting Sunny up onto the running board of the truck.

"Yessir, Mist' George, she's going a lot more smoothly now that we have replaced the front and rear universals, Mist' George." Banjo said as he walked around to the driver's side of the truck.

"Yes, well, I suppose they were the original ones, and you would never know what she had been through, although she probably never left the States," George replied.

She was one of the early Korean War Surplus vehicles. George had purchased three at an auction, one assembled, the other two still in their packing crates in greaseproof paper. They had brought them home in their boxes in the back of this one, a Ford CMP four-ton 4x4.

It was only in the last year or so that they had removed the second one from its crate and assembled it. George thought quietly to himself that he would never see the third one up and running. Oh well, he was lucky to survive as long as he had. He had no regrets. Life had been wonderful in every respect. The only thing that really affected him was that he would never see his children grow up.

They drove slowly out to the Bend, so as not to jostle the six immaculate punts in racks on the back of the truck. They were wooden, and had been made years ago before the war in The Lagoon carpenters' shop. They were only used all up once a year on the big day, but from time to time they were used singly if anyone on the staff wished to go into the swamp shooting. They were beautifully maintained, and varnished to a high sheen. They each had two poles about ten feet long, each was twelve feet long, and with two-and-a-half-foot beam.

"Ideal for the swamp," said Unc, who actually designed them. They had a foot of freeboard.

They were about two minutes from the grassy expanse where they were to leave the punts in readiness for the coming day when George quietly began to be flooded with an overwhelming sense of emotion. The Canard was one of the few things that he was involved in that he really loved out of all proportion. He suspected that Alice knew this although they had never really discussed it that way, but he was aware that she had over the years deferred to him in respect to anything to do with the shoot. It had of course been Unc's big thing, and he at first had felt that he had been imposing and that he had only been asked to take over as a matter of form. Whatever the original intention, it was his as much as Unc's now, and this would be his last.

Initially the shoot was known as the "Duck Shoot." However, shortly after the war, Unc invited a Frenchman who was staying with one of the regulars. He was a lovely fellow and became terribly excited when he saw how many ducks they had shot, and began calling out aloud, *"Canard canard, 'coup canard."*

He became so excited that he actually collapsed and died. This of course rocked everyone. The only redeeming feature was that he was nearing eighty and his wife told their hosts that he had heart trouble and she was quite relieved in a way that he had gone, being so excited and doing something that he enjoyed so much.

They all agreed that they would rename the Shoot the "Canard," in his memory.

Banjo pulled the Ford onto the patch and eased it over to a knoll and not far from water's edge he pulled up and cut the gas. He then clambered down, with Sunny tumbling out beside him. They had removed the driver and passenger doors years before, and George put one foot out onto the sill of the step and looked out over the water to the other bank. The reeds were nice and high and would afford plenty of cover for the punts, particularly further up where they would be concentrated.

He sat there and his mind wandered back to the days before the war. He had been told by Unc that they had relied on everyone bringing their own punts, although it had been difficult for some, and developed into a cussin' match when they were trying to set themselves up in the dark, as quietly as possible on the morning of the shoot.

Unc had announced one year when they were sorting out the "divide," that he had pondered long and hard and decided that he would provide the punts from then on. All they all had to do was decide how many they needed, and they could leave the rest to him. He would have them made in the carpenter's shop by the young apprentices and some of the young deckies from the "Swashbucklers."

His mind wandered to the Swashbucklers. Oh, what a tale that was. During the Civil War the Union forces had overrun this part of Marilina. A troop came in one day and against all pleas on the part of the few old men left still looking after the fishing fleet of eight boats, had smashed them and burnt them, and ridden off. Well you can imagine the outrage this caused as it became known even beyond The Lagoon. Apart from that, there were no fish for a very long time. The old men, however, were biding their time.

One night, when there were four Union frigates anchored in the "Roads" out beyond White Oak, they rowed out in three small boats under cover of darkness to where the flagship of the flotilla was, where there were eight or ten small craft moored alongside. There was obviously a meeting taking place on board, with officers from the other three ships attending. The men found that there was a veritable hoard of craft to choose from.

The smallest of them were alongside, however there were three magnificent 30-foot cutters hanging off the stern. They took one of the smaller boats a "whaler," and the three cutters in tow, and set off for the other three vessels to see what else was in the offing, having cut the mooring lines of the remaining craft. They eventually managed to make off back to the comparative safety of the town with seven cutters complete with sails and masts, although they were unstepped.

The whole exercise had been beautifully planned and executed and by daybreak, all the boats were out at The Lagoon, and hidden in various barns and buildings well away from the water. The following morning of course shore parties were sent off from the "flagship" which was the only one which had a boat hoisted aboard. The "swashbucklers" had scuttled every other boat that they didn't make off with.

How they managed to achieve this under the noses of the "Watch" that would have been mounted on each ship amazed everyone. How the crews of each visiting cutter survived the courts martial that must have resulted was never discovered. They were very heady days.

The shore parties scoured the shore around White Oak, but of course the boats were well out of the way and well off the waterways and hidden in barns on The Lagoon. They didn't go back into the water for some weeks.

Eighteen months later, during Reconstruction, one of the cutters was moored alongside a Union vessel taking on supplies to ferry across to the shore, when an old crewman who was leaning over the rail smoking a pipe complimented one of The Lagoon fishermen on his boat. The fisherman thanked him and went on to say that they don't build them like this anymore.

The reply floated down to him that he could only agree with that because he had actually had a hand in building that very same boat, and furthermore he had been on one of the vessels that it had been stolen from nearly two years before. He was the ship's carpenter, and he was going to report it to the Captain.

It was then that the Legend of the Swashbucklers was born. The Captain, upon being told that there was a "pirated" Union boat alongside, arrested it and the crew of six. He then sent a shore party across and they found three other cutters which they correctly identified as having been Union craft as well. The Captain confiscated all the cutters and laid charges against the men.

This of course took several days to transpire, and of course Unc's Great Grand Pappy did not take it lying down. Several of the very best legal minds in the state were retained to represent The Lagoon men, and the upshot of the whole business was that the case was thrown out of court on the basis that the boats were legitimate spoils of war.

The press coverage was sensational, with the County paper reporting the escapade as one of "swashbuckling proportions," and of course the men and all those down the years who have crewed on the fishing fleet, have been only too pleased to have that sobriquet.

George felt a pulling on his trouser leg, and snapped out of his reverie to see Sunny standing by the side of the truck pulling his cuff and softly calling.

"Whath happening Dadda?"

"Oh, what's happening darlin, absolutely nothing!" He brought himself back into the present.

"Dadda!"

"Yes darling, I'm sorry I was just sitting here thinking a few things and one of them is, 'How did you know that pink was my favorite color?'"

"I didn't Dadda! Why ith it your favorite color?"

"Weellll," he drew it out, "because when you were born, you were all pink, you were pink all over, and I thought that you were the most beautiful little bundle I had ever seen. And you still are," he added with a smile.

Banjo was down at the water's edge and suggested to George that the punts would be quite safe if left right there. George agreed and they began pulling them off the back of the truck and laying them out and then proceeded to drag them down to the water's edge.

The boats had been securely tied down on the truck so it took a bit of time and Sunny began playing by the water's edge. When the first boat was placed on the bank it had a little over half its length in the water, and of course Sunny hopped into it.

They were lugging another punt down to the edge when Banjo said to George that they would have to watch her as "Chillen, boats, water and rubber boots are a bad mix!"

"I know Banjo, we'll certainly keep an eye on her," he responded, looking down at Sunny who was sitting in the punt.

They continued to drag the other punts down, and had two to go when they heard Sunny scream, "Dadda!" They looked down and there she was standing up in the middle of one of the punts as it slowly turned around in mid-stream.

"Sit down, sit down," George screamed as he and Banjo rushed down to the water. She seemed not to hear and appeared to be transfixed, although she was screaming, "Dadda, Dadda."

They plunged into the water but the boat by this time was too far away for them to catch. They were not far from the bend in the stream and she was still screaming as she slowly drifted around and out of sight. George clambered back up the bank again and set off across the narrow strip of headland in order to cut her off on the other side.

He felt he was in his worst nightmare as he ran sobbing with exhaustion, mingled with a dread that he had never felt before, through the tangled undergrowth, hotly pursued by old Banjo. He fell heavily several times and it took several minutes for them to cross the headland, and to their horror saw the punt, empty and just circling lazily mid-stream. He gave an anguished howl and plunging in, half-swam, half-waded out to it. It was empty. Howling as he made his way slowly upstream, he waded through water that was about four feet deep.

He came upon her when he was a few yards beyond the punt. He managed to gather her up without too much trouble and holding her well out of the water he and Banjo got her to the bank and carried her up. Laying her down gently George went to work resuscitating her as a feeling of absolute devastation overcame him.

He didn't know how long it was before through his crying and tears he heard Banjo's voice saying, "Mis' George, Mis' George," and felt his hand gently on his shoulder. He looked up into the face of Banjo who had tears streaming down his cheeks, gently shaking his head.

"Oh Banjo, oh my God," he moaned. Banjo put his arms around him and held him for several minutes.

He eventually disengaged himself and staggered to his feet, and then bending down slowly gathered up the lifeless little body. Holding her up close to his face he gestured to Banjo and they set off back across the headland towards the truck with Banjo leading the way and holding aside any branches that may impede them.

Alice and Unc were at the front of the mansion when they were alerted to the noise of the truck entering into the driveway. Alice was picking flowers and Unc was putting them into a large basket he was carrying. They looked around and as one the two of them moved to the truck which slowly rolled to a halt.

Taking in the sight of what was in the cabin, Alice fell against Unc and then swooned. He caught her and lowered her gently to the lawn, with his heart pounding and a feeling of absolute despair sweeping over him. He moved over to George who was just sitting there with a look of sheer devastation that seemed to encompass his whole body.

George just kept sitting there shaking his head with tears silently streaming down his face. Unc looked on through at Banjo and saw the same expression with Banjo shaking his head slowly from side to side.

Reaching up, Unc held out his arms but George shook his head and began maneuvering himself, still holding the little body, so as to get down out of the truck. Unc steadied him as he lowered himself to the ground near Alice.

George placed her beside her mother and then gently began stroking Alice's hair. Banjo who had waited for him to alight from the truck, did something he had never done before: he ran across the drive up the front steps of the mansion, and in through the front door and ran smack bang into Norman, who needless to say began remonstrating with him. A split-second later they both ran back down to the kitchen and burst in on Mary, who for all her softness was made of very stern stuff.

Telling Norman to get two blankets from the linen room, through tears, she quickly made up two jugs of iced water with glasses, put them on a tray and sent Banjo back to the lawn with them. She and Norman weren't far behind.

All this had only taken a few minutes and whilst Unc had retained his composure, relatively speaking, he was just standing there looking quite bereft, thinking what he should do next when Banjo reappeared with the tray and Mary with the blankets and Norman.

"We should get them inside, Mis' Ted," Mary said, virtually taking control. She put one of the blankets beside Sunny and looking up nodded to Unc. Like an automaton Unc hunkered down and lifted her onto the folded up blanket and then gently gathered her up.

Mary gave a look to Norman and nodded towards the mansion. Taking Unc tentatively by the elbow Norman led him over to the steps and up into the front hall.

Mary had by this time turned her attention to Alice and George. She whispered to him that they must get Alice inside, as she was in a state of shock. Alice was slowly got to her feet and, having the blanket put around her, led slowly over to the house. Standing inside, she seemed to gather some composure, and looking at George with an aching look she slowly put her arms around his neck. They were both brought up short a moment later when she absently picked something off

159

his collar which turned out to be one of the "cut out flowers".

Actually it was the "butterfly" that they had glued to the gumboots only a short time ago. Alice let out a little whimper and fainted clean away again.

Chapter 12

The next few days passed in a blur. Unc had gathered himself sufficiently to ring the doctor and report the accident. Dr. Holmes drove out to The Lagoon and, after inspecting Sunny, was given an account from Banjo who had been asked to wait until this formality was dealt with.

The doctor also gave Alice, George and Freddie a sedative. Alice was put to bed. George and Freddie asked to be left to their own devices. Unc refused a sedative and asked if the doctor would like a whiskey, as he could certainly do with one. They sat in Unc's study and over their drinks wondered just what life was all about. There was nothing else they could say or do.

Later that afternoon, the doctor took a bottle of whiskey, one of the special Balmenachs, and after dropping his wife out at The Lagoon set off to see Alex. He pulled up in front of the cabin, only to find that Alex was not there. He had gone over to the door with the bottle in his hand, so he returned to the car and, putting the bottle on the hood, got back into the car and waited. Again he wondered what life was all about.

He snapped out of this with the scratching of Savage on the door. He wearily got out and, tousling Savage's head, looked across the clearing to see Alex. Alex, taking everything in—the doc. and the bottle—without any greeting said, "What has happened, Eric?"

"The very worst," he replied, falling into step with Alex as they both strode towards the cabin.

Alex held the door open for him and, following him in, put his gun down, got two glasses and, as he was putting some water in a jug, Eric said, "Sunny has drowned." The news hit Alex like a thunderbolt. He staggered; Eric, who was just about to sit down, steadied him and guided him to his chair.

Giving Alex time to take this in he poured two stiff glasses and gave one to Alex, noticing tears silently streaming down his face. He squeezed his shoulder and sat down opposite to him. He caught Alex's eye and, giving him a desultory raising of the glass, took a sip, and grimaced. He noticed that Alex didn't grimace but kept looking at him steadily.

Launching straight into it, he recounted what Banjo and George had told him. There really wasn't much more to say.

"How are the family?" Alex looked at Eric.

"As can be expected. Quite numbed, Annette is out there with them, although she may have gone home by now. I gave Alice a sedative and we put her to bed. I don't know, it just makes you wonder." The two men sat there and over the course of perhaps half an hour the bottle was almost finished. It had about two more neat nips left in it when Alex got to his feet and with purpose moved across to his bed. Getting down on his hands and knees, he groped about under the bed and dragged out a small trunk which he pulled across until it was between the two chairs.

Sitting down he leant across and opened the lid. Inside, Eric surmised, were a little girl's treasures. Trinkets, a teddy or two, a lovely doll, and some clothes.

The smell of camphor wafted up. There was also a bunny rug which Alex took out.

He sat back clutching it.

"Eric, could I stay the night with you and Annette?"

Eric sat back and opening his palms said or mouthed, "Of course you can."

"Thanks. I'll put a few things together and feed Savage and lock him up. Give me a few minutes." He poured the rest of the whiskey into Eric's glass and, pulling another bottle from the shelf, poured himself a stiff shot, placing the bottle close to Eric. Eric looked at him, thinking: *he looks stone cold sober. Well, that's how I feel too.*

They drove slowly towards White Oak, and were still on the gravel road and were nearing the outskirts when a car on the other side of the road which appeared to be stationary flashed its headlights once. They nosed over to it to find it was the Sheriff, Dale Smithers. The Sheriff was Chuck's grandfather; he was around Eric's age and was not far from retirement.

As they came up to him, he got out of the car and, leaning through the front driver's window, asked them if they could spare a few minutes. "Sure," Eric said, indicating the back seat, "would you like a swig?"

"Sure, but I'll get mine out of the car, otherwise we may run out!"

He returned and settled into the back seat. They sat in silence for a few minutes, each having a nip, lost in their own thoughts. Eventually Dale gave a deep sigh and said, "I haven't cried for a long time but I did today!"

Eric responded, "Well I think that makes three of us!"

Alex chimed in with, "And a lot of other folks as well!"

"You know," said Dale, "the younger they are the more precious they seem to be, and very rarely is there one who stands out head and shoulders over everyone else." A grunt came from the front seat. "When the whole thing gets out of whack and you lose a child it is frightful. When you lose a grandchild it lends another dimension to it."

"Mah Pappy fought in France and whilst he came home he lost a brother which devastated the family. Ah fought in Europe and spent some time in the islands and came out of it, as did my brother. As you fellas well know, our Pappy was on edge the whole way through, and then Ian as yo' both know lost David in Korea. As devastating as it was; looking back on it, Ian didn't seem to be as upset as Pappy, who cried for a week. He didn't last long after that actually, as yo' might remember. It has taken me this long to realize why; and although Sunny was close, she wasn't a relative. Ah put it down to their relative innocence, and the fact that yo' are more protective in a funny sort of a way. Grandchildren have an extra special place in the scheme of things, which, without diminishing yo' feelings for their parents, is an almost tangible thing." He sighed. "Ah don't know, Ah've probably had too much to drink." There were dissenting grunts from the front seat.

"Ah feel exactly the same way," said Eric.

"Well you both know where I sit in the scheme of things," said Alex, "I suppose that is why I have taken to the five boys, and little Sunny. I feel the same way. I have always been an optimistic hombre, but to be honest the pain I felt when I lost my family back in the 'twenties, put me in a frame of mind that wouldn't ever allow that to happen to me again. I suppose that's being selfish but, there you are. I have no regrets, but I took up with a beautiful person after the war. She wanted to get married and have children, but this old fear dogged me and I dithered, and I lost her. I suppose taking up with these young ones is a way to try and regain something that could have been. I just don't know. There you go, I've said it. Too much to drink!

"You know it really makes you wonder if the old men who always seem to be the ones who start these wars, have grandchildren themselves."

"Amen, Amen," they chorused.

"You really wonder if they ever stop to put things into perspective," sighed Alex.

They sat in silence for a few more minutes and then Dale said that he would appreciate some advice from them.

"Hang on for a moment," said Alex, "I've just got to get out for a piss."

"I'll join you," said Eric.

A few minutes later back in the car Alex said, "Now where were we? Oh I know. Off yo' go."

"Before we do," Eric said, "now Alex, what you've just told us is perfectly natural, I can tell you. That's a fact. Now Dale?"

"Well, we got three other officers here in White Oak, not nearly enough to direct the traffic I reckon is going to come into town for the funeral. Two things—at this stage while we don't know when the service will be. I suspect it will be in around four days from tomorrow. The Kershaws and Gardiners will have to allow time for Ted's family and also George's to come from outa town. Four days at the most. We don' know where it will be held, the church in town is too small, so I suspect they will have it out at The Lagoon. How am I doin'?"

"Keep going, you're doing fine," said Alex.

"Yeah," grunted Eric.

"The trick as I see it is to come up with an approximate number as who will turn up."

"Well," said Eric, "we got two thousand in town, there will certainly be half."

They tossed this around for a while until Alex commented: "There are all sorts of things playing into this. The interest in the family, whether it will be held in town or at The Lagoon, the respect for them outa town. I reckon we could be looking at three to four thousand. A thousand from town at least twelve, fifteen hundred from outa town, the family, the folk who work at The Lagoon, and there you could be around three without the straight out gawp factor. Particularly if it is held at The Lagoon. A lotta folks are never likely to see the mansion any other way."

"Then again, it could be private, but I don't think so," Eric added. "But we can't bank on it."

"Well that all makes sense, I reckon," mused Dale. "I suppose if I organize five State Deputies together with the four of us, we will be able to control them. No one will get ornery at a little girl's funeral, particularly with people like the family. Well, if you guys are comfortable with that, I am. I'll now have to apply first thing to have five deputies assigned for the day, and oh, the local law won't be wearing side arms and I'm going to ask the deputies to do the same. They can wear their belts but not the arms. I reckon in a way it could lend a lotta dignity to the occasion, it will certainly be noticed and also show that we aren't always trigger happy. What do yo' all reckon?"

"It sounds fine Dale, sounds good," they agreed.

They sat and had a few more swigs without speaking, in a comfortable silence, until Dale said that he had better let them go on their way. "Night fellas," and he was gone.

They arrived back at Eric's place about fifteen minutes later to find Annette waiting up.

"Hi Alex," she said giving him a kiss, "I thought that he would bring you back, so I have made up your bed."

"Thanks, Nettie. Now I have been thinking about tomorrow," he said as she ushered the two of them into the kitchen, and pulled two plates out of the oven.

"Now, will I get you something hot to drink, or will you finish the way you started? And I must say you both look terribly well for what has been a dreadful shock. Although I was getting worried about you. Did Dale hold you up?"

"Yes and no," said Eric, as he got a couple of glasses and another bottle. "We talked a while on life, and things that make yo' wonder, and such like."

"And of course there is no real answer, is there?" rejoined Annette.

"No," said Alex, "but it's out there anyway, just a little beyond anyone's reach. Dale wanted to talk about the service. He is worried about crowd control, for want of a better word, at the funeral. The problem was to decide on how many would attend and how many State Deputies he would need in addition to his meager force."

"What did you settle on?" asked Annette.

"Up to three thousand, with five deputies as well as Dale and his three boys."

"I'll have a think about that," she responded. "Now you boys, don't stay too late as I know we will have a big day tomorrow." She gave them each a kiss and said to Eric, "Don't wake me darling when you come to bed!"

They didn't finish that bottle as it happened, and after a couple of glasses each they turned in. The following morning over breakfast, as Annette was quietly thinking to herself how well they both looked considering, Alex asked if he could borrow a car. "Of course," said Eric, "take one for the next few days if you like."

"Alex," Annette chimed in, "we were thinking that if you would like to stay with us for the next few days, it would make a lot of sense, so why don't you?"

"Oh Nettie, that would help a lot."

She cut in, "And we could put Savage in Jock's pen. I cleaned it out thoroughly after he died and it is quite large, as you know."

Alex pondered for a moment. Jock had been their foxy that had died of old age about three months ago and his pen would suit Savage to a tee.

"That would be great, thanks; you do think of everything, Nettie. Now I was just about to say, if I can scoot off shortly as I have a few things to do, I reckon I can be back with a suit and a few changes of clothes and now Savage. Say about in time for lunch! Is that OK?"

"Alex dear, just treat this as home," said Annette.

Alex's first stop was the undertaker who, needless to say, he knew. He then went to the barber and had a neat haircut and a shave. He then set off for The Lagoon.

He arrived mid-morning, and was greeted at the door of the mansion by Freddie, who burst into tears when he saw him. He just held him tightly and until the sobs subsided, and told him he simply could not believe what had happened, and would like to see his mom and dad.

Freddie led him down the hall into the kitchen, and out onto the patio, past the sniffling Mary and the ashen Norman. When Mary saw him she immediately put the kettle on the large range again.

On the patio he found Unc, George and Alice just sitting listlessly around the table. Unc smiled and stood up and moved towards Alex and they both hugged and shook their heads. Unc threw a sideways glance at George and with one of those looks of concern Alex moved over to them. He and George exchanged a warm embrace and then he sat down in the chair beside Alice that Unc indicated to him and took Alice's hands in his. He put some flowers on the table before her that Annette had made up for him. Their hands met and they gave each other's fingers a gentle squeeze. They just sat looking at each other with tears streaming down their faces silently.

Alice, who hadn't really put two words together that morning up until then, said, "Thank you for coming, Alex."

Alex sighed and said, "I'm sorry for coming unannounced. It isn't like me at all. I do however come on a most sensitive matter, quite apart from my, our obvious distress. The only trouble I have, now that I am here, I don't quite know how to start."

"Ah've always thought the beginning is as good a place as any," Unc said, giving Alex's knee a squeeze.

"Well, how can I put it? I don't want to jump the gun or intrude in any way at all, he sat back and paused, but I can't really express how much that little girl meant to me. I know, I know she meant everything to everyone she touched. What I mean is everyone she did touch was touched in their own personal way. I'm not doing a good job of this, am I?" he looked lamely at them.

"You are, you are," said Unc, before Alex continued.

Thinking to himself that this would break the ice, Unc said "Afore you arrived we were going over a few things, and Ah know that Ali and George won't mind me saying, but they were wondering if you would consent to be a pallbearer? Ah should also say that it was Freddie's suggestion to which everyone agreed."

Alex screwed up his face and sighed and almost choked. "Yes, yes, I would be honored, thank you, and it is this aspect if you like that I was trying to broach. You see, I was wondering if I could offer you a casket for Edie, for Sunny. I have one!" The four of them immediately realized how he would come to have a casket, just as they thought to themselves that he must have had it for years.

"Oh Alex," said Alice, slowly rising as she looked at each family member in turn, and getting their unspoken affirmation. She went on, "It is we who will be honored."

Mary then arrived with more drop scones, tea and coffee, and they settled back discussing the course of action and the order of march over the next few days. Alex tried to take his leave but was prevailed upon to stay. He left an hour or so later.

The next few days were an absolute nightmare; however, everything went like clockwork, The Canard, needless to say, was put off; the extended family stayed at The Lagoon, where they had decided to hold the service; the local church women got together and, having arranged a marquee with Unc's permission, organized refreshments.

The turnout was around an estimated thirty-five hundred. The Law didn't wear guns, in fact they commented later that they were there under false pretenses, the crowd were so orderly. The pallbearers were Alex, Unc, Freddie, Billy, Chuck, and to the amazement of a lot of the folks, Lofty and Ben.

A lot of locals were whispering amongst themselves that they didn't know the distinguished looking man in the beautiful dark grey suit. When it was whispered back to them that it was in fact Snakesbreath they were amazed.

They had erected a small canopy beneath which they had placed the casket. To one side was a single chair for the minister. On the other side were five chairs, one for each member of the immediate family, and Lettice, Freddie's friend. Out from the canopy were placed some two hundred chairs for the extended family friends and the elderly.

There was even a microphone on a stand, off to one side near the family.

Also off to the side and well behind was the large refreshment marquee. Beyond and down a perfectly manicured sweep of lawn lay the lagoon. The day itself and the scene were picture perfect as only it can be in that part of the world.

The eulogy was a most painful affair, with those giving it holding together well under the circumstances, but then George rose again to speak. He spoke beautifully in that he thanked everyone for coming, and how touched and honored the family was to have so many people attend. He then had a long pause and went on to say that he also wished to add something else.

Alice with a look of concern rose to her feet and moved towards him. Those close to them could see a complete look of anguish on her face that seemed to transcend the expression that she had worn up until then. Tears were freely streaming down her face. George gently put his arm around her.

An uneasy murmur rippled through the gathering.

"Please forgive me but I feel it is appropriate that I make mention of it today." He took another long pause. "Also as many of us know there is never the right time to pick your moment, as it were, whereas there is an appropriate moment, and it is now with us. So I ask you all to understand why I am taking this opportunity. I can only tell you straight, without any embellishments, as you will find.

"You see," he said, "an old war wound has caught up with me, and a tumor has developed, and I have been given a negative prognosis, for want of a better term, and how can I put it, I will soon be with Edie once more." The shocked silence from the gathering was absolute. He held up one hand. "We have known this would be the outcome for some months, and have come to live with it. That our darling Edie would precede me brings another dimension that almost defies reality, but there you are. Under the circumstances we or should I say the family, at my request, will hold a small service for just the family when I actually do go. I know you will understand, thank you.

"Again, thank you so much for coming and we will catch up with some of you in the tent. You will understand if we retire early at some stage."

Everyone was transfixed; they just stood there. Some were beginning to shuffle as if to move, but not really wanting to be the first; others just stood stunned. Looking back on the moment, no one could quite remember how or where in the crowd it began. Just the faint humming of the first few bars of "Swing Low Sweet Chariot."

It began ever so softly. It was as though the first to hum was looking for encouragement or confirmation. Progressively more and more joined in. Some probably in spite of themselves. The black contingent joined in unconsciously, and then they began to slowly sway from side to side. This of course caught everyone up, and with everyone in the crowd knowing the tune and lyrics, it took hold.

They hummed through the entire tune and most thought that was that. Suddenly right on time, on key, rose this beautiful baritone voice actually singing the first verse. If everyone wasn't completely tingling from all this, for the second time in a few minutes the hair on their scalps rose again when another voice from a different section of the crowd came in on perfect pitch. Independently of each other Alice and Ole Neville the painter thought that the first voice had a familiar ring to it, there was something just barely discernible to the timbre of it. It then struck them virtually at the same time. It was Sam, Neville's assistant. The hairs rose again.

Alice was straining to recognize the second voice which sounded familiar, when it struck her that it was

Banjo. She looked at Gordos out of the comer of her eye and he nodded imperceptibly.

The two of them continued with the entire gathering softly humming. When they had finished, there was another silence. Everyone was emotionally drained. There wasn't a dry eye in sight, police and deputies included.

The minister presiding held up his arms. His mind had been working overtime. He knew that no one there had experienced anything remotely approaching that before, and he also knew that that he would have to be the next to speak, and he had better get it right. What should he do? He had to act quickly.

When he had everyone's attention, he solemnly bowed, and moving to George and Alice he moved his arm in a sweeping gesture towards the tent. He said a very soft Amen. Everyone responded and then stood for a few moments in silent reflection and then in small groups and singly began to slowly drift towards the refreshment tent.

They had decided to have refreshments after the actual service which was held at 11 a.m. and have a private family internment later in the afternoon with just the family, a few friends and The Lagoon folk. This amounted to well over four hundred.

Whilst Gordos managed to keep himself together for the formalities over the few days, the headaches gradually took hold and he was gone within two months. The family held a private service at The Lagoon, and surprisingly Freddie, his mother and Unc held up very well, much to everyone's relief.

Before George died he held a meeting with the three of them setting everything in context, explaining things in a way that Unc marveled at and then shortly after he was gone.

A week or so before he actually died, he woke up one night and stirred, trying to get out of bed. Alice, who was not sleeping well at all, was awake and asked him what he was doing. "The jug's empty," he murmured. "I'm going to get some more water." She said that she would get it and leant over him and picked up the jug, giving him a kiss as she did so.

Walking down the hall to the bathroom she passed Freddie's room and could hear him tossing around in bed. Returning with the water she heard him give a little cry as she passed again. Placing the jug on George's bedside table she whispered to him, as she poured a glass of water, that Freddie seemed to be unsettled and she would go and attend to him. George just mumbled.

She returned to Freddie's room and got into bed with him and snuggled down along side of him. "Is that you Mom?" He murmured sleepily.

"Yes my darling, are you alright?"

"I don't know Mom."

"Why darling is anything wrong?"

"Mom, am I leaking? I feel all sticky!"

Alice's head spun. Oh my God. This on top of everything. Right now. Couldn't it have waited? What, what next?

"No, oh no my darling you are just, you are just becoming a man," she managed to say.

She lay with him until his breathing eased into a sleep rhythm, and then slowly crept out from beneath the covers and back to her bed where she thankfully found George fast asleep.

It was some months after George had died before Alice mentioned the night she had in bed with the unsettled Freddie to her uncle. Unc didn't really comment at all; he just pondered on the matter, Alice thought in retrospect.

They continued to live in town for the rest of the school term, planning to move out to The Lagoon the coming year.

*****

Chapter 13

Freddie stayed a night out at The Lagoon. He stayed in what was always considered to be "his room." It had a beautiful view over the water, although by the time Unc had collected him and brought him out the previous evening it was too dark to see the sun setting over it. He wasn't quite sure as to why he had been suddenly, or so it seemed, been whisked off to The Lagoon on the pretext of driving around, and inspecting the cattle with Unc. He seemed to have been doing it on and off all his life; why again, now? Anyway he wasn't too fussed, he always enjoyed the time that he spent with his old uncle.

He had been awakened by Mary. She had placed a cup of tea on the bedside table, telling him that Unc was expecting him downstairs in twenty minutes, and that they would have breakfast when they arrived back later in the morning.

It was half past six she said as she disappeared out the door. He sat up and gulped down half the tea, and then flung himself under the shower, dressed quickly and finished the tea as he walked down the stairs, arriving in the kitchen with five minutes to spare. Unc was a stickler for punctuality, and oddly enough, so was Freddie, two generations younger. Perhaps this was another reason as to why they were so close.

Mary smiled and thrust a bacon sandwich at him, "Here yo' are darlin, keep de wolf from de door." He had no sooner finished it than Unc came into the kitchen offering an easy good morning, and spotted him having the last mouthful. He gave a mortified look at Mary who grinned and said, "Comin' right up Mr. Ted." She hurriedly made two more and passed them to each of them.

Thanking Mary they then walked, busily munching in a comfortable silence, to the brake which had been brought around to the front door of the imposing mansion. As they crunched across the drive towards it Unc said, through a mouthful, "Ah'll drive, and yo' can drive back if yo' like." Freddie just looked up at him, smiled and nodded. Unc seemed his usual cheerful but earnest "mornin'" self in that you didn't speak unless you had something to say. This suited Freddie fine as since the camping trip he had found the mornings to be so much more enjoyable if you didn't have to talk. Particularly at seven o'clock in the morning.

They drove in silence for a few minutes and Freddie asked which cows were they inspecting. "The five-year-old studs," responded Unc. Freddie knew that these were Unc's favorite cows. Any not up to his demanding standard had been rigorously culled out over the previous four years, either back down into the commercial herd or off the place completely, in some rare instances.

The Lagoon had a commercial herd of thousands of Angus cattle, and a highly regarded stud of the same breed. Freddie's grandfather had established the stud years ago in order for them to have replacement bulls for their significant commercial herd requirements.

When Unc had taken it on, he had initially thought of it as another chore that quite frankly he didn't need, but went on to find that he actually enjoyed the involvement, and whilst he would never let on, he thrived on it. He had gradually built it up over the years, "hastenin' slowly," as he used to say. He was not at all averse to seeking out other bloodlines which he felt may lead him to the ultimate conformation.

Whilst he had an extensive gene pool, he wasn't at all one for a closed herd. In a nutshell this program sought to produce bulls that had good feet, were well boned, well-muscled, threw progeny that had these characteristics, had scale, straight backs, had good weight gains, were easy calving, plenty of milk, and had excellent temperament. And as he was fond of saying: "Be pleasing to the eye!"

He had no qualms in making these endeavors or aspirations known, and was well aware that some Angus breeders considered him to be an absolute radical in his views. In particular, that they should be big-framed cattle. Traditionally Angus as a breed were not large cattle, due of course to where they originally came from, Scotland. The mighty Aberdeen Angus. Tough, hardy, but small framed. To him, scale was what it was all about, all things considered. He never tired of telling folks that it cost just as much to process a carcass that weighted in at half the size as it did for one as heavy as you could produce at the same age.

"Yo' couple that in with the fact that if the pasture they are runnin' on, is the most productive yo' can establish, then the most efficient conversion is runnin' fewer but bigger beasts on it."

It had given him pleasure over the years to occasionally find some of his earlier critics, fellow breeders, coming to him to actually purchase these bulls. Every year they had a small number of animals surplus to their requirements which they offered for sale. So the worm was turning.

They drove into the field and Freddie commented on how well the cows looked and asked how many there were. "Around one hundred, and yes they do look well, but so they should," said Unc. "They have everything going for them. The calving is going well and this lot are about halfway through." In the distance they could see two riders slowly poking through the cattle on horseback checking the calves, and putting tags in the newborn calves' ears. They needed to be able to match each cow and newborn calf in order to record and so gauge the performance of each cow.

Unc who seemed outwardly serene was feeling anything but. In fact, whilst he was making appropriate noises from time to time his mind was on other matters entirely and he was beginning to have second thoughts about the whole thing. Why had he been so cocksure and dogmatic with Alice about him being the one to enlighten Freddie on the facts of life, the "Birds and the Bees"? *Why do Ah make these undertakings?* he mused to himself.

"It will be quite straightforward," he had said, quite airily. "Nothing to it."

"Well how do you intend to actually broach the subject?" she retorted.

"What do you mean?" he said.

"Darling, you have to start somewhere. You have to have a game plan, a strategy in order to lead into the actual mechanics of it."

"What!" He looked at her.

"Ooh look," she said. "He is a thirteen-year-old boy. He will tie you in knots. Now come on, tell me. Children of this age can be trickier than a bag of monkeys, come on." She wasn't going to be put off.

He thought for a moment then said, with a certain amount of exasperation, "You forget, Chickie, I made sure that you had it all explained to you at an appropriate age."

"Oh I know, I know, but this is a little different," she said, putting her arms around him, reaching up to give him a kiss. "Now come, tell me."

"Ah'm going to take him around the stud cows," he said, looking at her a little imperiously.

"And pray tell me how this is going to pave the way?"

"They are going to be calving," he said triumphantly.

She stood up. "Well, you're going to do some sort of 'reverse back through the life-cycle' thing, are you?"

"Exactly," he said. "Happy?"

"Delirious," she said, "but I suppose it may work."

"It will, it will." He immediately cheered up.

"Ah hope so," she said without much enthusiasm. "Ah hope so."

Now here he was at the coal face, the moment of truth was fast approaching. He stole a quick glance across at Freddie. *Look at him,* he thought. *This beautiful looking child, the palest of olive skin just like his mother at the same age. Just the merest hint of, what is it, down on his cheeks, head of brown, dark brown hair. Just like Alice.* He felt an almost overwhelming surge of emotion sweep over himself. *Ah'll have to get a grip on myself,* he thought, *otherwise Ah'll lose it.*

Freddie for his part was quite oblivious to the turmoil that Unc was going through. He had his window right down and was taking in the smells of the morning, the heavy dew on the grass, the droplets of water on the fence wires the smell of the grass, and occasionally the rich smell of fresh cow pies. By now the, sun was well above the horizon, and he could even see steam or body warmth rising off the cattle. In the morning air the chill was just taking its leave from the earth. In the far distance he could even see a large flock of birds, flying low to the horizon.

They were driving very slowly, just crawling along so as not to disturb the cattle when they came across a cow that had calved some minutes ago. The cow had licked the afterbirth or placenta off the calf, and had nudged it to its feet and around to its udder, where it was wobbling away most unsteadily on its very shaky legs. *It is a nice looking calf,* thought Freddie. The cow looked at them disdainfully for a few moments and then proceeded to wrap its tongue around the edge of the placenta and began to eat it. The two of them sat there for a few moments, silently taking this in.

"Unc, why do cows eat the placenta?" Freddie asked. He had seen it happen dozens of times before but had never thought to ask why. Perhaps it was because there were only the two of them.

Ha, Ha, Unc thought, *Ah got him. Just the opening Ah needed. Ah knew Ah shouldn't a' worried.* "Well o' course yo' could read about it in one of the many books Ah have," he said as nonchalantly as he could, "but as we know there is nothing like a practical demonstration. The developing calf gets its nutrition from its mother before it is born, and it is through the placenta that it occurs. Through those button-like thangs on the membrane: Cotyledons, they call 'em. The placenta also has a cushioning effect for the calf in the cow's womb. When the calf is born the cow will sometimes eat the placenta to regain some of the nutrients that would otherwise have gone to its calf, or of course just go back into the ground, so one school of thought has it. They really don't know why.

"This o' course is at the end of the birth cycle, Freddie," he went on, wanting to get to the crux of the matter. Like a lemming, it could be said. "So! Now how do you think the whole thing starts?"

"What do you mean, Unc?"

"Well how do you believe that the cow comes to be having a calf in the first place?" He had regained his confidence, by now, and was in complete control.

"How?" said Freddie.

"Yup," said Unc, "how?" as he looked nonchalantly out the window.

"Oh that's easy," said Freddie. "Bulls fuck them!"

The numbing thud, shock, call it what you will, that hit Unc like a baseball bat quite caught him off-guard. He wasn't sure whether it was in the back of the head, or in the solar plexus. It was something he had rarely experienced. He gripped the wheel tightly, and looked quickly at Freddie who was sitting there with the most innocent look on his face, with not a trace of guile. He looked up at his uncle with an innocent disarming smile. Unc was no prude, he could cuss with the best of them if and when required, however he had a golden rule of never swearing in the presence of women or children. He well knew that they in particular would be exposed to it enough, later in life.

Before he could collect his thoughts he muttered, "They what? No, no, don't tell me. And who told you that?" It was out before he knew it, and as soon as he heard himself asking the question, he already knew the answer.

"Lofty!" said Freddie. Before even Unc knew it, let alone Freddie, Unc was out of the vehicle.

"Unc what's wrong, what are you doing?"

"It's OK," he called back. "It's OK." With as much dignity or casualness as he could summon. "Ah jes' need to see something a little further over. There is no need to get out, Ah won't be a moment." The nearby cow looked up, disinterestedly, took a slow look around at its calf and resumed eating the placenta. Freddie sat there without any sense of concern, but conscious of the scent of the waft of gas fumes that ghosted through the vehicle when Unc turned the engine off.

His uncle walked a few yards away from the brake, craning his neck at some non-existent object. His mind going like a threshing machine. He eventually turned back towards the brake looking as casual as he could. As he climbed back in, Freddie asked him what it was. "I think it must have been the light," responded Unc, "there was nothing there. Ah thought it was a calf." They were in quite high feed. He had partially recovered, however thought that he couldn't leave things hanging like this. He took a deep breath and plunged in again, hoping that nothing would come up behind him and bite him. Better to be up front he thought.

"You're quite right." He shrugged, looking lamely but squarely at Freddie. "They do. Of course."

"They do what?" said Freddie.

Give me strength, thought Unc. "What you or," he felt he couldn't get out of it, "Lofty said they do!"

"Oh," said Freddie, "you mean…"

Unc raced in. "Yes, but it is not a very nice word." Thank God he had got that across.

"Not a nice word," said Freddie innocently.

"No, no, nice folks really don't use it. It's one of them bad cuss words. Ah know young boys use it a lot, but it's not the sort of words yo' use in front o' ladies, or in our kinda company. Its, aaah, it's one them things like how yo' all use a knife and fork. Yo' know. How yo' dress. Stand up for the ladies. That sort o' thing. Yo' see with animals you use other words." *There, that should defuse things a little,* he thought.

"What sort of words?" asked the simply angelic-looking child.

"Well, in the case of cattle you say the bulls are… they are… are joined to them… they are… mated to them… they cover them… aww… they are put out with them," *what else, what else?* thought Unc, "or perhaps you could say they run with them, and in some instances you could use the expression—they mount them, you could even say they ride them." He knew there were other terms, expressions, but... they were being elusive.

"Could you say that they sleep with them, Unc?"

"No, no, you would never use that expression with animals. That is only used..." He trailed off. Dang it. What now? He was looking out over the cows in desperation. "Oh, what's that, ah... Oh look over there, the men are beckoning us. They must be in real trouble, it must be a cow." He felt quite weak, and lost no time in driving over to the men who were attending to a cow that was having difficulty calving. *Thank God, thank God,* thought Unc.

"Mornin' Mr. Ted," they nodded to Unc.

"Mornin' Seth, Cyrus."

"Mornin' Freddie," they chorused.

"Mornin'," he responded with a smile.

"What you guys got here?"

"A breach birth by the feel o' thangs, Ah reckon," said Cyrus.

"Do we have many breach births Unc?" Freddie asked.

"No, Ah don't thank so, but effen yo' fetch the Stud Book on the back seat o' the brake we'll have a look. What do you fellas think?"

"We wuz just sayin Mr. Ted, afore yo' arrived, this old gal's number, what is she, 48/89, we thank we come across her afore, effin y'all know what Ah mean," Seth drawled.

"We been thinking, Mr. Ted, that she's passed this way afore," said Cyrus. Freddie returned with the stud field book.

"Freddie son, look up cow 48/89 effin yo' be so kind."

Freddie thumbed back to the cow in question, and said, "Well Unc, have a look at this."

Unc glanced at the previous seasons entry, turned to the two men, and, handing them the book, said, "Ah don't know, you fellas, Ah'll jest have to put y'all on short rations." They all had a good chuckle. "Freddie, will yo' fetch mah big knife out from under mah seat please, like a good fella.

"Now, old girl, we better hunker down and help yo' get rid of this calf. Yo' know o' course that it's the end of the road for yo',' once o' course we weaned yo' calf. Yo' is fo' the chute." Unc, Freddie knew, would not abide breach births. Once of course. "It could happen to anyone," he used to say. But not twice. A cow could be relegated to the commercial herd, on all sorts of things. But not breach births, twice! If she couldn't calve unaided twice, she had her throat cut. That was that. Off to the slaughterhouse she went.

Unc was quietly thinking to himself that if ever he needed a distraction, it was then. He had been saved by the bell well and truly. Thank God for small mercies. The cow was a big one, and they all, that is the men, were working on getting the calf out and had been at it for around a quarter of an hour when Unc gave a grunt and said that he would have to stand up to have a stretch. They were all either kneeling or sitting around the rear end of the cow. Unc of course was a lot older than the two men. They had each of them been with him for well over twenty years, and were his senior cattle men, but he was probably over twenty years older than they were. He slowly rose to his feet as the men muttered something to the effect that that would be fine. He was nearly straightened when the cow slightly moved its back leg; the movement tripped him up, as his right foot was right beside it.

He went sprawling. The grass needless to say was very wet from the dew, in fact all of them with the exception of Freddie were quite wet almost from the waist down, from sitting in the grass wrestling with the calf trying to get it out. He fell over the cow and hurriedly got to his feet again, as the two hands went to his assistance. "Ah'm fine, Ah'm fine," he said. "Ah'll jes sit in the brake fo' a few minutes an' git mah breath back. Yo' fellas go on. Freddie son, yo' may be able to help."

"Sure Unc, what can I do, Seth, Cy?"

"Freddie, jes' sit by her head, yo' shouldn't come to any harm sittin' there," said Seth.

"Tha's right, Freddie boy," said Cyrus. "Keep yo' legs out of the way of her head. She might try an' toss it around, an' she could rasp yo' on the ground. That's right; now jes' soothe her like yo' would a calf. Jes' talk to her, all syrupy. Talk to her and stroke and pat her. Tell her she's givin' us one hell of a lot o' trouble."

"And on such a fine mornin'," added Seth.

The cow was lying on its side and was fairly immobile and there was no way it was going to get up with the birth as advanced as it was. They only hoped that the calf was alive when they got it out.

It wasn't long before Unc was back down with them and it took them, all four, the best part of another half an hour, to have the calf on the ground, and finish the job. They managed to save the calf, and had just as much trouble getting the mother back on her feet.

"Anyway, it was a job well done," said Unc, asking Freddie to dock the tail, after they had her on her feet and steadied. She would be much easier to identify in the yards when they came to cut her out for culling.

"How much longer yo' fellas be in the saddle this mornin'?" Unc drawled as they prepared to leave.

Seth and Cy looked at each other, shrugged and Cy muttered, "About three hours Ah reckon, Mr. Ted. The ole gal seems to have taken her calf."

"Well what say yo' all come up to the house, an Ah'll git Mary to patch us up a mess o' summat?"

"Thank yo', Mr. Ted," they chorused, nodding slightly, their faces lighting up.

"Say one o'clock. Gi yo' time to clean up," said Unc as he and Freddie took their leave.

They drove slowly back to the house. Unc was praying to God that Freddie wouldn't start up again on anything at all about breeding. He needn't have worried if he had only known Freddie hadn't been conscious in any way of the significance of what had passed between them. He did, though, accept the distinction as to where and when one could say certain things. When they eventually arrived back, after a pleasant though uneventful drive, they could see Alice's Chevy parked in front of the house. They went in and Alice said, "Look at the two of you, what have you been up to? Calving troubles by the look of it."

"Yo' don't miss a thing, Chickie," said Unc as he went up to her and gave her a distance kiss. "We better go and change. Tell Mary were sorry we're a might late, but when a cow's down, a cow's down. Anyway we got her up again, didn't we, Freddie? Give us twenty minutes."

"We sure did, Mom, we've had a great morning," said Freddie. Alice looked at her fast disappearing uncle but he didn't look back.

Alice had arranged to have their breakfast, which by now had become a brunch, set up on the patio outside the kitchen. Mary and old Norman bustled about and made a great fuss over Freddie, and to a lesser extent Alice. Unc seemed to be in his element, although Alice sensed that he was evading her direct looks. She

187

intuitively suspected that whilst things had not turned out disastrously, they had not gone perfectly either.

After they had finished, to Alice's amazement Unc jumped up from the table and bending down gave her a quick kiss, tousled Freddie's hair, and told him he had been a great help. Looking directly at Alice told her that he had to get over to the nerve center, the main office, to do a few things and that he would see her later on in town. *The old devil,* she thought. It obviously didn't go so well.

Chapter 14

It was probably some eight months later, when Unc was sitting at his desk in the farm office, that there was a knock on the door and the farm office manager entered and asked if he could have a few words with him.

"Sure," said Unc, "take a seat. Wilson, what is the matter, anything Ah can help with, something about the spread?"

"No, no Mr. Ted, nothing like that at all, it's about one of the office staff."

"Oh, which one?" Unc responded. "Do they wish to leave?"

"No, no not at all, in fact I am not sure myself what it is about, but it appears to be very important to her."

"Her," interrupted Unc, "what do you mean her?"

"Well sir, you know the German woman we put on recently to assist with the bookkeeping?"

"Yes, yes, Ah do," said Unc, "although Ah haven't had much to do with her."

"Well, she has told me that she would like to speak to you about a delicate matter and she wouldn't enlarge on that."

"She's the one whose daughter married the Unthank boy isn't she?"

"That's her, sir."

Ted pondered. "Yes, that was a sad business, a very sad business." He remembered going to the funeral, and could vaguely recall seeing the young widow and come to think of it an older woman as well. He hadn't introduced himself after the service, he had only signed the book.

"Well, Wilson yo' know very well that Ah really don't like getting involved with personal issues with the staff, why with the two hundred or so we have Ah would be for an early grave if Ah got too close. To be quite frank, Ah don't believe they could have money troubles, young Mike ran a good operation, and yo' know any troubles pertaining to money generally filter through. You just tell her that Ah would prefer not to and we'll leave it at that, Ah'm sorry son."

"Righto Mr. Ted, sir."

"Anything else, son?"

"No, sir I'll be getting back now, good morning."

"Mornin'," responded Unc.

That afternoon Wilson knocked on the door again and upon entering told Unc that the woman refused to accept that he would not receive her. He looked embarrassed and almost agitated. Unc looked at him and said, "Wilson, Ah can see that you are taking this very much on board yourself. Ah can understand, don't be too concerned."

"No sir, it is just that she won't entertain the fact that you will not receive her."

"Well, son, you just go out and tell her again, that the answer is no, an emphatic no! Ah do not wish to. Ah have enough of mah own personal affairs to contend with without becoming involved with anyone else's!"

"Yes, sir, Mr. Ted."

Five minutes later there was another knock on the door which was hurriedly opened to reveal the woman with a completely agitated Wilson looking over her shoulder. Unc stood up and, coming around the desk, said, "Thank you son," to Wilson. Wilson beat a hasty retreat. The woman, looking even more agitated, said in a beautiful British-sounding voice, "Mr. Kershaw, please have the grace to hear me out. I need five minutes."

Whilst she worked in the same office and for him, he had not actually put her on the staff. The accountant had.

Unc looked more closely at her. She seemed most refined although hassled and carried herself well, and to suggest to him, under his own roof, even obliquely, that he lacked grace meant that there was more to this than he could have expected.

"Come in madam, and you are Christina Schmidt, are you not? The Unthank boy's mother-in-law!"

"I am, Mr. Kershaw."

"Well, come sit here, and compose yourself. Would you like a cup of tea or coffee?"

"A cup of tea, thank you."

"Just a moment please," he said. He opened the door to the outer office to find, as he suspected, Wilson hovering about. Beckoning to him he said, "Son, will you organize a large pot of tea, two cups and all the trimmings please?"

He returned to his desk. "Well, Christina Schmidt, what is this al all about?" He was thinking to himself that she actually looked quite beautiful, and would be in her early to mid-fifties.

"Thank you. You may know, Mr. Kershaw, that my daughter married a boy from near here during the occupation of Germany."

"Yes," said Unc, "and that boy was Michael Unthank who was sadly killed recently, and that you and your daughter and child still live on his small spread. Ah attended his service. Is that correct?"

"Yes Mr. Kershaw. My daughter has inherited it, and as it happens Michael, who was a wonderful young man, has no near living relatives."

"Yes," said Unc, "It is all coming back to me. Now where am Ah expected to fit in to all of this?"

"Mr. Kershaw, my daughter is only in her early twenties and happens to be quite beautiful, and she is being pestered, no that's not the word, hounded by a local man, a neighbor, who quite frankly scares her, and I am nearly beside myself. We cannot cope, and I am here begging for you to intercede on our behalf. Apart from the people at The Lagoon we really have no one to turn to. I might add that I have never begged for anything."

Unc sat back, thinking to himself, *Germans, opportunists, the whole thing's backfired, and they want me to step into the breach, it's all too easy. Look what the bustards have cost my family! Still, there is something about this woman that intrigues me.* "Mrs. Schmidt," he settled back a little in the chair, "Tell…"

There was a knock at the door. "Come in," he said, and one of the office girls came in with a tray with tea and all the trimmings as he had requested.

"Thank you, Violet. Just put it on the desk, dear."

"Yes, Mr. Ted sir. It's a pleasure, Mr. Ted." She then withdrew.

"Permit me, Mr. Kershaw," the woman asked. He nodded at her.

"Strong white, thank you. And a couple of drop scones with apricot jam, thanks."

"Now where was Ah, Mrs. Schmidt? Oh yes, tell me a little about yourself!"

"Mr. Kershaw," she pondered for a moment. "Are you toying with me?" *Jesus,* thought Unc. *She is matching wits with me and she is really on the back foot.* He made up his mind.

He cut straight to the chase. "Mrs. Schmidt, what is the name of, how shall we describe him... the, 'The unwelcome suitor?'"

"Brian Perry," she said.

"Consider it done," he said, not without a moment's hesitation, she thought. "Give me two to three weeks."

"You can really stop all this, Mr. Kershaw?"

"Well, Ah would like to think so," he said. "Now tell me, how are you making out on your... your new property?"

A quarter of an hour later after she had gone Unc was still sitting at his desk pondering on the best way to tackle the problem. Softly, softly, he decided. Eli Perry wasn't a bad sort of hombre. How much does he owe me? He groped around in the top drawer and pulled out a small book. Where is it, where is it? Aha, Eli Perry initial loan. Two thousand dollars. What to do, what to do? He slowly got up out of his chair, and walked over to the shelves, pulled out a file from the shelf, and looked up the code for Eli Perry, down to twelve hundred. Not bad, not bad.

Now Eli, what is the best way to cut the balls off your boy? Your boy, who from what Ah have seen is just as much a fine fellow as Michael, however certainly not as good looking.

He was still pondering over how to broach the subject with Eli Perry, when a week later he was driving through White Oak, and he saw Eli getting into his pick-up truck. He pulled in beside him and waved to him to stay there and walking around got into the seat beside Eli.

"Well, Mr. Ted, how is you?"

"Ah'm fine Eli, Ah'm fine. Now how is yourself?" They talked about the crops, the price of cattle, where tobacco prices were heading, and then settled into a comfortable silence.

"Mr. Ted," Eli said, "Ah could speak to you any old time, yo' know that, but we've seen each other a hundred times in the street before and you've never taken the opportunity to devote so much time to me."

"Eli, 'devote' that's a mighty big word." Unc gave him a playful slap on the knee. "Ah know, Ah know, Eli. Ah have come to make you an offer Ah reckon is too good to refuse."

"Mr. Ted yo' already done that some years ago when you loaned me the money to buy that extra land."

"Well Eli, it can get better, but there is a little bit of other stuff involved."

"What kinda stuff Mr. Ted?"

"How can Ah put it, Eli? Your son Brian, Eli!"

"How can he come into this, Mr. Ted?"

"Well Eli, let me cut to the chase. Now hear me out. We all know love is a very powerful emotion, particularly young love; which we all know can almost verge on lust.

"For want of a better word, your boy is lustin' after that Unthank girl, that young widder. To be frank Eli, the girl is mighty scared of him. She has not long been widowed, and along comes Brian. It is all too soon for her Eli. Ah'm askin you to get him to back off. In the fullness of time, well you never know what may develop, but right now he is making life a misery for her."

Eli sat there for a few moments before replying. "Dang it Mr. Ted, he's a full-blooded boy and he's mah son. And the gal is a right beauty."

"From all accounts Eli, from all accounts. At the same time, you got a mighty pretty daughter yourself. Eli, yo' know where Ah'm coming from, Ah don't like getting dragged into this any more than you do. Young people are young people and where affairs of the heart are concerned, it can often lead to tears. Yo' know that as well as Ah do, Eli."

"What do yo' suggest, Mr. Ted?" Eli asked.

"Well Eli, let's have a think about this. Do you have a nest egg?"

"Why yes, yo' mean money for a rainy day kinda thing?"

"Ah ha," said Unc. "Eli, does yo' boy have anything that he would like to do more than anything in the world... Apart from chasing girls that is, something that is virtually outa reach?... At least for the time being?"

"Well yes, Mr. Ted, maybe he does."

"What's that Eli?"

"Mr. Ted, yo' know we got a pretty good herd of cattle."

"Ah know, Ah know Eli, what are yo' saying?"

"Well he's always wanted to go down to Argentina and spend a bit of time and seeing how they manage their grass fed cattle. He's even learnt how to speak Spanish. As yo' know we're moving towards feed lottin' here in the States, but of course those cattle gotta come from somewhere. He would dearly love to go down there and do some work on optimizing the weight for age factor as he calls it, and compare it with what we do or should be doing at home. He says we should be bringing objectivity into it, whatever that means. Cattle are his life, and he's a much better cattle man than Ah am. Ah'm quite prepared to admit. Ah'm more into the croppin', and machinery. In fact, mah Daddy used to say 'If cattle had spark plugs we'd have the best herd in the state.' Any ways, Brian's making up for it now."

Unc sat back with a stunned look on his face. "Good Heavens, Eli, Ah can't believe it. This is just the very thing that Ah have been mulling over for the past few years mahself. Well now, how does this appeal to yo', it came to me in a flash. Ah think we have already solved the problem ourselves, and do yo' know what, Eli?"

"What's that, Mr. Ted?"

"Eli, we'll be the only two to know. Now, one word of what Ah am about to say Eli, to anyone, and Ah'll have your ass. Get it?" and he slapped him on the knee.

"Yes of course, Mr. Ted," he said, grinning with a pronounced grimace. "What do we do?"

"Well, Ah'll tell yo'. Here's what we'll do."

Some days later Unc was going through his mail one morning at the mansion when a very expensive-looking envelope caught his eye. He ran his thumb over the paper's grain and nodded to himself. *It's probably even got a watermark to it as well,* he mused. He inserted the paper knife inside the slit on the back and ran it down. Removing the paper, he had to admit that he wasn't at all surprised to find that there was an embossed letterhead across the top of the page. It appeared to be a German address which had been crossed out and a local one handwritten below it. He had to admit that it was one of the nicest letters he had ever received, even more so because it was written by one who had fallen so low in the scheme of things. This was obviously apparent from what had passed between them before and the quality of the paper to say nothing of the address, although he couldn't quite understand it.

He quickly went through the rest of the mail and finding nothing pressing, got up and, thanking Mary, walked over to the nerve center. Returning the multitudes of "Good morning, Mr. Ted," he made his way through to the rear into another slightly smaller office where he found Christina Schmidt sitting at her desk, attending to what looked like an intimidating range of papers.

"Good morning, Mrs. Schmidt, how are you?"

"Very well I must say, Mr. Kershaw, and you?"

"Yes Ah'm fine. I received your letter, thank you. Would you like to come and have a cup of tea with me?"

"Thank you, that would be nice. I can be with you in a few minutes."

He nodded and moving into the main office spotted Violet. "Violet dear, will you make up a pot of tea with two cups and the trimmings and bring it to my office please?"

"Yes Mr. Ted, right away, sir."

A little later they were having their first sip when Christina broke the silence saying.

"Mr. Kershaw, I have no idea as to what you did with the Perry boy, but I understand that he has even gone to the Argentine."

"As Ah understand it Mrs. Schmidt, yes!"

"Well thank you again, Mr. Kershaw."

"Let's put that all behind us shall we, not a word about it from now on, eh?" She began to say something but he held his hand up and smilingly shook his head.

They sipped their tea for a few more minutes in silence and then he said, "I hope you don't mind me saying, but from when we had our first, what Ah can only describe as our first encounter, and then your letter, which I won't reply to but can honestly say is perhaps the nicest letter Ah have ever had. Coupled with all this and the address on the letterhead, the paper quality…"

She began to interrupt him.

"No, no, let me continue please. All this indicates to me that whereas on the face of it someone like you and your daughter coming here, finding a new life in this great country of ours, would consider it to be to be a golden opportunity, on the face of it of course. Now without trying to belittle what you had here or have, it seems to me that it in no way comes up to what you have left behind or lost in Germany! Ah'm not sure whether Ah put that correctly." She put down her cup, screwed

197

up her face, nodded and pulling out a handkerchief wiped away the tears that were beginning to form.

"Now now, Ah don't wish to intrude at all, but if at some time in the future you would like to have a chat to me about it, a confidential chat, Ah might add. Having someone to confide in, may in some way ease the burden. Now now, don't cry. Ah have a few things to do now, so you sit here and when you're ready, you leave, and not until. You won't be disturbed." He beat a hasty retreat.

He walked back over to the mansion thinking, *How on earth do Ah get myself into these situations?* He was at the same time, however, mulling over a statement that Alice had made just prior to George's death. She referred to it as, Freddie's unsettled night, as she enlarged upon it.

"Freddie's now fifteen, we've already been through that dreadful experience going around the calving cows some eighteen months ago. Where was Ah at the same age in regard to this kind of thing? Well Ah was just about to lose mah virginity. Mah Paw saw to it that these things had to be handled delicately. Ah remember mah darling mother at the time, when Ah walked in on them having overheard some of the conversation. She didn't appear to be too happy at the time and shortly after 'the event.' But she never said a word. Ah suspect that she knew, as most people it turned out knew at the time that it was a rite of passage."

Chapter 15

Whilst he had not quite formed a view as to how he was going to tackle it, he was coming around to the fact that Christina Schmidt may be the key to it. Around two months after the last meeting with her he saw her in the car park one evening after work, and after the usual pleasantries, commented on the fact that he suspected that she only worked four days a week, and that if this was the case, he would like to have a word with her in the not too distant future if it was convenient.

She responded by saying that it would be a pleasure, and suggested the following Wednesday. He arranged to call on her at 10 a.m. that morning. He asked her if she could meet him out at the road. She was a little surprised at this but could only comply.

That morning she walked out the half-mile or so to the road and there a little before ten she found him waiting beside his car, a beautiful 1930's La Salle. He removed his hat, gave a slight bow, and opened the passenger door for her. She noticed a wicker basket on the rear seat, and thought to herself that this was certainly leading up to something, a something a little out of the ordinary.

They drove in a comfortable silence for a few minutes, and then he cleared his throat, and told her that he had a picnic lunch on the back seat, and even a chilled bottle of white wine which he hoped she would like, and that they would be going to a remote secluded place on the far extremity of The Lagoon, where he knew they would not be disturbed, and he could explain something to her. (As if she hadn't already suspected. *He of all people obviously wants something from me.*)

She sat back and relaxed, feeling completely at ease. The luxurious feel of the seat, the purr of the engine, the perfect ride down what became quite a rough road, evinced feelings in her that she had not had for a very long time. They almost verged on a sense of security that she had long given up on. She felt that the next few hours or so would be both confronting in a way, and how she reacted or responded would perhaps be the catalyst for how her future would shape.

This whole, almost smug lifestyle she now was observing exuded a confidence that was in a way conceited and oddly refreshing. She couldn't quite put a finger on it. She would have to be very much on her mettle. She gave a little inward shiver. She may have become accustomed to survival, but was never comfortable with any form of intrigue.

They drove for quite a while. She really didn't know for how long; she really didn't care. The car eventually came to a gate and Mr. Ted got out, unlocked the gate, drove through and got out and locked it again. Not a word passed between them, only the occasional smile. They then set off on a well formed but gravel road, through some of the most beautiful scenery she had seen since she had arrived in America, which she felt was the most beautiful naturally endowed country she could imagine.

Prussia where she came from was beautiful in—how could she put it?—in a pristine, chocolate boxy way, although structured, very formal. It was also a little claustrophobic when compared to here. This country had a raw untamed beauty by comparison. It also had an energy that she had never experienced before. The energy was just below the surface, and it would escape the casual observer, but it was there nevertheless, and vibrant to boot. She could appreciate it, but she yearned for Germany. (With a broken heart.)

She wasn't sure for how much further they drove other than to be vaguely aware that they drove through another gate, and then off on what felt like a much rougher track. They eventually pulled up and he announced that "We are here." He got out of the car and walked around to her door opened it and helped her out. *This is old Southern Charm,* she thought, *just like the old days back at home.*

He led her to the front of the car, and invited her to "Take a look." It took her breath away. The sun was almost at its zenith, and they were almost by the water's edge with the shore, the grassed shoreline arching away in each direction, for half a mile or so. Away directly across the water was what appeared to be a headland jutting out towards them from the far shore.

"Mr. Kershaw, this is absolutely beautiful, I am quite transfixed by it."

"Mrs. Schmidt, can Ah say at the outset that Ah would like you to call me Ted, and Ah'll call you Christina. In public we can observe the proprieties, if need be, but between the two of us… Ah feel it is appropriate in view of what Ah have to ask you." She smiled and nodded to him.

"Well, what say we get the hamper from the car? Would you like to do that and Ah'll get the rug out of the trunk." He took the rug out and walking a little way from the car spread it out. "Ah've got a couple of chairs in the trunk too. Ah'll get them as well. Ah can't sit too long on the ground, Ah cramp up. Looking at it now Ah

201

realize Ah have forgotten the table. Ah'm a little nervous!"

He didn't have to tell her. She could see that. What on earth could he want from her that had brought this on? Well at least he was being frank about it. They both sat down, and were taking in the view, when she looked down, and suddenly said, "We will have to move."

"What, what do you mean?" said Ted.

"Look at the ants," she cried, jumping up.

That broke the ice. They hurriedly gathered up the rug, shook it out and moved it to a spot not far away where there didn't appear to be any. Fortunately, they hadn't got into the hamper so nothing to worry about there. They sat down again, and looked at each other and burst out laughing.

Ted said, "Well Christina, Ah'll cut straight to the chase. You see," his voice trailed off. He looked at her lamely. "You see, now that the moment is here Ah have gone all to water."

"Mr. Kershaw. I would really prefer to call you that or perhaps Mr. Ted as everyone else does. Will you mind? It is just that the intimacy which attends my calling you Ted, is something at this stage at least, I feel a little uncomfortable with. I hope you understand. Anyway, Mr. Ted, tell me, it is quite alright." She knew instinctively that it would not be some romantic attachment to her that he had suddenly developed, although it certainly seemed to be a most sensitive matter.

"It's about Freddie, mah nephew. Ah can appreciate your reluctance, Mr. Ted will be fine."

"Oh, Mr. Ted," she said tentatively. She was still coming to terms with this sudden familiarity. "I don't know him at all, I've only seen him a few times. He is certainly a fine cut of a boy; how old is he?"

"He's nearly fifteen."

"Well,' she said, 'he is going to be a big man when he grows up, how tall is he?"

"He's five eleven."

"My," she said, "he'll be well over six feet, won't he?"

"Yes, yes, Ah suppose so," muttered Ted.

He's still having trouble, she thought. She went on, "Is he doing well at school?"

"Oh yes he is," Ted responded.

"He has good friends?"

Again, "Yes, yes he has." She had certainly thought that this would be a process of elimination, but there were only two matters left that she could think of at the moment.

"Ted, please forgive me for being intrusive."

"No, no you're not. It is quite OK. Ah'm being no help at all."

"Ted, I know he was very close to his sister and father; I didn't ever get to meet them, but do you think that he is grieving for them?"

"Christina, Ah know he is, we all are in our own personal ways, but it is not that." *Well that fixes that,* she thought; *now there is only one thing left.*

"Ted, can I ask you? Has he discovered girls? As you know he is at a very difficult age in this respect, but I can assure you it is much trickier with a girl."

"Girls, well yes and no. He has had a lovely young friend for years, and we hope that something may come of it eventually; but that really isn't what Ah'm on about."

"Ted, dear," she said, jumping the last hurdle to familiarity. She felt that under the circumstances she had to. He was looking more uncomfortable by the moment. "I would venture to say that with what I have experienced, nothing is going to surprise me."

"No, perhaps not," he said, "but yo' will certainly be shocked."

"Well, what is it, Ted? It is girls, it is not girls; we seem to be going round in circles. Should we have something to eat and then perhaps a glass of wine?"

"That would be wonderful."

"Well you sit there and I will prepare it, now what do we have here? Ted, would you like to open the bottle? Do you have a corkscrew? There doesn't seem to be one here!"

"Ah have one in the car's glove compartment. Ah'll get it," he said, he said jumping up, obviously happy to have got off the subject if only for a short time.

"Mr. Kershaw... Ted," they were happily taking the first sip of wine. "Do you know that I haven't done anything like this since 1941!"

"Gee, that's a long time Christina, although an awful lot has happened in the interim."

"It has Ted, it has. Now Ted, I don't think either of us can relax, until someone has grasped the nettle."

"Ah know, Ah know and it is me. The thing is Freddie is growing up mighty fast, and well, well. There are some things a boy has to learn before he really becomes a man, and this requires the assistance... Aw, Christina, Ah'm finding this terribly difficult... because..." and he petered out again.

She felt a tremor run through herself. She had been beginning to get inkling that it was something like this he was trying to get out. She cut in on him, now quite sure.

"And Ted you were wondering if my daughter may be able to help him with his, what shall we say, rite of passage; is that correct?" Her heart was thumping and felt as though it was nearly in her mouth.

He threw a sidelong glance at her, and mumbled, "Yes."

She actually felt quickly that in any other circumstances she would have been so indignant as to state an emphatic *No!* This situation was really quite different. She surmised correctly that if she had said no then that would have been the end of it, but his whole approach had not the slightest hint of control or expectation. He was quite humble about it as though he really found the whole issue distasteful, and had only approached her because he considered her to be in a way, a kindred spirit.

"Oh, Ted dear, this isn't the end of the world, it has been going on down through the ages. All cultures, all nationalities, not just here in this country of yours." She looked at him. "Now look at me," she said. He was looking quite ashen.

"I understand. I am not shocked. I must say, however, that when you have fallen so far in your station in life, as we have, you have to be prepared for anything that happens your way. Things that would not have happened if, if things were different. I do have to say at the same time, my daughter and her child are the most precious things to me, and I will never compromise their wellbeing." *Phew,* she thought. *Thank heavens I managed to get all that out.*

A not unnecessary and understandable silence settled upon them.

Some minutes later she said, "This has been exhausting hasn't it?" looking up at him.

"It sure has," he said, looking directly at her for the first time in perhaps half an hour.

"Ted, I have to ask you, this is a very sensitive matter. Subject to one matter we have to clarify. I will say that I am prepared to ask Ilse. What her reaction will be I don't know. She is nearly ten years older than your great-nephew. I just don't know, I really have no idea. All I can really say is that if she does it will be with my blessing. Simply because I understand."

"The other aspect before we proceed, however, is does his mother know? Does she have any inkling that you are up to this cloak and dagger business, for want of a better term?"

"Good heavens no, no she don't. Of course not."

"Well, Ted, don't you think that it is unwise to even contemplate this kind of thing? I mean it is what goes on, but there is a great deal of difference between what you are setting out to do and what his father would do, or perhaps even want."

"You have hit the nail on the head, Christina!"

"What do you mean?"

"Ah myself am not altogether happy with it, but Ah swore to his daddy before he died that Ah would arrange something that would be most respectable, and to be honest Ah did not know where to start. If you weren't able to help out mah next stop would have been the doctor, and Ah really didn't want to go down that path.

"Yo' know in mah day and in his daddy's day, things were little more out in the open. Particularly between the men. The women, mothers, didn't have a say in it. It's only because his daddy was insistent, he brought the subject up, and Ah swore to arrange it, that we are sitting here. No no, Ah can't bring Alice into it. If she ever finds out heaven forbid, all hell would break loose. Ah will deal with it then, at the time, but not now.

"Yo' know, Christina, Ah am fairly worldly for this part of the world. The only thing is, it is a pretty small one in the overall scheme of things. Ah know, Ah have traveled abroad a lot, but Ah'm really only at home in mah own little comfort zone. The thing is, Ah have never met anyone like you at all, even on my travels. Ah know Ah was fairly uppity and patronizing when we first met but that's me. Inside Ah'm not like that at all."

"Oh Ted, anything like this is never easy, so thank you very, very much. What you have just said certainly puts a different complexion on it. You are obviously honor-bound. I suppose your nephew-in-law knew that his wife would be upset."

"Yes, yes, he certainly did; but there you are, what can yo' deny a man on his deathbed?"

"Oh dear… Ted, I will get back to you in good time. I expect within the week. And Ted…"

"Yes, Christina."

"I am flattered that you would ask me to assist in this what can only be described as a most personal sensitive matter. And, Ted…"

"Yes."

"We are people of the world, so please try and relax."

"Yo' are very kind, Christina."

"No Ted, you are very much a gentleman! Oh dear, I thought when I came to this country, life, whilst it would not necessarily become easier, would at least become a little less complex. Alas."

"Oh look at me, you could think that Ah would find things a little easier, but it doesn't seem to be mah lot either. But really, thank you for helping me through this, Ah have been on edge for some weeks and haven't known where to start, and then Ah thought of you, you and your daughter are quite beautiful, in more ways than one and all this helps, and, Christina, my offer to you to be a friendly ear, in telling me about your past is still open, yo' know! It is entirely up to you. As Ah have said before, Ah don't wish to intrude, so Ah won't mention it again."

She looked at him. "I know, thank you. Actually I am becoming reconciled to the fact that it would be a help to me if I did. Perhaps before long. Perhaps when we have this current business sorted out!"

"Christina."

"Yes, Ted. There is one little thing?"

"Yes."

With a smile on his face he asked, "Christina, how do you come to speak such perfect English?"

With an impish but almost wistful smile she replied, "I went to school in England! I was educated there!"

Some days later, Christina saw Ted in the car park, and asked him if she could see him in his office.

A little later over a cup of tea she told him, much to his relief, that her daughter would be prepared to meet with Freddie. Whilst she could not guarantee anything would come of it, as she felt that whilst she was prepared to make the running it does take two after all, and Freddie may not in any way be attuned to what was expected of him.

"Well Christina, Ah'm most grateful to her, and she is correct, it does take two to tango. Please give her my heartfelt thanks. How do you feel we should proceed from here, Christina?"

"What I suggest, Ted, is that as the school holidays are coming up in the next week you could deliver him to our place.

"Tell him that you have to drop off some papers to me; you'll need some pretext to actually have him in the car with you. I'll leave that to you. When you arrive I will invite you both inside. It is likely to be quite hot, so ask for a cool drink.

"I will then say, I must be off as I have to take the grandchild in to play with some friends not far away; which we can arrange beforehand. You can then gallantly offer to run me and the child over in your car. Ilse will invite Freddie to have a look at the cattle yards, and hopefully something will happen along the way over the next two hours. We must allow this amount of time as nothing is going to happen at least for the first hour or so.

"We will arrange some sort of a signal to let us know if it was a success or not before we actually arrive back. A drawn blind or the like. That's the theory, anyway. What do you think?"

"Well, Ah have to say, Christina, it all sounds simple and straightforward. Ah'll arrange for him to be with me, what will it be—next Wednesday? And Ah'll get back to yo' as soon as possible. Yo' know, Christina, most of what Ah do or am involved in is pretty straightforward. From time to time one may have to tread like a cat and be a little bit more sensitive than one otherwise would, but in all mah born days Ah've never experienced more intrigue than this, and Ah've brought it all on mah self!"

"Oh you sweet man. Of course, but remember you are doing it for the very best of reasons. One, you promised his father, and two, you are going about it in a most sensitive manner. And three if you like, you happen to have approached someone who is in a position to help, and understands your predicament completely." *I just hope I don't ever have to confront his mother over this,* she thought to herself. *I'll have to draw on every reserve to handle her, I imagine.*

Chapter 16

The day came and at the appointed time Ted and Freddie drew up in front of the Unthank ranch house. Christina and her daughter came out to meet them, together with a small child and Ted's heart gave a bit of a thump when he saw the two women together. They were as beautiful a pair of women as could be imagined. He could understand how the young neighbor fell for the daughter, to say nothing of her dead husband. Interestingly, she looked quite composed and friendly, not as he thought she would at all. For some reason he felt that she would look a little put out and prevailed upon, but not at all.

On cue, Ted, after the pleasantries had been exchanged and he had handed over the satchel of papers, asked if he could have a cool drink as it was mighty hot. Inside they went and Freddie was offered one as well. Christina then picked up the child and told Mr. Ted that she would have to be going as she had to drop the child off, and then go on into White Oak to do some shopping.

Ted, casting an eye at Freddie, said that he would be only too happy to take her, much to Ilse's bemusement looking at her mother with raised eyebrows, which wasn't missed by Ted. Freddie, to Unc's horror, told his uncle that he would be happy to go with them. Christina said that Ilse would then be left behind to which Freddie rejoined that she could come too.

By this time Ted was looking as though he was going to have a heart attack, when to his great relief, Christina asked him if he would like to see the new steel cattle yard design which they had erected.

"Yes." He would.

"Well, why don't you and Ilse go down and have a look at them Mr. Ted and I will be back in no time?"

Much to Ted's relief, Freddie agreed. They were all thinking to themselves that this whole exchange went on completely over Freddie's head; he was quite oblivious to the angst he was causing. Both she and Ted felt how lucky they were that Ted had told her about Freddie's passion about anything to do with the handling of stock.

Also, whilst all this was going on Ted, for all his concern, was observing the body language and looks being exchanged between mother and daughter. Studied but concerned control by the mother and studiously controlled mirth by the daughter. *The little minx,* he thought. Still the ball would be in her court before long. Could she handle such a delicate situation as this? *Well, the fat was in the fire now, we will know before long.*

They eventually set off and Ilse looked at Freddie and asked him if he would like another drink before they went off down to the yards; he said he would and to her relief commented on how hot it was. *Well, he is certainly not going to be difficult to talk to,* she thought.

She agreed that it was, and it was something that she was finding easier to cope with than her mother, who was quite affected by the heat, whereas she quite liked it.

"I feel it quite a bit," said Freddie, "in fact, I would like to take my shirt off. Do you mind?"

"No, not at all," she responded, thinking that this may be easier than she had imagined. She wanted to say she would like to take hers off also but thought that would be moving a little too quickly.

They walked side by side, he by now carrying the scrunched up shirt and wearing a pair of old dungarees and a pair of old boots. He looked quite beautiful, she thought, walking as close as possible without it being too obvious. *He will break a few hearts before he is through.*

She was dressed in a similar fashion with shorts and a white blouse knotted well above the waist which accentuated her figure. And she was wearing sandals. She wondered if he found her attractive in any way. She had decided to put her hair in pigtails; they added to the girlish look she wanted to convey. He may be too young. She wasn't wearing a bra. Which would be obvious to anyone—it had been to his uncle, she could tell. Men!

She had used just the smallest amount of perfume, and felt that her overall appearance was as attractive as she could make herself. She was just wondering where the whole thing would go when they had finished looking at the yards.

They arrived and she explained to him that Michael had decided on a set of yards that you could work cattle by yourself if you had to or with another one or two people. It consisted of a large yard which led to two smaller yards which fed into a circular smaller yard with four gates off it: two back to the feeder yards and two to separate yards either side of a race which could hold twenty odd animals and with a crush at the end of it which could be exited in three ways.

"It is all most impressive," said Freddie, and they discussed the virtues of them when Freddie then asked if he could see the approach to them.

"Over here," she said quite beginning to enjoy herself.

"So you have the entrance to them in the middle of a fence, say two hundred yards long from what I can see," said Freddie.

"Yes we do." She looked at him.

"Well you need a wing coming in at an angle in order to funnel them in, so there is only one way to go. If I can come back at some time I would love to help you plan where it should go." In spite of herself she said that would be marvelous and gave him a kiss.

He blushed bright red, and she said, "Oh come on silly, it would be wonderful if you could help plan it. Actually I have quite a bit of trouble getting them in at times; my horse and I are quite often in a lather by the time they are in, particularly with cows and calves. I have taken to putting bales of hay further into the yards which I find helps and I suppose we would have a wing if Mike was still with us, but it was not to be. Well off we go, we need to get out of this sun and back to the sweltering house."

In the past few minutes she had decided exactly how she was going to go about it, and she felt it was as foolproof as could be and was quite looking forward to it. It had been such a long time. They arrived back a few minutes later and found the kitchen to be even hotter than when they had left it. In no time at all her blouse was wringing wet again and she was most conscious of her breasts straining against it.

They were both sitting opposite each other with a jug on the table sipping from their glasses, and perspiration streaming down his bare chest and her by now heaving bosom, when she said, "Come on, Freddie, you need to have a nice cool shower. I will have one after you." She headed off out of the kitchen without giving him a chance to reply, as though it was the most natural thing to do. Much to her relief he meekly followed.

Leading the way into the bathroom she asked him if he had ever used a shower closet before. He replied that he hadn't but said that he had heard of them. She said that it was the only thing she had asked of Mike when she first saw his house. The bathroom was quite large

213

enough for a bath and a separate shower, which she much preferred; she went on to say that her mother still preferred a bath. Of course a bath is much nicer for a baby.

"We have a shower over every bath at The Lagoon, so I am quite used to them," he muttered.

"Now here you are, here is a towel and I'll put this one on the floor," she said, pulling a large heavy towel from the cupboard.

"There is plenty of water, and there is soap on a rack in the shower, so there you are. Take as long as you please." She almost skipped out of the bathroom, closing the door behind her.

*****

Ted and Christina dropped off her granddaughter at her little friend's house, and told the mother that they would be back in about two hours if that would be alright.

They drove in silence for about ten minutes and then Ted pulled over to the side of the road. "Well," he said, "I found that utterly exhausting, although it went well enough."

"I know, Ted dear, it wasn't going to be 'Yes sir, no sir, three bags full' but just the same it did go well. The poor darling, I don't think he had any inkling whatsoever."

"No he certainly didn't, and I must say your daughter was wonderful, although she could hardly contain herself at my apprehension."

"And mine," added Christina. "Oh to be young."

"Dare I say it, she did appear to be comfortable with the exercise, even though I say it to you her mother."

"You're right Ted. I think once she had reconciled herself to it she was. You know it has been a long time for her, your nephew is a beautiful boy, and we all have our needs."

He started the engine again and drove a short distance and pulled over.

"Christina, Ah," he faltered "Ah was thinking, yo' said," he broke off again.

"Yes dear."

"Yo' said we all have our needs." His hand was quite close to her on the seat. "Ah, Ah," he couldn't go on.

"Ted, it is I who need a little help." He looked at her with that soft anguished look she saw when he was trying to broach the Freddie business.

"Ted dear, I did and I said it deliberately; it has been years for me and I suspect a long time for you?"

She placed her hand over his.

"Yes, yes it has. Can we find a secluded spot if you know of one?"

"Christina, Ah know of dozens of them."

"Well I am in your hands, is it far?" He looked across at her with a smile on his face, and shook his head.

They drove for a quarter of an hour when he suddenly pulled off the road onto a little used track, and in a few minutes they were in the perfect spot she exclaimed. "We won't be disturbed here," he said.

"I have been thinking about your offer to hear me out about my background. I think this is about as good a time as any, would you mind?"

"Christina Ah am only too happy to hear yo' story, fire away."

"It all seems a lifetime ago, and in some respects I suppose it is, but looking back on it I don't think we were too different to a lot of people living in our part of the world really. Both my family and my husband's family were Junkers, landed aristocracy who were also with military backgrounds. Both our families knew each other and I married my childhood sweetheart. Three generations before, one of my family married into the English aristocracy, and both sides of the family were very close.

"Most of the young generation on the German side were educated in England, and I was no exception. That has given me a different perspective to those who were not afforded this opportunity. Whilst the first war put a strain on the relationship between the two families this was overcome between the two wars. However, after the Hitler War no reconciliation was possible.

"You see, my husband's family achieved high rank in the Wehrmacht, and my husband and my family achieved high rank in the SS."

"The SS," interrupted Ted.

"Yes, the SS," she went on. "To our English relatives the Wehrmacht may be one thing, but the SS put us irrevocably beyond the pale. So when the whole terrible conflict had ended, I had lost not only the English side but my husband together with my young boy, who was only a year older than Freddie at the time. To add to that, my immediate family, my father and uncles, who were all in the SS, were captured. My father, and uncles were indicted for war crimes. These charges were eventually dropped due to their pitiable condition due to the torture. The mitigating reality with them was that they had been captured and tortured by their own SS before the Allies got to them, and now they have all gone anyway. Needless to say our whole world came tumbling down. Do you mind if I have a cigarette Ted?"

"No no. Do you have any?"

"Yes." She lit up. "To add to all that our extensive landholdings on both sides of the family came to be in the east of Prussia when the victorious Allies drew the line between east and west. Fortunately, Ilse and I had moved west ahead of the advancing Russians and were in Berlin when the Allies arrived. Fortunately, we were in the British Sector so I was able to tell our English relatives where we were, by mail, but the letter was returned with a not known sticker on it. Now of course I am telling you all this in a rather condensed form, but that is it. On the face of it, I might add."

"Phew," said Ted. "That is quite a story and not a pretty one. What do you mean on the face of it?"

"Well Ted, I am not an apologist for what went on, particularly within the SS. However, my family had a plan to thwart Hitler and his designs from a very early stage, I must stress. My father and his brothers had a pact. They joined the SS relatively early, in the thirties. Actually, they were in the Wehrmacht anyway. And with their background were welcomed of course, as they lent an extreme amount of dignity to the organization. My husband and my brothers and cousins on my side of the family joined also. My husband's family also were part of it, so whilst it was quite extensive the network could not have been much more secure. You see, we were all very close. In the end we all paid a very heavy price. All the men folk, one way or another, were lost.

"Their pact was to enable as many people as possible, Jews in particular, to get out of Germany initially, and then Europe. This is what they did, and it worked terribly well, for years, until it caught up with them, and working from the bottom up as it were, the Gestapo executed my husband and my cousins and only caught my father and uncles when the war was drawing to a close. Fortunately, they survived, but with the SS millstone around their necks, however only for a short time."

"Christina, whilst I believe you, haven't yo' any proof of their activities? This surely would absolve them of any SS guilt."

"No Ted, nothing, there is absolutely nothing. You think about it: everything they did was done in secret, not only from the SS of course, but from the people whom they assisted to flee. That is why they were so successful for so long. No one could do a trace on whoever it was carrying out this escape route. It was all in the family. It was only by an inadvertent statement a cousin made right towards the end that brought the whole thing down. He and my other cousins and husband paid the ultimate price. My son died in one of those schoolboy battalions fighting the Russians."

"You're quite sure there is nothing? Not one little snippet?"

"No there is nothing. I have wracked my brains on and off over the years. There is absolutely nothing."

"Good heavens," mused Ted. "That is some story. You have actually lost your entire family and fortune."

"My mother, aunts, everybody. Yes, and the few remaining women, if any, are well behind the Iron Curtain. I haven't been able to contact them since the end of the war. Don't worry, I have tried.

"I know the whole story seems improbable from so many angles—my family, the Junkers, the estates, the wealth… the SS, the escape route. How can I explain it in my defense? The reality is that we were a population of nearly seventy million, and from where I am coming from, hundreds of thousands would have been against Hitler. Perhaps millions. Many people, families were against him, though few more than my collective family, who were extremely well organized and had a sophisticated approach to it. By God, we paid for it. They were dreadful years.

"Also with my English education I have perceived that Germans, particularly we Prussians, are considered by those who come into contact with them to be a little too truculent on occasion. You, I am ashamed to say, may have found me like that when I first barged in on you. I am between a rock and a hard place. It is very difficult."

"Oh Christina, what have you been through, what have we got ourselves into? Ah feel completely drained, to be quite frank. And no, Ah didn't think you were truculent; feisty perhaps, but to be honest if you had come simpering to my door you may not have got past it."

"Ted, you are very kind, but I also feel that you will view me in a completely different light from now on, and how long that will last I cannot say," she said, looking across at him with her lower lip beginning to tremble.

"Oh Christina please," he said placing a hand over hers, and looking at her with his eyes beginning to water. "I suppose, my dear, we should be getting back." She just nodded. "What we'll find when we do is anybody's guess. Ah just hope it works out."

He started the engine, and slowly drove off. *Well,* she thought, *I suppose one of my needs has been met.*

Few people were more intuitive than Ted, but what she had told him called all his instinctive powers into play. His mind had been working like a threshing machine needless to say, as her story developed trying to take all this in. Her story seemed preposterous. Was it plausible? Yes! Was it implausible? No! And when you really thought about it, she certainly wouldn't make something up, anything like that. Why construct a damning story like that, if it wasn't true? There was no point to it. It must be true. He looked at her again, smiled and put his hand over hers reassuringly.

*****

She ran down to her bedroom and quickly stripped off; taking a quick look in the mirror, she thought to herself that she couldn't look much better. She saw a bottle of aromatic baby oil on her dresser, and quickly put a small amount into her cupped hand and rubbing it gently into the soft down between her thighs, and then over her breasts. She padded back to the bathroom, and, taking a deep breath, opened the door and walked in. He heard the door open and called out from behind the screen that he had nearly finished and with a quick couple of steps she crossed to the screen and, drawing it aside, stepped in with him.

"No no, Ilse. I'm not ready, please I haven't finished," he blurted out.

"Freddie darling, it is alright, we can shower together."

"No, no."

"Don't worry, where is the soap?" She reached around behind him to the rack. Her heart was nearly in her mouth. Facing him she gently began to move the soap over his back and then to his chest. She continually soaped both hands, and could gradually begin to feel his concern give way to a surrender to the situation. He buried his head in her hair and began to moan ever so softly. He was beginning to tremble all over. She slowly began to turn her back on him and as she did could feel his hardness against her. Reaching behind her she slowly guided his hands to envelop her all the while soaping both of their hands. She began to feel an urgency in him and thought to herself that she would have to get the timing of this just right.

She moved one of his hands over her breasts, and the other down over her stomach and beyond. By now she felt that she could drop the soap and he would take over. She turned around again, replaced the soap and reaching up wrapped her arms around his neck, and kissed him tenderly on the lips, as he began to make soft whimpering sounds, and continued to thrust against her.

With no time to lose she drew him from the shower and turning him around told him to get down on the floor on his back, quickly. As he eased himself down, she followed him, straddling him and as he stretched out she lowered herself, enveloping him completely. Oh such bliss, it had been so long. She moved with an old familiar rhythm that gathered in intensity as she met his every plunge and thrust.

He uttered a little cry. "Oh Ilse, what is happening, what are you doing?" This trailed off as he began to rise up against her again and again. They were both panting and clinging to each other, as they melted into one another. He eventually arched up and went into a convulsion, moaning all the while.

Afterwards they lay for some time getting their breath back. She kept him inside her for as long as she could remain comfortably astride him. Eventually easing up over him, she brought one of her breasts to his mouth and suckled him as she stroked his hair; he began muttering slow moans again.

She suddenly thought, *my God the shower,* and gently rolled off him and stood up and stepping inside the closet and turned it off.

Kneeling down beside him she was relieved to see a sleepy smile on his face as he looked her directly in the eye.

"Oooh Ilse, oooh," he gave a little shiver. "Do you know what Ilse?"

"No, darling."

"Oh nothing. Ilse. Ilse, when can, when can we do it again?"

She gave a little chuckle, "Oooh let's see, in about a quarter of an hour, how does that sound? We will have to be quick though, they will be back in about 45 minutes." She helped him up, and taking him by the hand led him down to her bedroom.

The big La Salle moved slowly down the drive. Ted wasn't sure what the signal would be, but as they drew closer Christina suddenly gave Ted a look of concern. "No successes dear."

"How do yo' know, Christina?"

"The blinds across the front of the house are down! That was to be the signal. Look they are all down, so it must have gone badly. We always have them down in this hot weather. She was going to put some up if it worked out."

They pulled up and gave a short toot of the horn. A moment later the two of them came to the door. Little Trudl jumped from the car and ran to her mother who picked her up, hugging and kissing her, and Christina thought she just looked positively dreamy. Freddie was close beside her with a similar expression.

To Christina's amazement Ted asked Freddie what he thought of the yards. "Oh Unc, they are good yards, thanks for suggesting I check them out."

"That's fine, Freddie, that's fine, it's all good experience fo' yo'."

"Mr. Ted, would you like to come inside for a cool drink," Ilse asked.

"Well that's mighty nice of yo' Ilse, Ah don't mind if I do. Then we better be off, don't you think Freddie?"

Ilse turned and led the way back into the house with Trudl running ahead, Freddie close behind with Christina and Ted bringing up the rear. Ilse managed to tell her mother that she had forgotten the blinds. As they reached the door Ted gave Christina a hug and a peck on the cheek and a whispered: "Thank yo'.' Ah'll see yo' in the morning." They had a drink and then took their leave.

Ted and Freddie drove slowly back to The Lagoon, and were about half way when Freddie broke the easy silence by asking, "Unc?"

"Yes, son," said Unc, fairly relaxed.

"How do cows actually have calves?" Ted threw him a startled look and found himself looking directly into the eyes of an impish-looking Freddie.

Ted thought hurriedly that he would have to come up with something that both gave a reply, and matched Freddie's wit, and hopefully throw it back onto him. "Well Freddie, now that yo' a man, Ah shouldn't have to explain thangs like that anymore, don't yo' thank?" he drawled, looking at him with a smile and his head cocked to one side.

Freddie just nodded. "I suppose so, Unc."

A little later. "Unc!"

"Yes son?"

"Unc, Ilse showed me the map of the ranch."

"Yes, Freddie."

"It is two thousand or so acres, and there are no laneways."

"Is that so, Freddie?"

"Yes, now I was wondering if I was to draw up a plan, could you have a look at it and give it to Mrs. Schmidt. You never know, we may be able to even help them with the work entailed in a new layout."

"Freddie that is a mighty big word, son, 'entailed.'"

"Well Unc. It is a word I first heard Snakesbreath use, and Unc, I do go to school, and I do read a lot."

"Ah know, Freddie, Ah know. Yo' just never cease to amaze me, that's all. Now that would be wonderful, we can do that. How did yo' come to be talking about fencing layout?"

"Well, Unc, we had a look at the yards, and they look pretty good to me. There is no wing leading into them, and that needs to be sorted out first. If you are going to do that you may be better off with a clean sheet, as Ilse said, when I spoke to her about it. The thing is, I wonder if they have the money to put towards new fencing."

"Well, Freddie, we'll see, we'll see," said Unc.

"And Unc."

"Yes, Freddie?"

"They do all or most of the cattle work themselves, and they really have no background to it. Ilse couldn't even ride a horse before she came here."

They continued on back to The Lagoon in silence, each in contemplation.

Chapter 17

A fortnight later Alice went over to the main office and poked her head in, seeing Ted disappearing into his office with their local solicitor. She also saw Mrs. Schmidt speaking to a couple of other people as they looked at a sheaf of papers she was holding. She thought to herself, *Where can that boy be?* Perhaps the workshop.

She set off towards the workshops which were about three hundred yards from the mansion area, and happened to run into Wilson, on his way back to the office.

"Good day Miss Alice, how are you?"

"I'm fine thank you Wilson, you don't happen to have seen Freddie have you?"

"Why yes Miss Alice, Ah took him over to the Unthank place again this morning at about ten, and I have to pick him up at two."

"Oh, he's working on the fencing layout already is he?"

"Ah suppose so Miss Alice."

"Well don't you worry about picking him up, I will, thank you Wilson." They walked back to the main office chatting and then he took his leave of her.

Her mind turned to Mrs. Schmidt, an absolute beauty, although slightly fading. Her daughter in the prime of life and a younger version of her mother, and probably more attractive. Freddie, beautiful young blonde woman: equals chaperone. Where is the chaperone? There is none. She walked over to the Chevy got in and drove straight down the drive and over to the Unthanks' ranch.

As she approached the front entrance to the spread she could see the cattle yards in the distance beyond the house and sheds, and as she suspected there was no one there. *This is just ducky,* she thought, *although just the same I will have to be very careful, and not blow a fuse.* She drove quietly down to the rear of the house, and quietly got out of the car and didn't close the door.

She walked on in through the extremely neat garden she thought, in spite of herself, and up to the rear door and knocked on it firmly, stepping slightly back and to the side to be out of immediate sight of anyone opening it. She was just about to knock again, when a slightly disheveled Ilse poked her head out, and, seeing her, promptly burst into tears. Freddie was right on her heels and managed to blurt out a "Hi Mom."

"Hi Mom indeed!" responded Alice, managing to put a good face on it, in spite of the fact that she was seething, felt hurt and betrayed, all in one.

"Ilse," she said straining to keep absolute control of her emotions, "Where is your baby?"

"She is with friends in town, Miss Alice," she managed to blurt out through the tears.

God, she looks beautiful, thought Alice in spite of herself. "Now Ilse you go back inside and make yourself respectable, you too, Freddie, and both be back in the car with me in five minutes, now scoot."

She retired to the car, thinking—*How could Unc have done this to me, how, how, and why, to us of all people?* The two appeared a few minutes later, and Alice told Ilse to sit in the front and Freddie in the back, and they set off back to The Lagoon. When they arrived she put the two of them in Unc's study and asked Norman to go over to the office and ask Mr. Ted to come over and bring Mrs. Schmidt with him. "When they arrive will you direct them into the big room please? Not to the study."

She went into the beautiful main room of the mansion, taking in everything, the flowers, portraits, couches, other paintings, the book cases, easy chairs; the only thing she thought that was a little incongruous was the baby grand which Unc was very fond of, although he couldn't play it. The wood was too light in color for her; why he bought it a few years ago was beyond her, but there you are.

A few minutes later Unc walked in, preceded by Mrs. Schmidt who although looking concerned was certainly taken by the room which apart from its furnishings was beautifully proportioned, and opened out onto the patio overlooking the lagoon itself. Before anyone could say anything, she had turned and, looking in the direction of the piano, uttered a low moan, staggered towards it and fell down in what appeared to be a dead faint.

"Unc, quickly," said Alice. "Her daughter is in the study with Freddie, send them in here and get Norman and Mary quick. With smelling salts if we have any." The two young appeared, and seeing her mother on the floor Ilse uttered a little cry and with great haste knelt beside her. She took one of her hands and began to rub and kiss it and then uttered another cry, and burst into sobs.

Unc reappeared a second later and, taking in the two women—one comatose, the other racked with sobs—could only look at Alice and shake his head. Freddie was just standing there transfixed.

"Freddie," his mother said, "will you go and ring Doc. Holmes and ask him to come? Tell him it is not an extreme emergency, but someone, a woman, has fainted,

227

and we don't know why. Also her adult daughter is taking it very hard.

"Unc, we will leave Freddie helping out with the fencing for the time being, OK? Until we sort this business out, there appears to be more to it than meets the eye," she said in low tones.

Mary and Norman appeared and between all of them they managed to lift Christina onto a couch, and Alice waved a little smelling salts under her nose which seemed to have some effect. Unc managed to catch Alice's eye and motioned to the door. Satisfied that nothing could be done for a few minutes, she followed him out and into the study.

"Chickie, what did yo' mean by Freddie's fencing? We have only talked about it."

"I found him there today with Ilse, they looked, how shall I say, extremely compromised, to put it mildly!"

"Oh my God!" was all he could say. "We had better get back."

They found Christina sitting up and with a little color coming back to her face, but was sitting looking longingly at the piano with tears streaming down her face. Fortunately, Ilse had settled down, although she too was crying silently.

Unc looked at Alice shaking his head, and knelt down beside Christina, throwing caution to the winds, he said, "Christina, dear…" *I might have known it,* thought Alice.

"What is wrong, are you alright?"

"Yes, Ted." Alice looked at the ceiling, in spite of herself thinking that they would make an attractive couple regardless of the age difference. "I am alright or I hope I am."

"Well what is the matter?"

"The piano," said Christina.

"What do you mean the piano?"

"It is mine Ted, or at least it was." He looked at Ilse. She looked him fair in the eye and nodded.

"Look, here is Mary with a cup of tea," said Alice. "We will all feel better having had one and we will continue this business when the doctor has checked you over, Mrs. Schmidt."

They hadn't finished the tea when the doctor was ushered in. Over another cup of tea Alice explained what had happened and told him that she and Freddie and Unc would wait outside on the patio while he checked her over. Christina said, "You are very kind Mrs. Gardiner."

Alice nodded and told her she could take the doctor into whatever confidence she chose to. "Actually, I suspect he is already your doctor! We will now leave the three of you." She then led the others out onto the patio and closed the door.

They went over to some casual chairs and sat down. Unc began to say something, but Alice checked him.

"Please dear, I find this whole business exhausting, can we wait until say tomorrow after we have had time to sleep on it? OK, Unc, Freddie?"

"Yes, Mom."

"Alright, Chickie."

Alice thought they seemed quite relieved at the suggestion.

A few minutes later Eric appeared. "Firstly," he said, "the woman is in perfect health, I have no concerns for either of them. She did however begin to tell me about what brought it on. The piano, as you already know; but there seems to be quite a lot to it, so I think you had all better come in and hear it. I actually stopped her before she told me much at all. Most of it was preamble anyway, so I thought." They all trooped back inside to find Christina sitting in an easy chair. She began to get up but Eric stopped her. "You stay there, Christina. You are free to tell us your story when you are ready."

"Thank you doctor. Mr. Ted, Mrs. Gardiner and Freddie, I am sorry for my most unfortunate display of emotion, but as I told you before: the piano is actually mine, or perhaps should I say was mine. It was given to me on my 21st birthday, nearly 30 years ago. I can readily prove it."

"You can prove it, Christina?"

"Yes, Mr. Ted. If you lift up the lid, and prop it you will see halfway up the prop, inside out of view, painted in black paint the word 'Christina.' Also whilst you are doing that cast your eyes down to the claw on the ball of the rear leg and you will see half the rear claw broken off an inch and a half down from the top. Also the fourth ivory in on the left is slightly darker than the others, if you lift the keyboard cover.

"Please all of you have a look; I feel it will settle things down a little." They all carried out the inspection and returned to their seats with incredulous expressions on their faces. Ted was shaking his head slowly from side to side. *This is incredible,* thought Alice, *the woman is, apart from this Freddie business, a pleasant, beautiful woman who has fallen on hard times, but has never really let herself go, and has maintained her dignity. As well as that she holds down a very responsible job in The Lagoon office, so she is obviously very good with figures. And now with this piano business she seems to be slowly emerging from what could be described as a chrysalis.* It was almost imperceptible but there nevertheless. She looked across at Eric, and from the expression and look he returned her, she felt that he realized the same thing. The woman was slowly becoming energized. *Well whatever it is, it must be big,* she thought.

Eric asked if he could have a smoke. "Sure thing," said Ted, "anyone else, Christina would you like one?"

"Thank you; Ilse I have some in my bag."

230

"Freddie will you get some ashtrays please?" asked Alice.

"As I said it was mine, once upon a time; how on earth does it come to be in your possession, Mr. Ted?"

"Well, it's quite simple really. Ah have always been interested in antique auctions, and whenever Ah am in a major city or center, Ah go to them. Back in the late 'forties they were auctioning the effects from a deceased estate, the piano was one of the items and there you are I bought it for two hundred dollars, Ah seem to recall. It seemed a lot at the time, but Ah liked it. Ah thought the color of the wood would fit into the color of the room. As it turned out, almost but not quite."

"Do you remember the actual background of the estate?"

"Oh, at the beginning they said that it had belonged to a veteran of the European Theatre, and he and his wife who were childless were killed in a motor accident. The extended family happened to be there and I spoke to one of them when the piano was knocked down to me. They seemed to be a very well to do family. He said that his cousin, the one who died, had brought it from some Russians in Berlin."

"He said, the story goes, that he came across them near a truck which the piano was on. They had broken the crate, lit a fire and had actually tossed on one of the legs. He saw that there was a piano in the crate, and managed to cajole the Russians into giving it to him in exchange for some dollars and a few crates of rations. He had been seconded to his unit as a Russian Interpreter so he had no trouble conversing with them. Apparently they had come across the truck when it had broken down, and had told the driver in no uncertain terms to 'disappear.' He didn't need much encouragement. He said he quickly pulled the leg out of the fire when he realized what it was. The charring on it bore testament to

231

this. As you can see it is a Schimmell, one of the very best."

Christina just sat there with tears streaming silently down her face. *And it has come halfway around the world to this beautiful man, to this beautiful family. I simply cannot believe it but there it is. I am looking at it. There is some good in the world after all.*

"Christina, yo' said that it was yours. It still is, Ah'm giving it to you. It is what fate had in store for yo', and for Ilse."

"Mr. Ted, I have to be quite frank with you. Do you mean that? I have to tell you, our whole future, and our whole wellbeing is in that piano."

"Christina look at me, look at us, the piano could be full of gold. We are about as wealthy as one can get. Ah don't know why Ah am saying this, it's just mah way of speaking, Ah suppose. Ah know Ah nearly drive Alice mad at times but there yo' are, the piano is yours. Freddie boy, go over to the nerve center and get Mr. Brady, will yo' please? Bring him back here pronto. Alice will yo' get Mary? Oh there yo' are Mary."

"Yessir Mr. Ted. Ah'm jes' holdin' the door open for Norman, he's bringing in another tray of tea with all the trimmin's!" Alice took the tray from Norman who scuttled back with Mary to the kitchen to get another tray.

"Jack, there yo' are. Get yourself a cup of tea or coffee if yo' prefer, help him, Alice dear. Jack, yo' know everyone here except Christina Schmidt and her daughter Ilse. Christina, this here is Jack Brady, one of the finest Attorneys outside of New York." Jack chuckled and nodded all round.

"Jack, see that piano over there? Will yo' please get a piece of paper, there is some next door, will you get some Freddie boy? Ah'd like yo' to draw up in longhand, in one paragraph, an irrevocable deed of gift, of the piano from me Edward Kershaw to Christina Schmidt, named as the original owner. One paragraph, mind yo' Jack, in longhand, and two copies please. Leave room for all of us to witness as well. Also please put in today's date.

"Now Christina, I suspect that we will all sleep tonight, but at the same time Ah reckon yo've got another rabbit or two to pull out of the hat. No, no don't say anything. Yes, Ilse."

"Mr. Kershaw, sir, could I please ring to see how Trudl is and tell them we may be a little late picking her up?"

"Freddie, that was quick, now take Ilse to the phone in the study, off yo' go now, but don't be long. Christina we seem to be moving towards something, now is there anything else we need?"

"Yes Mr. Ted."

"Could you send for George the carpenter please and ask him to bring a heavy screwdriver and a sawhorse?"

"Of course Christina, Ah should have anticipated that. A saw as well?" He finished with a smile on his face.

Alice, who had been quietly sitting there undergoing this sense of unreality, snapped out of it as she heard herself saying, "Unc, I need some air, I'll go and get him," quickly standing up, shaking her head. "This is almost getting too much for me."

"Now Jack, how are yo' going there?"

"Nearly finished the second copy, Ted. You can have a read, and then a couple of yo' can witness them. If you're happy."

"Let's see, Jack," Ted said taking one of the pieces of paper, which he quickly perused. "That's fine, that's fine Jack, Ah'll sign and then if you other folk sign, and we'll leave one for Alice when she comes back."

"Now Christina, is there anything else?"

"No Mr. Ted, not until George arrives."

"Well. what say we all stretch our legs out on the patio? It's getting a little stuffy in here anyway." He walked to the door into the hall and called out to Mary to come and fetch the tea things. He then led the way out onto the patio through the French doors.

A little later Alice arrived back with George who was introduced all around, and Ted enquired, "What is next?" Christina was still a little weepy, and a little unsteady, but she was standing up, and she moved closer to Ted saying, "First I would like to make a little speech."

"Before yo' do, Christina, hear is yo' copy of the deed of gift. No, No, not a word," he said, shaking his head.

She began, "Ted, everyone, I am almost at a loss for words. None of you, not even Ilse, can appreciate just what this means to me, and to her. It is quite honestly our salvation, as you will shortly see. On one hand I can't thank you Ted enough for your generosity in giving the piano back to me."

"Now Christina…"

She held up a hand. "No Ted, Mr. Kershaw, you are a thorough gentleman and I want to thank you from the bottom of my heart. I could not mean that more sincerely. Over the past few years I have had to control my emotions for my two girls, and it hasn't been easy: at times I have been taken to the limit, though I have battled through, but as we know nothing worthwhile ever is easy. I should also say I am aware that your family has not in any way had an easy row to hoe. In fact, a most unenviable one. Today I am sorry, but I allowed my pent up emotions to get the better of me. Again I am so sorry.

"On the other hand, for me to actually find the piano again is quite literally a one in a more than million chance. The conditions when I last saw it were chaotic in the extreme; it was on a truck twenty odd miles from Berlin when it simply disappeared. It was quite shattering to me personally, as you will shortly see.

However, I couldn't bring myself to tell Ilse the true significance of the loss, as she would have been devastated also, and we didn't need the two of us to have a breakdown. The piano also bears a more testamentary acknowledgement to the sacrifice that my dear family made, as we will shortly discover. I say this in all humility.

"Could you allow me to play a little something for you, before we continue? I haven't actually touched it for years, so I'm not sure how it will play. Actually I have resisted touching it even now…"

"Christina, I have it tuned every so often, just in case someone can actually play! What are you going to play, is it anything we may be familiar with?"

"I would like to play 'A Spring Morning.' My grandfather was a gifted amateur composer and he composed this for me for my tenth birthday. I hope you aren't disappointed as this is also the last piano I played, so I may be a little rusty."

She walked over to it, sat down and lifted the lid, moved the seat slightly, and then flexed her fingers a little. She began to play. The notes wafted out through the doorway through to the kitchen, causing Mary and Norman to look wide-eyed at each other. With Mary leading the way they tiptoed back through to the big room and crept in. Freddie saw them out of the corner of his eye and gave a slight toss of his head beckoning them to come right in. Ted looked around as they came in and said, as Christina finished, "Just a moment, Christina please. Norman, bring two chairs from the dining room for Mary and you. Freddie be a good fella and get the girls. Tell them to each bring a chair from the dining room." Ted was referring to the four house girls: young girls from the plantation who do all the cleaning, dusting, fetching and carrying in the house, ably supervised by Mary.

The girls weren't far away and they eventually crept in with their chairs. All four, Rosie, Dolly, Elsie and Joey, looking at Ted expectantly. In return he gave them a reassuring smile.

"Ah'm sorry Christina, can you play it again please?"

Alice looked at Ilse who had tears streaming down her face silently, and then around the room and everyone's eyes were brimming with tears. It was only a short piece, but when it ended there was a hush and no one moved, until Alice with a choked voice, said, "It was quite beautiful, simply beautiful, and I'm so pleased, and I suspect everyone else is too, that it was back with its rightful owner. It is as emotional moment as I have experienced in a long time. Also the fact that you played it after so long without appearing to miss a note. And the fact that you have rediscovered it under such unusual circumstances is really quite incredible."

"Hear Hear!!" said Eric.

Ted walked over to Christina. He put his arm on her shoulder and gave her a light kiss on the top of the head. Turning to the small gathering, he took a few moments to collect himself. "Well," he said. "Wasn't that just something. Ah can't say much more at the moment but thank yo' Christina, thank yo'."

He moved to the center of the room and clearing his throat, started again. "Now, we haven't brought George over here to have a cup of tea. Yo' can't get off that easy George." George just stood and looked fondly at Ted, with a slight smile. "You girls can stay too. Now Christina, what have yo' in store for us next?"

Christina stood and said, "Again it is I who am the grateful one, thank you again. I'm sorry I can't stop shaking."

"Don't worry, don't worry, there is no rush. What would you like us to do?" said Ted.

She looked at him. "What we need to do is lift the piano at the back leg and unscrew the single eye screw recessed into the top of the leg, keeping the saw horse handy so that the piano can be put to rest on it when the leg is removed. Perhaps you can do that Ilse, you have already seen it done once. The screwdriver may help. And if the men can lift the back. We will have to lower the lid first. It won't have to be lifted very far, around two to three inches. And then perhaps if I slide the horse under it. It is just the correct height."

"No Christina, I will slide the horse. You sit down please, at least until we have the leg out," countered Alice.

They all hunkered around the piano, and without any trouble at all soon had the leg off and with the piano balanced squarely on the horse, they turned their attention to the leg.

"Freddie son, go and get Mary and Norman will yo' please? They have disappeared and they may as well be in on all this excitement too. Now what, Christina?"

"George, you can see the brass location peg on the top of the leg. There are two heavy screws holding the mounting plate to the top of it." As an aside she muttered that that is what her father called it.

"Yes Ma'am."

"Can you remove the screws please?" They were removed without any trouble.

"Do I remove the plate now Mrs. Schmidt?" said George.

"Thank you George."

She then to everyone's amazement got down on her hands and knees and after taking a handkerchief out of her hand bag, unfolded it on the carpet.

"Now George will you be so kind as to gently tilt the leg but as near as possible to it, over the handkerchief." He knelt down and she cupped her hand and, as he tilted the leg further, a dozen enormous diamonds rolled out onto the handkerchief. A gasp went up from everyone. She sat back and looked around at everyone with tears streaming down her face. Ilse, who was kneeling beside her, put her arms around her and silently sobbed uncontrollably.

"Ah'll take mah leave now Mr. Ted," George said.

"Son yo' can stay if yo' like."

"Thank yo' sir, Ah will."

Ted said that he had no idea what diamonds were worth, but that lot could be worth a king's ransom! Everyone muttered agreement. They were enormous stones. Christina gathered them up in the handkerchief and handed it to Ted who put it on top of the piano.

Alice was as stunned as the others, but had to turn away, it was almost too much. Suddenly she heard Christina's voice say,

"There is more!"

Ted muttered, as much to himself as anyone else, "How could there be more?"

"Ted, look into the cavity," Christina said without looking herself. She motioned Ilse to have a quick peep. Ted motioned to George to carry it over to the light, and peering in he saw what appeared to be a small scroll of paper.

"Freddie, be a good fella and go to the study and in the rack on mah desk is a long pair of veterinary tweezers, will yo' fetch them please son?" Turning to the others he said that there appeared to be a letter or a note in the cavity.

Freddie returned and passed the tweezers to his uncle. Ted turned and looking at Ilse said, "Ilse girly, why don't yo' pull them out? It's all to do with yo' when it's all said and done."

Alice sighed to herself. *You dear old fellow. You are always thinking of somebody else.* Ilse pulled it out, and handed it to Ted who in turn handed it to Christina.

"Well, Christina?"

Wiping the tears from her eyes and choking back words that would not come, she eventually managed to compose herself and read. "'To whom it may concern. Will the bearer of this letter please call Mendelson and Green, Attorneys at Law, New York City, U.S.A. Relate the circumstances and offer the code Christina Schmidt.'

"Signed, by my father. All in my father's handwriting." Off she went again.

Ted put his arm around her and asked, "What does all this mean?"

She looked up at him. "Right towards the end of the War, my father told me that we didn't have long to go and the result was a foregone conclusion. Germany would lose. He himself had to fight as it were until the end.

"This whole piano business began back in the 'thirties. He had decided that he should leave something secreted away that may assist some sort of family re-establishment. He said he felt that we were moving towards something and he felt would all end in tears, again he said, German tears. He had always been interested in diamonds. Back in the mid-'thirties he had been speaking to a Dutch Jewish Diamond merchant friend he always dealt with and convinced him that things were going to become very dire for the Jews of Europe and that he should get his family and as many others out and to hopefully America before a flood began.

"This he said took some months, on and off. Eventually his advice was accepted, but the fellow told my father that this would take a lot of dollars which were virtually unprocurable, although he had a lot of diamonds. My father in his position had no trouble in getting American dollars.

"To cut a long story short, my father said that whilst he believed he paid as it were a lot more than the diamonds were worth, they were saving people's lives and that is what he was out to do. He led me to believe that these diamonds were just a token of what they actually represented. I'm not sure what he meant by that.

"He also told me that these stones were a gift and played no part in the diamond dollar transactions that had taken place over the years."

Ted looked around and spotted Mary. "Sorry, Christina. Mary can we have tea all around again please? Yes, Christina?"

"He, my father, was always keen on carpentry, and always one for intrigue felt that the piano would be a good place for the diamonds and the note. He swore me to secrecy. I was not even to tell Ilse for obvious reasons. We had no idea that we would have to move the piano at that time, but that sadly became obvious eventually with every passing day. Why a piano, why not some other hiding place? I honestly don't know. I put it down to my fathers' sense of intrigue, humor, call it what you will."

"I suppose you could say, well, why didn't you remove the leg, the diamonds and the note. It wasn't as simple as that. I couldn't physically remove the leg myself. Even if I could have there were too many people around in the house. As soon as anyone saw that there was focus on a piano leg, the cat would be out of the bag completely. No, it was move the piano entirely or not at all. I had enough trouble finding someone to move it as it was. It was only our standing locally that got it onto the truck in the first place."

"By that time I even suspect the SS were closing in on the family anyway. It was a dreadful period in more ways than one. From the time the piano was packed up and we set off, life became a blur. There were still enough old-fashioned types about who regarded me as an eccentric rich woman who wanted to save a piano for me to carry it off! I had hoped to find a safe place for it far away from the Russians, but it was not to be."

"I suppose what we have to do now is ring the Attorneys and see what eventuates," mused Ted. "Freddie, be a good fella, there is a plug over by the table there by the window, will yo' unplug the phone in the study, bring it in here please, and Jack can make the fateful call. God this is exciting, don't yo' all think?" He rubbed his hands in anticipation. No one disagreed.

The phone was plugged in and Jack was given the number from the exchange and made the call. He afterwards said that it was one of the most memorable he had ever made. The upshot was that the person who took the call put him on to someone who was electrified by it. Christina was put on for a few moments to answer a few questions that only she could answer, and then they asked for Jack to be put back on.

They asked if it would be convenient to call here in two days, and if accommodation could be arranged for two people. They would make a booking to arrive by train, and would ring back when they were confirmed.

"There was one last thing," Jack said, when the visit was confirmed and he had rang off.

"What was that?" asked Ted.

"He said that they say 'Kaddish' for Christina's family!"

"Jesus," said Ted, as the older ones looked quite startled. "That means, fo' yo' young ones, in this context they say a prayer for the dear departed. A prayer of mourning. People very special to them. Yo' cannot get much closer than that." Christina just sat there, quietly sobbing at this latest revelation.

"Ah think we should all have a breath of fresh air for a while until they ring back," said Ted rising, they all agreed. Alice looked at her uncle and inclining her head indicated a quiet word with him next door. The others moved out onto the patio and she and Ted went into the study.

"Unc dear, all this is simply incredible, and how did you know all that about the 'Kaddish?'"

"Oh, Chickie!"

"But," she went on, "it has all come about through me calling the initial meeting and…"

"Ah know, Ah know Chickie. Yo' have stumbled on the fact that Freddie and Ilse are having an assignation!"

"Oh that's what they call them now days, is it dear?"

"Chickie," his eyes beginning to fill with tears, "please believe me when Ah say Ah didn't want to do it, but Gordos made me swear on his deathbed, that at the appropriate time Ah would arrange it for him in a respectable manner."

I might have suspected as much, thought Alice. "What, well, how did you settle on the Schmidts?"

"The young Perry boy was hounding Ilse and she was scared of him, and Christina asked for mah help. Eli packed him off down to Argentina with mah help. We made a pact.

"Ah asked Christina to help, and she was not at all happy but Ah overcame that when Ah told her of mah promise to Gordos, and that he didn't want you to know. That's the honest truth, Chickie," and he began to cry.

"Oh dear, oh dear," she said, "you poor old thing. All that on your shoulders, and now this piano business. Very well, I accept it all in good heart. OK Unc; now give me a kiss. I'll go out to the others and you come out when you are ready."

She had to keep moving and, on top of this, she couldn't let herself go. That New York call should come through shortly. Her head was spinning. It was just the sort of thing Gordos would ask Unc to do, and of course she hadn't helped by telling him about Freddie's unsettled sleep. Dear oh dear, he was always doing the right thing, but the other incredible thing was that it all seemed to be stuff right on the edge.

They were all close to the doors into the big room, and filed back in as Jack picked up the phone. "They can arrive on the noon train the day after tomorrow!" He looked at Ted and Alice.

"Yes, we will meet them!" said Ted.

"We will accommodate them here!" said Alice.

Christina looked a little startled and said "Mrs. Gardiner, you…" She trailed off.

"No Mrs. Schmidt, my uncle and I will be happy to put them up." She nodded to Jack. Jack spoke for a few more minutes, then rang off and sat back.

"He said that the fellow on the other end of the phone advised that there was one other thing he would like to say, and that was they had dealings with a lot of Germans through this dreadful business, and the Schmidt people were acting with more altruism than any others they had encountered. That is something to think about. Well, we'll all be here, late morning the day after tomorrow." Alice looked across at Christina. She was sitting back with Ilse at her knee, silently trembling with tears streaming down her face. *God, what she must have been through,* she thought.

"We can't do too much more today, so thank yo' George, we'll leave the piano as it is for the time being and call yo' when we want to put the leg back on it."

"Thank yo' Mr. Ted." He nodded to everyone and took his leave.

"My my, what a morning. Eric, yo'll stay for lunch?" Ted asked.

"Ted, I feel I should get back to the surgery."

"But Eric, can you come for lunch the day after tomorrow, it may be mah turn to collapse."

"Unc!" said Alice.

"Oh Ah'm sorry, Christina, Ah'm sorry, here Ah am trying to be funny again, Ah didn't mean it."

Eric gave a chuckle and said, "I'll see you all then. Bye ladies, Jack, Freddie. Will you see me off, Ted?"

"Christina," Alice looked at her. "What say we take you home now and tomorrow afternoon both you two and your granddaughter come here for the night?"

"Mrs. Gardiner, I have my car here already."

"Yes of course, I had forgotten, anyway the invitation still stands, that way we can all prepare ourselves for the gentlemen from New York without any rushing around on, what will it be? Thursday."

"Oh Mrs. Gardiner you don't…"

"No, I think that would be the most sensible thing to do," said Alice. "We will prepare two rooms upstairs. We have plenty of room. Don't' you agree, Unc?"

So it was settled.

Chapter 18

After breakfast on the Thursday morning Alice caught Christina's eye and suggested that they have a walk around the garden.

They met the train at the appointed time and drove the two lawyers out to The Lagoon. One, Mr. Solomon, was the head of the firm. The other, Mr. Green, a younger man, was the firm's expert on antiques and precious stones.

After lunch in the dining room they all went next door to the main room, most of them taking chairs with them.

After they were all comfortable Alice announced that it was perhaps time to show the diamonds to the gentlemen. She looked at Christina and Unc who both nodded. "Freddie darling, will you put the coffee table in front of the gentlemen please. Christina, will you do the honors, please?"

Christina picked up her handbag and, walking over to the table, took her handkerchief out placed it on the table and opened it, revealing the diamonds. "They may look a little better if I remove the handkerchief," she muttered, and gently scooped them across to the bare tabletop.

Both men leant forward and studied them intently. Mr. Solomon eventually leant back and looked expectantly at Mr. Green. For his part he was not going to be hurried. He held up a hand momentarily, and continued to sit deep in thought and then slowly arose from his chair, and then just as slowly walked across to the windows and gazed out.

Eventually he turned around, still seriously bent in thought. He moved back to the diamonds and, taking in the whole gathering, announced that this was perhaps as fine a collection of stones that anyone could imagine, let alone actually see.

He had been in the diamond industry most of his life and had never seen anything like this collection. They were in fact Golconda diamonds from India, where these types of diamonds were first discovered. They differ from other diamonds in that they are alluvial. They are the finest category in the world.

"Quite often with anything rare, the whole is worth more than the sum of the parts. This collection is quite different and I honestly don't know what it is worth. Either the whole or the individual stones.

"Without knowing anything about diamonds everyone here would have to acknowledge that they are enormous stones. They are all over five carats, which refers to their weight. They don't have a modern cut. They have what is referred to in the trade as a 'cushion cut.' Without even examining them I can tell that they are flawless.

"With regard to the value, each stone is worth a fortune. Only the wealthiest people could afford even one. To contemplate purchasing the entire collection, even a wealthy institution would be hard pressed to come up with the funds.

"Having said all that, I am pleased to say that since you have contacted us we have been in touch with the person who your father dealt with, Mrs. Schmidt. We have arranged for you to meet him in the near future. I must say he too was electrified at the news that you had survived. Mrs. Schmidt, Ilse, you are most fortunate, indeed. I might add I consider myself most fortunate to have been involved, and to actually view the stones at first hand."

Mr. Solomon chimed in: "On top of all this we have a trust fund for you and your two girls established by some of these people and you are in fact a very wealthy woman, quite apart from these stones. May I suggest that you put the stones in a place of safekeeping, such as a bank or a safe? Collect your thoughts, your options, and I suspect from what I have seen here, you will have the very best advice possible, and will arrive at the correct decision. Again, there is no hurry, take your time."

Well, everyone sat back and just looked at each other. The servants quietly picked up their chairs as they crept out of the room, nodding to Ted and Alice.

Later that day Alice asked her uncle if she could have a chat to him in his study, and she would bring Freddie.

They sat down and she launched straight into the Ilse business. "Freddie, I just want to say two things. What has passed between you and Unc and Ilse, I wish to put to one side. I don't agree at all with what went on behind my back, however I accept the reason why. And as far as I am concerned I don't wish to speak about it again, when we leave this room, OK you two?" She looked quizzically at each of them. "Now come on, Freddie?"

"Yes Mom!"

"Good! Unc?"

"Yes Ali!"

"Right, now if you two think that I have been cross or hurt by what we have just been talking about, it will pale into insignificance if you, Freddie, compromise Lettice. I want your solemn word that you won't become involved with her in that sense, Freddie. I mean it, Freddie. You will ruin her life and yours. It will bring shame on both families, and you may even go to jail."

"Aw Ali!" Unc interjected.

"No Unc, I mean it, and you well know. With our pull we may be able to keep him out of jail, but the shame would be there nevertheless!

"She is the most beautiful girl, and you may not quite realize it just yet but she has eyes for you, and you alone. And dare I say it, these things are wont to happen, and I am not going to allow it to happen in my family. Freddie, it would be the stone end. I mean it!

"Phew, that is all I have to say, now both come and give me a kiss!"

Ted accompanied Christina and Ilse to New York to meet with the man who had dealt with Christina's father. It was a most emotional meeting as you can imagine. They were then advised as to what the trust fund held. It amounted to several hundred thousand dollars. A fortune, in fact.

There seemed to be so much to do. Christina told Ted that she would like to travel to London in an endeavor to contact her English relatives. The law firm suggested that they arrange this and pave the way through their London Associates. They felt that she would only get one last opportunity to do this and it needed to be gone about correctly. Christina accepted this advice.

She discussed all this with Ted of course, and he suggested that he accompany her. They decided to book passage on the Queen Mary two months hence.

Ted suggested to both Christina and Ilse that they must take a long-term view as to what they would like to do with the farm. He went on to say that it should really be kept until such time that the baby could make up her mind as to what she would like to do with it.

Why not lease it? It will appreciate in value, and he had a suspicion as to who may like to lease it with to the view of eventually purchasing it.

"Who would that be, Mr. Ted?"

"The young Perry boy," was the quick reply.

*****

And so it came to pass. Young Perry came back from the Argentine, and even brought a blue-eyed blonde girl with him, who he then married.

All these measures were put into place over the last few frantic weeks. Alice and Freddie went to see Unc and Christina off on the Queen Mary, and had to admit that she wasn't surprised to find that they had two of the very best staterooms available with an interconnecting door.

Oh well, she thought. *They are both old enough and Ilse is there to chaperone. I wonder if this is a new chapter opening or an old one closing.*

She need not have worried. Unc was back at The Lagoon within six weeks. He gave Alice a fond hug in the cabin when they met him, and told her that he was well over any romantic relationships. "But it was fun," he added with a twinkle in his eye. "Ah'm pleased Ah went Ali. Actually her English relatives were extremely welcoming once they got over the initial shock. Particularly her female relatives.

"The head of the family arranged a weekend gathering on his estate. It was really something, you would have enjoyed it.

"He made a speech over dinner which dealt with people's natural inclinations and the more impersonal perceptions, which in their family's case were in fact misconceptions, 'Which I must say,' he went on, 'led to some particularly bitter arguments within the family.'

"His speech went on to say, 'Without raking over it I must say I was one of the strongest proponents for cutting you off, and I have to say I feel ashamed and I apologize to all concerned for taking the most intemperate stand that I did. I really could not be happier that you girls have now returned to the fold. I really feel quite frightful about the whole business.'

"Well, Ali, you can imagine we were all in tears. Christina and Ilse got up and went around to him and they embraced. Ah was wondering what was going to come next, as Ah didn't feel that Ah should say anything.

"Blow me down if another male relative then asked me if Ah would give an account as to how Ah fitted in. How Ah came to have the piano. Actually most of them actually knew the piano. This Ah did. Yo' can imagine when Ah got to the bit about Freddie's rite of passage…"

"You didn't," Alice interjected.

"No, no, o' course Ah didn't. Anyway the whole thing ended up on a happy note. And there, Ah suspect they will stay Ah might add. They still haven't decided what they're going to do with the diamonds."

Chapter 19

Looking back over the years, Freddie and the others always marveled at the timing of their association with Snakesbreath as much as the time they had actually spent and the things they had done with him.

He was the most wonderful mentor, and everything was so unobtrusive. They had no idea really that they were following him by example. They were coming into their most formative years and whilst the lead they took from him was obvious to their parents, the boys only came to be conscious and grateful for the significance of his friendship some years later.

They even in the main followed his professions. Chuck and Billy became doctors, Lofty and Freddie engineers and Ben differed in that he did constitutional law. They all became expert bridge players, as did the girls they married who were all professionals in different fields.

Freddie was the first married and of course he married Lettice his childhood sweetheart. The others married girls they met at University.

Freddie's marriage took place at The Lagoon, and to no one's amazement Lofty was the Best Man. The other three boys were groomsmen. There were about three hundred people in attendance and whilst some of the guests were slightly bemused to see Freddie with a black best man, whose speech quickly made everyone sit up.

After acknowledging what a pleasure it was for him to be standing there he went on to say that he could not have imagined the way his life would change the day that he and his good friend Ben had gone into the woods together.

He then outlined what had taken place, how they had met Freddie, Billy and Chuck and how they had then met Alex. He went on to say that his life had then changed forever, and he could not thank Miss Alice, Mr. Ted and Alex and the boys for the way they had taken him and Ben into their hearts and homes.

To be standing there being able to speak on behalf of the bride's maids and young Louise the flower girl, Lettice's cousin, and convey how much they enjoyed helping Lettice, who he adored, on her big day, gave him so much pleasure.

He went on. "To conclude, I would just like to offer a little saying that came my family's way many years ago.

'Lettice and Freddie may your life together,

Have just sufficient clouds,

As to give your marriage,

A glorious sunset.'

Thank you."

He sat down to a sustained and generous applause. He looked over at his family and he could see their faces glistening with tears and pride.

They were all eventually married over a relatively short time. Whilst Chuck and Billy had their weddings at reception houses, Ben and Lofty had theirs at The Lagoon at Unc and Alice's request. Of course all this close association of the boys carried amazingly through to the girls that they married, and whilst they did not live in each other's pockets they saw each other for a long weekend or holiday at least twice a year.

Freddie and Lofty, however, some years after they had graduated and worked for large engineering firms, decided to go into business together and established what went on to become a successful heavy and civil engineering firm. They specialized in steel work for large buildings and bridges, and hydraulics.

Early on, when they were still establishing the business, they had been sitting having a jaw one day, wondering what else the firm could do, and Lofty suggested to Freddie that he design steel cattle yards, and they could make them. They could have different designs, prefabricate them and even erect them. Why, they could even make cattle crushes.

Freddie thought this to be a brilliant idea. He had already redesigned The Lagoon yards, and whilst they were wooden, they could just as easily have been made out of steel.

"You never cease to amaze me, Fly Boy, that is a brilliant idea."

The idea, before long, when put into practice, came to be a significant part of their business.

In the years between graduating, marrying and growing their various businesses, both Unc and Alex passed away.

Freddie felt the passing of Unc very badly. He, together with Chuck, Unc and Alex and the doctor, who had semi-retired. had attended a meeting one night in White Oak that was convened to discuss what had developed into a contentious issue.

Lettice and Freddie were staying at The Lagoon for a few days.

Unc had said to Freddie that if he would like to drive, they could take the La Salle. Unc and Freddie loved it. Unc had had it from new and looked after it like a new pin. Freddie liked the purring sound it made. It had the smoothest engine sound of any he had heard, and it never let them down, and could not have been more luxurious.

They set off from The Lagoon, and picked up Chuck. Unc said that he would hop in the back and Chuck could sit beside Freddie and the other two who they were picking up shortly could sit either side of him. That way he could arrive in style.

There was quite a crowd at the hall, and of course whilst everyone knew everyone, they weren't necessarily on the same side. In fact, the council seemed to be equally divided. Unc said that they would sit in the front row as he wanted to be near the action. He muttered an aside to Freddie that he would bring on a bit of action himself if he thought it was required.

The meeting got under way.

One of the large national chains was going to build what would be the town's first supermarket, on a large area of land that they had purchased on the edge of town. They had applied to the city fathers for permission to have an extensive car park, and this had been granted. However, it then emerged that to gain access to the site, two trees that were part of an Avenue of Honor to locals who had fought and died in the First World War would have to be removed.

Incredibly, it appeared as though the trees would be removed with no objections, and then one of the councilors mentioned the matter to Unc. Unc had been on the committee which had planned the Avenue initially. He immediately set about having the removals stopped. In this he was supported by the local Legion, and they all attended this meeting.

The outcome was not looking favorable for the retention of the trees. Unc, though, was becoming more strident in his objection to the removals, in spite of moving that the entire plan be realigned. This would give ready access to the loading docks through the car park, and have the actual blank wall of the building along the side where the Avenue was. There was an easement on the other side of the land that was in effect an unmade road; this could readily be sealed and the entrance could be off it. He even tabled the town plan showing the easement.

He also suggested that a lawn be sown along this wall and be established together with shrubs planted to soften the blank wall.

Freddie suspected that whatever people's recollection of the meeting would be, they would center on what came next.

Whatever Unc put forward, the lawyer for the company countered, as glibly as you please, they all agreed afterwards. This, needless to say, riled old Unc no end, until after one such remark, Unc retorted with, "Now yo' listen here young man, Ah used to eat fellas like you, for breakfast in mah day!"

Everyone sat up at this, and you could have heard a pin drop; then the out-of-town lawyer said, taking off Unc's hitherto slow drawl, "Ah can well believe it Suh, an Ah venture to say those good ole boys wouldn't even tetch the sides on the way down!"

Well, Freddie felt sick, and he supposed most people there did also. After a stunned silence of a few moments, he began to feel Unc beside him beginning to quietly giggle under his breath.

The retort coming to anyone thirty years or so younger than Unc would have been seen for what it was. Terribly slick. Coming to Unc it showed a distinct lack of respect for someone of his age let alone standing. His sense of humor then came through.

He eventually erupted into loud but restrained laughter, and congratulated the lawyer on it, summing the whole thing up by saying that he would rest his case. The upshot was that Unc's motion was carried and the whole plan was realigned according to what he suggested.

After the meeting when they were all standing around having a light supper, the young lawyer approached Unc, and apologized for his retort. He said, "You know sir, it was out before I knew it. I suspect I'm a little too used to the cut and thrust of the debates up North. Sometimes to my own detriment. Again, I do apologize."

Unc had looked him squarely up and down and put out his hand. "Well young feller, Ah accept your apology, it's most gracious of yo'. It can't have been easy to come over here and say that. Ah wish yo' well, and Ah suspect yo' will go far, and thank yo'."

Well, a lot of people saw and heard what passed between them, and the whole night finished on a happy note, with no face lost all round. Unc for one could not have been happier.

They had a good laugh about it when they all got back into the La Salle. "That was quite a feisty debate, Ted," Alex said, chuckling away.

"Well yo' can't allow these city lawyers to have their own way all the time. Ah must say though, Ah thought our argument was lost, after mah outburst."

They all laughed again, and Eric said, "Well, he certainly shot himself in the foot with his quick retort. Anyway, all's well that ends well."

The following morning, a Sunday, Alice was woken by a quiet knock on her bedroom door. "Come in," she called. It was Rosie; she entered and just stood there with tears streaming silently down her cheeks. "It's Mr. Ted."

Alice quickly got up and looking at the bedside clock saw that it was just after 6.30. Unc in these latter years had always stuck to his old routine of having a cup of tea brought to him right on 6.30. A feeling of utter grief came over Alice as she gave Rosie's arm a squeeze as she went past her and whispered to her to wake Freddie.

She went in to Unc's room and there he was lying looking perfectly serene, with the most beautiful smile on his face. She bent down to kiss him and he was only slightly cool. He must have gone only a short time ago she thought, *Oh dear oh dear. What a way to go. You beautiful old thing... And now we are two!* She knelt beside the bed.

After Ted had gone Alice decided that it was time to have a family meeting. Over dinner one night, she filled Lettice and Freddie in on how Unc had dealt with the lynching and his subsequent rejection of his grandfather. How she had Unc wrong for years as to his true attitude to blacks and how proud of her he was when she confronted him.

This of course was a most sobering revelation for them both, and led to much discussion and reflection; but as Alice said, now that he was gone and the fact that she could go at any time soon, she would not be doing his memory justice if she didn't tell them.

All these years on, Alex still flatly refused to move into White Oak, and once every week he went in to the Holmeses to have a bath. The only part of the routine that had altered was that he would stay the night and attend to any business the following day. Prior to returning home.

Whilst Eric would ferry him to and fro, sometimes one of the boys would collect him. Late one afternoon Freddie thought that he would take the La Salle for a run and picking up Lofty, who happened to be at his family home, and having let Eric know that he would do the run, they set off.

"Well, we've come this path a few times," he murmured to Lofty, as he carefully negotiated the big car while it purred its way down the narrow track. "I don't think I'll bring Sally again. I don't want to scratch her. I can almost hear Unc having a fit."

"I have to agree," said Lofty, "but Alex likes it so much. I know he appreciates it."

They arrived to find the door of the shack open with his new dog, a miniature fox terrier, which the Holmeses had given him when Savage had died, nowhere in sight. He usually rushed out to meet callers.

They crept in and there on the big armchair was Alex in his good clothes, with his packed bag, on the table but still open. He had the most wonderful expression on his face and had been dead, they thought, for an hour or so. "Towser" the foxy was curled up in the crook of his arm looking up at them, quivering.

On the small table beside him was an unfinished glass of whiskey.

"Well, it's all over, Freddie," Lofty said in a choked voice. They both looked at each other with tears streaming down their cheeks.

"We'll have to tell the doctor," Freddie said. "I'll go, if you stay with him if you like; we can't leave him like this. Look at poor little Towser."

"Can we start the gas mantle before you go? It's nearly dusk, and they can be tricky things if you're not used to them!" Lofty muttered. "Freddie!"

"Yes, what?"

"What a wonderful way to go. Such a sad but fulfilling life, and now it's all over."

"I know," said Freddie. "He deserved to go like this if anyone did!"

Eric told them later that evening that there was a letter at the bank addressed to him and that he would meet them next morning if they could make it.

Whilst it was addressed to Eric, it was also to the boys and was one of the most beautiful letters that they had ever received. In it he outlined how terribly fortunate he had been to meet them that day at the cabin, all those years before. How much they had enriched his life, which up until that time had certainly been full but lacked the something that his friendship with them had brought. He went on to say that Edie's death had hurt him like nothing before. This had amazed him because losing his own family had been traumatic.

He reminisced about the time that he and Unc had taken them to California to see first-hand the Grunion Run. How they drove to Chicago and inspected a consignment of bullocks that Unc had railed there. How he and Unc had a good laugh at Lofty's and Ben's expense when they were too scared to get onto the horses and had to ride behind Unc and Alex when they were taken on a tour of the sale yards. The trip in part to California by train where they spent time in the mail car. It was all such good fun and all seemed a long time ago. All the shooting they did. It went on and on.

He then wound the letter up by telling them that he wished to ask a favor of all of them. Normally, he said, he would leave a nest egg for each of them, but as they had all become successful he felt there was no need to. However, there was quite a bit of money in the bank and some stocks. He nominated them as Trustees of his estate, and set out a plan to establish a scholarship to university for a boy and a girl each year, whom they would choose from his relatives who lived in Florida.

He went into great detail outlining the parameters within which they had to choose the lucky ones, and it also provided the sum to extend for the duration of their individual courses.

Well, they thought, *that is a most generous gift; and it will certainly put us on our mettle.*

Chapter 20

Some eight years after Freddie and Lettice had been married and had had two children—Freddie Jnr. and Winona—Lettice's aunt contacted her and asked her if Louise could stay with them for a while as she needed straightening out. She adored both Freddie and Lettice, but her mother was concerned that she had become quite aimless. She just might take some notice of them. She was eighteen.

She said in fact that Louise seemed to be going the way of too many of these young girls who whilst quite beautiful were inclined to becoming simpering and fawnlike, working on the presumption that their beauty would take care of everything. She was hoping that between them they could give her a bit of direction. She had extremely good grades at school and would have no trouble getting into university, but was not remotely interested.

Whilst they didn't promise anything, they agreed to have her to stay for as long as it took.

Louise fitted in quite well and was a great help with the young children and, wonder of wonders, due to Lettice's strategy of leading by example and not direction they managed to convey to her that it would be a great help to her if she were to do a course that would lead to her financial independence, come what may, as one never knew what was around the corner.

The upshot of this was that she went off and studied pharmacy, and did very well.

It was some years later, when the engineering business was really humming, and they were all having one of their annual get-togethers over Thanksgiving, that Freddie announced or put a proposition to Chuck, Billy and Ben and their wives.

"Lofty and I and the girls have been thinking of buying a plot of land up at Squaw Lake about a hundred miles from here. We were thinking that we build three cabins and a main house, and we can all use it whenever we get the chance.

"I saw a small five-acre lot up for sale recently and have taken the offer on it, in the expectation that you will all say yes. I know it will be a bit cramped, all of us being on five acres, as we don't get along at all well! It is surrounded by forest, which gives us plenty more space, its right on the lake, and I know that whilst none of us like trout fishing the lake is full of them! I just thought I'd throw that in."

The others all looked at each other, grinning from ear to ear. Ben looked at the others and said, "Well you know the trout business has no attraction, Haw Haw!" Next to bridge it was the main pastime for all the boys. "So why don't we all go and check it out A.S.A.P."

One way or other someone from each family should be able to get away, for a day or so. Lofty asked Judy if she knew a reputable architect, who could put something on paper for them. Chuck said that he supposed there was no electricity up there, and Lofty said, "No, but we can have a generator; one big enough to power the four buildings, and then some.

"The other thing about it is that it is quite remote. The closest place is a mile or so down the lake and has a similar compound arrangement. We don't have to have anything to do with them. We can keep completely to ourselves."

They eventually built three cabins, each with three bedrooms, a main house with four bedrooms and servants' quarters, laundry and storeroom. Freddie and Lofty had the big house which they referred to as the Lodge and the others each had a cabin.

They had a shed which housed a large 20KVA generator, a small 6KVA as a backup which was portable and kept in a large cupboard, together with canoes, two yachts, boats, different games and a ride on lawn mower. It even had a gun rack with all their guns. They had a stove in each cabin which was powered by bottled gas. They kept their fishing rods in their respective cabins.

The area that they bought was in fact cleared with just the odd conifer. The land ran down to the water and in time they built a small jetty for the boats. The cleared area was well grassed and the compound was used about once a month. The lawn was well kept and the whole complex looked an absolute picture.

They had been going to the Lodge for some fifteen years and always made it a point of spending Thanksgiving there. It happened to coincide with Freddie's fiftieth birthday.

Some two months prior to the date, Lettice rang Lofty.

"Hi Fly Boy," she called him.

He chuckled. "Now I wonder who that is."

She had always called him Fly Boy. "Is there any chance of meeting you in the next day or so?"

"Yes of course. I'll pick you up if you like. What say tomorrow?"

"No, I want to buy Freddie a nice something for his birthday, and I'd like your opinion on it, and it has to be a secret. I'll give you the address. It's in the city and easy to get to with good parking."

They met at an antique shop. Lettice had seen it a few days previously, put a deposit on it and asked for it to be held for a week. It was a split cane fishing rod, a trout rod, and was in a box with a brass plate on it: T. R. Roosevelt.

"What do you think, Fly Boy?"

"Oooh Lettie. I think he will be thrilled, let's open the case." There it was, almost in mint condition. There was also a paper in with it, that set down the provenance, which Lettice had read.

"It was the real McCoy alright," she said.

"Would he use it, do you think?"

"I don't know, it really is a collector's item. He may practice casting with it on the lawn but you have two things coming into play. The actual line itself which is terribly old and the runners. The binding on the runners would probably give out, and any failure of one or each of them would compromise the mint condition that it now enjoys."

"I see what you mean Fly Boy, darling, that's just what I wanted from you. She went on. What do you know about reels, is it a good one?"

"Well, in the context of the whole thing, it really doesn't matter. It once belonged to Teddy Roosevelt, but let's have a look." He took it out of the case. "Look here. It's a Hardy St. George."

"Now, I don't know a lot about reels, but I have certainly heard of the Hardy. They are English and were the very best in their day. The St. George, I don't know of, but if Teddy had one you can bet your sox that it would be a good one. Look Lettie, I don't think you can go wrong. He will be over the moon. It will be a simple matter finding out more about it by taking it to a specialist fishing shop, once he has it."

"Now, Fly Boy, one more thing." He looked up at her. "Would you mind taking it home with you and taking it up to the Lodge? I don't want him to see it. When we are up at the Lodge I will wrap it and put the card in it. OK?"

With that she paid for it and they walked out of the shop, up the street and kissed each other goodbye.

Later that day Freddie rang Lofty to say that Lettie had been run over and killed as she was crossing the street.

They had the birthday that Thanksgiving at the Lodge as it was planned. Lofty felt in a spot as to how to tackle giving the present to Freddie, in the context that it was in his possession. How does he explain that if they hadn't met that day in particular, Lettie would still be alive, as she had been killed as it happened some five minutes after they had said goodbye?

He and Sue Ellen, his wife, decided to consult Alice. Alice being perhaps the most common sense person that they knew, said she could understand their concern, but if you look at with the view that you were not going to give it to him this birthday, it would be no easier to do so at some time in the future.

"Then again, why not think about giving it to him privately, Lofty, with no one else about? You and he can talk it right through, you can tell him how and why you happen to have it, and you can both have a good cry.

"Why don't you take it to the Lodge, let the birthday pass and then at a later date, perhaps just before the Thanksgiving weekend, give it to him then. That way, he can have it there, and he can show it to all of you, with the story behind it."

"And then we'll all have a good cry," said Sue Ellen.

"I suppose so," said Alice. "Whatever we do it is never going to be the same, and the fact that her present to Freddie arrived after her death will just lend another dimension. Now I'll quite understand if you don't wish to have me for the few days."

"No no," they said. "We've booked you and Winnie in."

Chapter 21

When Lettice died, the whole family descended on Freddie, including Louise, who by this time was nearing her mid-thirties, an absolutely beautiful girl who hadn't found the right man. Freddie's home was in the city where the business was. Alice still lived at The Lagoon with her grandson Freddie Jnr. Both he and Winona had returned to their respective homes and Freddie was left with Lettice's mother Susan, Alice and Louise.

Needless to say they were still in a state of shock and nothing the three women could do seemed to shake Freddie out of the loss. The two older women, whilst thinking that Louise was trying to get too close to Freddie, were too bereft to say anything to her but at the same time could see that she was doing everything in her power to jolly them all along without being too obvious. And of course she had always adored Freddie.

She was doing all the cleaning, shopping and organizing all the meals although they had a live-in maid. She was in fact running the household.

As usual Freddie excused himself early one evening and after giving them all a still teary goodnight, went off to bed.

Later on Louise, who could contain herself no longer, crept down the passage to Freddie's room and slid into his bed, having slipped out of her nightie. Ever so gently she moved over to him and cautiously lay beside him touching, running her hand gently up his flank. She moved up ever so quietly and presented a breast to his lips which he accepted eagerly, although as if still in a drugged sleep.

She felt him harden against her, and throwing caution to the wind, straddled him and enveloped him. She eventually eased out of the bed, and slipping back into the nightie, made her way back to her room.

He didn't ever say anything to her about that encounter although he had given her an extra squeeze the following morning and seemed to accept her presence more.

His mother and mother-in-law left him some ten days later but not before they had found a nice apartment for Louise to live, although not far away.

About two months prior to the anniversary of Lettice's death they were all having dinner at Chuck's home one night to discuss the weekend at the lake, and Lofty was late. They waited as long as they could when he rang to say that he was not far away, but to start dinner before him, if it would help.

A quarter of an hour later in he walked, with his face almost beaten to a pulp. Freddie, Chuck and Billy almost barged Sue Ellen out of the way, getting to him, as they all asked what had happened.

Sheepishly he told them, over a stiff whiskey, that he had come out of his meeting, and had time on his side and was walking past the Albion hotel, where there happened to be a man and a woman arguing.

Just as he drew up to them the man pushed the woman and she staggered and fell. "She had picked herself up, the man lunged at her again, and I decided to stop him."

"You what?" said Freddie.

"I decided to step in, and look at me."

"For your troubles," said Freddie. "Don't you know you short-assed schlock," the women looked at him in alarm, "you never barge in on an argument like that. You ass."

Monica said, "Now Freddie."

Freddie went on. "Was the doorman there?"

"Yes he was," muttered Lofty.

"Well, you leave something like that to him. Man Mountain!"

"I was only trying to protect her," he lamely went on.

"Well you can't!" said the agitated Freddie.

Chuck went to Lofty's aid. He was only trying to help.

This went on through the whole dinner, with Freddie obviously most concerned at Lofty's injuries. He wouldn't let up.

"Who patched you up?" he asked at one point.

"The hotel staff."

"What did they say?"

"Actually, they said I was an ass too."

"There, what did I say? You never involve yourself in anything like that unless you can dictate the outcome, head them off at the pass or steer them off," he went on.

They were all looking at Freddie with concern, realizing that whilst he had had a terrible fright, he was going on about it too much.

"It's all very well saving a woman who you know, but you never step in like that."

"Well," said Billy, "thank God we have established that, but pray tell us how you would influence events your good self."

"Come on man," said Ben, "we need to know."

It was Freddie's turn to become sheepish.

"Oh, great seer, what wouldst thou do thine self?" asked a piously sounding Ben. They all chuckled.

"To be frank, I don't know. It would depend on the circumstances."

"Come on, mastermind," said Chuck.

"No, no, I just don't know." They all looked at him and grinned. All except Louise who had been sitting and not saying a word, but drinking too much, and suddenly blurted out.

"You would always save me, Freddie, wouldn't you?"

The others rolled their eyes, as Freddie looked crossly at her. "It's time I took you home, my girl. Come on."

"Sorry tough guy, you gave me a terrible shock!" He gave Loft's shoulder a gentle squeeze.

"I know, I know," he responded and gave Freddie a playful punch. "I'll wait until you come along next time." That broke up the party.

Freddie took Louise by the arm, and saying, "Off we go," and rolling his eyes, was met by the odd shake of the head. He took her straight home.

After they had left, Billy, who had the driest sense of humor, said. "Would one say that the pheromones are in the ascent?"

The following day, Louise awoke with a splitting head ache, and lay there thinking of the previous night's happenings and it gradually came back to her that she had disgraced herself and made a complete fool of herself.

She took her time getting up, and having decided what to do, although still slightly befuddled went off and had a light lunch, having made an appointment with her hair stylist.

She arrived on time and sitting down asked him to cut all her hair off.

She had a beautiful head of long golden hair and was very proud of it. When she first started going to the stylist, he asked her if she would have it cut off and sell it to him. This was met with an emphatic no. Every time she went there he asked the same question and it had become their private joke. This time he was stunned, and

269

thinking that she looked a bit the worse for wear, refused. This was to no avail.

She was a stunning looking girl, and, with her hair cut in a short poodle cut, looked even more delectable if that was at all possible.

After leaving the incredulous hair stylist she made her way to Sandra and Chuck's place where she knew there was a lunch party with two tables of bridge, just about to start.

Knocking on the door she was greeted by an incredulous Sandra, who she apologized to and asked if she could have a quick chat to her in the study.

Sandra led her off to the privacy of the study, after excusing herself from the others and beckoning to Monica, Billy's wife. Thinking to herself that whilst she knew why Louise was so het up, she felt that to go off and make such a statement by having her beautiful tresses cut off was only exacerbating the whole business.

Louise took quite a bit of settling down and seemed most concerned that she may have compromised herself with Freddie. It took all of their persuasive powers to settle her on all counts, but Sandra did convey to her that she may be moving a little too fast with Freddie.

"People take time to come to terms with a loved one's death, and it is better to let these things take their course. In the fullness of time, perhaps, but just let him work through it without any pressure."

Monica said, "He is a very attractive man, and you are a beautiful woman, but you have to ease back a little. I really can't express it any other way. Lettice's death has been a great shock for all of us. For Freddie, it could not have been worse; they had been childhood sweethearts. He just needs time."

Sandra went on. "Amongst other things she was so much looking forward to hopefully becoming a grandmother, and of course that would never come to

270

pass for them to share. You just have to slow up, darling. Now I don't wish to go on about it, but you shouldn't have cut your hair! It makes a mountain out of a molehill. Next thing someone will be asking you where your hair shirt is."

She looked at Louise, whose face had fallen even further.

"Come on dearie, It's not the end of the world," and gave her a hug.

Chapter 22

They were all getting excited about having a few days up at the Lodge, on the anniversary of Lettice's death, which coincided with Thanksgiving. When Ben arrived home one night he found Judy with the drinks ready as usual. She said to him, "You would never believe what Conchitta asked me today."

"I'd have no idea," he rejoined.

"She asked me if you wore pantyhose over your panties or under the panties."

"I wouldn't have thought she wore them!"

"She doesn't, she was just wondering!"

"Crazy Mexican," said Ben grinning.

"Oh no she's not a Mexican!"

"What do you mean she's not a Mexican? What is she?"

"I don't really know."

"What do you mean you don't really know?"

"Well, I don't. I think she said she comes from Colombia."

"Haven't you seen her papers, her Green Card?"

"No, I didn't think!"

He began stomping about the room. "Give me strength, how do we come to have her, and her husband I might add?"

"She was recommended by one of the girls at the readers' group!"

"I can't believe this. If this gets out my reputation will be shot. I'm number two in the administrations department which handles, amongst other things, Illegal Immigrants. I would even lose my job, to say nothing of what it would cost the Administration.

"This is appalling; don't you ever think. Are we living in some kind of dream world? Almost every other night on television there is some tale or other about illegal immigrants, and here am I almost the top dog with two of them living under my roof. I can't believe it!"

She was ashen. "Darling, I'm sorry, I just didn't think. It simply didn't enter my head."

"It certainly did not; anyway, they will have to go!"

"Oh Ben, can't you do something? We have had them for eight months or so, and they are wonderful!"

"I know, I know, but that's it, they go!"

"Can't we keep them until after the weekend at the Lodge, and you never know something may crop up, please Benny, please. They are the only ones any of us have had who fit in so well, and it's only another two weeks or so. Please? We are going to have everyone there and Winona is also coming too."

Freddie and Lofty set off in two cars three days before the big weekend with Conchitta and Manuel, to prepare for the influx. Ben had relented on the deportation, but "Only until the weekend is over," as he put it.

Conchitta was airing all the cottages and the Lodge and Freddie and Lofty decided to go fishing right in front of the Lodge. They had sat up all night looking at the Roosevelt rod and reel again. Needless to say Freddie was moved to tears when Lofty gave it to him on one occasion when just the two of them were at the Lodge, and the others could not have been more impressed with it. It really was a collector's item.

They had taken the bulk of the food with them. Two legs of pork to have on the Friday night. Also two turkeys and a leg of ham for Thanksgiving. Plus all the vegetables. All this was put into the refrigerators.

The day was perfect and Freddie had prepared his fishing gear and was putting on his waders when Lofty said that he would take a few photos of Freddie first from water level. He also had his waders on which were too big for him, and as Freddie used to tease him he looked like "Puss in Boots." Manuel was mowing the lawn on the magnificent new ride-on mower they had recently purchased, both he and Conchitta completely oblivious to the fact they were on borrowed time.

The two walked halfway down the jetty and, sitting down on the edge, gingerly lowered themselves in to the water, which came to Freddie's waist and Lofty's chest, in fact almost lapping the top of the waders.

They walked slowly away from the jetty and at right angles to it with Freddie casting a fly out towards the open water. After several casts he had a strike and began to play it, much to Lofty's delight, who was madly taking pictures trying to get a good shot of the rod bending; and bending it was.

He moved further out. "It feels pretty big, Fly Boy," he called back.

"It certainly looks a big one," called Lofty, and suddenly disappeared.

Manuel was coming back down the lawn and saw the whole thing happen. He was not far from the bank and without pausing knew he would have to act fast. Screaming, "Señor Freddie, Señor Freddie," he leapt from the mower having cut the gas, and ran for the jetty, screaming out to Freddie all the while.

The mower stopped short of the water's edge, by which time Manuel was halfway down the jetty still screaming, and praying he had marked the spot where Lofty was in his mind's eye.

He launched himself off and swam the few strokes to where he thought Lofty was.

He was right on and lifted him up, to find him still struggling but nearly all in.

Freddie turning around took the whole scene in and flinging the rod away, waded as fast as he could back to Manuel who by this time was holding Lofty's head out of the water, but could do little more. Together they got him back to the jetty where they were able to bring him around. Manuel rushed up to the Lodge to get a blanket, as Freddie pulled the waders off the gradually recovering Lofty.

Lofty looked up at them, and asked them what had happened.

"You must have stepped in a hole," said Freddie, "and Manuel fortunately saw you and dived in, and the rest is history."

Lofty, still getting his breath back, waited until Manuel returned, when Freddie repeated the story again.

Manuel smiled down at Lofty. "Si, señor Lofty!"

"Oh Manuel, oh dear, thank you, thank you." He muttered listlessly. "What else can I say?"

"Nothing, Lofty," muttered the shaken Freddie. "God, you have been in the wars of late."

"What do you mean?"

"Oh, you know!" he responded.

They decided not to tell the others about the episode until they arrived in a couple of days' time, although that night the four of them had dinner together, and they all toasted a blushing Manuel.

Freddie realized Lofty was back to his old tricks when at one stage he asked a momentarily stunned Manuel, with a straight face, what he had done with the camera?

Needless to say when it all came out, Judy looked across at Ben who grinned and winked at her, giving her a thumbs up. No one else noticed the exchange, although to Judy's delight Ben called Conchitta and Manuel in and proposed a toast "To Manuel!"

Chapter 23

In another place and another time…

For half an hour after the emissaries from the Mob had left, they sat around quietly sipping their beers. All except Lincoln, who preferred red. They had been approached because they were black, and had no affiliation whatsoever with anyone connected, even remotely, with the Mob. Lincoln looked up as Emmy came into the room with an enormous platter full of chicken fritters which was their favorite. She put the platter on the small table in front of them, and good-naturedly slapped Fude's hand as he leant forward to take the first one in his enormous fingers.

They were all pretty comfortable with one another, all being around their late forties, and they had been at it for years, some having been raised in Harlem, had done it tough. The thing that never ceased to amaze them, however, was that in all these years they had only had the odd brush with the law, and whilst they had been in a few bad scrapes; were all still intact, even though they had taken out a few along the way.

In the scheme of things they were not very high up in the pecking order, even in the Black Underworld, but they had a reputation as true professionals, whatever they undertook to do. Whatever contract they accepted, it was carried out to the letter, with a minimum of fuss, and right on the money with nothing ever being traced back to the client.

"Well man, wud yew think?" said Emmy in her slow drawl, as she snuggled up to Lincoln.

"Ah think Doll, that our reputation has got out."

"So do Ah, man," drawled Fude as he reached across the fourth in the group for a fritter, passing one each to Jethro, and Alby.

They all looked at Lincoln, who was the undisputed leader of the group; he was also the eldest, being nearly fifty.

"Seems too good to be true on the face of it," he responded to the unasked question.

"There must be a catch. Let's spread the map out and have a look at the lie of de land. Man, Ah haven't looked at a map since 'Nam."

They all grunted assent. Fude put the platter beside himself on the couch, and the others rolled their eyes.

Emmy said, "Don't worry guys, Ah got mo' where dis' came from."

"Where is it again?" said Fude.

"About three hundred miles from here," said Alby.

"In hilly, wooded country, wi' plenty of lakes apparently," said Lincoln.

"What does it set out exactly?" he leant forward to the map; by now spread on the table. "Here, they have marked it in red."

They had been contacted by an intermediary two weeks ago to see if they would kidnap the young son of a rival mobster, who was trying to muscle in on the territory of the Mob that had approached them. They knew that with kidnapping being a capital offence the contract would have to be exceptionally high, but as it was being kept within the "family," as it were, they were on reasonably safe ground. The snatch was to be carried out at the country retreat of this mobster who had a compound of five houses on an estate that was isolated on one hand and not common knowledge on the other. Even to the extent that it was not even heavily protected, according to their prospective employer.

The upshot of all this was that they carried out a comprehensive reconnoiter of the whole area over the following ten days. And their conclusion was that they could give an undertaking that they would accept the contract, subject to a payment of $40,000 upfront, with a further $160,000, upon the successful completion of the operation, which would be deposited into their account. This was accepted by the client.

It goes without saying that the prime objective of the exercise that they had entered into really only required them to get the target out and into the custody of the client. Whatever went on with the "collateral damage" was not an issue. If required, the whole family could, in theory, be taken out! This, of course, to the "A" Team, put them into the category of abductors which curiously gave them a greater degree of comfort. Three days before the deadline was up, they contacted the client and the money was deposited into their account the following morning.

Emmy was "de book keeper!" As she never forgot to remind them. "Ah'm de wizard, de financial wizard." She stood up and leaning down picked up the empty platter, saying that she would bring some more. As she went out, her mind took her back, as it had numerous times before, to the night she had first met them, the night that had changed her life forever.

Emmy was a "High yella" from Baton Rouge. She had arrived in Harlem after leaving the South following a miscarriage of justice that ruined any respect that she may previously held for City Hall. She arrived with a degree in Business Administration and had been the P.A. to a high-flying merchant banker. He had developed a penchant for other people's money, which he embezzled by the pirogue load and he also implicated her in it to save his own skin. He was a cracker who, with her, was having his cake and eating it. She was being led by the nose and as is often the case didn't realize it. She was well and truly roped in and by the time she did realize it, she finished up going to the State Pen., for four years for embezzlement.

Some believed her, of course, some didn't; either way she was tainted, finished, out. Of course the "Establishment Man of the Moment" went off without even being arraigned. Consequently, she in turn lost any respect she had had for the business community in general and the judicial system in particular, to say nothing of the Establishment. She decided that a change of scenery was needed, together with a life of crime, if life took her that way. If they were going to try and crucify her for something she did not do, next time they tried anything on her, it would be for something she had done! All this had been twenty years ago.

She had been in town three days and was sitting in a bar, taking in the scenery. The unfamiliar smells, the people going about their business. People enjoying themselves. All too long denied her. The things she ached for. God, she felt lonely. Although she had to admit she was enjoying the freedom from the claustrophobia of prison life. The two-day bus trip north had been quite grueling. She had found a hotel which she knew was a flea house, but had been happy to sleep for hours on end, and eat only when she needed to. Today she had stood for what seemed like hours under the shower and washed away all the pain of the last few years, or so it seemed.

She wandered down to some exclusive boutiques, and gradually put together a small wardrobe of the things she had been dreaming about. She checked out, taking the only thing from her past that meant anything to her: her Louis Vuitton shoulder bag. She had only ever had three, and had purchased this one just a month prior to being charged. Handing it over to the Prison Authorities when she went inside had more of an effect on her than the actual clanging of the cell door. She was admiring it when the barman slipped her a note, saying that it came from the table with four dudes sitting over in the corner. The note was quite innocuous, inviting her over for a drink, and hopefully for dinner.

She thought, *Well, here we go again*; mindful as she always was that she was as striking a woman as most folks had ever seen, be they either black or white, men or women. She slowly turned around and surveyed them. The first impression she had to admit was good. They were all very big men; they looked cheerfully at her but with none of the usual leers that could accompany approaches of this kind. She thought to herself that there was strength in numbers with the bar being full, and still sipping her drink, she slid off the stool and slowly crossed the room towards them, thinking all the while that if she didn't feel comfortable, she could always retreat back to the bar.

One of them, the one who she suspected sent the note, stood up as she approached and swung a fifth chair over from a nearby table. He introduced himself as Lincoln and the others as Alby, Jethro and Fude. A funny name, she thought, but didn't feel confident enough to enquire of its origins.

As they sat down together, he said, "Well, Missy, what brings you to town, and may we have the pleasure of knowing who we have the pleasure of the company of?"

She noticed that two of the others gave just the slightest change in their facial expressions which indicated that they weren't used to this kind of palaver from Lincoln, and she thought that he really was putting on the dog, he's out to impress. Well, why not?

"Ah'm Emmy Lou from some place South. As for why Ah'm here, are y'all really interested?"

"We sure are, Honey," said Fude, who up until then had not moved a muscle. She thought, *There's more to this cat than meets the eye.* She gazed around the group. She looked at each one of them intently as she took a long sip of her drink. *Well, why not?* she thought. It was probably of no real interest to them, they were just killing time, and any way she had done her time. She also wondered if any of them had done a stretch. She suspected not, as they didn't have "that" look about them. Unless they had done it in the "style" that she had. But of course that was another story.

Well, why not? "Well," she said, "Ah've been in the State Pen. for the past four years." They didn't bat an eyelid, but she noticed they pursed their lips without a glance running between them.

Lincoln asked, "Wo fo', Honey?"

"Embezzlement!" she responded. "And do you know what, Ah didn't do it."

"No, no, o' course yo' didn't do it, honey. De pens are jes' bulging wi' folks who didn't do it. Ain't that right, guys?" He gave a chuckle. They all gave good-natured laughs.

Alby said, "Ah thank yo' is jes' putting us on, Honey, Ah thanks yo' is one o' dem comedienne frails from de South." Whilst she didn't take too kindly to all this she knew she had to rise to the occasion and went on.

"But!"

"Oh, dere are buts are dere, Honey?" said Lincoln, grinning from ear to ear.

282

"Sure are," she rejoined, gaining confidence. "If Ah go down again, it will be for something Ah done, no' fo' what someone else done."

"Oooh it's like dat is it honey, yo' thank that may ever come to pass?"

"Time will tell, time will tell," she said. They all laughed.

She then asked them what line of business they were in. They murmured amongst themselves without any sign of concern, but said that they really couldn't put a name to it.

"Ah s'pose yo' could say that we're kind of facilitators. Yeah baby, that's what we are – facilitators." Lincoln eventually responded.

"Oh," she said. "Wha' kind o' things yo' facilitate?"

They pondered for a moment, and Jethro said. "Jest about anything Honey, jest about anything."

"Fo' a fee, o' course," said Alby.

"Oh o' course," she said.

They sipped their drinks for a while, in what she became aware of, was a comfortable silence. As though she had been one of the group for years.

Suddenly, but languidly, Fude announced that he was hungry. The others chuckled. Alby said that he was bein' polite tonight. He usually said ravenous, or even just food, and actually he didn't know how he had taken so long to mention it. She looked at Fude, and smiled.

"Well don' Ah know that? Such a fine strappin' fella."

Fude's face lit up. "Ah's come from a family o' big men, so Ah's know they need a lot to keep 'em jes' tickin' over." So from then on she had Fude, who sat there and simply preened.

"Where to, Fude?" said Jethro, "dat German place around de corner where they has de 'favorite fruit?'"

"Can Ah ask Missy wha' her favorite is, and what she missed most in prison?" said Lincoln, ever the diplomat.

"Why dat's easy," she said. "Chinese."

"Ah declare," said Lincoln. "I feel a Chinese comin' on. It's mah favorite too!"

She barely detected the expressions that passed between the others. But it was code for you fellas have German, Ah'll have Chinese.

"Wha' say we," said Lincoln, "meet back here in an hour an' a half, af'er we've all had our favorites? De Chinese is jes' up from de German, and dat way, evra one'll be satisfied."

"Dat's jes' what Ah was thinking," said Jethro. "De three of us will jes' go an' hog down on de German. An' you two can have a nice delicate Chinee." He stood up and gave Lincoln a friendly slap on the shoulder, and said, "C'mon le's go, de sooner we go, de sooner we git back."

Lincoln stood up, and looked down at Emmy who hadn't had any input into the discussion whatsoever. She was in good humor, but felt she couldn't let him get away with it so easily.

"Y'all thank Ah'll be safe?" she asked with a disarming smile on her face, putting on her deepest drawl. They all looked at her, as if they had taken it for granted.

"How can yo' say such a thang, honey?" said Fude. "Y'all be jes fine. But don' let 'im eat too much Sezuan powak!"

Lincoln walked to the bar to pay for the drinks, and told the barman to keep an eye on her bag which he effortlessly picked up and handed across. Without a backwards glance at the others, he took her gently by the arm, and guided her through the bar and out onto the street. It was mild and quite pleasant being outside after being inside for over an hour. As they walked, he leant down and told her that the best Chinese in town was about five minutes away.

"Ah hope Ah'm not givin' you the rush, honey!" Well she thought. He couldn't have been much faster but she had a nice confident feel about the whole thing. About all of them, and about him in particular. She just looked up at him and smiled. She suspected that it was her earlier frank admission that she had been in the pen that had intangibly, somehow or other, put her into their camp. It had put the seal of approval on her. What their "camp" was, she felt, would be revealed in the fullness of time.

Chapter 24

They walked for a few minutes through the early evening throng, and before she knew it was being ushered through the door of the restaurant. The one thing she had been acutely conscious of and had trouble resisting was that once or twice she unconsciously found herself just about to put her arm through his. She couldn't believe it. It was years since she had felt this way about anyone.

The restaurant was called the "Lotus Flower," and it had an atmosphere of opulence even before the door opened. It was, she felt, almost another time when she had last been in a place like this, and whilst she was not at all intimidated by it, in fact she felt quite comfortable, she felt it quite uplifting and showed her appreciation by giving Lincoln's arm a good squeeze, and a look of pleasure. Lincoln appeared to be a regular patron, as she noticed several waiters nodded soberly, discreetly to him as they were led to a table in a quiet corner of the room. She also noted that the waiter who escorted them, deferred to her in a way that indicated his approval.

The dinner passed in a daze. She honestly couldn't remember what she had had to eat when she was lying awake in bed later that night. They had chatted about all sorts of things, and she was conscious of the fact that he did most of the talking, or questioning; but it was only after he had made mention of the fact that she appeared to be without anywhere to stay that night, that she really began to focus again. Prior to that, she had virtually no recollection. Of course she didn't, in fact it had slipped her memory completely since the note came. She thought that she should be a little communicative on that score and agreed that she hadn't, and did he have any suggestions, at the same time thinking that she would really have to be on her guard in this respect.

He responded that there was a nice looking boutique hotel a few yards back the other way, and beyond the "bar," and that they could check it out on the way back. He had never been inside it himself, but the folks that patronized the place looked to be sharp.

She began to open her bag, and pulling out a mirror, checking herself said, "Well, le's go man!"

Lincoln looked around for the waiter and settled the bill, and before she knew it they were out on the street again, as she thought, hoofin' it back.

Again her natural reticence began to assail her, but "In for a penny, in for a pound," she found herself saying to herself. She honestly couldn't be feeling more comfortable. Whilst her mind was racing she tried to rationalize the situation. She had longed for an experience such as this, a meeting like this, through all the long years in prison, which to her had been, she often confessed to herself, not too bad at all. To the extent that she quite understood how folks become quite institutionalized; and few could have done it in the style that she had. For all that, she was only just keeping on top of proceedings the way they were developing, and it frightened her a little.

What had happened? She went over it again. She had been sitting in a bar, looking delectable, well she couldn't help that. Suddenly the barman had slipped her a note from four dudes inviting her for a drink. The reality, as she was well aware, was that it would have been even more amazing if she could have sat there for much longer without an approach of some sort being made, even if it had been the barman.

The fact that the most attractive one to her seemed to have a mutual attraction for her wasn't verging on warranting a case study into the mating habits o' homo sapiens. So what was all the fuss about? No, she would just have to relax. She would go with the flow. The fact that she had "Twinkle" discreetly taped in "his sheath" upside down inside her left thigh, certainly gave her an added sense of security.

Her Russian friend had given her the name of the knife master craftsman, who made Twinkle. He was her first call after she had been released from prison. The knife was six inches long overall, and a masterpiece. The blade and handle were made from one piece of the finest steel, and the blade was sharp for only the first two inches. It was modelled on a throwing knife, and the sheath was made from the finest leather.

After two days of wearing the knife she found that she had become accustomed to it, and was not at all self-conscious. In fact, she had almost forgotten about it on several occasions through the evening. The only problem with this was that you had to be wearing a skirt, if you wished to be able to pull the knife out quickly, and tonight she was. When she had first inspected it, she commented on the configuration and he said that if ever it had to be used, she could only expect to get one, perhaps two if she was lucky, thrusts with it, and there was no need for a good heavy handle. Surprise was going to carry the day, and surprise meant concealment. Hopefully you will never have to use it, but it will certainly give you a measure of security. She hoped that tonight of all nights she would not have to use it. He was too nice, but one never knew. You never can tell.

The Russian girl had told her that the knife smith would look after her, with a slight raising of the eyebrows. Whilst she understood and was prepared to play the game she was hoping that he was not some grotesque little creature reeking of cigarettes and drink.

Actually to her surprise he was quite a looker, in his mid-forties she suspected, with a shock of unruly blonde hair. She detected a look of undisguised approval from him when she walked into the shop and told him that the Russian had sent her. She eventually had to ask him what the price was for the one he selected. He said that there would be no fee at all for it, if he could put the "Closed" sign up in the doorway right now, and then again in the morning when she came back to collect it as he had some adjustment to do on the sheath.

She stepped back saying that she would put the sign up herself, quickly thinking that this couldn't be a better way to break the drought. What had it been? Four years? She didn't count the pen. She walked out some twenty minutes later, quite looking forward to collecting the knife next morning, and what would be an athletic start to the day.

In no time at all or so it seemed, they arrived at the hotel, and it was all she was hoping it would be. Small, exclusive, up-market. There were a few people at the desk and in the lobby, and the two of them blended in without any trouble. Lincoln went up to the desk, and after waiting his turn asked if the lady could inspect a room on about the fourth floor. He also muttered something else which she didn't quite catch. A moment or so later a bellhop appeared and invited them to follow him. Lincoln declined, saying that he would wait. Emmy went into the lift with the bellhop, and was whisked away to the fourth floor. She returned a few minutes later to find Lincoln sitting in an armchair flipping through a magazine.

"Wha' yo' think, honey?" he asked, bounding out of it.

"Well, it's very nice but Ah'd hate to think what it would cost."

"Don' yo' worry yo' pretty li'l head about that." He went over to the desk and catching the clerk's attention, said that they would take it, and the lady would be back within the hour.

The next thing they were out on the street again, and she found that things were getting a little beyond her and she would simply have to make some sort of a stand. She stopped dead in her tracks. He continued for about four or five strides before he became aware that he was chatting away to himself. He stopped, looked down, and around, and saw her standing there with her head slightly inclined. He walked back.

"Why honey!" he exclaimed. "Wa sa matta?"

She looked up at him. "Lincoln man, Ah's have to be frank wi' yo', man." She had come to the conclusion that she had to be straight and up front. He wasn't the one to be hoodwinked or pussyfooted around with, for all his apparent bonhomie.

"Man, Ah's gettin' outa mah depth. Ah's quite frankly losin' de plot, in fact man, Ah's becoming scared, Ah really am. Man, yo' talk about givin' me de rush. Man, yo's just takin' me up an', well man, Ah don' know rightly how to put it. Man, yo's steam-rollin me. Man, we'z only known each other for about five minutes. An' man, while it's great, Ah think yo' should slow down a li'l."

He looked at her closely. "Aw Emmy, Ah'm sorry, honey lamb, yo' quite right. Ah suppose effin Ah'm frank wi yo'.' Ah've never passed this way afore. An Ah'm a li'l outa mah depth too. Ah'v never met anyone like yo' afore, an Ah, Ah suppose Ah'm a li'l excited.

Ah'm sorry, honey!" He bent down and gave her an awkward kiss on the cheek.

"Ah'm about ready to catch de next Greyhound. Yo' wasn't oversteppin' the mark at all. Yo' know, but it was all happenin' too quick."

He stopped and turned to face her. "Ah know, Ah know, honey. We, Ah'll cool it a li'l." She was conscious of him giving her a little more space as they set off, so again she put her arm through his, looked up and smiled, and they walked arm in arm into the bar. The others were already there.

"Wad yo' thank o' de Chinee, Missy?" Fude asked.

"It was as good as Ah've ever had," she replied, smilingly.

Lincoln pulled out a chair for her and as she sat down, asked her what she would like to drink.

"Do yo' all suppose they have tea?"

"Tea!" said Lincoln incredulously.

"Yeah man, tea," she said demurely. She saw the others looking at each other limply shaking their heads. "Aw, well, honey. Ah, ah."

"Try 'em man, try 'em!"

He wandered off. He took a little longer to return than one would have imagined, but arrived back grinning from ear to ear.

"Well, do de?" asked Emmy.

"De do an' de don'," said Lincoln.

"What yo' on about, man?" she said.

"One o' de staff does, but she wants to know, how yo' like it; so she said."

"Oh," said Emmy. "Tell her, strong, but wid a li'l milk."

"Strong, but wid a li'l milk?" said Lincoln weakly.

"Yeah man, it's code, it's rocket science," Emmy drawled.

He looked at the others for some kind of support; they just looked back. They were all on unsure ground.

"Go on man, jes' say what Ah tol' yo',' see what yo' git." He wandered off again, and she turned and gave them another' smile. Alby and Jethro also looked at her weakly, but she could see Fude sitting there nearly killing himself. His enormous belly quivering with mirth.

The tea eventually arrived and she took a sip, to the rapt attention of the four, who gave the impression that they had never seen it being drunk before, let alone by someone who went to great lengths to make sure that it was "jes' right."

"Beeautiful!" she announced, beaming at them.

Emmy finished the tea, by which time they had all had a second drink and Lincoln announced that they should all push off. *Here we go,* she thought, *the moment of truth.* They all stood up, and Lincoln announced that he wouldn't be long; he would "jes'" take Emmy to her hotel and would be home shortly.

They all said, "G'night, honey," and they paid their account and all drifted out together towards the door.

Emmy looked at Lincoln and he caught her look, and said he would take her to the hotel, and be on his way. Hopefully he could see her in the mornin'. She thought to herself that maybe she really was on her own tonight. Maybe he was playin' it cool. She hoped so. She was suddenly very tired; the attention had caught her by surprise, and while it was stimulating and flattering, she had to come up for air.

"Ah haven't asked yo' where yo' all live, Lincoln man?" she asked him as he collected her bag from the barman, and they set off back to the hotel.

"Honey, we live jes' around the corner an' up a bit in a big lodgin' house, not far away." She didn't feel it appropriate to discourage him at this stage. They had

292

almost declared their attraction for one another. There was no point in standing on ceremony too much.

"What time in de morning, man? Not too early, Ah hope."

"Wha' yo' think, honey? Ten?"

"Ah'll see yo' then," she said. They walked into the lobby a moment or so later, and he put down her bag, and just looked at her.

"Yo' really will be here in th' mornin'."

She looked up at him, stood on tiptoe, gave him a quick but nice kiss on the cheek, and looking him squarely in the eye said, "Ah'll be here, don' worry. Ah won' walk out on yo'." She smiled and walked over to the desk, and the clerk gave her the key to her room. She turned and looked and smiled at him as she walked towards the lift. He flipped a hand at her, and walked out.

This really is one of them nice boutique hotels, she thought as she unlocked the door and walked into the room. It was beautifully appointed, and as fresh and clean as a whistle. *What a night,* she mused as she put her bag on the couch, opened it and took her toiletries out. She slipped out of her clothes, removed "Twinkle," and walked into the en-suite. She looked at herself in the large mirror. *Will I be up to it in the mornin', when he comes a-callin'? Some sleep after a hot shower will do de trick, Ah reckon.* Shower she could. Sleep she couldn't.

She drowsily looked across at the window, and there in a beam of moonlight she could see the slightly illuminated outline of Twinkle on the low table by the wall. Twinkle! Was that Russian girl a force in de market place.

She had been placed in her cell on a Saturday, and by Sunday they were like two rubber ducks. Their bodies were mirror images of each other apart from the color, and she was a stunner to look at.

It was she that gave her the name and address of the knife-maker.

She wasn't sure what time she drifted off, restlessly, but she could remember thinking, "When he comes a callin' in the mornin', there'll be no dew on de cotton fo' him!"

Chapter 25

Lincoln walked out of the hotel and back up the street in a daze.

Man wha' have Ah go' onto heahr? Is she de one? Well effin she ain't, Ah'm fo' de long drop! He almost skipped his way back through the crowded street. He breezed up the few steps to the door of his house and bounded up the stairs two at a time to the first floor, to his apartment. Unlocking the door, he bounced in. He could see the other three, sitting over by the window on two great sofas, having a nightcap, as they were wont to call it. They had grins on their faces, and were shaking their heads. Fude was the first one to open up on him.

"Ah's neva seen anyone go down like a rack o' tenpins, man, as fast as yo' did, Lincoln baby. Awwww yo's smitten, man."

"Well, where do we go from here, man?" said Jethro. Alby just sat there playing an imaginary violin.

The thing with these four individuals was that amongst themselves they were like lambs or puppies. If they took to you, you were in, you were OK. If you were on the outside they just put up a brick wall. In their own neighborhood, where they knew a lot of the folks, they were relatively relaxed. They knew they could automatically depend on the others in any sort of a scrape. It was them against the world. They were however conscious that they were not getting any younger, and some day their cosy little foursome may be intruded upon, by someone, and it could only be a woman.

Is this the one? She would have a bearing on all their lives if Lincoln for example wanted to go off with her. It was not the last thing that could happen. It was of great interest to them, and they were trying to be quite nonchalant about it, in that they were ribbing Lincoln, but it was serious stuff. Lincoln poured himself a drink and flopped down beside Fude.

"Well Ah's bin askin mahself. She's sure a honey, an Ah don' think Ah've ever felt so, what do ya say, smitten, but there's a li'l bit of extra something."

"We can tell man, we can tell, now yo' just git off to bed and git some sleep," said Alby. "Yo' goin' to need strength, man, stayin' power, effin yo' goin' to do dis gal justice."

"He's right," said Jethro, "we can have a committee meetin', ever it comes to that."

"Yo' never know," said Fude, "once yo' get it outa yo' system, yo' might see her completely different. Why don' we all git some shuteye?"

They all lived in the apartment, which took up half of the first floor. Whilst it was relatively open plan, it had four separate bedrooms, with two en-suites. The living area and kitchen dining was spacious, certainly for their needs. The only other folks they had in there from time to time were women, and most of them didn't last long. Once they had been "got outa de system," as they used to say, they were outa there. They din't do it rough. Those days were past. So it always looked reasonably presentable.

As they all rose to go to their respective rooms, Lincoln looked around and went over to the sink. He looked around.

"Yo' guys got Missus Tonkin comin, yo' gone and done de dishes." They always went to an extra bit of effort to have things a little more respectable than usual when the cleaning lady was coming.

"Yeah man yo' in luck effin yo' bring de gal back heah sometime tomorrow, she'll be heah. De place be spankin' clean. Yo' can make a good impression man."

Lincoln also took a shower to clean up. And he too couldn't sleep. He wondered what she would be like, and if this is really why he wanted her. Fude had whispered in his ear, "She'll make de sparrows fly out of yo' ass!" He could almost believe it.

They had really only taken flight twice before. The first time was when he was nearly fifteen. The girl was about thirty-something, an ole woman he thought, and "Right into virgins," so she said.

It was a long time ago, and whenever he thought about it, he shuddered. The fetid room, the tar paper on the walls of the shack. Anyway it seemed half a lifetime ago. Although he wondered from time to time over the years, what had happened to her.

The second time was with a beautiful cracker. She was blonde everywhere, and had a figure like one of them Nordic princesses. She had a thing about black men, and couldn't get enough. For all that, she wound him up and led him on for about a week before they saddled up. He was nearly out of control, and she knew it, and she played him like a harp. She could certainly deliver though. He was pleased that they parted on good terms. They both got what they wanted, so there was no reason why they shouldn't have.

For all that he was almost on fire all night, and drifted into an uneasy restless sleep. He woke with a start. He could see broad daylight outside. He always kept the watch on the table beside the bed, and reaching over found to his relief that it wasn't quite nine o'clock. He looked down the bed. Not that he really had to look; he had a head of steam he rarely experienced.

He hobbled next door to the bathroom, and went through the usual routine, and after he had had a shower and got dressed, he only felt marginally better. He had dressed in the baggiest loosest clothes he could find, while still retaining his sharp look. No one else seemed to be about. The place looked fairly respectable, and would look more so after Mrs. Tonkin had finished. She had yet to arrive. He began mulling over whether Emmy would be there. Would she have done a runner? If he was the praying type, he thought he would certainly be praying she hadn't. He went off down the stairs quietly. He didn't want to run into the landlady, Mrs. Schinkell. If he did amongst other things she would know that he was on a serious mission and hold him up. That was something he wanted to avoid at all costs.

He made it out onto the street, and set off a few doors away for a cup of coffee. He didn't want to go calling on a full stomach, particularly, in view of what was going to take place. As he was having it, he planned his strategy.

Should he take something with him? What should he take? *Ah know, Ah'll take a bunch o' flowers. Tha's wha' Ah'll do.* There was a flower vendor just near the hotel, so that shouldn't be any trouble. He finished the coffee, left the morning paper where it was and slipped out of the coffee shop.

There weren't many people about, and he hadn't seen anyone he knew, and hoped he wouldn't. Particularly as it was nearly ten, the flower vendor was right ahead, and the hotel was right there. If he was in luck he could be inside the hotel in two minutes.

He thought later that he had lingered over the flowers too long. The problem was he had never bought flowers before. He settled on a bunch of violets. He was just about to pay, when the all too familiar voice of Fude, in cooing tones whispered, "Dey like roses. Don' yo' know dat' man? Roses!"

He gave Fude a hooded good-natured look, handed the violets back, and said "Roses, a dozen!" So near and yet so far. He must have had that "sprung" look about him.

Fude slapped him on the back. "Loosen up, man. Ah can be walkin' down de street, and come upon a cat Ah've never seen afore, a cat wid lust in 'is eyes, and help 'im out in de flower departmen,' can't Ah?" Go Fude!

Lincoln took the roses, paid the money and walked into the hotel. Taking the lift up to Emmy's floor he arrived at Emmy's door feeling like a schoolboy. He was as nervous as a cat. He knocked on the door, and in a moment or so it opened. He felt an involuntary intake of breath. The room was dimly lit, and whilst she had her hair properly made up she was standing there in a heavy bathrobe, with, he suspected, nothing on beneath it.

He had been holding the roses behind his back and slowly brought them around in front. He offered them to her. She took them from him with both hands, which he thought were slightly trembling. She looked up at him and smiled and he could see that her eyes looked misty.

She held them up to her face and inhaled. Then she turned and slowly walked across the room to the table to where there was a water jug, in which she placed the flowers, turned and said, in a low voice trembling with emotion, "Do yo' know, no one has ever given me flowers before, thank yo'." She gave a slight shrug and the robe fell off.

He nearly fainted. She just stood there in all her magnificence, and slowly, ever so slowly bought her arms up straight in front of her with her palms outstretched. He felt the pulse in his neck almost as much as his heart beat. He moved across the room towards her, never more conscious of his need. He took her hands in his and drew her to him, and with her hands still partially enclosed in his own, cupped her face, and slowly tilted her head back, and gently kissed her. Another thrill swept through him and he felt her shift position imperceptibly.

Just as she withdrew her arms and began to place them around his neck, with time seeming to him, to stand still, he reached down and picked her up and ever so slowly carried her to the bed which he had noticed, was neatly made with only a top sheet.

He knelt on the bed with her in his arms, and gently laid her in the middle of it. He stepped off, and back, and looking straight at her, removed his jacket and shirt, at the same time slipping out of his loafers. He thought for a second that he had been pretty cool deciding not to wear socks, and so it turned out.

Still looking her straight in the eyes he undid his belt and dropped his trousers to the floor, and with a quick flick removed his shorts, and for the first time since he had seen her, he felt free and comfortable. When his shorts were removed, he could see her take a slight intake of breath, and then her mouth slightly opened, and her tongue slowly snaked out and began to roll ever so slowly around her lips. He could feel his temples pounding as he moved back and down onto the bed beside her.

As he moved down, she turned slightly side on, and rose up a little to meet him. His left arm slid beneath her and they melted into each other. He could feel the whole, it seemed, soft but firmness of the entire length of her body; she then wrapped her perfectly formed left leg around his. She felt unbelievable; cool but warm, her skin smelt intoxicating. She seemed to be moving against him, with him, without even moving at all.

A little later he lay back thinking that it was only just after ten in the morning and he quite honestly felt exhausted, but in a way he had never known.

There they lay, in each other's arms, not moving or speaking, apart from Lincoln entwining his fingers in and out of her hair, and she, giving his chest the occasional smoothing pat. Several times he found himself nearly dozing off, and eventually, after he had given himself quite a start, lazily murmured, "Wha' say we go an git summat to eat honey? Dis has given me an appetite."

She moved her head and looked up at him pouting her lips in a kiss, and just nodded.

"There's no hurry," she murmured.

"Ah'll jes' go to the bathroom." She pushed herself up off the bed, and leant back over him, smiled and bent down and gave him another kiss, and whispered. "Yo' know, yo' really are, such a nice nigga." Drawling it out again. He hardly moved a muscle, just lay there watching her as she padded across the room and disappeared into the bathroom. *Oh mah Mammy, yo' sure woulda' loved her,* he thought to himself, with a great lump in his throat. Also thinking at the same time that he would have killed anyone else calling him a nigga.

Her voice snapped him out of his reverie, he must have nearly dozed off again. She was standing near the bed getting dressed, and she had said something like they were wasting the day. He got off the bed, and gave her a kiss as he walked through to the bathroom.

He knew just the place to take her to, and was of course a regular there. He felt quietly as pleased as punch when he walked in with her. She looked sensational, wearing camel-colored tailored pants, beige short-sleeved blouse, silk scarf and low heeled loafers. The Louis Vuitton hung from her shoulder.

The regulars all looked up, and he could see from the barely concealed rolling of the eyes, that she was quite a hit, to put it mildly. He acknowledged their felicitations with a condescending good humor; he was having a great time, really putting on the dog.

He tucked into his usual breakfast of eggs sunny side up, bacon, sausages and tomatoes, with rye toast, followed by waffles and maple syrup, and she just had croissants, butter and honey. They both had black coffee to follow. The only coffee she had each day. The one with "sting!" They were sitting comfortably finishing the coffee, when she asked him what he had in mind now.

"Ah'm in yo' hands man," she said.

"Ah was thinkin' that Ah could take yo' home, and show yo' off to de guys," he said tentatively.

"Why that would be nice," she said in her "street voice."

"Come on then," he responded in kind. *She certainly wafts in and out of the drawl,* he thought to himself. They left the diner and set off again.

"How far?" she asked.

"Just a minute or two," he said and before she knew it he was indicating that they were to go up these few steps into what struck her as a very well maintained lodging. He held the door open for her, and looking down at her placed a finger over his lips indicating that he wanted no sound.

He set off towards the staircase, across the lobby slightly on his toes, beckoning her to follow. Bemused by all this, she followed him, and whilst she thought that they hadn't made any noise at all, she soon found out that this wasn't the case. They were half way up the stairs to the first landing with Lincoln perhaps a step ahead, when suddenly she heard something that literally took her breath away.

"Oooiii good for nottin' niggers!" It was rasped out. She looked at Lincoln in alarm. "Sun's hardly up and you're bringing frails inno mein house!" Lincoln turned, looked at Emmy, she wondered later on if he had given her a surreptitious wink, and slowly began to descend the stairs. She then turned her attention as to where all the commotion was coming from, and could hardly believe her eyes.

Standing between an open doorway and the bottom of the stairs was the diminutive figure of an old woman, wearing an apron, a skirt with a hemline that barely covered the tops of her shoes, with her arms akimbo, glaring up at them. Emmy took the whole scene in at a glance. Lincoln got to the bottom of the stairs and began to move like a cat towards her, crouching a little lower with each step.

Emmy, in spite of the invective that had been flying around a few moments before, became quite concerned as Lincoln bore down on her. She stood her ground, she didn't move a muscle, she stood firm. Just as Lincoln's arms flashed out, Emmy uttered a little cry, "Lincoln!"

Emmy was horrified, she started back down the stairs, and lost her footing and had to grasp the railing with both hands, to stop her fall. She quickly recovered, and made her way down the last two steps. "Lincoln you musn't," she blurted out without quite taking in what had happened.

Lincoln actually had lifted the woman right up to eye level and was holding her comfortably in one arm. He was waggling a finger right before her eyes, and saying. "She aint no frail, Momma... Git it!" All this through clenched teeth, but with the semblance of a smile on his lips.

For her part, the woman seemed quite unruffled by all this, and lowering her glance to Emmy took her in with an unhurried studious appraisal from top to bottom. She then returned her eyes to Lincoln, and gave him a firm nod. *I don't believe this,* thought Emmy. *They're actually baiting each other.*

Lincoln gently lowered the woman to the floor and she began smoothing out her clothes. She was tiny. She must have been around four foot two or three.

"Vell boy, introduce me!" Emmy looked at Lincoln in amazement. Lincoln didn't flinch, in fact he gave every indication that he was oblivious as to how the request was put.

"Emmy Lou, Ah'd like yo' to meet Missuus," he drawled it. Emmy looked at the woman who had drawn herself up and was looking sternly at him. *What is all this about,* thought Emmy.

"Miss Zelda, Momma Ah'd like yo' to meet a friend a' mine, name Emmy Lou."

Emmy looked at the woman and thought that it was incumbent on her to say something, so she said, "Good morning, Miss Zelda," with an obligatory nod of her head, and a nice smile. Miss Zelda returned the greeting with another nod, and a "Hrumph!"

"Vell the goil's vell brought up!" *Glory be,* thought Emmy.

"And yo' like to know summat else, Momma?"

"So there's more?" She looked at Lincoln.

"She drinks, she prefers tea."

The woman looked at her as if for the first time.

"Now you tell me. The goil drinks tea." She became quite relaxed. "Now you come vit me, goily. Lincoln you go upstairs, I vill bring her up shortly. Avay, avay, off you, go. Vamoose!"

Without further ado Emmy, after a helpless look at Lincoln, which was returned with a shrug, a grin and a look of encouragement, found herself being ushered in through the doorway that was open near the foot of the stairs. It was like walking into another world. It was

304

opulent and baroque. There was just the merest hint of that very subtle smell that furniture polish, waxed floors give off. She had never been in a room like it. There were even several vases of what appeared to be very fresh flowers, there were paintings on the walls.

It had everything Emmy felt Zelda considered to be an expression of wealth. There probably wouldn't be another room like it in city blocks from here. Although she conceded that there probably would be, but you would never know. Whilst it wasn't to her taste at all, she had to agree that the old girl had somewhere along the way, made an awful lot of money, why, each painting would be worth the cost of a few weeks in Miami. She even had an aspidistra on an incredibly ornate stand, which itself could have cost a fortune.

She was taken gently by the arm by this now smiling, bustling little woman, through the apartment which, she suspected by the layout, would take up a third to a half of the ground floor. They went through to the kitchen which Emmy noted was spotless like everything else she had seen on the way through. For all that, there was no doubt it certainly gave off the feel that it was lived in, in the intangible sense that such homes give off. Zelda invited her to sit at the kitchen table, and excused herself, saying that she was going to get the good teapot. She disappeared back to where they had come from as Emmy sat there and looked around the room.

She could see that everything in sight was obviously expensive. There were pieces of silver, silver cutlery, there were Venetian glass ornaments, some delightful looking glass containers with different kinds of cookies in them, and the kitchen had the aroma that is given off when there is something baking in the oven. There was a shelf with what Emmy suspected were cookbooks, and they looked well used. The whole thing had an air of serenity to it, of permanence. Nothing at all like what she would have expected from their initial encounter. She heard a slight noise behind her, and there was her hostess with the teapot, which she was pulling out of a green soft felt bag.

"Now goily, ve can relax in a moment together."

She put the kettle on the stove gave the teapot a good rinse in hot water from the fawcett, dried it meticulously, and asked Emmy what kind of tea she would prefer. She then rattled off about six different teas, half of which she had never heard of, and Emmy settled on the Dilmah.

"The Dilmah," said Zelda, "the Dilmah! Vich one? English Breakfast?"

Oh my God, thought Emmy. "Yes, the English Breakfast!" she responded again a little tremulously.

"Goily." Zelda came and sat across from her, clutching her hands in hers. "Oh vat beautiful hands," she exclaimed. "Dilmah English Breakfast is mein favorite too!" She got up and went over to one of the tea caddies on the bench, and opened the biggest. She looked over her shoulder. "Lincoln of all people vit a goil like you." Emmy looked at her, with her head inclined. "No, no, no, no. He is vun of my favorites. He is a very good boy. Actually he is the vun!"

She spent nearly an hour with Zelda, and had to confess the time flew. She was also conscious of the fact that by the time Zelda actually took her upstairs she had almost bared her soul to the little old lady, yet she was really no wiser on any aspect of Zelda herself, apart from the fact that she embodied what can only be described as a proprietorial air in regard to the whole establishment.

As "the tea party" was drawing to a close she said, "Goily…" She went on, "May I call you Emmy?"

Emmy inclined her head, and responded. "Please do." Thinking to herself, *This is quaint, but it is really quite nice.*

"Gut, I must get you back to your man!"

"Can I help you with the dishes?" Emmy asked.

"Not at all, zere is nothing to do," was the reply. A few minutes later she was standing beside her as she knocked on a door on the first floor. She turned to Emmy, "It's mein house, I can go anywhere; but ven you haf lodgers you haf to respect zem." She gave an expressive shrug.

"Vot haf I got myself into?" Emmy mimicked to Lincoln after she had gone.

Lincoln chuckled. "Honey, yo' sure made a hit there. The ole girl is hooked on yo'."

"Well, Ah don' know about that. What is her story? She could now write a book on me, an' Ah don' know a thing about her."

"It's an amazin' story." He sat back. "She came here after the war as a displaced person, an' actually got the job as cleaner of this house."

"She what?" exclaimed Emmy.

"Yes," Lincoln went on. "She did, an' did a wunnerful job. It was run as it is now, as a roomin' house, an' she ran it an' kept it up as though it was hers. Some of the lodgers from that time were still here when we came, so we have heard it from dem."

"She would go to the synagogue once a week, do the shopping, and they were her only interests. Apparently she lived here in a single room at the back, and even had to share a bathroom. But…"

"There is always a but," said Emmy.

Lincoln went on nodding. "The story goes that she kept telling people that one day men from the government would come and give her a lot of money, and she could retire. Well, as you can imagine, none of the lodgers believed her, but humored her."

"Of course the reality, honey lamb, is that, the men did come, and they did give her a considerable amount. Under the Swiss Government release of Jewish Bank

Account monies in the 'fifties, 'sixties. Monies deposited during the Nazi era. No one knows how much, but certainly enough to buy the house which just happened to come on the market at about that time, and plenty left over from all accounts. 'Cos she went right on and commenced restoring it, and look at it now."

There was a knock at the door, Lincoln bounded out of his chair like a cat, which gave Emmy a little thrill. A gun appeared in his hand as if from nowhere, he put his finger to his lips and moving over to the door. "Yo'!" he called out.

"Vat are you liffin in, a fortress, come, open up!" He turned around, looking at Emmy with an enormous grin on his face, and, putting the gun high up on a shelf, opened the door. Emmy sat looking in wonder as the little old lady came bustling in carrying a small wicker basket. As she walked over to the table, she beckoned to Emmy. "Come Emmy, come. I haf zomzing for you. You too, Lincoln my boy."

She put the basket on the table and took out a small item wrapped in tissue paper. She unwrapped it carefully saying that she had only just washed them. They were a magnificent, fine porcelain cup and saucer. There was also a beautiful teaspoon with a magnificent colored enamelled bowl depicting buildings of some sort, with a small banner with Gdansk, Danzig. She said, "Where I come from." She then proceeded to open another green felt bag from which she produced a small silver tea pot. "There," she said. "Gut for two cups!" Emmy and Lincoln looked at each other across her with eyes wide. "Und now ve have the tea caddy full of Dilmah."

"Oh Zelda, they are beautiful," said Emmy.

"Yes they are, und you look after them."

"What…?" said Emmy.

"Yes, yes. If you are to be coming here you must have zumzing nice to drink your tea out of."

"Well Ah," Emmy started again... "Lincoln do yo' happen to have another cup or two?" She glanced across at Lincoln again with a raising of the eyebrows.

"No, no we don', we only have mugs."

"I knew it! Ah was thinkin', Zelda, that it would be very nice if you would have the first cup of tea, here with us," said Emmy, getting into the spirit of things.

"I vill go und get two more cups!"

"No, no Momma, no' fo' me thanks," blurted out Lincoln.

"Ah'll get them for you," said Emmy, walking to the door with her.

"No, no," Zelda looked at her winking, as she gave her arm a squeeze.

Emmy walked back over to Lincoln, and leant on him. "Am Ah a hit or am Ah no' a hit? The old match-maker, it didn't take her long did it."

"Wha, Wha' do yo' mean?" said Lincoln.

"She's doing her level best to pair us off!"

"Really, honey lamb?"

"Yeah man, she must have some sort o' sixth sense, that tells her that yo' absolutely mad about me." She giggled, and Lincoln took a playful swat at her.

He chased her and caught her in a flash and, wrapping his arms around her, looked down and said. "Yo' know, Ah thought Ah was hidin' it rather well."

"Oh Lincoln, yo' mean it?"

"Yeah Ah do. Am Ah outa line?"

"Lincoln honey, Ah feels exactly the same way too. De ole goil must know something!"

The ole Goil arrived back a few minutes later with another cup and saucer together with a jar of cookies, which Lincoln zeroed in on. She lightly patted his hands away, and told him to get some plates, and didn't he know how to behave like a gentleman?

"Zees are made to my Auntie Rachel's recipe, Emmy, und they are always a good hit with zees monsters."

They had boiled the jug, poured the tea into the pot, Lincoln had made some coffee and was eyeing off the five cookies on the plate – three for him, and one each for the others – when the door opened and in walked Fude and Jethro. Like lightning Lincoln snatched up two of the cookies and jammed one of them in his mouth.

Zelda looked at Emmy, and went off on a good-natured diatribe on how her boys could smell her cookies a mile off, and whenever they were put on the table, it brought the worst out in them. The three of them just sat there and grinned. Jethro having taken the third cookie, pushed the plate with two cookies left, over the table towards the two women. Emmy withdrew philosophically, thinking to herself how special it was for her to be accepted so readily by these enormous men, and this simply delightful little woman.

Zelda stood up and giving one of her customary shrugs, told Jethro who she pointed out was the only gentleman in the bunch, to follow her and they would get the cookie jar.

"Vy should I be expected to carry great loads of cookies around, ven I hef all zis help?" With another shrug full of emphasis. Off they went, with Jethro grinning from ear to ear.

Fude looked at Emmy, sat back and asked her how she felt, finding herself in this madhouse situation. She felt that coming from him, she had to offer up a considered response. Lincoln also appeared to be intently interested.

She was also conscious of the fact that whilst she knew virtually nothing of these four, five, individuals whose lives she had stumbled into, certainly by their volition not hers, she was so comfortable with the situation, turn of events, call it what you will. She was

310

also, above all things, so terribly lonely, and she was doing her best to maintain perspective, to maintain dignity in circumstances that seemed to be always just a little to be verging out of control, if only a little, but, she had to admit, in the nicest way.

She looked at Fude, and at Lincoln and back at Fude. She felt that the question warranted a formal response. She was in a quandary, she couldn't afford to be too keen on one hand and certainly was not going to be dismissive, offhand, on the other, she had to be careful. The little she had gathered about him over the past few hours indicated to her that when he spoke he was rarely being chatty, he wasn't given to small talk. He, perhaps more than any of the others, appeared to have depth to him. Or so it seemed with her limited exposure to them.

"Fude, it is a question I have been asking myself," she heard herself saying. She went on to say that during the long years in prison, she had dreamt of eventually finding herself in a happy situation like this and she was still coming to terms with it. "I really can't put it any other way at this point."

There, honestly spoken without giving a thing away. She couldn't bring herself to say more, under the circumstances. What she would have liked to say, and strongly resisted was that the reality was on two levels. She had happened upon it straight off the bus literally, quite literally; and it is beyond anything she quite honestly could expect, perhaps even deserve. At best she could only realistically ever expect to happen upon one person, let alone a whole clutch of you guys after weeks, months, if ever. To actually say so however would have been too much too soon.

She got up off the sofa, and moved over behind Lincoln putting her hands on his shoulders. She looked at Fude and inclined her head, and just looked at him. She also desperately wanted to say to him, to all of them

311

and Fude, I'm having real trouble with it, and contrary to what you may think, I'm not really a good time girl, I play for keeps. Just as she couldn't bring herself to tell them that she felt so very lonely, so terribly vulnerable. She actually thought that she was going to burst into tears.

She stood there, she had almost bared her soul. Fude sat there and was just raising his head to look at her directly, and the door opened and in they walked followed by Alby.

"Vat I tell you. Out cum z'cookies, out come z' cookie monsters!" Lincoln reached up and patted Emmy's hand. He then grasped it and gently led her around to sit on his knee. She felt exhausted. She stole a quick glance at Fude, but he wasn't looking in their direction, he had sat back in his chair, and was looking into space.

Zelda broke the party up. All the cookies had gone their separate ways, when she stood and announced that she was going down to the wharf.

"Yo' what!" said Lincoln, "yo' goin to de wharf!" She gave another of her expressive shrugs, that by now Emmy was becoming quite used to.

"So all z' cookies haf almost gone. There is anozzer boat comin in, full uv veat, unt oats." They all burst out laughing including Zelda, who leant across to Emmy and gave her a kiss, and whispered, "I have more Dilmah."

Emmy stood up and walked her to the door with Alby. She turned and said "Don't come down, I will be alright," and off she went. Emmy wanted to say a lot, but felt it should come from one of the others. Fude looked at her as she sat down near Lincoln.

"Emmy baby, yo' sure a hit wid ole Zelda."

"Dat's wha' we'all bin thinkin', honey," said Alby.

"All I can say is that the feeling is mutual," Emmy responded.

"When are we'all goin' t' eat?" yawned Fude. "Ah'm ready t' pass out."

"Come on," said Lincoln, "those cookies have made me feel th' same way."

Emmy said. "Ah'l jes' do th' dishes first. Ah got time?"

"OK," said Lincoln. "Yo' guys go on, we'll catch yo' up. Murphy's?" They nodded and drifted out.

Lincoln looked at her, and said. "Yo' know what Ah feel like, honey lamb?"

"We got time yo' think?" She put her arms around him.

"Yeah baby."

"What if they come back?"

"Dat's one thin' dey just won' do. Come on, le's have one, right here now!"

"Dat din' take long," said Fude when they arrived at "Murphy's."

"De's thing never do," said Lincoln. Not really to anyone. Both of them could not have looked more relaxed. This of course wasn't lost on the others. They didn't linger over lunch, and the others drifted off singly over about twenty minutes or so, leaving Emmy and Lincoln to themselves. She commented on how interesting Zelda appeared to be, and went on to say how much her whole apartment, which appeared to be enormous for just one person, appeared at the same time to be really lived in.

Lincoln filled her in. He said that she lived a very full life. According to the old original lodgers, after she had the house renovated and redecorated, she began having a few of her friends come visiting. They came once a week to begin with, and then she began going out quite often herself. Anyway the upshot of it all was that she went off and played cards, and it had reached the stage now, where seven or eight old folk came here, around once a week.

"Well," said Emmy. "She sure keeps out of mischief then."

"She sure does," he replied.

Emmy looked at Lincoln. "Wa' yo' like to do, honey?"

He looked at her with a silly grin, with his eyes wide, fluttering his eyelids. "C'mon, le's go, Ah do too!" She cooed.

They almost fell out of the lift at the hotel, and tumbled through into the room, and onto the bed, leaving a trail of discarded clothing. Afterwards, Lincoln, to Emmy's bemusement, then dozed off, gradually. She was sure he tried to stay awake, but as neither of them, it seemed wanted to say the first word, he obviously found it difficult to keep his eyes open.

She lay across his chest gazing at him, and was afraid, suddenly, that he may be disturbed by the beating of her heart, which she felt was beating like a tom-tom. Her heart welled up with an overwhelming sense of love, affection, desire; together with fear that this could be too good to last. Whenever, through her life, something that was wonderful came her way, something else wasn't far behind, to upset it.

She wasn't sure how long she lay there; his whole presence seemed like a security shield to her. She wished it could last forever. Her whole existence, or so it seemed, was like being on a great swooping roller coaster.

She had never known stability. She clung to him ever more closely, his rhythmic breathing seeming to envelope her, her tongue languidly reached out and caressed his almost hairless skin. Early images of her childhood came eerily to her; they were almost devoid of her parents. Her father beat her mother, or so she was told.

She was taken in by her father's sister when she was five years of age, at the insistence of her grandmother, who lived there with her daughter, son-in-law and her five cousins: three boys several years older than Emmy and their two sisters, two and three years older than her. The first few years were idyllic; her grandmother adored her, but unfortunately lavished too much affection on her. This became apparent after she died, when the atmosphere in the household, never happy at the best of times, began to deteriorate, unfortunately to the detriment of Emmy.

Her grandmother's death, which was sudden, "Of a Heart," as they used to say, came at a time when Emmy was beginning to blossom. Up until that time she was to all intents and purposes, a gawky, lithe of limb, unself-conscious fourteen-year-old. Her grandmother, herself no beauty, had seen the coming storm early on.

Astutely, she also recognized that there was no one in the family who she could confide in. Someone with whom she could rely on to see it through, what had become her obsession in life. To enable Emmy to claw her way out of this day-to-day existence, and to provide, if only in a small way, the means to accomplish it.

She pondered long and hard over the early years, as to how she could achieve this end, and hit upon it all of a sudden. A devout Christian, she had taken to the new Preacher who had come to their congregation. She confided in him. He was old enough to appreciate the concern, and young enough to be "tending," the little flock for many years to come. He was one of those rare souls who could not have been more honorable. He invested her "nest egg." He put it into the care of an old college friend, who was a stock broker, and he was one way or another, able to turn the initial investment into several thousand dollars, and then some, in the space of six short years, all for Emmy.

Her grandmother, however, was very astute. She also instructed the Preacher that whilst her concerns extended to Emmy as far as providing for her, Emmy was only to have enough money to enable her to go through college. Emmy's share would be forty percent of the residual after she had graduated. The balance of the money, sixty percent, would go to her aunt, two years after Emmy had received hers.

The old grandmother thought that Emmy could put enough distance between herself and the rest of the family in two years to be safely enough out of the way. Also if her aunt contested the will, her sixty percent share would automatically revert to thirty percent.

When the time came for Emmy to go off to college there was, needless to say, an unholy row. However, the Preacher "the trustee," had the whip hand, and was able to talk the aunt and her husband out of over-reacting, for reasons that they were later able to appreciate. The aunt must have had a little bit of her mother in her after all.

Some time after she became involved with the foursome, or fivesome, she began to become a little reflective. Over the years, the others had girls from time to time and she had lost count of who had come and gone. They were fast, flashy, good-looking, good time girls and if she really thought anything about them it was that they progressively got younger as she and the boys became older.

None of them, of course, had her intellect or education so they had nothing to offer in that respect. However, she took good care of herself and was always neat and trim; in fact, she was what they used to say on the street—sharp, in fact she could give many of these girls a run for their money in virtually every respect.

316

You never knew what was around the corner with her. The other thing that she was grateful for was that when she first became involved with them they were living from hand to mouth. They were always short of money. Whenever they collected on a contract they spent up— they spent big.

One night, about four years after she had joined them and they were all sitting casually looking at their last few bucks, she bent forward and said that she would like to say something.

"Go ahead," they said in agreement.

She then took them through the last few hits, the amount they had been paid—how it had slipped through their fingers and now they had nothing to show for it. They would no doubt agree on this, as it had happened too much of late of. She had kept the wolf from the door and was even paying the rent right now—she had a part-time job as a typist, and really there was no need for it.

The amount of money they made several times a year was stupendous, and if they would trust her to manage it, she could pull them out of this hole and make them a lot of money by investing it. To be, why—in a few years they could in all probability retire if that is what they wished. Well, the upshot of that was a day or so later they sat her down, told her that –

"That means we will each receive 20 percent of each job."

She interrupted. "There are four of you; that means twenty-five percent."

"No, baby," Fude said emphatically. "There are five of us! No arguments!"

So the deal was done and after a few years or so they were all nicely set up. She ran the whole operation professionally, she had a portfolio for each of them, provided them with monthly accounts, had their Powers of Attorney and the whole arrangement was working perfectly. After this operation they would each pocket $40,000—not too bad for a few hours' work.

All that was almost a lifetime ago, and she had subsequently become the girl of the leader of the bunch, Lincoln.

Chapter 26

Emmy returned with the platter and tuned in on the conversation once more. The Mob had given them an excellent map of the district where the compound was— on a dirt road several miles from the highway and ran off into the Lakes Country, the roads were well formed and well signposted. The roads did not seem, on the one proper reconnoiter that they carried out, to be used a lot. Probably only in the season, they thought. This suited them just fine as they didn't really want any close neighbors.

The Mob had included a map of the immediate vicinity around the compound, so the boys felt that the whole plan would be foolproof. They drove past the driveway to the property on the day in question and were surprised that there was only a post at the entrance. They almost could have driven past. They decided to get out and walk back in until they had found the buildings. They were meticulous planners and on a contract like this they needed to be sure of the lie of the land.

They would not have the luxury of daylight when they made the hit and to be familiar with the layout was an imperative. It took them half an hour or so to walk in the distance from the road to the complex of buildings. When they arrived they stayed back a little in the trees surveying the scene. They didn't want to give themselves away needlessly, although the complex seemed to be deserted. It was pretty much the same as on the layout that they had been provided with, although one of the buildings seemed much larger than depicted on the plan. There were three smaller lodges or cabins and also one set back from the others that was the same construction but appeared to be the tool shed and generator room.

The property was too remote to be on the power grid and they obviously generated their own electricity. There were overhead wires running out to the other buildings for this purpose. Jethro commented that they probably had boats, canoes and mowers in there as well. There appeared to be no sign of life so they decided to risk breaking their cover.

The buildings were of solid construction and very well put together, they concluded. It would have cost them a fortune to have this set up established miles from anywhere like this, but then money would not really be an object to them. They walked out into the open, spread out in a line abreast of around thirty feet, but not before they had checked their handguns. The land sloped ever so gently down towards the lake with the buildings set on it. They estimated it to be a five-acre open space of lawned area.

The lawn looked as though it was maintained fairly regularly but needed cutting as it was between three to four inches high. It had the appearance of a lawn that was cut to a shorter length.

"One good mow and it would be back in top shape," said Jethro out loud.

"What would you know about cuttin' grass?" muttered Fude, good naturedly.

"When we was chillen, down Alabama way. Ah used to be de king of de lawn mowers." He bounced backed in an exaggerated rap talk. They all laughed.

They gave the three cabins a cursory inspection and then moved in the direction of the main house. It faced the lake and was about 150 yards back from it. It had a wide verandah each side and was enormous, and rectangular in shape. A few yards out from the rear, was a twenty-foot square area with a six-foot trellis fence around it.

"There is a clothesline inside it," said Alby.

"And five will get you ten, there are garbage cans too," said Jethro.

"Your powers of observation never cease to amaze me," said Lincoln, rolling his eyes at Fude who was looking at them in feigned amazement nodding his head.

The house had a door on each of the four sides, each door leading out to the verandah. The lawn ran right up to the house on all sides, except where the back door was and, between it and the utility area there was stone paving which continued on out to take in the trellised area. They walked on down the lawn towards the lake and off to the side they could see a magnificent white wooden flagpole about halfway between the distance from the lake to the house.

"They obviously wish to retain their national spirit without affecting the view," said Alby.

The others looked at him, their faces bursting into grins but no one said anything, as they continued down towards the small jetty that they could now see. It ran out about forty feet and then along for around another twenty feet. It was a good twelve feet wide.

"Not a word," said Lincoln, "not a word." Alby cleared his throat, as though he was going to comment on the jetty. "You were going to say they could tie up half a dozen small boats here, weren't you?"

"Of course," said Alby, "and with a few canoes on the deck to boot—you gotta know these things, man," he said imperiously.

They sauntered out onto the jetty and along towards the far end.

"Hey," said Alby, who was bringing up the rear. The other three looked around and there he was lying down on the deck leaning over the side with his arm in the water.

"What are you doing, man?" said Fude.

"The water ain't that cold," said Alby.

"So what?" said Jethro as they all turned and continued to the end of the jetty.

"You know, this looks mighty fine, this could be what heaven is, do you think?" Lincoln muttered.

They heard a splash and looking around saw Alby floundering around in the water. "I'm having a swim," he shouted. They looked at each other, shook their heads and watched him work his way back to the bank.

He reached it and gingerly climbed out. His great physique looking like an ebony seal, one of them muttered as he pulled himself out of the water and up onto the bank.

"More like something else," said Fude as he watched Alby rise up from a squat and turn to come towards them.

Lincoln said "I know what you mean," and the three of them burst out laughing. They were all very big men but none of them was bigger than Alby in all departments. He came along the jetty towards them with water glistening over his body, and as he came up to them his face opened up with a grin and he said, "What's wrong with you guys, don't yours shrivel up in de cold?" executing a little jig. They all howled with laughter and both Fude and Jethro lunged at him and pushed him back in, screaming with laughter.

When Lincoln was out at the end of the jetty he stood, hands on hips taking in the whole vista. The lake was enormous with several reaches, it seemed, disappearing into the middle distance. There must be some beautiful secluded spots out there and the fishing must be about as good as it gets.

He moved to the edge and looking down thought that he could quite easily see the bottom, and even thought that he saw a fish. Quite a nice one too. He moved his gaze right around, and it struck him as to just how isolated this place was; he could see no other sign of habitation.

His gaze wandered off to the right beyond the far point, about a mile away along the lake, and he thought that he saw something white, above the trees just in from the point. He looked again and couldn't see it and thought that it must have been a trick of the light.

Walking off the jetty the three of them called out to Alby as he was nearly back to the bank to come on, they had to get going. They were half way back to the main house by the time he caught up to them, clutching his clothes and shoes under one arm with the gun in his free hand.

"Man, you sure can put on a turn," said Lincoln.

"With a little bit of help from some friends," was the response. By the time they got back to the tree line Alby had dried out sufficiently to get dressed and catch them up again and they all set off back to the car keeping off the track. When they arrived at the car they restudied the map, checking the coordinates to everyone's satisfaction, and were happy.

All they had to do now was contact the client and authorize the money to be put into their account and then await the notification for the hit. It was to be one of the days over the Thanksgiving long weekend. They drove back out to the highway checking every track and signpost against the map and were comfortable that the complex that they had inspected was the same as the complex set out clearly on the map that they had been given.

Chapter 27

At the Lodge they were all nearly ready for dinner when Conchitta announced it would be served in five minutes. Two of the men decided to go into the garden to relieve themselves.

This was just after Lincoln and the boys had arrived, planned their attack and got out of the car.

They discovered that there were six cars and felt that they could handle the occupants. Lincoln had instructed that under no circumstances was there to be anyone killed. They would be going into certainly a hostile situation as it were, and whilst there could be plenty of rough stuff—no killing, and no drinking. They were all happy with this.

They were to go in within five minutes of now. The two villains around the rear of the main house came upon the two bridge players relieving themselves and gave each of them a slight knock on the head to show them what was what, and then told them to move back to the house which they entered through a door opening into a passage, in what was the utility area of the house. One of the villains stayed outside. The rest were just inside walking down the passage, when a side door to the john opened on the right and out came another bridge player. He was quickly grabbed and then told to lead the way quietly into the body of the house.

It should be pointed out at this stage that all the men were Vietnam veterans, with the exception of Lofty, and in their way very tough dudes. This went for Lincoln and the boys as well. Ben, leading the way and obscured partly by the other two, patted his hands either side to get them to slow down a little and as they turned the corner into the rear of the laundry area, he took a dry chemical fire extinguisher from the wall, and pulling out the pin turned around to face the three coming behind him.

His timing was perfect. The first two parted to enable him to spray the villain in the face. This of course completely incapacitated him. The three of them then took the gun from him and led him over to the trough to wash the powder out of his eyes.

They were all concentrating on this, when the second villain, Alby, walked up and disarmed them, but not before he had given Ben an almighty crack on the head. When Jethro had cleaned himself up, although looking as though he had crawled out of a swamp, they all moved to the front of the house, making their way through the kitchen into the dining room where they were met by Lincoln and Fude who had all the bridge party sitting up against the wall. The men were looking sullen but unconcerned, the women were looking terrified. The Latinos were doing as they were told.

Lincoln looked at Jethro, shaking his head slightly when he and Alby appeared with the others. The rest of the occupants were all sitting on the floor, with a good eye being kept on them. Lincoln indicated that they were to sit on the floor too, and beckoned Alby and Jethro over to him. "This is not the hit," he said softly.

"I agree. What do you want to do?" said Fude. "These cocksucking garlic munchers have given us the wrong location."

"That is what we were thinking," said Alby and Jethro.

"Exactly," muttered Lincoln. "It's too late to go again tonight, and we're miles from anywhere, what say we have a feed here, and then leave? We can have a bit of fun, touch 'em up if yo' like, and be on our way. Only one thing; A'll call de shots, OK? One other thing," he looked at them. "One drink!" They all nodded in agreement.

Lincoln made a little speech and told everyone that no one would be hurt provided they all did as they were told. He then asked what was for dinner, and was told that it was roast pork. This he said was his favorite meal. The villains ate the meal with the men sitting on the floor, with the women waiting on them.

Louise and Conchitta, who were the two young attractive ones, were getting leers, particularly from Alby who had fondled them a couple of times. Two of the men tried to stop this but had been pistol-whipped for their troubles. The meal being well and truly over, Lincoln knew that Alby, who was an animal—a trained one, but nevertheless a real animal—wanted more than the meal. He announced that Alby would now give a demonstration on how to really finish off a meal.

"Wa' y'all thank man, a little white meat, or de Latino." With two sweeps of his great arms he swept everything off the table in front of him and nodded to Alby who picked up Louise. Alby was nearly beside himself, and threw her down onto the table. Taking the top of her dress in one hand tore it right down the front to the waistline. With two hands he then took the hem and tore it up and open. Three of the men muttered oaths and tried to stand up but were pistol-whipped again. Four of the women gave little sobs. Conchitta began to wail and was given a hit by Fude and told that she would be next. Louise lying back on the table was shaking with fright but had not uttered a sound.

"Jes' so yo' good folks knows where de man's comin' from, it might interest y'all to know dat a long time ago, he had to watch while six crackers, wad yo' call dem, Southern Gentlemen, raped his Mammy, who was four months wid child. His Mammy died two months later. So all yo' wailing carrying on, don't cut no ice wid us. Carry on, man."

Freddie to all intents and purposes appeared unmoved by the whole business, although the others were looking at him appealingly, he kept his peace. Lofty who had been sharply hit in the solar plexus, was beside Freddie on the floor, and was looking decidedly grey. Alby reached forward for the top of Louise's panties and as his hand touched her bare skin she gave a little sob and a shudder ran through her. Lincoln who by now was sitting at the other end of the table seemed to be enjoying himself immensely and said, "Go man, show us how much you really appreciated the roast powak."

Freddie's cool clear voice cut through the fog. "Too yellow to do our own dirty work are we, C...?"

There was a stunned silence, no one moved. There were stifled sobs from the women. Everyone who could actually see Freddie sitting on the floor slowly turned their faces towards Lincoln, who a moment or so before was looking quite jovial. A look of bewilderment turning to malevolence slowly crossed his face. He could barely control himself, but he did, remarkably. "What did you say?" he said in a cold clear response.

"Oh, we're deaf as well as yellow, are we? C...!" retorted Freddie.

Lincoln slumped back in his chair and a look of bemused utter bewilderment descended on him. No one said a word. There was first the odd sniffle from some of the women. Lincoln gazed down the table at Alby as if

328

devoid of all emotion, and flicked his head to one side. Alby reached down, grabbing Louise by the arms and pulled her up and off the table and sent her flying into the corner, into the other women who steadied her. He then, without a word, indicated to the others to put Freddie into the chair beside him.

Lincoln then slowly rose from his chair like a man in a trance and walked almost wearily down through the room and out into the kitchen. He was only gone a moment or two and returned with a beautiful heavy knife, Manuel's favorite, from a kitchen set. It had a blade around eight inches long.

He put it on the table as he walked slowly, sauntered is probably more the word. He went to the other end of the room where there was a bookshelf built into the wall above a long bench built in with cupboards beneath it. There were also books on the bench top, he took his time and eventually selected a coffee table book which was about two inches thick. It had quite a lot of weight. He then sauntered back to his place at the head of the table. "Now you good folk, you just listen to me. Now where do I start? This will do!" It was not missed on anyone, that he spoke in perfectly enunciated English. Which made it all the more chilling.

"We're all out here in this fine house, and my friends and I have just partaken of what I can only describe as a most beautifully cooked meal of roast pork. Now the fact that it happens to be my own personal favorite meal is of course a coincidence. You good folks couldn't have possibly known that it was my favorite. Now all I was setting out to do was show my appreciation. How I show this is surely my affair. What happens?" He opened his hands beseechingly. "What happens? Our friend here is offended. He doesn't like the way we show our appreciation."

Everyone was riveted on him, he had their undivided attention. "So where does that leave me? I mean, after all I am a guest in the house. Your hospitality has broken down." He appeared to have regained his composure and seemed to be enjoying himself once more. "I will tell you where it leaves me. It leaves me no alternative but to demonstrate my appreciation in a much more personal fashion. So what are we going to do, or what are you all going to do? You are all going to do nothing, get it! If any of you make one move, one squeak, you are dead. Get it!"

Freddie looked around the room and mouthed at them silently—"This is my call!" Lincoln looked down at Freddie, caught his eye and beckoned him to sit beside him. He then reached across and took Freddie's left forearm and interestingly took a little time positioning it on the table in front of him on his right. After again telling everyone to be still, Lincoln had Alby steady the knife above Freddie's arm with the point gently pressing in two thirds of the way up his forearm.

"Now have you anything to say?" he enquired of Freddie who looked straight through him. "Now before I proceed, Ah have to say," he said, wafting in and out of the drawl, "Ah'm getting a lil ahead o' mahself." He rested the book in front of him.

"Is there a doctor in de house? Ah don wan' to cut his arm up too much. Ah don wan' to cut through what yo' call it, it's a long time ago. Oh Ah know, de radial artery, dat's watit is, de radial artery. Trouble is, Ah've never done this afore, an Ah was thinking effen any o' yo' good folks are medicos, an' would be prepared to give what shall we say, a li'l direction, de man may come outa iy a li'l bit better than if Ah was to go it alone. Now how's dat for an offer? How's dat fo' consideration? All outa respect fo' de ladies, Ah might add." He looked around the room, and Fude caught his eye, giving him the wind up look.

Billy and Sandra looked at each other, and Billy gave a slight shake of his head, as he started to struggle to his feet. Sandra ignored him and stood up as well. Lincoln sat back and exclaimed, "Well, Ah declare, we have two doctors in the house. We can only hope yo' all can remember where de arteries are, can't we?"

"Now man give 'em de knife," he said to Alby, "An we'll see how good they are. Now yo' two fine medico folk, yo' jes nod to me when yo' all think yo' got it right, and don't mess around, as Ah's getting jes a might impatient," he added for Fude's benefit, looking over at him.

Freddie looked up at the ceiling, averting his face from the other two. Sandra had tears streaming down her cheeks as she gently moved Freddie's forearm over. She looked closely at Billy who was concentrating on getting the correct alignment of the knife, so that it would pass between the radius, and the ulna, without cutting through the radial artery. Billy looked at Sandra raising his eyebrows, Sandra looked down, pursed her lips and nodded. They both turned slightly and nodded to Lincoln.

Lincoln, acknowledging their look, held the book up with both hands over the top of the knife and then raising it up further suddenly brought it down hard driving the knife straight through Freddie's forearm, in fact splintering through the table top.

Louise moaned, the older women gave little choked sobs, and Conchitta gave a wail that was cut off as Jethro made a move towards her. The men looked malevolent but resigned. Freddie actually felt very little pain as the knife was extremely sharp. The pain and numbness would come later, as he well knew.

One of the women helped Louise tear strips off her skirt to staunch the flow of blood as Freddie reached out with his right hand to pull the knife out. He had not uttered a sound. The two women moved forward with the bandages but were stopped quite roughly.

Winona had been sound asleep in the enormous bed that she and her grandmother shared. She was most uncomfortable with the baby which felt as though it would come at any moment.

She had been quite unsettled had eventually dropped off and had now awoken. She went to the en-suite, put on a dressing gown and then sleepily wandered out into the passage and on into the main room where she saw the bridge tables set up but no one in sight. She then wandered over to the dining room door. She entered, much to the amazement of the villains.

She shuffled in looking wrung out, and terribly pregnant, but with a beautiful serene look on her face. She looked around smiling and said to no one in particular, that she thought the baby was due, any minute, and that she had been calling out.

Lincoln looked at the others as much as to say, *And what other surprises are we going to have tonight?* and received the same looks in return. He can't have known that he had in fact checked out the main bedroom where she had been, but the light was off and she had gone into the en-suite when he had checked out the room. Whilst he had noticed the turned-down bed, he had placed no emphasis on it. It all looked too neat. He had in effect only turned the light on and straight off again, missing her completely.

Winona gradually brought the whole scene into focus, and looking down the table at her father, uttered a little cry.

"What... what is going on?" She staggered a little. Fude moved towards her.

"Don't you dare touch that girl." Sue Ellen and Monica flung themselves between Winona and the advancing Fude. Sandra and Judy took Winona gently and drew a chair out for her to sit on. Fude looked at Lincoln in an exasperated fashion, giving him another almost withering, wind up look. He, like all of them thought that things were going from bad to worse. They were now going to have to contend with a baby before too long, by the look of the girl. He wanted out of the whole thing.

Lincoln was, of course, feeling the same way. However, they had to extricate themselves from the situation in good order without losing any more face than they had, which for Lincoln was too much already. He usually had no compunction in taking people out for far less than some of the things that had happened tonight. This group, though, intrigued him. They were obviously all successful, to the extent of being extremely wealthy, which was obvious from the buildings, the cars, the way they dressed, and of course the furnishings. All this in Lincoln's opinion was secondary to the way they all seemed to be extremely comfortable, almost intimate, and extremely supportive of one another.

Lincoln may have been a cold-blooded killer if required, like his friends, but he, like them, had a sensitive side, and he could tell from the odd look from the others that they felt the same way. All this had flashed through his mind in seconds. It had been gathering pace for some time. Now was the time to move out.

He looked across at Freddie who was gazing down the table at Winona and it struck him, that she was his daughter. Freddie was looking at her with intent, but reassuring look. For her part Winona was traumatized and in a state of shock. As the whole dreadful scene began to sink in she started to say something when

Lincoln, who had finished his summation, cut across everything. Mustering as much dignitas as he could under the circumstances said. "We will now wind this up!"

The women had been continuing tearing off bandages, and began to move towards Freddie again when Alby stepped in. Louise slapped his arm and said that they were all animals, even surprising herself. Lincoln waved to them to continue.

Looking around the room he spotted the bookcase again containing dozens of books. He went over and pulled out a Bible. Making the comment that it was quite appropriate under the circumstances. He then turned to everyone as he moved towards the curtains which he drew back. There was a level area of lawn which then gradually sloped down to the lake. There was a floodlight shining over the lawn but they all could see the moon on the water. It looked quite beautiful. Lincoln took Alby into the corner and spoke to him for a few moments and then bidding everyone goodnight thanking them for a delightful dinner he took Freddie by the arm and together with Jethro they went out through the house to the lawn.

At the sight of Lincoln with the Bible and his pistol, everyone reasoned that this nightmare was going from bad to worse. The upshot of this was that three of the women were given a nasty backhander and this included Alice and all the men were belted down again with another pistol whip. As they walked out of the room Winona leaning forward but being restrained called out—"Dadda, Dadda oh no, no, oh Dadda, please, please."

This of course shook everyone to the core including Lincoln and Company and whilst Freddie held his head high without giving any indication that he was affected by this, he certainly was and was also conscious of

Louise trying to crawl towards him and Lincoln, begging, "Please, please leave him, leave him." As he passed through the main room he commented on how nice it looked all set up for the three tables of bridge. They left the room; Louise, choking back tears, begged Lincoln to take her and do whatever they liked.

Lofty and another two fellows were badly hit again and of course it was all to no avail. Freddie was marched out of the house and around in front of the window, and they could all see him looking steadily ahead quite stoically but holding his arm which by now was beginning to throb. He was then turned around and made to lie face down on the grass; Lincoln knelt beside him and asked him if he would like to kiss the Bible. "Not for you, cocksucker." Lincoln and Jethro looked at each other and rolled their eyes. Lincoln nodded to Jethro to move off. Freddie and Lincoln stayed there for another minute or so which seemed like an eternity to Freddie. He had no sooner spoken to Lincoln than the cry of a new-born baby came down to them through the still night air.

Lincoln could see Freddie give a little shudder. Just before he heard the generator dying and the floodlight fading out, Freddie thought to himself that this was it, as he heard the cocking of the revolver, the "So long, cat" and heard the explosion of the shot in his ear. He gave an involuntary shudder and was conscious of the fact that he had urinated and his feet came up and then with everyone watching from the house, the villains pulled the curtains.

As they went out Fude told the gathering to remain where they were until they heard the sound of the car moving away. They had already cut the phone line. There were mobile phones of course, but reception was very patchy in that part of the world. The tires on all the cars had been slashed too.

335

The villains didn't speak until they were over a mile or so down the road and one of them said, "Well Lincoln man, next time yo' want something to eat, yo' can get it yo'self."

Another said, "Man, they were one group of cats if ever I've seen any. That top one sure was a cat."

"What do yo' mean?" Lincoln said. "What do yo' mean was a cat, he still is. He was too good a cat to chop."

"Man, you mean he's OK?" from the back seat.

"Sure, he's got one hell of a sore arm but he'll be all right."

"Well man I'll be doggoned," said Fude. There were high-fives all round as chuckling away they continued down the road.

Chapter 28

After the shot had rung out Freddie couldn't believe that he was still alive. He had wet his pants but that was the least of his worries. His arm hurt like hell and the Bible was resting against his head. It had protected him from the blast. He lay there for some minutes smelling the dewy grass as if for the first time.

Suddenly he heard the small auxiliary lighting plant start up and getting slowly to his feet he looked over to the house and saw that the curtain to the lounge room had been drawn. He staggered back as he was nearly knocked over by Lofty and Billy. They let go panting little sobs when they realized he was on his feet, and hugged him not saying a word.

Billy led him back into the dining room looking like a ghost, and on seeing him all of the rest of the party began to cry; Louise was distraught. The men weren't much better. Winnie, who had fainted, was still nursing a beautiful newly-born baby that her two grandmothers and Conchitta were helping her with.

Freddie gave Louise a hug and went over kneeling down, gave Winona and Alice and his mother-in-law a kiss. There was subdued pandemonium. Monica and Sue Ellen enlisted Susan and Conchitta to the kitchen to make coffee for everyone and for Conchitta to get clean sheets and towels and the medicine chest. Billy went off to get his medical bag where he had some morphine.

He returned and gave Freddie a shot and asked if he had had a tetanus boost recently. He had. He then called Conchitta and asked her how sharp the knife was. She replied that Manuel had sharpened them all earlier in the day.

Billy looked at Manuel who replied that he had sharpened all of them that afternoon—they could not be sharper, and he had also washed them all in clean soapy water. He had also cleaned the rack that was magnetic.

He was pleased with this news. Freddie disappeared and then returned to where they all had gravitated. They were in the sitting room where they had flopped down although Freddie sat on a wooden chair as his trousers were soiled.

Freddie said, "Look at me, I've disgraced myself," indicating the soiled trousers. They all just shook their heads. He then asked for a whiskey which he said he felt he had earned. They all looked a bit dubious at this, but Billy just looked at Chuck, and put up his right hand, with forefinger and thumb, close together indicating a small whiskey. Freddie said that he would take it with him to the bathroom as he needed to have a shower.

Louise went with him telling him that she could get some clean clothes for him if he would like to go straight to the bathroom. She looked up at him with tears in her eyes and he just put his arm around her and gave her a nod and a hug. Billy came after them with his bag saying that before he had a shower he would tape up the arm and after he had had the shower to give him a call and he would attend to it properly after he was dried and dressed.

Freddie eventually made his way back to the main room looking much better to find everyone still there and with Winnie and the baby settled on the couch. He sat down beside her and put an arm around her and kissed her on the forehead and said, "Missy you haven't called me Dadda since you were a little girl." Winnie had been snuffling and this made her begin to sob out loud. She looked at him, her grandmother and Susan who both rolled their eyes and shook their heads. He then hugged Winnie again and said, "I'm sorry darling, I'm just trying to be funny to jolly you along a bit."

"Oh," she sniffled.

"That's right, darling, we have had a frightful time and here am I with only a knife wound and look at all you guys. There is probably no one without a laceration or a frightful headache. Billy, Chuck, have you attended to everyone?"

"Of course we have, you ass, of course we have, what do you think we've been doing, sitting here, having a whiskey?" said Chuck.

"Thank God," said Ben "you two almost seem back to normal; and can I make a suggestion?"

"Yes of course you can, darling," said Sue Ellen.

"Look, it seems like one o'clock in the morning but it is only 9.30—too early to go to bed. Why don't we all take half an hour off and clean ourselves up and we'll meet back here at 10 p.m?"

"Good idea," said Freddie, "we may have an appetite by then. There were two legs of 'powak' weren't there? And we can have a rubber or two."

They all howled him down but he insisted and Alice said that they would decide when they got back.

Freddie continued, "Oh, and there is one other thing, I must apologize for my intemperate language, earlier on."

"Jesu," said Lofty.

"Lofty!" said Alice.

"OK, OK. Everyone settle down," said Sandra. "Freddie, don't ever say that again, don't even think it!"

Chuck thought to himself that he had the sensitivity to not mention his theory of "heading someone off at the pass."

Sue Ellen said, "Come on everyone, let's get the show on the road. Winnie should really go to bed as she had had next to her father, the most trying time." The bassinette had already been made up and was already in the room she was sharing with Alice. The two grandmothers got the message and moved over to Winnie with Louise who stooped and helped her up off the couch, at the same time offering to take the baby, which was given to her.

Freddie asked if he could nurse the baby who was sound asleep, until all the arrangements had been put in place. He then exclaimed, "Holy mackerel, do you know what? Oh," he said, "I am so selfish, here we are, the baby has been born for half an hour or so and I don't even know what it is. I've been so caught up in my own thoughts."

"Dad don't say that—good heavens, no no!"

"When I was facing the firing squad and heard the baby cry, I was so relieved that it was alive."

"Don't joke like that, Freddie darling," said Alice.

"OK Mom. I then quite frankly forgot about any concerns regarding the next of kin. Well what is it, a boy or a girl?"

"A girl," said Winnie.

"Oh, how wonderful, you clever old thing. Do we have any name?" said Freddie.

"Lettice Alice Edith," she replied.

"Oh," said Freddie and burst into tears.

They all met back at around 10.15 and Alice spoke.

"Now before we all get too settled, why don't we decide what we are going to do? Are we going to mill around for another hour or so and go to bed or are we going to have a bite to eat and then bed or what?"

"Why don't we have a bite and then go to bed after a rubber of bridge?" said Freddie.

"No, no," said Alice. "Bridge is too much after all we have been through tonight."

"Well," Freddie said imperiously and getting to his feet, "I think that after my star performance tonight, I am, or should be allowed to have a rubber." He looked around the gathering. "Another whiskey, some food—if the swine have left us much and then a rubber. What do you say? Mom, darling, why don't you ask Conchitta if there is anything ready to eat?" Alice shook her head wearily and went off to the kitchen with Susan and Sandra.

"Freddie boy," said Chuck, "I must say I have to agree with you. There is nothing like tonight's performance to give you a thirst and an appetite and a need to refocus one's attention on something like a rubber or two—what do you say, gang?" They all agreed.

Ben and Billy had disappeared and now came back into the room.

"We have had a look at the vehicles," said Billy.

"And we have slashed tires in every one of the seven," said Ben. "We reckon we can 'salvage' three wheels from the spares that will fit one of the cars but will have to repair a puncture on the fourth."

"It is too late and too dark to be jacking up cars and repairing punctures, at this juncture," said Billy. "So why don't we do it in the cold clear light of day, and someone can go into Bears Pass in the morning and report the 'intrusion?'"

They all heartily agreed.

Susan came back from the kitchen to say that yes, Conchitta had cooked two legs of roast pork actually, intending to have the second one cold for tomorrow, and whilst she had thrown out the remains of the first leg and all the vegetables, the turkeys were still in the fridge uncooked. The second leg was completely untouched by the recent visitors. She, Sandra and Conchitta would rustle up some nice pork sandwiches for the boys and the women would get something lighter for themselves like a boiled egg and toast.

Sandra said, "Come on girls," to the others, "we'll set up the table."

This made sense to everyone and after the meal they all settled down to two tables of bridge as some of the older women were too worn out. They would just sit around and chat.

They all drew for cards and Freddie drew Monica against Louise and Chuck. Freddie felt about halfway through the rubber that he probably shouldn't have made an issue of having forced the game onto them, as they all appeared to be only going through the motions, to accommodate him. They seemed to be in the same frame of mind at the other table as well.

Freddie's table was very low scoring and the other table had finished their rubber, whilst Freddie and Monica had only won one game, Freddie was dealt what he thought would be the last hand and then, picking it up couldn't believe it. A hand with four aces. Louise looked at him and asked if he was alright. "Yes yes, I'm fine." They all looked at him quizzically, and at each other. "I'm fine," he echoed again.

He opened one no trump, they all looked at him, Chuck, holding sixteen points in his hand, doubled one no trump, grinning at Freddie. The grin faded when this was redoubled by Monica, Chuck resignedly then led with a four of diamonds and Freddie went on to claim the rubber with an overtrick.

No one could believe it, certainly not Freddie. There were claps and cheers all around and he was showered with kisses. "Well, what a night and what a way to finish it," said Billy.

"Yes," said Freddie, "a nightcap and then all off to bed."

"Freddie, do you really need another drink?" said Alice.

"Ooh, Mom," he said, "I've only had two since my return from the dead."

"Don't say that Freddie, please," cried Alice.

"OK, OK, but one more won't hurt. It is my right, after all."

"Hail, Freddie," said Chuck.

"Will he be OK, Billy?" said Lofty, who hadn't said much at all since he had brought Freddie back in from the front lawn. He actually looked more emotionally drained than Alice.

"Yes, yes, he should be OK," he responded.

"Freddie, you sit over there and I'll mix you one," said Billy. "Would you like a three or four finger job?"

"Billy!" said Alice.

"Now, now Miss Alice, where is your sense of humor?"

"Just about had it, Billy darling—another night like this would be the death of me."

"All's well that ends well," said Freddie getting up from the card table and walking over to the two old girls, giving each of them a kiss.

"A new day dawns tomorrow and we can all enjoy our new little Lettie." He went over to the comfortable armchair and sat down.

Louise took the glass that Billy gave her and walked over to Freddie and bent down and handing it to him gave him a kiss saying, "Just sit there and enjoy this, you wonderful thing." He gave her arm a squeeze and settled back holding the whiskey between two hands on his lap.

His mind began to go back over the evening's events. He took a sip of whiskey. His arm which had been beginning to hurt just before he sat down, began to feel better.

"Isn't it wonderful that Winnie has decided to call the baby Lettice?" Her mother would have loved that, he thought to himself. He looked over at Alice; she looked quite wrung out. He looked at Sandra. What would she and Lettice be thinking about all this?

Alice and Louise were just sitting side by side looking at him. He looked over at Ben who was sitting beside Monica with his eyes glued to him. He caught Ben's eye, and smiled. Ben winked at him, and returned the smile with a slight shake of his head and a widening of his eyes. Ben, probably next to Freddie, had been more knocked about than anyone, but for all that, they had all copped it almost in equal measure. A point not lost on any of the women.

Freddie toyed with the drink. He began to think of what Lettice would have thought of all this. What his father and Edie... His mind wandered. Unc, even Alex too. His mind wandered to Ilse, and the first time. Phew, what an experience that was. Was it better than with Lettie the first time? No, it was quite different. Lettie was the one.

Oh Lettie, Oh I miss you, but do you know you are now a grandmother. We have a granddaughter. Perhaps it is time to join you. I wonder. His head swam a little. Bright colors flashed through his mind. His arm began to throb again. He tried to take a sip of the whiskey. The throbbing ceased. The glass was too heavy. He tried to lift it in two hands. He tried to open his eyes which had closed. He couldn't. He became aware of a crushing weight on his chest, and then it eased. He settled more comfortably in the chair. A beautiful smile came across his face as he uttered ever so softly, Lettie.

She moved towards him with that beautiful almost enigmatic smile that had always captivated him, although it did appear to be a little wistful. There was a very bright, whitish, yellowish light surrounding her, recognition glowing from her. Her eyes were welling with tears. She seemed to hover in front of him, going in and out of focus. Her image cleared. He brought his fingers up to his lips and kissed them and ever so slowly reached out and ran the backs of them across her lips. He was aware of actually touching her. She shivered slightly as he was bringing his other kissed fingers up to her other cheek. With both hands cupping her face he moved her closer and they melted into each other.

The glass slipped from his fingers and spilt the whiskey in his lap. He was quite oblivious to the stain.

Louise, who had been watching him like a hawk, quickly crawled across the few feet to him and took the glass, with a smile.

"You poor dear, you are all out to it. It's time for bed." She shook him slightly.

Lofty bounded across the room to Louise. He gently took her and held her.

"He has gone," he gently whispered to her. "Oh dear. Oh dear." He helped her up as it dawned on her too, sobs wracking silently through her. He held her tightly. He then moved her back to Susan, and sat her on the floor at her knee. Then, sitting on the arm of Alice's chair put his arm around her.

"It is all over, Miss Alice," he whispered. "He has gone."

The others looked at each other in bewilderment as it slowly dawned on them what had happened. No one really said a word. There were tears flowing with abandon and whilst no one moved they held hands with those nearest to them.

Alice just sat there with her eyes closed and her face turned upwards. Tears silently flowing down her cheeks, with her lower lip trembling. Her whole body seemed to be quivering. She eventually began to rise out of her chair and with Lofty's help moved across to Freddie, and sat on the arm of his chair cradling his head in her arms. Shudders seemed to pass through her.

They sat quietly watching for some minutes with no one wishing to speak before Alice spoke. As if in a dream, in a low voice she said to no one in particular: "I was looking at him as he went and I am sure that his last word was Lettie." Tears streamed silently down her cheeks, she stroked Freddie's head.

"I have always looked ahead," she went on. "However, tonight I had a premonition that nothing good would come of it. When he returned after the shot, I felt that all would be well, but something niggled me. And now.

"He had never got over Lettice's death, I think we all recognize that." She gave Louise a reassuring smile, "And I think tonight was perhaps too much for him, and he just let go. I don't know what else to think."

Eventually Billy looked at his mother who was consoling Louise; she nodded to him. He cleared his throat and in a faltering voice said that they had better take him to off to his bed. His mother nodded again and moved over to Alice. Their tears mingled.

Louise was quite hopeless. She had always known that she could never compete with Lettice, who she utterly adored, and had given up hope that Freddie would come to her, although she had been doing her level best to bring it about. Lofty asked her to turn down Freddie's bed as they would carry him in in a moment or so.

Alice squeezed her shoulder and Susan helped her to her feet, and led her off into the bedroom.

Judy asked Alice what she thought they should do with Winnie. Alice replied that she had been thinking just that, and to wake her now after what she had been through would achieve nothing, and to be quite frank would upset everyone even more. They all agreed.

Moving as if in a dream after giving Alice a kiss and several hugs, they all drifted off to their respective beds.

The four friends returned to the kitchen. Conchitta heard them and came in. They assured her that they would be OK, but she said, "Please, I need to do something. Could I make some more sandwiches?"

They acquiesced. She bustled about, and after a while and over the sandwiches they decided that it was too soon to work out what they would do in respect of the intruders. It was felt they should get an independent view on what caused Freddie to die sometime after the event. They agreed that it was cardiac arrest but it was not proper for one of them to sign off on that. They should have an independent third party.

Chuck said that he and Sandra would drive into Bears Pass in the morning after they had got a vehicle set up with the spare wheels, and report the whole business to the police. Then they should find a doctor who would no doubt come out, but they would also need to organize an ambulance to take Freddie's body back to the hospital, where he suspected they would carry out an autopsy.

"I don't think they will discover anything that we don't already suspect, but you never know."

"You know," said Ben, "we will also have to decide what to do in relation to the actual intruders themselves tomorrow. It was tricky as they had not actually committed a murder, although had inadvertently brought the death on."

They cracked their second bottle of red, and Billy muttered that he was concerned about Alice. "She would have to let go at some stage."

How she seemed to have the strength, they all marveled at. "It's her faith," said Ben.

"It is," agreed Chuck. "She has never worn it on her shoulder. But I don't know anyone who has suffered the knocks that she has."

"From when she was a young girl," said Billy. "She is incredible; for all that she just seems to keep herself together.

"And at the same time she can be emotional. Look at her when Freddie came back, and after the baby was born and we heard the shot. She just seems to gather herself so quickly. I for one consider myself so fortunate to know her, in fact the whole family, virtually all my days. As bad as today has been, I'm not looking forward to tomorrow. Tomorrow will be like no other day." They all agreed.

"I really feel," said Lofty, "that there is a little more to it than her faith. She is or has been a very spiritual person. She has this, what would you call it, an 'inner grace' that even the most religious people rarely have. She is to me, one of a kind. Oh I love her; in fact, I couldn't love her more!"

"Amen," said the others.

Alice couldn't sleep and sat up beside the sleeping Winnie who had the baby, who looked absolutely beautiful, beside her in the bassinette. There was a magnificent full moon which shone over the lake and through the window on the two girls.

From time to time she peered into the basinette, wondering just what the world had in store for her. She prayed that Winnie wouldn't wake, and decided that if she did and was to ask her why she wasn't in bed, she would just say that after all the business of last night she felt better staying dozing in the chair. She would let the 'morrow take its course.

At the same time she thought that, as dreadfully as her father's death would affect her, she was very young, happily married, was financially secure and had a new

348

baby to care for. She, Alice, of course, would be there to give all the help that was needed. As always she was frighteningly practical.

She was just dozing off when suddenly she became aware that the sun was beginning to come up. The first ray was creeping across the water, and moving across the lawn. There was an incredible almost blinding flash, and then it was gone. She shook her head and rubbed her eyes.

What was that? She had to find out. She moved quietly out of the room, down to the rear of the house and out onto the lawn, thankful that she had a gown on. There was a slight dew on the grass, but that didn't bother her on her bare feet. She was still rubbing her eyes from the flash.

She sensed someone ahead of her. "Lofty," she whispered. He stopped and she caught up. He put an arm around her.

"Are you wondering what that was?"

"I was!"

"We'll soon find out!" she responded.

Ahead all they could see was the expanse of lawn and then a dark shape which took form, it was the Bible. They looked down at it, and it slowly dawned on them. The Bible was sitting upright slightly opened, with the cover, a bold cross in gold lettering on the front of it, angled towards the house.

Lofty picked it up. He handed it to her. "It's actually quite warm!" he said. "Does this mean, Miss Alice? Could this mean…?" Lofty whispered.

"It must, it must," she said in a faltering voice. "Oh yes, Oh yes!" Her head swam, she staggered a little. Her mind wondered. "Oh, The Great Truth, The Great Truth! Everything, everything. Oh, oh…"

He held her.

They both wept, silently.